HUNT

Lion's Lineage Book One

ROHAN HUBLIKAR
DAKOTA KROUT

To my mother

PROLOGUE

The King had been forced to his knees before the powerful dark cultivator that stood before him. Even with the violence of the moment, his eyes were merely tired. He looked out over the kingdom that he had been building for the last few hundred years, and wished them a fond farewell.

"I hope you understand why we are doing this." The Master joined the King on the floor, and placed a hand on his shoulder. "I swear to you, I will not intentionally bring harm to your child. Prince Henry will be safe so long as the situation doesn't change, and he does not rise against me."

The King shook his head and met the eyes of The Master, no fear showing on his face. "Precisely why I agreed to this, instead of waging a full-scale war against you."

"Admittedly, that was somewhat… surprising to me." The Master smiled softly and offered the King a memory stone; one of such purity and quality that the King's eyes nearly bulged out of their sockets. "This is for you. A way for your legacy to continue on. I'll pass it on to your son if we ever meet."

"Not before looking through it yourself for any additional secrets, I suppose." The King snorted and looked out at the completely peaceful Kingdom below him. Peaceful from this vantage, at least. There were no *truly* peaceful places in this world; he had searched longer than most. "I'll let you know, I was very forthright. I have no interest in seeing my people as undead."

"I trust you." The Master told him seriously. "I do. I will *also* verify this for myself."

Letting out a nod and a shrug, the King touched the memory stone to his head and allowed it to collect his entire life into it as memories that others would have access to so long as they had possession of the stone. Everything that was stored in his head, every struggle, triumph, joy, and sorrow... all of it flowed into the stone. Hundreds of years of memories from the cultivator collected in nearly an instant.

He handed the stone to the Dark Lord, the leader of the necromantic hordes that had ravaged this world not once, but twice in the King's lifetime. The man that would be his murderer, The Master.

The dark cultivator took the stone and carefully held it in his left hand, even as he used his right to take the King's head and store it in a spatial bag. As the floor was painted red, the memory stone was held to The Master's forehead, and for an instant that lasted hundreds of years... he lived the life of the King of the Lion Kingdom.

CHAPTER ONE

"Your tea, milord." Garron, the servant boy, held the tray out; his head bowing so that he didn't look directly at the Noble. The rattling of the cups shaking in their saucers was the only sound in the room for a long moment. His weak arms were betraying him, and he was going to drop the expensive tea if they didn't—

The weight was lifted off of him, and the emaciated servant lowered his arms with a near-silent breath of relief. Today was a bad day; the pain was much more intense than it usually was. He bowed a little deeper, feeling his bones cry out in protest, and turned to beat a hasty retreat. He froze like a rabbit as the familiar commanding voice rang out. "Hold on, Gar."

Garron stifled a small smile creeping onto his face at the acknowledgement of his lifelong friend. As much as he wanted to show his appreciation, that wouldn't work with the present company. Thanks to plenty of practice, he smoothed his facial expressions before he turned around.

"Yes, milord?" Garron was only fifteen; he hated how his voice sounded like an old man's. No matter how he tried, today he just couldn't keep the rasp out of it. Still, he knew from experience that coughing would just make everything worse. It might even get him chased out of the room with a kick if he managed to upset... He tried not to think of that.

Garron found himself looking straight into a pair of dark eyes framed by a face furrowed in concern. Young master Andros had just hit a growth spurt, and looked like someone had taken the slightly pudgy boy Garron had known since birth and stretched him out into a lanky teenager. Long black hair fell to his shoulders; at the moment it was matted with sweat and stuck close to his scalp, but even when it was dry it was always messy.

The young Noble spoke quietly, but with the same confidence he'd always had. "You don't sound too good today. Do you want some of my tea?"

Before Garron could so much as open his mouth, a scoff from the man standing next to Andros interrupted him. A voice dripping with annoyance sent a chill down Garron's spine. "Don't be *foolish*, boy. That's *Essence-infused* tea. No sense wasting it on a *servant*. Especially not one so... pathetic."

Garron winced at Captain Jackson's harsh words. He remembered when Andros' father, Lord Tet, had been the one to sit in that chair. Though he had been a busy man, powerful and important, he'd never said an unkind word to Garron nor intentionally scared him. The same couldn't be said of the seat's current occupant, the Captain of the House Guard. Jackson didn't mince words, and he knew exactly how vastly different their respective social positions were.

After a moment of hesitation, Andros spoke again, a controlled rage creeping into his voice. "He needs it more than I do. *I'll* be fine, but he—"

"Wouldn't *appreciate* or even *understand* what he was wasting." The Captain's eyes flickered to Garron again, and the young servant's chest restricted painfully. He'd never quite known why, but Jackson had always treated him with disdain. When Lord Tet had left to go fight in the war, and Jackson had become steward of the estate, life had only gotten worse. While Lord

Tet was away, even Andros couldn't contradict the man on matters of the estate or his own training. In Jackson's eyes, that meant that he could treat Garron however he wanted.

On a positive note, Andros didn't seem to agree. "It's *my* choice to—"

"Not *another* word, boy." Jackson's eyes were suddenly burning with rage. "Just drink the infernal tea so you can get back to training. I want you on the verge of the C-ranks when your father returns. As for *you*…"

Once again, Jackson's eyes rested on Garron, and this time it took everything he had for Garron to just barely hold back a chest-wracking cough. The man was incredibly intimidating. Jackson kept his hair cropped close to his skull, and always had a singed look to it as though he'd burned off the bits he didn't want instead of cutting it. In all other ways, Jackson's face seemed like a harder version of Andros', all sharp lines and deep shadows, the jaw just a little too long for his face. The main difference was the perpetual sneer that was a stark contrast to Andros' pleasant demeanor.

The Guard Captain waved a disdainful hand. "Ugh. Just… get out of here before I need a cleaner to move you. Oh, and try to die somewhere outside so the staff don't need to clean the floor."

Garron bowed again, panic making him forget the pain he was almost always feeling these days. He hurried off, hearing Jackson's words floating through the air behind him. "As for you, Andros. I'll have to have a word with Lord Tet about that servant; he's distracting you. But perhaps I won't *need* to, if you…"

The servant made it out of the room, closing the door with a sigh of relief. The sigh quickly turned into a hack, and then a cough, and before Garron knew it he was spasming on the floor. The fit only lasted for a minute or so, which was better than this morning, but he still grimaced as he struggled to his feet.

Jackson's scrutiny was always a trial, and his presence always seemed to exacerbate Garron's condition, but seeing his only real friend was *almost* enough to make up for it. He was pretty sure that the head cook always sent him to deliver the tea just so they could stay in contact, and he was grateful to her for it. Especially since... it felt like he wouldn't have many more chances to do it. Garron let out a sigh, shaking his head. "I gotta stop being dramatic. I think Jackson is getting to me."

No matter how bad his illness was getting, he knew for certain that failing to get back to head cook Hila in time would kill him faster. He started shuffling down the halls of the manor, beelining for the kitchen.

Minutes later, he pushed open the wooden doors at the end of a narrow servant's corridor, a wave of warm air and clamor washing over him. He spotted the plump woman standing at a counter across the room, chopping herbs even as she shouted instructions at the bustling workers surrounding her. She tasted a spoonful of soup from a passing cook, then shot a glare at Garron. "Took you long enough, didn't it?"

"You wanted me to spill the tea?" Garron smiled a little as he said the words, but he kept his voice stern enough to match Hila's. The cook snorted, a little puff of flour rising from her uniform at the rush of air.

"You're quick enough when swiping rolls from my oven, aren't you?" She tossed the words over her shoulder as she swept the herbs from her cutting board into a waiting pot, stirring with one hand as the other felt at a passing tray of sweetbreads. She gave the man carrying the tray—a new hire—a nod; the man barely acknowledged it as he continued on to the cooling racks.

"Can't spill rolls, can I?" Garron caught the hint of a smile on Hila's lips, and not from his banter. He was certain the new hire was going to do *well* in the kitchen. The smile was replaced by a scowl as she looked up at Garron once again.

"Jenny didn't make enough for seconds, you know. You got one, but that's all you get."

"I need to keep my strength up!" Garron put on a piteous

expression, making a show of coughing into his arm. He managed to hold a real one back, but only just.

His acting was only met with another snort. "Well, boy, you know what'll *really* keep your strength up?"

"Stew?"

"You stay away from my stew." Hila shook a wooden spoon at him, a little splatter of soup speckling the uniform of a passing cook. "What you need is *exercise*. Why don't you go on and see if those boys out in the east wing need help?"

Garron couldn't hold back a wince. "But don't you need a taste tester? I have a very developed palate, you—"

"Get to work developing those noodle arms instead, why don't you?" Hila turned back to her soup, dismissing Garron from her mind.

A laugh rang out from another counter. The sous chef was expertly breaking down and deboning a large fish for the night's dinner, but he had Hila's knack for multitasking. "Hah! You'd better get going before she gets nasty!"

Garron suddenly remembered that there were at least a half dozen other people going in and out of the kitchen, and considered whether or not he'd want to engage in a public sparring match with Hila. "Good plan. I'll see you all later then!"

Jameson's laughter followed him out of the kitchen, but Garron still smiled as the doors closed behind him. His levity vanished as he moved away from the kitchen and back into the claustrophobic halls of the Tet estate. He always breathed a little easier in the kitchen, though honestly anywhere indoors was harder than outside. Garron didn't really mind going out to the east quarter for that reason, but if his cough was any indication, he wouldn't be doing much in the way of exercise today. It didn't matter what the cook said.

"Hey there, Garron."

Garron looked up into a pair of tired eyes crinkled in a weary smile. The man had his guard uniform on and a sword belted at the waist, but Garron could see that his tunic was stained with a viscous fluid.

"Hi Ulysses." Garron raised a hand in greeting, fighting to keep it steady. "You've got something on your tunic."

"Oh, abyss." Ulysses brought his own hand up to his uniform, then winced as it touched the fluid. Tiredly, he reached for his sword, and pulled out a little embroidered handkerchief from between the crossguard and sheath.

It was already stained with the fluid, and Ulysses spent a fruitless moment dabbing at the stuff on his tunic before Garron handed him his own cloth. "How's the baby? Myra, right?"

"Thanks. She's doing well, I think. Her stomach was bothering her a bit though. She won't stop *crying*." Ulysses took the cloth with a sigh. The last words were said with the sort of frustrated despair that Garron had only ever seen from new parents. Not that there were many in the estate, but there had been a few lower-ranked guards like Ulysses, as well as kitchen staff or houseworkers, who'd come in and out of service, sometimes bringing families with them.

"That's rough, buddy." Garron patted the shoulder not stained by baby vomit.

Ulysses nodded appreciatively, though his face remained glum. "Thanks, but Mylena's got it worse. I can't really complain. Just wish I didn't have to pull night watch on top of—"

"*Ulysses*! Break time's over, get back to your post!"

Garron winced at the voice booming down the hallway. Abyss. Lars was coming.

He could almost feel the ground shaking before he turned to see a mountainous man in the uniform of the House Guard lumbering down the hallway. Garron knew he was small for his age, but Lars' size made even Ulysses look like a youth. The snarl perpetually twisting his face didn't help make the guard lieutenant look any less intimidating either. "Oh, of course it's *you* distracting another person. Shouldn't you be doing something useful, instead of standing around freeloading? You've got to earn your keep for a little while longer at least."

As the man drew closer, Garron felt his chest tighten slightly like it did when he was around Jackson. In some ways, Lars was worse; every time he looked at Garron, his face showed... distaste. It was as though Garron were physically painful to look at. Garron didn't think he was particularly handsome, but he wasn't *that* ugly.

Garron didn't point out that, like most of the senior guards, Lars did very little other than sit around 'gardening,' or 'cultivating,' or whatever they called it. He thought Hila did more real work than any ten of them combined. Instead, Garron bowed slightly. "Yes, sir. I'll get go—"

"I mean, not that you can really do anything worth keeping you around, but the boy won't let us kick you out." Lars' voice was edging toward spiteful now. "And after you spent all that time getting Skyspear-tutored, world class training with him for free... for not a single abyssal *reason*!"

"Right, I'm *so* lucky." Garron barely held the words back, remembering the 'training' Lars had talked about. It hadn't seemed that exciting to him. He'd been Andros' sparring partner, and done most of the exercises with him as well, but when Lord Tet went away, Jackson had refused to include him. Of course, his illness came in soon after that, rendering the point moot. He took a deep breath, trying to cool his annoyance.

It caught in his chest and he let out a hacking cough, and another, until he was doubled over, only on his feet because Ulysses was supporting him. "You alright there, Garron? Do you need water or anything?"

Garron couldn't respond with anything but a cough, but Lars cut in over the noise, sounding even more disgusted than before. "Just get back to your post. Isn't like *water's* going to help him."

Ulysses hesitated for a bare moment, looking at Garron in concern, but with a sigh, he gave a sharp salute. "Yes, sir. I'll be right there."

Lars grunted, and Garron could hear the sound of his heavy footsteps moving away even as he continued to cough.

Ulysses stayed until the fit died down, for which Garron was grateful, but he couldn't help being preoccupied by the knowing tinge to Lars' last comment. Why *not* give him water? Wasn't that a normal thing to help a cough?

When Garron finally managed to walk out and around the estate to the east quarter, he was met with the sounds of stone grinding and men shouting. The construction work being done to build the new wing was, frankly, incredible. Jackson had hired a stonemason, a carpenter, and a few specialist builders for the task; but that meant much of the brute labor had to be done by the estate staff. He walked up as close as he dared to the construction site, where a pair of burly men were pulling a huge block of stone into place along the growing wall; scraping away imperfections and creating smooth joints in the process.

A man holding a stone tablet and scrap of paper came over to him, eyes calculating. Garron liked the man, who called himself an 'engineer.' He claimed to have learned his trade from Dwarves, though Garron wasn't sure he believed that. Still, he had to admit that the anchored pulley system that he'd had built next to the wall was nothing short of amazing. Even now, there was only one sullen guardsman manning the rope. The rope itself looped around a series of pulley wheels and held up the stone that was being added to the wall.

The engineer waved a stylus in Garron's direction as he approached. "Hey there, boy. You're here to help, are you? Hm, why don't you go over and help out that fellow on the pulley rope? He says he can handle it, but an engineer always plans for the worst-case scenario. Remember that, boy."

He tapped his nose, smudging it with dirt before walking back to the wall. Garron privately thought that 'engineer' was probably a made-up word, but he agreed in principle. The thing was, even if he wasn't exactly sure how Joris—the guardsman currently holding the rope—was managing to lift all that weight by himself; he was certain that his contribution would change absolutely nothing if something went wrong. Garron just tried his best to stay out of the guardsman's way.

He could tell Joris was just as disdainful of Garron as most of the senior guards, and there was no sense inviting yet another scolding.

Garron managed not to have another fit for the rest of the day as he helped with the construction, and planned to have an uneventful night when he went to bed. The manor had barely settled before that plan for relaxation was rudely interrupted, and he was shaken roughly awake.

The engineer would have been disappointed. He should have planned for the worst-case scenario.

CHAPTER TWO

"*Gar.*"

Garron blinked the sleep from his eyes, somehow managing not to panic at the rough shaking and frantic whispering.

"*Garron.*"

Something *solid* nudged him again, and his eyes popped open and focused on a face *far* too close to his own. Garron shot up and knocked his head into a set of teeth that felt like iron. "*Oww.*"

"Oh. Sorry about that. You okay? Never mind that, we have to go *now!*" the familiar voice demanded. Garron managed to struggle out of his covers and stand, wiping a hint of blood off of his forehead from where the teeth had broken his skin. He took a deep breath, noting with relief that the air went in and out easily. Today was good, then.

"What's going on?" He couldn't see much of anything in the darkness, but he thought he recognized the voice. "Andy?"

"Not so loud!" Andros waved his arms in a blur of motion. Garron ignored that his 'whisper' was quite a bit louder than Garron's normal speaking voice, focusing instead on his Noble friend's blurry form.

"What are you doing here?" A hand landed on his shoulder.

"I'm here to save you, Gar. We have to go, now. I'll explain when we're clear." Apparently, Andros had also given up on whispering. Garron sighed and began pulling on his boots. He didn't have a prayer of stopping whatever scheme this was.

"Andy, if you'd just said it we could have been on our way by now, whatever this is."

Silence. Then, a reluctant answer from the young Noble. "I've stolen some money and important supplies from the family repository. We have to leave, and get you to a dungeon so you can swallow a Core to fix your cultivation base, or else... Garron. Everyone knows it, everyone except for you. You're going to die in a week. Two at the most."

A cold feeling came over Garron. Most of that had gone straight over his head, but two things stuck. The first was that he was dying. A deaf, blind old man with a drinking problem could have told him that one, though it was surprising that there was an end date. But the second... "You stole something from the repository? From your *family*?"

"No time, Garron!" The hand on his shoulder gripped him with a strength that seemed out of proportion for Andros' size, and suddenly Garron was in the hallway, stumbling along behind a shadowy figure, too startled to protest. They were moving surprisingly quickly, and Garron half expected a coughing fit to overcome him. Maybe today was just a *really* good day. Except for the whole 'risking his life and possibly the life of his best friend' thing, but Garron knew better than to stop and question someone that was trying to save him.

They took three turns: two lefts and a right. Garron was moving under his own power, though he was struggling to keep up with Andros. Almost to the south exit now, the one Hila and the other cooks used for picking up raw ingredients. They were through it in a flash, though the kitchen felt eerie to him; barely illuminated and dead silent as it was. Two more turns and...

"Halt! Who goes there?" The voice cut off with a choking sound, but Garron noticed that it had sounded... muted somehow. Almost like he was hearing it through a wall or something. There was a dull thud, and a dark figure collapsed to the ground.

"Sorry about that, Ulysses," Andros whispered, tugging Garron along behind him. "You'll be fine tomorrow, but I don't envy you the headache."

They moved past the still huddle of shadows, and Garron grimaced. "What are we doing? Andy, why—"

"Trust me, we *have* to do this. Now, come on. If Ulysses was there already, we must have missed our window. Thank celestial it was him on duty tonight—I wouldn't have wanted to run into Lars." They made it to the exit, a large door set into a stone frame with a worn brass handle sticking out. Andros grabbed the handle.

Garron opened his mouth to tell him that it was locked, but before he could, there was a stirring of wind and a *click*. The door opened and the sweet scent of the open air filled the room, then the wind washed over him and a chill ran down his back. "Andy, I don't have a cloak or anything."

"I've got all that ready. We just have to get to it. I'm sorry." Andros *did* sound sorry, but he still pulled Garron through the doorway and onto the paved patio around the entrance. Garron sighed, only rasping a little, and moved to the path that would lead to the gate of the estate. Andros' hand stopped him. "No. This way."

Wondering if he was in a very strange dream, Garron followed his old friend, ducking low and stealing across the perfectly manicured lawn of the Tet estate like an assassin from a bard's tale. The estate itself was large, but the south exit was fairly near the edge; soon they found themselves in the light woods that grew on the outskirts. Garron was gasping, each breath only coming with a great effort, when Andros finally slowed. "Alright, we're here."

It was an interesting feeling, working so hard in the cold. Garron's face, hands, and feet were all throbbing in time with his heartbeat. He felt flushed, but whenever he sweated, the water grew cold against his skin and set him shivering.

"I'm so sorry, Gar. Here, put these on." Andros moved to the base of a tree, a young willow whose branches swayed despite the dead leaves, and rummaged for something. After a moment, he pulled something out and took a sharp breath. "Abyss, an animal must have gotten to it."

A tattered brown cloak was just visible in the moonlight, barely held together. Huge swathes of fabric had been torn away. "It got the food? Celestial *feces*!"

Garron smiled a little, still shivering. "You left a bundle of clothes and *food* out in the woods without any protection? Nice."

"Oh, shut up, you. I didn't think we had that many animals in the woods here." Andros' shadowed form hunched slightly, and Garron knew he was crossing his arms like he always did when he was annoyed.

"You're right. Animals in the woods... that *does* seem unlikely." Garron nodded sagely. Then both of them were laughing. It lasted a good few seconds before Garron started coughing, and Andros pounded his back lightly. It didn't help, but Garron appreciated the effort. Once his breathing had calmed into its normal labored pattern, Garron looked at Andros, trying to inject some urgency into his expression. He trusted his friend implicitly, but they had broken out of the *manor*. He needed answers. "What's going on, Andy?"

Something settled around his shoulders. It was a smooth fabric, not too thick, but certainly better than nothing. Andros' cloak? "There you go, that's made from Beast hide and fur—I pity the animal who tries to chew *that*. Sit over here for a minute."

Andros moved to a root that was protruding up out of the ground, motioning for Garron to sit. "I'm sorry. There wasn't anything else I could think to do. Jackson's away tonight, but he'll be back tomorrow and I don't know if we'll have another chance before you..."

"What, die? I mean, I know it's coming, but how do you know *when*? What does any of *this* have to do with that?" Garron kept his voice matter of fact. Plenty of people had tried to comfort him when it became obvious how bad his illness was. He'd gotten tired of it quickly, and even more tired of consoling *them* about his own impending death. Being frank with his words helped avoid that.

Andros gave a light cough, looking oddly guilty. Almost… ashamed? "Uh, yeah. Well, you know how I started opening meridians a few years ago?"

Garron shrugged. There had been a big party in the house, he remembered that much. He wasn't clear on why, exactly, there was cause for celebration. "Sort of. I don't know what mandarins have to do with it, though. They're out of season, aren't they?"

"*Meridians*. Anyway, now I can see the Essence in the world, and the corruption. You… ugh."

"What? And what do you mean, 'Essence'? And why does everyone make that sound when they look at me?" Garron had heard that word, vaguely, especially back when he'd trained with Andros. But there were more important things to worry about in life than what Nobles babbled about; even Andros could be a little silly sometimes, but he chalked that up to him being a year older and wiser.

Andros sighed heavily, rested a hand on his shoulder, then pulled him to his feet. "We don't have that much time. They're going to find Ulysses and raise the alarm if we don't get a move on. I can give you the memory stone later. The point is, I know why you're sick. I have something that can make you better, but we have to go to a place where you can take it safely, or you'll die even faster."

"You have… something that can *cure* me?" Garron blinked. Full disbelief. He blinked again. He reached a hand out, not really knowing what he was doing. "What is—"

Andros grabbed his hand. "Let's start moving. We're close to the wall here, and I think I have enough Essence to get us over and make a break for it."

They began dashing through the woods, Garron shivering somewhat less under the cloak, and following Andros in something of a daze. He'd long ago accepted that he was meant to die young. It was simple reality, and honestly he didn't mind so much. Fifteen years wasn't long enough to really know what he was missing out on. But now, there was a way to *live*? Somehow? He didn't know how to handle it, except to try as hard as he possibly could to keep up with Andros.

They got to the wall in short order, Garron breathing much easier than he had all week. He looked up at the stone barrier with a numb sort of worry. He hadn't really registered Andros' words before about where they were going. "So, what are we going to do about this?"

"Alright Gar, now it's time for the tricky part. I'm going to cultivate a little more wind before we go. Just so you know, I'm going to have to lift us over the wall, and then we have to *move*. The alarms on the wall will trigger when we get over it, and we have to make sure that we can get away before the guards catch us. I'm a higher rank than pretty much all of them; since Jackson's out doing his own training and Lars went to the town for the night. We should be able to get away before they can call either of them. But I'm going to have to do something a little, uh… painful. I'm not really the best with it yet, but there's no other way."

Garron frowned, considering Andros' form. His outline was rigid, almost thrumming with contained anxiety. He was terrified, but Garron heard the determination in his voice. This was important to him. And, apparently, to Garron. "Okay, Andy. I trust you."

"Okay." Andros took a deep breath and began walking around aimlessly, jumping occasionally.

"What the abyss?" Garron kept his voice down, but he couldn't help but wonder if he'd taken a bad fall sometime the previous day. After all, he still wasn't clear on how Andros was going to get them over the wall, and now he was doing some sort of… dance? "Did you just pirouette?"

The wind stirred, then slowed. Garron noticed that the trees around them had stopped swaying so much, and he felt a familiar tightness close around his chest. Maybe it wasn't such a good day after all.

"That's enough. There wasn't much here anyway." Andros hurried back over, securing the little pack by his waistband, then spreading his arms out. "It's time now, Gar. We're going to go flying over the wall, but I'm not so great at controlling the way up yet. It's going to be rough."

"Uh, okay." Garron uncertainly embraced his friend, and he felt long arms wrap around him very, *very* tightly. Too tightly. He choked out, "Andy, you're—"

The rest of his words were ripped away as wind *gusted* all around them. Garron felt an immense pressure pushing on him, not from above, but below. When he tried to gasp, nothing happened. There was a rushing sound filling his ears, and abruptly he realized that he wasn't on the ground anymore. They were actually *flying*.

This was nothing like what bards had sung about. Garron didn't have time to appreciate beautiful landscapes or marvel at the freedom of the skies. He felt wind tearing at his body, his clothes began humming as the wind ruffled them. His cheeks were vibrating as well, and every inch of exposed skin felt like it was being pounded by a million little hammers. Garron's ears popped, and a moment later popped again. Suddenly the noise, the wind, everything, stopped.

"*Sorry.*" Andros' voice was muffled, but Garron hardly paid attention.

Now he could see, and it was, well, strange. They weren't very high, but even so he could still see most of the estate from this angle, and it looked so… small. The place he'd spent his entire life in wasn't even large enough to take up his whole field of vision. He could see tall, grassy plains where they would land, dense forest nearby, and beyond it—were those mountains?

Then they started falling. Garron was too surprised for a

proper scream, and by the time he got ready for it they were slowing down again; then his feet were touching the ground. Andros was panting, shifting around but not letting go of Garron. "That's done. I heard the alarm go; they'll be after us soon. Actually, I think it'd be better if I carried you."

Without waiting for a response, Andros changed positions to scoop him up as though he were a baby. *What?* Yes, Garron was small for his age, but Andros wasn't huge. The other boy was holding him just as tightly as before with no apparent effort. How in the abyss was he this strong?

Andros took a deep breath, unceremoniously hauling Garron's weight into his arms. "This is going to stink worse than a bucket of demon blood. Just keep your face close to me or you won't be able to breathe."

Garron opened a mouth already half-covered by Andros' shirt; but then realized that in the distance he could hear a high-pitched tone and—he imagined—men shouting. He shut his mouth before any words escaped, seeing Andros staring at the stars.

"Okay, we're lined up with the Gnome's Bellybutton and… Let's go!" The world became rushing noise and wind again, but this time Garron didn't have the benefit of open air around him. He was being compressed, squeezed as flat as an apprentice cook's first attempt at breadmaking. Garron wondered, somewhere in the back of his head, why that was the only metaphor he could think of… then the screaming wind drowned out even his mental voices.

It took far, *far* too long; and the worst thing was that they kept stopping and restarting every few seconds. The first dozen times, Garron hoped that it would end. Then he began hoping he would pass out. The only reason he didn't vomit was that he couldn't get anything out past the constant acceleration pushing his bile back.

After a while, he retreated into his own mind, and began thinking more closely about the situation. Had he really just escaped the estate with Andros? Jackson was going to be furious.

Were they really going to cure his illness somehow? Was Andros really *still* going?

Finally, blessedly, they stopped. Garron tensed again, waiting for the horrible moment of acceleration, but it never came. Instead, the world spun and he fell to the ground with a light *thud*. After a moment of just laying there, dizzy and confused, with tears streaming out from his closed eyes, Garron began struggling weakly to his feet. He only made it to his knees before he vomited.

Then he made it to his feet, and fell over again, more bile dripping down his chest. On the third try, he finally stood, breathing heavily and painfully. He looked over to curse at his friend and felt his heart go cold. Light had started tinging the horizon, and he could see that they'd stopped in another forest, much more unkempt than the one contained in the Tet estate. He could also see a gangly form laid out on the ground, and a face framed by a mess of black hair. Andros looked as pale as death, and when Garron tried to rouse him, the young Lordling didn't respond.

CHAPTER THREE

"This had better work." Garron muttered in between gasps. He'd panicked for a few minutes, coughed for another, then vomited a little more. Somewhere in between, he'd thought about what was going on.

Andros had done impossible things that night. Leaving aside the flying and the infernal *running*, he'd also managed to knock Ulysses out without touching him, then unlock the door leading out of the estate with… magic? Based on the dancing in the forest, and the way he'd felt the wind respond whenever Andros had done something impossible, Garron thought that the air had something to do with it. Andros had said something about having enough 'Essence' to make it this far. Maybe he'd been wrong?

He recalled Andros mumbling that there 'wasn't much here.' The air had been still, so Garron figured he should get Andros someplace with as much wind as possible and hope that would be enough to save him. In a forest, that meant they needed to go up a tree. Of course, Garron had about as much hope of carrying Andros up a tree by himself as he did of winning a footrace against a racehorse. He recalled the pulley system the engineer had put in place, the one that had let a single man do the work of ten. Garron didn't have the time or materials to set up a system like the one the masons used—he didn't even have a rope. But Andros had a knife in his pouch, and his cloak was made of *very* strong material.

Hand, hand, foot, foot. Or was it the other way? He didn't quite remember. It had been a long time since he'd had the time or constitution to climb trees. This one had plenty of little branches to make hand and footholds, but Garron hadn't done anything so physically taxing for *years*. It was a very good day for his chest, thank celestial, but that didn't stop the burning and shaking in his limbs after a few minutes. He kept going. Garron had no idea what would happen if he didn't hurry. It had already been too long, and the air around where Andros was lying was completely dead. He was still breathing, but he hadn't recovered or roused at all, even when Garron tied the 'rope' around his shoulders.

Garron moved his foot, already getting ready for another torturous haul upwards, and he heard a *snap*. His cheap boot scraped against the tree bark, his knee smacking painfully into the trunk. His heart tightened in panic, and he held onto the other branches with a death grip. Then the branch holding his *other* foot broke away.

There was a terrible moment of *wrenching*, as his shoulders, then his arms, took on the weight of his entire body. Then it got to his hands, and suddenly his grip didn't seem nearly tight enough. His forearms started burning, and he held back a scream. Garron looked around wildly and spotted another branch right above his right hand. If he could get his hand there, maybe he could get his foot up to his handhold? It looked like it was just barely in reach. With only his hands supporting him, that might be too far.

As he *pulled*, a yell escaped him. His hand shot upwards, and fingers caught on the little branch stub. Scrambling with his legs against the trunk, Garron managed to get higher and grab a good hold of the wood. Without pause, he *pulled* again, getting his leg up as high as he could. One advantage of being small and sickly—maybe the only one—was that he didn't have much weight to pull up, and he was flexible to boot. He got his foot on the open branch and breathed a shaky sigh of relief.

Garron took a moment, just standing there. He was high enough that a fall would have certainly broken bones and probably killed him. It was one thing to know that you were going to die of sickness in the near future, and quite another to go out and risk your life for an insane plan that had almost no chance of actually working. But…

He thought about what he'd seen in Andros, just before they'd gone over the wall. Fear. Andros knew that he was risking everything to help Garron, risking truly angering *Jackson*. He'd done it before, too, when they were both not even thirteen years old. He'd screamed for days and refused to eat when Jackson had tried to kick Garron out of the estate. Garron knew he'd taken a few beatings for that, probably more than he'd heard about. He owed Andros too much to give up out of fear now.

He kept going, the shaking worse than ever, until he found a large enough branch and the cloak-rope started losing its slack. After a moment's consideration, he carefully took off a boot and rubbed it against the branch, smoothing out the wood as best he could before laying the rope across it. On the way back down, remembering the way the stone-workers' rig had been set up, he looped the rope around two more branches.

Soon, he was pulling against resistance, but not so much that he couldn't get anywhere. Thankfully, whatever the cloak was made out of, it was both strong *and* supple enough that it didn't get much resistance from the branches as it rubbed. About halfway down, chest heaving, Garron started leaning against the rope as a counterweight, and began sliding slowly down the trunk, feeling the weight on the other end get pulled up at the same time.

When he reached the ground, Garron didn't quite know what to do, except hold onto the rope for all he was worth, using the roots at the base of the tree to brace himself. He could see Andros up there, dangling from the rope Garron had knotted about his shoulders like a human scarecrow. Time was passing quickly, and soon almost an hour had vanished. Still, Garron couldn't move.

He was intensely grateful for the times he'd had to work with the stablemaster, and to the man himself for taking the time to teach him all of those knots. Everything seemed stable, now all he could was wait and…

Coughing fits were never fun. Up in the tree, he'd suppressed a few out of pure terror and determination, but now he was back on the ground and there was so much *pollen* in the air. The infernal wrenching in his chest came back in full force. Garron coughed so hard that he was convinced he could feel things ripping in his chest. He covered his mouth and hacked away, the sound strangely dull in the life of the forest, for what felt like a quarter hour. For a moment, the fit subsided, and he looked at his sleeve, to see specks of blood, combined with something… black. "What the—"

Then another great cough tore through him, and he reflexively brought his hand up to his mouth to cover it. The same hand that had been holding on to the rope. Garron barely had time to realize what was happening before he heard a whizzing sound and a crack as the rope slipped off the first two branches.

"*Ahhh!*" There was a shout and a gust of wind; then something fell on Garron, not as hard as he would have expected, but not gently either. He fell to the ground with a yell of his own.

"What the abyss!"

Andros wriggled, rolling off of Garron and trying to stand as Garron did the same. They both fell over when the rope tripped Garron up and pulled at the harness on Andros' shoulders. It took more effort than it probably should have to disentangle themselves, but both of them were pale and shaking now. Andros actually seemed worse off than Garron, which was, in some ways, a welcome change of pace.

Once they were finally free of the rope, Garron shot his

friend a hesitant look. "Are you okay now? I, uh, didn't really know what to do and—"

"I think you saved my life, Gar," Andros interrupted him, still panting with the white showing around his eyes. "There was enough Essence up there that my passive technique filled up my Center a bit faster. Just wish you hadn't dropped me."

Garron felt slightly awkward at the words, though whether from Andros'—his liege's—obvious gratitude or the reminder of his mistake he wasn't sure. "Yeah, I don't know what any of that means. Maybe you should go dance around a bit until you're back to normal?"

Andros opened his mouth, then closed it and shrugged. He went off and started dancing again, eventually climbing up a tree with an ease that made Garron a bit jealous and hopping around the branches there. The whole while, Garron simply sat and tried to calm himself a little, until finally Andros settled down next to him.

That lasted for only a minute, before Andros shot to his feet, eyes focused on the distance. "Okay, we've got to go. I have a feeling Jackson found out we left."

Garron's body protested, but he lifted himself up as well. "What? Why?"

Andros sighed. "A pillar of fire flared into the sky, down about where the estate is."

Garron felt his own eyes widen. "Celestials, Jackson. Right, we should go. Uh, where are we going, anyway?"

Andros started frantically jumping around again, eyes going out of focus but still speaking in a fearful tone. "Dad told me about it, before he went away. There's a new dungeon up this way, but they couldn't set up Guild offices on it before the war started up—it's got an earth affinity, but there's a river running through it, so apparently there's a good bit of water Essence in it too. It's not perfect, but it's the best option we have. And it's still young, so hopefully we'll still be able to get through it and have you use the Beast Core."

Garron blinked, his fear sidetracked at the new information. "Wait, a *dungeon*?"

Even the sickly peasant had heard about dungeons. He'd wondered if they were real, or just a bard's fanciful tale, but he'd reasoned that there had to be some way Lord Tet could be as scary as he was. He must have been through many dungeons throughout his life. Still, even if he recognized some part of Andros' words, he was getting rather annoyed at his friend's incomprehensible explanations. "When are you going to explain what's going on?"

Andros came to a halt again in front of Garron, and started fumbling at his discarded pouch. "You're right. Wait a second… Okay, here we go."

The young master pulled out a stone that glimmered in the light of the sun peeking through the foliage. It was still early morning, and from its current angle not much could make it through to the forest. Still, Garron could see that the little gem didn't quite match any of those in the fancy jewelry he'd seen on women who used to come to the estate for parties. "I'm going to press this on your head, okay Gar? It's going to feel weird, but just stay calm. You're going to learn a lot of information, so brace yourself."

Garron's eyes followed the stone in Andros' hand, crossing slightly as it moved toward his forehead. "Wha—"

Knowledge *poured* into Garron's mind. Suddenly, he knew that 'Essence' was the energy of the world itself, and that 'corruption' was the taint that it accumulated from the environment. He knew that humans held their Essence in their 'Centers,' and that 'cultivating' was the word for pulling Essence into oneself and purifying it. He learned a 'cultivation technique' that would let him pull in and purify Essence; then make it into a 'spiral' in his Center. Most importantly, he learned how to perceive his own Center.

He looked right away. If he'd had anything left in his stomach, he would have thrown up again.

From the gem—memory stone—Garron knew vaguely

what Essence should feel like. He could barely perceive a hint of it in himself, but oh, the *corruption*. His Center was a seething pit of foul earth and tainted water, like a forest gone to rot, or a latrine pit that got too full, all bubbling and oozing through him.

He tried to move it like he'd just learned, but nothing happened. The corruption filling him seeped into every part of his body, and he could *feel* how it ground away at his being, binding his chest in chains of mud. Earth and water. A dual affinity, pulling in tainted Essence from the world around him so fast that it was a miracle he wasn't dead yet.

"Why? Why didn't they *tell* me?" Garron gasped, falling to his knees. He now knew the basics of what they were about to do. These were Andros' memories; Garron could feel the anger, the despair, and the pity that had colored his thoughts as he formed this stone. Not all of the information was clear—some of it had been muddled in the making of the stone—but Garron could see enough.

Andros took in a shuddering breath, and when Garron looked up he thought he could see tears in his friend's eyes. "Jackson—"

Garron held up a hand. "I know it's him. But *why?*"

"I don't know, Gar. He hated that you were training with me. Dad was planning on granting you a Beast Core, after your mom died and everything. But when he went away, Jackson wouldn't hear of it." Andros' fists were clenched, his knuckles white.

For the first time in Garron's life, he felt true, deep hatred well up inside him, out of his pit of a Center. He'd been condemned to years of pain, years of believing he was meant to die, because of the maliciousness of one man.

He looked up at Andros, and he could see his rage mirrored in his friend's dark eyes. Now he knew why the other boy had looked so angry for the past year. He'd been fighting for Garron the entire time. "Andy, thank y—"

"Don't mention it, Gar. He's cost you too much already. You

deserve this." Andros stepped up to him, laying a hand on his shoulder.

Garron felt his tears begin to dry, and he was surprised at the note of weariness in his own voice. "We have to go now, don't we?"

Andros nodded decisively. "We're really close now. My movement technique can get us there in a few jumps."

Garron felt the blood drain from his face. "Or—"

Then they were moving.

CHAPTER FOUR

Garron didn't really know what to expect from a dungeon, but once his eyes cleared and he finished dry-heaving... he wasn't very impressed. It just seemed like a hole in the side of a grassy hill. They were on a slope, and the ground seemed muddier than it should—that must be the underground river Andros had mentioned. With his new senses, Garron could tell there was much more Essence in this place than anywhere else he had been; primarily earth but also hints of water. He could feel his Center pulling in the power, and the corruption, faster than ever.

Next to him, Andros winced. "You know, being here has shortened your lifespan. You've been taking in more Essence, but also more corruption. If you go to a low Essence area now, you'd probably be bedridden. If this doesn't work..."

"Huh." Examining his new knowledge, Garron saw that Andy was right. It was a good day, but that was because of all the Essence he was pulling in. The corruption he took in along with it would stay behind, and accumulate even more, until it killed him. He would feel great all the way until the end, at least. "We'd better get going fast, right?"

"Heh. I guess." Andros seemed... nervous?

Garron stopped walking, shooting a suspicious look at the young lord. "What's wrong?"

"It's just, I've never been inside a dungeon alone before. The report I read said this one's only F-rank seven or so, and I'm D-rank three, almost four, so it shouldn't be too dangerous but... dungeons can be weird."

"Rank... yes. I'm..." Garron looked at his Center again. "Actually, I can't tell."

Andros nodded. "Neither can I. Somewhere in the low-to-mid F, I'd guess, but all the corruption makes it pretty immaterial."

Garron supposed that made sense, considering what he knew now. The memory stone had really contained a lot of information—Andros' knowledge of cultivation had included plenty of interesting tidbits. Besides the general information about cultivation, Garron could parse some things about a basic cultivation technique, even some earth and water techniques he'd learned from another memory stone. Those seemed interesting, but he'd save them for after he'd purified his Center.

"Well, either way, we've got you, right? Let's do this." Garron clapped his hands, then winced.

"Really? That's the best you could come up with? You're slipping." Andros turned from examining the dungeon entrance to look at him, and took a deep breath before nodding. "Okay. I've already taken in about all the air Essence there was here anyway. Just keep safe. Hopefully we can get some weapons or armor for you as loot."

With that, they stepped into the cave. They walked down a winding tunnel in complete darkness for a bit, before it started to lighten. A few moments later, the tunnel opened up into a dank stone cave. Garron looked at the rock formations and grunted. "Wait, what's on the stalag... stalac—"

"Pointy stone things. I don't know." Andros didn't even turn to look in his direction.

Some of the pointy stone things were glowing with a soft

light that nonetheless showed them that there was nothing to worry about in this room. Garron moved to take a step forward, and Andros stopped him with a hand. Without saying a word, he reached out with his own foot, and the stone below it crumbled away, revealing a pit lined with more pointy stone things.

Andros shot him a meaningful look. "I think we have to stay close to the…"

Garron didn't hesitate to hug the wall. "P.S.T.'s."

They began threading their way through the cave, always sticking close to the pillars of stone. Occasionally a wrong step almost got Garron skewered, but Andros kept a tight grip on his arm as they continued forward. After a tense few minutes, they were clear.

"That wasn't so bad," Garron commented cheerfully.

"No, but we haven't run into any mobs yet. Much less loot. Actually, hold on a minute." Andros went back into the stone room, moving carefully but much more swiftly without Garron to slow him down. He expertly threaded his way around the treacherous floor, using a leg to break away the false bits and reveal the pit traps below. Eventually, Garron caught the glint of something shiny.

"There we go!" Andros straightened, holding something metallic in his hand. A few moments later, he was back at the end of the room, offering a slightly rusted metal sword out to Garron. "It isn't much, but it's something at least. I'm better at hand-to-hand, so you should hold onto this."

Garron hesitantly accepted the sword, noticing that, though the metal wasn't of the best quality, the edge was still sharp. "Okay. I can't say I'll be good at it."

Andros frowned. "Don't you remember our lessons, back when we were kids?"

"Uh, most of those just ended with you hitting me with a stick." As Garron recalled, he'd actually been a fair bit better at the actual sparring, but Andros had been fond of finding opportunities for 'sneak attacks.'

Andros shrugged, apparently remembering none of his own

antics. "Huh. Fair point, I guess. Try your best though, the next room will probably have mobs in it."

They continued on, the tunnel taking a sharp bend, and the smell of animal feces hit them. Andros took the lead, holding his hands up warily, and Garron awkwardly held his sword in front of him, trying not to accidentally cut himself.

They walked into another room, which also had a forest of glowing stone protruding from its ceiling, with a floor bare except for dirt and excrement from some small animal. Garron stepped cautiously, but Andros motioned him forward after a bit of experimental tapping. They both looked around warily, wondering what the challenge here was supposed to be.

Then something fell on Garron's face.

"Ahhhh!" he yelped, dropping his sword and clawing at whatever was on him. Sharp claws raked across his skin, and he felt pain blossoming. There was a wrench, and he was free. He looked around wildly, scooping up the sword and looking to see what was happening.

Andros was wrestling with the shrieking, hissing creature now. It had dark fur with white and black markings around its eyes. A raccoon? Andros raised the animal up, clearly intending to smack it against the ground, but suddenly his arms sagged, and he dropped the thing with a cry of his own.

The raccoon hit the ground with a solid thud that seemed out of proportion with its size, and four more identical sounds followed it in quick succession. It only took a glance to see that they were surrounded.

"Oh, *aby*—"

One of the little monsters jumped at them, far too quick for its size, and Garron took a clumsy swing at it, barely managing to aim it edge-on. He thought he would hit it, but right before his sword made contact, the creature suddenly dropped out of the air like a stone, landing with a thud in front of Garron and swiping a claw at his legs. Garron yelped and hopped back.

Behind him, he could hear the meaty sounds of flesh hitting flesh, the occasional crack of little bones breaking, and the yips of injured raccoons. It seemed Andros was busy. The raccoon in front of Garron snarled, and he swore he saw the skin beneath its fur lighten as it darted forward again. This time he was ready. When it jumped, instead of trying to hit it, he just moved to the side as quickly as he could, his sword slashing wildly at the same time. The raccoon did the same trick again, falling swiftly as soon as Garron's sword got close to it, so he took a swing at it on the ground.

The creature tried to dodge, but apparently whatever it did to fall made it much slower: it failed to avoid his strike. His sword bit into the creature's hide, but not nearly as deep as he expected. Instead of cutting to the bone, he barely saw the blade penetrate an inch before the creature yipped, its skin lightened, and it darted past him. Garron turned to chase it, but he saw that it had lost interest in him. It was joining its fellows in attacking Andros.

Garron's friend was being overwhelmed. Two of the monsters were lying dead on the ground, but that left three who were all attacking him at once. They were jumping at him from all angles, and whenever he took a swing at one, it dropped to the floor and one of its fellows took over the assault. Andros was dodging with exceeding grace, but he couldn't land a hit and keep himself out of harm's way. He needed help.

Another of the monsters dropped to the floor with a thud, and Garron took the opportunity to leap forward himself, sword flashing from behind. He just barely managed to keep from chopping Andros' leg off as the other boy took the same opportunity to aim a stomp at the mob. They both stopped short, and the creature scurried away.

"Watch out!" Andros' shout interrupted Garron's heaving breaths.

Garron winced. He hadn't even looked to see what Andros was doing before he rushed in. "Sorry—"

"No, *down*!" Andros shoved Garron to the side, and another raccoon jumped through the air where he'd been, only falling when Andros tried to kick it. This time, when the young Noble attacked the disoriented mob, it died; the wet crack accompanied Garron's rise from the floor.

Andros was already back to dodging. When Garron spotted an opening, he tried shouting before taking his swing. He swung down with all his might this time, and though the blade slowed quickly, the cut was still fatal. At the same time, another crack signaled that the final mob was dead.

"*Phew*! Those were a little tougher than I expected, but I'm glad I didn't have to use any Essence!" The young Noble turned from the raccoon's corpse. "There isn't much air Essence down here, so it's better if I save it for the boss. Oh, check this out! I think I see some silver!"

Garron was breathing hard, intensely glad that he wasn't feeling the worst of his illness just then. "What were they?"

Andros laughed, gathering up the silver that had popped out of the monster's corpses. There was no equipment to be found, unfortunately. "Raccoons."

Garron rolled his eyes. "Andy…"

"Well, they must have been soaking in the earth Essence from here. They had some sort of weight manipulation ability is all. Not a big deal on something so small." Andros shrugged, then dropped the coins in his bag with a clink.

Garron nodded slowly. "So, other monsters in this place might have the same ability, or something similar, right?"

Andros nodded amiably. "Right."

Garron nodded along with him. "Do you think they'll *all* be this small?"

"Sadly…" There was a long pause followed by, "Not a chance."

In the next room, Andros was forced to use his movement technique while carrying Garron again. Every time they took a step forward, a spike would fall on the spot. When Andros sped them through the room, they suddenly found themselves at the end, with a line of stone shards piled up in their wake.

"Hey," Garron commented as Andros released him. "How come you needed to cultivate after using that technique? The ones in the stone you gave me seem like they're supposed to loop back into you."

Andros laughed awkwardly. "Well, it's… uh, something I made. I haven't really figured out how to do the 'looping' thing, and besides, it's worth the loss. It uses up my Essence to boost me forward really, *really* fast."

Garron frowned. "Isn't that bad?"

His friend shrugged. "I dropped a rank or two on the way here, but my cultivation technique is really good, so it's not much of an issue to fill my Center back up. At my cultivation rank, it's still a pretty insignificant amount of power."

Based on what Garron had learned, he thought Andros was underplaying what he'd done quite a bit, and he felt his respect for his friend increase even more. In the next room, they found a different sort of challenge. Instead of raccoons, a trio of gray-furred deer were roaming about aimlessly.

The one doe seemed fairly normal, though Garron had never seen a deer with a predatory look of hunger in its eyes. The two stags had antlers that gleamed wickedly in the cave's light. The horns were made of stone, and ended in multiple sharp points.

"You keep the doe busy, Garron. I've got the stags." In a flash, Andros was off, jumping and executing a perfect kick into one stag's side. The other monster snorted, shook its antlered head, and turned to charge him.

Garron ran forward much more slowly, aiming an awkward slash at the doe's flank.

The monster whipped around, almost smacking Garron with its hooves before he stepped away. He held his sword out warily. As the doe reared up, he moved to stab at it and got a kick in the chest for his trouble.

Apparently, the deer's antlers weren't the only thing made of stone.

Garron fell back, losing his sword once again. The doe—graceful as any normal deer—gently laid its cloven stone hooves to rest around him with a light click. Then she raised them up again, and he rolled out of the way with a yell as she tried to crush him. His shout coincided with a dull crack of breaking stone from across the room. Andros was doing well; if Garron could survive long enough for his friend to save him, he would be fine.

"No!" Garron wouldn't rely on Andros for this. He could make do with what he had. His hands, his feet, his *head*, and a Center filled with corrupted Essence. When the doe came around to rear up before him again, Garron felt at his Center and—utilizing the knowledge he'd gained from the memory stone—pulled at himself, gathering up the disgusting power and flinging it at the monster.

He wasn't quite able to see what happened, but he heard the wet squelch, and felt the *stuff* rush out of him. It... didn't feel good. Vaguely, he heard a high-pitched snort, a little thumping. He didn't look, because he was too busy shaking on the floor, overcome with coughing. A few moments later, he felt Andros' hand pounding on his back.

"Just breathe, you're okay."

That gave him just the motivation he needed to control himself and sit up, chest still heaving, to laugh in Andros' face. "Oh... just... *breathe*? Thanks... for the advice. Maybe I could just *stop* being sick, too?"

Andros' weak laugh brought a smile to Garron's own face. After another minute, he stood. "That wasn't a great idea, Garron."

"I figured that out." Garron paused as another cough racked his body. "But... *why*? Those techniques in that stone used corruption."

"Did you know that it's well-documented knowledge that people *can't* use corruption the way you just did?" Andros laughed again, stronger this time. "Besides, those techniques are meant for cultivators with only a *hint* of corruption in their Essence. You somehow forced *so much* through your body, and pushed out some of the Essence you have along with it. Look what it did to the doe!"

Garron looked and had to hold back from gagging. The doe was covered in a black, tarry substance that bubbled slightly against its fur. The creature was already decomposing, and the corruption was fading into the surroundings. It wasn't a pretty sight.

"So, don't do that again?" Garron shuddered and looked at the hand that had cast out the *stuff*, noting a new ten-pointed black star on his palm.

"Frankly, I have no idea how you did it the first time." Andros shook his head firmly, dark hair whipping around. "If you *can* do it again, don't. You'll probably just die. You don't have much more Essence left in your body, and you won't be able to get much more without purifying your Center. Your whole body is *saturated* with taint."

Garron nodded, stretching his arms. Now that the coughing had subsided, he felt surprisingly… normal. Not much worse than he'd been the night they escaped. After thinking about it, he decided that was because of the amount of corruption he'd forced out along with the Essence. It had balanced out, but after considering the goopy spray technique he'd somehow managed, he knew his Essence would run out before anything else.

They collected the loot, which included a well-made steel helmet that Garron jammed on his head, a knife that Andros laid claim to, more coins… Then it was time to move on. In the next room, they could smell the dampness of the river permeating the stone. There weren't any animals, or obvious traps—the only thing in the little cavern was a trio of simple boxes.

"Hm." Andros glared at the crates in a way that made Garron tense up. "I don't think this place is advanced enough for Mimics, but I still don't trust when there's loot without a challenge attached to it. They could be traps or something."

"Oh. Why don't we just skip it, then?" Garron suggested easily. They weren't here to get rich.

Andros grunted in the affirmative, even though he seemed displeased. "Yeah… good idea. It's just… leaving treasure behind is… Forget it. I bet we're close to the boss already; since this place is small, it should be near the river."

They continued on, but instead of a simple open hole leading to the next connected cave, there was a solid stone door built into the opening with a gleaming handle protruding from it. Andros tried the handle… then the air stirred.

Nothing happened.

"Abyss. It's not responding to my push. This rock," he rapped the stone around the door, "is way too dense for me to be able to break and still take on the boss. The key must be in one of the boxes… I think this is a puzzle."

Garron frowned at the door before glancing back at the innocuous chests. "Oh. So we're supposed to just… pick one, then?"

Andros shrugged and started back toward the chests. "I guess so. Hand me your sword?"

Garron almost asked why, but Andros' intense expression forestalled him. Garron handed the weapon to his friend, who walked over to the boxes warily. Holding the sword out as far away from his body as possible, he used to slowly open the leftmost box's lid. Three stone spikes shot straight up out of the box, clattering against the ceiling before landing harmlessly to the side. "Ha! Try to skewer *me*? You gotta try harder than *that*!"

When Andros went to open the second box, the spikes shot out horizontally, straight at him. To his credit, he moved *fast*. With the grace of a gifted air cultivator, he twisted and jumped, getting the majority of his body out of the way a split second before the spikes ripped through him.

The arm holding the sword wasn't so lucky.

"Abyss!" They both shouted it at the same time, Garron rushing over to his friend's side. The spike hadn't actually impaled him, but the other boy had a massive gash on his forearm, and the wrist hung limp. Without hesitation, Garron took off his shirt and began binding the wound as best he could. Andros just stood there, hissing through clenched teeth and applying pressure to his own wound as Garron worked. "I deserved that one. Thanks, Gar. Remind me not to taunt the dungeon, hubris is a real killer."

Garron scoffed and tightened the dirty clothing around his arm. "Don't thank me. How is it? Your wrist—"

"It's broken. It knocked into the last spike after the first one cut my arm. Feces, I don't know anything about healing." Andros seemed more angry than hurt now, staring at his wrist as if he could *will* it to get better.

Garron didn't say anything as he finished binding the wound. A knot of worry began tying itself around his stomach. Finally, when it was clear the bleeding would stop, he spoke. "We have to go back, Andy."

Andros' head whipped around. "*What?*"

"If you fight the boss injured, you… you might die." Garron tried to inject his voice with as much urgency as he could. He'd come this far on a mix of trust and mad hope that he could be cured, but risking Andros… He couldn't.

But Andros was having none of it. "If I *don't* do this with you, you *will* die! I have a chance, you don't."

"This is all… too much." Garron sighed and gestured at the stone spikes and blood on the floor. "I made my peace with dying a long time ago, Andy. You still have a long life ahead of you."

The other boy hit him on the head. Hard. Not as hard as Garron knew he could have, but it still *hurt*. "Still being an idiot. Nobody 'makes their peace' with dying when they're our age unless they're forced to do it. My life isn't worth any more than yours. In fact, if one of us died here, it should be me. After all, you've been miserable the last few years while I've been cultivating. If anything, you should get a turn at happiness. If I go back, it's just more of the same."

Garron thought about protesting. He opened his mouth, then closed it. He tried one last time. "Fine. Neither one of us is going anywhere. We're going to kill that boss, and I'm going to swallow the Beast Core, and we're going to go home carrying big ol' sacks of loot over our shoulders."

Andros laughed and tried opening and closing his wounded hand. "That's the spirit! Let's get on with it?"

The last crate did contain the key, along with another sword of much higher quality. After a brief debate, Garron took the weapon, leaving his rusty blade behind. Andros couldn't use the thing with his wrist, and he worked better without weapons in any case. Garron did the honors, sliding the stone key into the door and turning it. The door unlocked with a grinding noise, and slowly slid open. "Ready?"

Andros nodded at him, and Garron felt the wind stir slightly. "Of course."

Garron had been thinking about what they would find in the boss room. It ended up being his first guess. It should have been obvious. Really, raccoons, deer, and now... "A wolf. Of *course* it's a wolf. You know, I was really hoping it would be rabbits."

Andros laughed. "Rabbits as dungeon bosses? That would just be ridicu—"

A howl cut him off as the wolf charged at them.

Garron moved to the side, holding tight to his sword. The monster's eyes tracked him for a second, and he felt shivers run down his spine. He'd never seen one of the beasts in person before, but he'd certainly seen plenty of dogs. Somehow, he didn't think that wolves were supposed to be his height at the shoulders, with teeth set in stone, and fur that glistened like crystal. For a moment, it seemed like the huge animal was going to pounce at him, but then Andros moved in.

He couldn't fight at maximum efficiency with a broken wrist, but he captured the boss' attention with a shout and a gust of wind to the face. Then he slammed a kick into the creature's side, which seemed to hurt *him* more than it did the wolf. When the wolf pounced, he slipped out of the way. In a moment, he was dancing easily around ponderous claw swipes. The wolf was slow, thank celestial, but it was so heavy that the floor shuddered every time it landed after an attempted pounce.

Andros was dodging fine, but the few blows he could land weren't doing anything.

"Hit while it's distracted!" Andros' shout echoed in the open cave, but it was drowned out in the next moment by a howl.

Right. He could be a part of this, too. Garron started moving in, raising his sword. The boss was completely engaged with Andros, so he had no trouble landing a full-power strike on the nape of its neck. His sword connected with a crunch, and Garron saw pieces of fur break away as the sword continued down to bite into the monster's neck.

It would have been much more impressive if the blade went in more than a quarter-inch. With a snarl, the wolf turned and took a swipe at Garron. When he was watching Andros fight the monster, he'd thought it was ridiculously slow. He'd been terribly mistaken: Andros was just *that* fast.

The back of the monster's stone claw hit caught him on the shoulder, sending him spinning away, but thankfully failing to do any real harm. The momentary stumble was enough for the wolf to get after him. Snarling, it bent its legs to pounce. With a rush of wind, Garron was suddenly several feet away, next to the rushing river that took up the back half of the stone chamber. His head spun slightly, and Andros' tight grip around his waist told him what had happened. His friend had used the movement technique to get them clear for the moment. But the monster was still there, and it had already seen where they'd gone.

Panting, Andros turned, still gripping Garron with his arm, eyes fixed on the wolf. "Can't get through its hide either, huh? Abyss, I really wish I knew how to do lightning or something, but you need more affinities for that stuff."

Garron nodded shakily. "This sword's not a good weapon for this. A hammer or mace or something would have been much better. I can't get enough force."

"I can't hold that because of my wrist. Look out, it's coming." Andros tensed, ready to shoot back into the fray.

An idea struck Garron, an idea that might kill him, but even so he shifted around in Andros' grasp so he was facing outwards, turning them until his sword was pointing straight at the oncoming wolf's chest.

"What the—"

"Andy, I never thought I'd say this, but you need to use that movement thing, now." Garron tensed, gripping the sword so tightly his hand ached.

"What? Oh, you want to—"

"*Now!*"

Wind rushed and the world shifted. A massive force slammed Garron forward, sword-first, into the wolf. With a resounding crack and a flash of intense pain, he felt the weapon impale the boss right through the chest. Then the rest of him smashed into the monster's body, and everything stopped and went black for a moment.

"Garron!"

The weak boy tried to roll over, his head spinning. Where was he? Was it morning already? He'd have to get up then, or Hila would have his hide. He groaned and opened his eyes. What was that sound? It sounded like… water? A river. Like the river in the east woods, where he'd liked to play with Andros. He'd always loved it outside, especially when his only friend was there.

Andros slapped him soundly.

"Ow!" Garron's eyes opened, and he sat up with a start. "The dungeon. I'm in the dungeon!"

Andros scoffed. "Oh, come on. You were *totally* milking that. I didn't go *that* fast."

Garron grumbled under his breath as he looked around the cave, wincing slightly at the pain shooting through his shoulder. "Whatever. Is it dead?"

"About as dead as you're going to be if we don't get that Core in you right now."

It took a bit of help, but Garron managed to stand. Together they made their way over to the river. Earth Essence permeated this room thickly, but this close to the water, he could feel his other affinity in almost as much abundance. At Andros' instruction, he drank deeply from the river, until he was full to bursting and unpleasantly queasy. It didn't take too much—it was well past breakfast time, and his stomach was already complaining. The pure water made the feeling worse, mixing with his stomach acid in a thoroughly unappetizing manner.

Andros looked at him seriously once he'd struggled back to his feet. "You know how this works, right? You swallow the Core, and when I tell you—*and not before*—you start cultivating. You have the technique all set? The Core's going to pull everything out of you, so we need to replace it with clean Essence, or you'll die. I mean, that's what I hear. I didn't really have this problem, but I've heard enough stories from Guild Officers that meet with father, and I did the research, so I—"

"Let's get back to the part where I don't die," Garron interrupted him, trying to sigh and wincing at the pain in his ribs.

"Right, sorry. So, once you empty out, you have to throw up the Core. I'm going to punch you a few times to make that happen, by the way. Be ready."

Garron shrugged and got ready for more pain. Pain was one thing he could handle. "You hit me enough as it is. Let's do this."

Andros nodded, suddenly seeming even more nervous than Garron. He pulled another gem from his pouch, one very similar to the memory stone, and handed it to Garron. Taking a deep breath, he realized that this would be the last time the air rasped on its way down, making him want to cough. One way or another.

He swallowed the Beast Core.

Garron had experienced a lot of extremely painful things in the last few hours. Andros' so-called 'movement technique,' his disastrous attempt at using an Essence technique, and, of course, his recent high-speed collision. But this… his entire body, everything that was *him*, was being pulled into his stomach.

Pain blossomed in a dozen points around his body, then a

hundred, until everything was agony. He knew he'd begun spasming, but he had no control over his limbs. He could feel the dense, viscous, somehow bubbling corruption sliding *inwards*. Some from his limbs, but most of it from his putrid Center. Then the sweet Essence—the few dregs of pure energy he'd managed to retain despite the taint—vanished as well, all sucked into the Core. Finally, the pain subsided.

Then something hit his abdomen *hard*. His stomach was already on a hair trigger from the day's activities, and the extra blow prompted him to vomit out all of its contents. He felt the greedy gem leave along with the bile, but for a moment, he still felt it tug his Center. A crunch sounded at his feet, and finally the pull vanished.

"Now, Gar! *Cultivate!*"

A large part of Garron was tempted just to glory in the bliss that was the absence of pain. He almost let go. But his words to Andros, his promise that both of them would leave this dungeon alive, came back to him. He remembered everything his friend had sacrificed for him, the risks that he'd taken, the blood that he'd spilled so Garron could have a chance at life. He began to gather the Essence, the power of the world itself, into his Center.

Immediately, he knew something was wrong.

He was pulling at the earth and the water Essence around him, drawing them both into his Center and refining the energy into threads that would go into forming his Center. But something about the process felt… off. Incomplete. He was following the cultivation technique perfectly, but the Essence wasn't merging into his Center properly.

"What the—oh, abyss. You've got another affinity? But I've never seen you drawing in… air. Abyss."

Suddenly, the Essence in the room blossomed, and a third type joined the earth and water, light like a summer breeze. Garron acted on instinct, drawing this new Essence into his Center, and finally felt complete. He refined carefully but quickly, rushing to fill the void at his Center.

He continued cultivating, pulling Essence into himself from three separate sources, refining it, and using it to form a chi spiral. There was a crunching noise from nearby, and a few words, but Garron didn't hear any of it. All he could feel was the pure freedom. He hadn't known what he'd been *missing*! It felt like he'd been mired in filth his entire life, and now he'd bathed for the first time.

Eventually, he ran out of Essence to pull from. It was the water that went first, surprisingly. There was much less of the third kind—which he recognized as air—but he pulled it in at a fraction of the rate of the others, so there was a bit left over when he exited his trance.

"Finally. I thought maybe I should have been cooking us up some stone wolf with how long you were taking." Andros' voice sounded tired, and when Garron looked over, he saw that the other boy was a bit paler than usual. At his feet was a shattered gem, where a bit of bubbling black corruption was still fading away into the environment around it. He must have smashed it on the ground before him.

"The air Essence, was that—"

"Yup, straight from my Center. I'm D-rank zero, now. All the way back at the start. Jackson would be so furious if he knew I traded all of my cultivation just to keep you alive. Past that, celestials *above*, Gar, *three* affinities?" Despite his words, Andros' face was split by a wide grin.

Garron felt a weak smile come over his own face in response. "The air one is way weaker than the others, though."

"Believe me, I know. Only reason I didn't notice it at the start. I pull in so much air Essence all the time, I never even saw that you were doing it too. Not to mention, all the water and earth taint masked it in your Center. If I was better with Essence sight… I'm sure *he* knew." Andros scowled for a moment, before his grin returned.

Garron didn't want to talk about Jackson just then. He stood, and though his body still ached from the damage he'd sustained, he marveled at the way his breath came in so easily, without any tightness or rasping. He didn't feel like an old man anymore, and when he raised a hand to Andros' shoulder, it didn't shake.

"Andros. From the bottom of my heart. Thank you. You saved my life. I don't know how I can repay—"

"It was for me as well." His best, oldest, and only friend hugged him, almost crushing him with Essence-enhanced strength. "I've always known I'd need to get away from him eventually. I should be thanking you for giving me the motivation I needed to do it. There's no *way* I'm going back now."

After a few moments where both of them pretended not to notice each other wiping at their eyes, Garron spoke. "So, what now?"

"First things first, you are disgusting and need to get clean." Andros wrinkled his nose and waved at the river. "Then, we'll get to a city with a portal and use all this loot to get passage to someplace far away."

Garron frowned at the plan that, frankly, wasn't really a plan. "Where?"

"I don't know, but I'm never getting back under Jackson's thumb." That declaration had a note of steel in it. Garron looked at his friend who was cradling his unresponsive wrist, but smiling through watery eyes. He took a breath, feeling no urge to cough as he let it back out. He was finally free, thanks to his friend.

"Let's go."

CHAPTER FIVE

"How… in the *abyss*… did two *teenagers* manage to get past all of you?"

Ulysses stayed silent, as did everyone else. Even Lars, who was standing quietly behind Jackson, looked a little shamefaced. Ulysses wouldn't have thought that was possible, given how the man behaved on duty. Of course, Jackson was worse.

"One of them is practically dead, so how did a teenager and a *corpse* sneak past *all* of you?"

Fire flared up around the slender man, bursting outward from him in a ring, and the wave of hot air felt at odds with the shiver running down Ulysses' spine. He'd heard of things like this, and he'd suspected when he began working at this estate that there was something… *different* about many of the senior guards. Even the young Noble, Andros, was incredibly strong for his age, and Ulysses had no idea what he'd had done to him a few nights ago that had knocked him out so soundly.

Ulysses regretted taking this position, but what was he to do? In the wake of the war, this had seemed like the safest posting he could have wished for, and the pay was good. Jackson had seemed *reasonable*, if disinterested, and even allowed living space for Mylena. But now… he couldn't quite justify it with reason, but he felt that trying to leave this place would be dangerous.

Jackson finished the shout by letting out an incoherent roar; before allowing calm to descend over him again. This pattern had repeated itself several times over the past days, but even though everyone had been working sleeplessly, they hadn't been able to catch the boys. Ulysses wasn't sure he even wanted to catch them. He didn't like the look in Jackson's eyes when he spoke about them. Especially Garron.

"We finally have a lead. You idiots did something right, at least. Every senior officer, pack up. We're going *hunting*." The guard captain's eyes blazed with determination and rage in equal measure. Even as he spoke, he strode toward the barrack's exit.

Ulysses let out a relieved breath—as quietly as he could—as the more senior guards began shuffling around. He was the most junior guardsman in the estate, and he certainly didn't mind holding down the fort while Jackson's men went out to get the boys back. He began to walk as quietly as he could back towards the quarters he'd been assigned. Mylena had been up far too much lately. He should take a turn caring for the baby as long as he could before—

"You! *Fishie*! Don't think I don't remember who let those two out in the first place! You're coming *with* us, to make up for what you did." Jackson's voice held a savage pleasure at those words, and Ulysses had no doubt who the man was talking to.

Ulysses turned, heart sinking, wondering if he should ask for a consideration for his infant daughter, or even if he should simply cut his losses and resign there and then. Yet one look at Jackson's flame-wreathed form and he pressed his fist to his chest as humbly as he could. "Yes, sir."

Jackson didn't acknowledge his words, but his flames began to die as he stepped through the doorway. "Hurry it up, boys, I want to be through the portal within the day. Bring everything you've got. They're not getting away again."

Garron brought the axe down with as much speed as he could manage, and finally managed to split the wood cleanly with a thud and a clatter. The pieces fell to the side, and he wiped a bit of sweat off his brow and grinned. An attention-grabbing light cough from across the yard interrupted his satisfaction. "Very nice. Now do you finally want to let me do it?"

Andros' voice held his usual cheer, but there was more than a hint of annoyance to it. That wasn't directed at Garron, he knew, but at the object in his hand. Garron leaned on the ax, a smile tugging at his lips. "You're *already* tired of raking?"

"I hate it." The flat note in his friend's voice made Garron laugh.

"Well, tough luck. Now that you're not a spoiled Noble, you're going to have to learn how to handle a rake if you want to eat dinner. Or, do you think the farmer will let us eat for free?" He kept his voice light, but Andros still frowned.

"It's not like I can't *do* it, it's not even hard. It's just so… *boring*." The young lord descended into incoherent grumbling, and the slither of dead leaves sliding across ground resumed, faster than before. Garron set up another log on the stump and hefted the axe.

This was still hard work for him, even without the corruption weighing him down, and in all honesty they should switch back soon. Even so, he had really wanted to use the axe. He hadn't had a healthy body long enough to get bored of working yet. Garron wanted to feel his muscles contracting, his breath flowing in and out of his lungs without issue as he slammed the axe down onto the logs.

They went through their assigned chores with surprising efficiency. Once Andros finally got Garron to switch, he went through the waiting logs with superhuman speed, the Essence suffusing his body making the job easy. Garron was quite the practiced raker from his time working odd jobs in the Tet estate. Once they moved on to shoveling manure and filling water troughs, he was able to show Andros how to handle the tasks without splattering himself by being over-hasty.

Andros gave Garron a queasy look as they finished with the manure. "Crazy old man, calling us off the road and making us do his work."

"Our money ran out from the portal fees and the healing for your wrist," Garron reminded him as he dropped the final cowpie with a wet *squelch*. "This is a good opportunity."

Andros grunted and grumbled about 'bandit portal Mages,' but it was good-natured. They'd both been grateful for the opportunity to earn a meal and a place to stay, even if the old man who'd offered them had been… *gruff*, to say the least.

Garron himself found the whole thing immensely enjoyable, as he moved through the tasks with ease, especially compared to his old infirmity. He appreciated being able to move, as well as spending time with his friend without the threat of capture dangling over their heads. Still, he was rather relieved when they finally returned their shovels to the shed and surveyed their finished work.

"That's the last of it, *right*?" Andros' voice barely sounded strained, but he looked almost childishly happy when Garron nodded. "Great! That old man said dinner'd be at sundown, so we've got some time… Why don't we do a bit of cultivation?"

Garron grinned as well, feeling his friend's excitement infect him. "Good idea."

They ended up settling by the water troughs. There wasn't much in the way of Essence in the area, but that had the best balance of earth, water, and air for Garron. Andros began his usual dance, though Garron was almost certain now that he didn't actually need to do that to get Essence. Garron himself settled into a cross-legged position to begin adding to his own Center.

They passed the time in peaceful silence, Garron pulling from the wisps of water, air, and earth Essence around him, stretching out the threads of power and adding them to his Center in the spiral formation he'd learned from the memory stone. It was a surprisingly simple process, but it required careful control, focus, and patience from him. They were no longer in a dungeon, and the purity of this Essence was sorely lacking. With the strength of Garron's three affinities, he had to be careful in refining the Essence he pulled in, or risk adding too much corruption into his chi spiral.

He would never make that mistake. Garron knew too well what lay down that road. His power still grew with relative speed, but all too quickly, Andros was tapping him on the shoulder.

"What?" Garron felt almost groggy as he came out of his trance.

"Uh, I can't really cultivate any more right now." Andros sounded apologetic, but as Garron opened his eyes and looked, he could see that the sun had barely moved from its position low in the sky.

He shot his Noble friend a questioning look, not moving from his seated position. "Why not? There's still air Essence around here, more than the water for sure, and I've still got a bit to go."

Andros sighed. "It's… well, if I wanted to cultivate more, I'd have to exercise a bunch to make up for it. My cultivation technique pulls in a lot of Essence at once, and my body needs an outlet to process it correctly. I'll start exercising more tomorrow, I guess, but I can't do more today."

"Oh." Garron wondered what exactly made Andros' cultivation technique so much stronger than Garron's own, but that was a question for another time. Andros was still looking at him expectantly, shuffling slightly from foot to foot. "What does that have to do with me?"

Andros looked mildly offended. "What, you want me to just stand around and watch you cultivate? That's so *boring*."

Garron sighed, not mentioning the several times in the past days that he'd stood and watched Andros cultivate. After all, his friend had been saving his life at the time. "What do you want to do?"

"Well, do you want to try moving your Essence around? You learned a few techniques from the memory stone, right?" Andros was already nearly hopping with new excitement—for all his abilities as a cultivator, sometimes he seemed half Garron's age.

His proposition actually *was* interesting. "I did, but I haven't really been able to—"

"Right, no worries." Andros waved his hand dismissively. "It takes a whole lot of time and practice to learn to apply proper techniques, so don't worry too much about it. We'll get there eventually, but the basic stuff is easier; like pushing Essence outside of your Center. You shouldn't do that yet because, uh… well, the whole 'you'd die' thing, but it'll be easier later on. Still, you can at least learn the basics!"

"Sure." That sounded fine to Garron, but his friend's speech had raised a new question. "Andros?"

"Yeah?" Andros was actually hopping now, each bounce taking him several feet into the air.

Garron coughed, unsure if he was being rude. "It, uh, seems like you know a lot of techniques."

Andros nodded and let loose a slimy grin. "Yeah, a few. More than most cultivators our age."

Garron waited for a second, then another. No point in talking when Andros clearly knew the question. Eventually, the young air cultivator settled down, and gave Garron a glance from his peripherals. "It's kind of… *easier* for me than most. I've been learning them for most of my life, so I had plenty of time to practice, unlike most cultivators at my… rank."

"Right." Garron suspected that Andros had serious talent in this area. After all, he had invented his own movement technique, which—while clearly costing him enough that others would curse him to an afterlife in the abyss—was probably rather impressive for someone his age. Still, the line of questioning was clearly making Andros uncomfortable, so Garron let it go. "Let's get started?"

"I also stole a lot of techniques from my family vault," Andros stated in a rush.

"What?"

Andros waved away any further questions, though he looked relieved to have finally stated what was on his mind. With that out of the way, he began teaching Garron to the best of his ability.

It quickly became clear that Garron didn't have the talent to match Andros. The sun crept closer to the horizon as they worked on Andros' first lesson, which should have been laughably simple—grab a specific type of Essence in his Center. The problem was, with his three affinities, Garron couldn't get a handle on which type was which: they all seemed to have been combined together.

Garron almost felt bad for Andros, but his friend only grew more intent as, one by one, his teaching methods failed. After a lengthy and confusing explanation failed to help, the air cultivator jumped to his feet and began walking in circles, hand on his chin. "Okay, try punching the ground!"

"What? Why would I do that?" Garron looked at the ground, it hadn't done anything to him?

Andros gesticulated wildly. "So you can, you know, *feel* the earth. And then, maybe try grabbing it in your Center and—"

"Maybe if I punch *you*, then I can feel how to control air Essence." Garron heard the tinge of grumpiness entering his tone, even as he tried once again to grab at the Essence in his Center. What was he even supposed to grab *with*?

Andros was still pacing. "Hm, maybe, but—hey!"

Garron raised a hand to block the kick he knew was coming, but a shout across the yard forced him to open his eyes.

"Alright you two! Git over here!" The voice, which managed to sound even grumpier than Garron's, shook them out of their budding argument.

They looked over at the old farmer standing in the doorway of the farmhouse. Every line seemed etched into him by years of work in the sun—probably rain and snow as well. As he surveyed the work they'd done in the yard—from the huge pile of split firewood to the troughs filled with water and the leaves neatly collected in rough sacks and laid out by the house—he let out a grunt.

"Not bad. I'd have come out and helped ya, but the missus insisted I spend the day with her." He tapped his craggy nose, and a crooked smile split his face. "I ain't sure who got the tougher job!"

He let out a chuckle, which surprised Garron. Not that the man's mirth, but the laugh itself. Somehow, he had expected it to be phlegmy and weak, barely distinguishable from his old coughing fits. That was what he'd seen from the few elderly people who'd come to the Tet estate. But *this* man had a laugh as strong and warm as any young man, and Garron found himself smiling along with him. Andros actually let out a few chuckles of his own, seeming to forget his earlier annoyance.

"Alright you two, git yourselves washed up 'fore you come in then. You smell like dung!"

The man let out another laugh, but Andros didn't seem to find it quite as funny when he shut the door in their faces.

CHAPTER SIX

After a quick and cold wash with some of the water they had already drawn from the well, they were sitting at a rough-cut wooden table inside the house. A grandmotherly woman—the man's wife—was bustling about in the kitchen, and the old man was easing into his chair at the far end of the table. Garron wondered if he should have asked them their names, but he would have felt strange using them in any case, and the two seemed perfectly content calling Andros and him 'boys' or 'lads.'

"It was good of you two to do all that work, you know," the woman called from the kitchen. "It's been tough for us to keep up with all of it since our boys went off, what with how old my husband's getting."

"Who're you calling old, hag?" the old man muttered, thinking he was too quiet for the woman to hear from the kitchen.

"*You*, ya piece of sun-dried leather," she called back on cue, sounding cheerful.

Garron thought the corners of the man's mouth twitched up, but it was hard to see for certain. He glanced at Andros to see his reaction, but to his surprise his friend seemed agitated rather than amused. After a moment, he called back, half-rising out of his chair. "Do you need any help with the food?"

Huh. Not what Garron had expected, but certainly not a bad thing to do. His question was met with a laugh from the kitchen. "Oh! Don't worry, you'll be doing plenty of work cleaning up afterwards! Don't want you stumbling about my kitchen while I'm trying to cook!"

Andros nodded, almost to himself, and sat back down, still looking a little uneasy.

"I'll give you some advice for the future, lad: when a woman wants you t'sit down and wait, take the opportunity and don't complain—it don't happen too often." The old man's booming laugh filled the little dining room. Andros laughed along with him.

"I guess you're right. I just haven't... Anyway," he cut himself off, a bit of the mirth fading.

Garron smiled at the fact that Andros was clearly feeling too much like a Noble who was waiting on the servants to bring him dinner. Garron had a feeling he wouldn't be quite so guilty when it came time to do the dishes, but he commended his friend's attitude. Truth be told, it seemed like Andros' recent giddiness was as much a function of his newfound freedom as his natural personality, as though living in a mansion with functionally unlimited money and time to train was one step from the abyss. But then, Garron remembered reading something about birds in gilded cages, back when he'd had the time to read.

Still, the old man was looking at Andros with a measure of respect in his eyes.

"Eh, good that you two lads are willing t'work. I'll say, too many young people these days want an easy life making money t'pay for food that other people worked t'get. 'Money ain't worth nothing but what you put in t'get it,' I always told my boys. Look here." He reached for his pocket, and after a moment of fumbling, pulled out a silver coin, slightly blackened and scratched with age. "This here's the only piece of silver from here to the big city, I reckon. Know what it's worth?"

Garron and Andros shook their heads on cue, though Garron suspected he did.

The old man gave them another crooked grin. "Nothing! Can't even use it t'wipe my—"

"That isn't talk for the dinner table, dear," the woman cut him off sharply as she strode into the dining room, carrying a tray with a steaming pot of rice and several succulent cuts of chicken balanced atop it. "Now, stop talking and eat before these boys die of boredom."

Silence, except for the tinkling of cutlery and loud chewing, followed for a time. The food was good, almost as tasty as what Hila's kitchen made for the estate staff, and there was more than enough for Garron and Andros to eat their fill. Garron found that his appetite had increased a great deal since he'd removed the corruption in his body—he supposed he was making up for lost time.

After clearing out every scrap of meat and grain of rice, they finally sat back, content. But before Garron could give in to the temptation to close his eyes there and then, the old woman clapped her hands and stood. "Now then, why don't you two get started on those dishes, eh? I'll help you put it away while the old goat cleans up the table."

With matching groans, they all hopped up and set to work. Garron ended up washing dishes, thanks to long experience in Hila's kitchen, but Andros did a credible job of drying them, and the woman swept them all up as soon as he was done, placing them in their proper places with practiced ease even as she cleaned up the rest of the kitchen. All the while, she chatted with them amiably about the weather, the area around their little farmhouse, and the likelihood of a difficult winter.

"We've got plenty of stores put by, of course. I'm not worried, but it is sad for some of the other families around here. There aren't many to the east of course, what with the monsters wandering that way, but between here and the city there are still a few other farms that stayed put." She sighed, but didn't pause in stowing a pair of large bowls in a waiting cabinet.

Garron wasn't sure what she was talking about. They'd passed a few of the farms she was talking about on their way out of the 'city'—more of a medium-sized town, even by Garron's standards. But the other part of her offhand comment had been far more interesting. "Monsters?"

"Monsters." The woman nodded as she wiped around the stove, sweeping up ashes and bits of food that had fallen in. "They didn't use to range so far out west, but back then those nice people from the Guild used to stop by here every year or so and clear them out a bit. With the war… well, I'm just glad my two boys are still alright. Joined the Guild just before it all happened, you know, but they ended up getting a nice safe station down south for the whole thing."

The war. Garron had heard it called the 'Undead War,' and he knew that it had been terrible. He wasn't clear on the specifics, but Lord Tet had been away for *years*, fighting for the Guild, and from what Garron knew now, he was a B-ranked cultivator. The conflict must have been massive if the contributions of all the Mages and cultivators in the Guild hadn't been able to end it for years.

From what Garron had gathered, it *had* finally ended a few months ago, but Lord Tet had still been forced to work cleaning up what had been left behind. Garron had never really understood what was meant by 'necromancers' before, but knowing what he did now, he suddenly had a few ideas about what exactly that meant.

Still, he couldn't ignore the other parts of the woman's comment. That meant there wasn't much past this point, in terms of people. Garron and Andros had gotten a portal to the farthest and most secluded location they could afford, and ended up in the little town these people called the 'big city.' They'd ventured out almost immediately, worried that Jackson would follow them anywhere there was a portal. Now it appeared they'd reached the end of civilization in this area.

With everyone contributing, the remaining work was done in short order, and Garron was once again overcome with sleepiness from the meal. Before he could ask if there was anything left to be done, the old woman gave them a smile.

"Alright, you two, that's enough. Let me show you your room!" She strode out of the kitchen, and they scrambled to follow.

It was a clean, spacious affair appointed with two beds on each end, a small dresser across from the door, and a pair of large windows fitted with shutters and no glass. Garron found he quite liked the feeling of fresh air that imparted, but he was glad that both beds also had blankets resting atop them.

"There you go then; let me know if you need anything." She still had the same cheerful smile on her face, but as she looked over them, he thought it drifted a bit towards… motherly? Garron felt himself flushing a deep red and looked down at the clean wood floor of the room. "You know, the geezer could use the help around here for a bit, since winter's coming. My boys aren't coming home any time soon, so we have room and food to spare… Think about it, won't you?"

With that, she shut the door, leaving Garron and Andros to stand awkwardly in the middle of the room. *Stay* here? Garron thought about the prospect and found it surprisingly attractive. They were in a secluded spot, with plenty of space and time to train, guaranteed meals, and a place to sleep. Even people to take care of them. It felt good to not be on their own, even for a little bit.

Andros interrupted Garron's thoughts. "Uh, we should sleep soon. Why don't you do a bit of cultivation first? I'll get the beds set."

The young Noble's voice was quiet, and a little troubled, so Garron just nodded. Fatigue was beginning to build up behind his eyes, but he wanted to add to his cultivation as fast as possible, so he opened the shutters to his window, exposing the remaining leaves of a great tree that had grown up next to the house. In the moonlight, the red and gold of the autumn leaves seemed to almost glow. Garron took in a breath of the fresh air and sat down on his bed in a meditative pose.

Essence began to trickle into his Center slowly as he refined what there was in the room. Andros was holding back his own passive Essence accumulation, Garron noticed, or else there wouldn't have been enough air Essence to cultivate at all. Doing it like this was slow and rather boring, but it was still worth the trouble. By the time he was done, Andros was already asleep on his bed. Wicking down the lantern, Garron laid down, wrestled for a bit with the covers, and drifted off to sleep.

CHAPTER SEVEN

"Gar."

"Not this again, Andy. If you are waking me up to whisk me away—" Garron paused his groaning as he sat up in bed and saw Andros' serious expression. "What's wrong?"

With a bit of clatter, Andros lit the lantern, although there was a very small amount of twilight filtering in through the windows. Garron blinked at the light, then looked at his friend. He seemed well-rested, but there was a hint of worry around his eyes. "Sorry, but… I think we should head out now."

Garron sat up a little straighter and folded his arms. He hadn't expected that Andros actually wanted them to leave. "Why?"

Andros gave him a look filled with guilt and worry in equal measure. "Jackson. I'm worried what'll happen if he finds us here. These people, they don't need that."

Garron thought it over, his heart sinking a little bit. However much staying here appealed to him, they couldn't put their hosts in danger. But… he still didn't want to agree. This place was *perfect* for them, and the old woman had seemed to want them around. "How would he even follow us?"

"The portal attendant would probably tell him where we went, and there aren't too many people out this way. It won't be long before he shows up. We need to keep running."

"You're right," Garron said after thinking on it. He shook his head. "We should at least wait until they wake up, maybe do a bit more work in exchange for supplies."

Andros shook his own head in return. "That'd just make it harder to leave. And winter's coming. We shouldn't be taking their food."

"But maybe—"

Andros gave him a sympathetic look, but shook his head. "Let's *go*, Gar."

Garron managed to keep his shoulders from slumping, but he had to look away from Andros before he stood. The other boy was already rifling through his pouch, making sure their meager belongings—just a pair of knives and a few spare strips of Beast hide from his cloak—were all there. "Abyss. I hate it, but you're right."

The very fact that Garron was so reluctant to agree showed *exactly* why they had to leave before their hosts woke up. He still cast a regretful look at the bedsheets below him, and another at the cozy room he'd known for such little time. With a sigh, he went to the door, where Andros joined him after a moment.

Going through the house was easy, but it reminded Garron forcibly of stealing through the manor a few nights before. Once they had carefully shut and locked the house, they began walking. Garron walked at Andros' side, but he gave his friend a questioning look. "East?"

Andros kept his gaze forward. "Can't go west, can we? We'll try to loop north a bit so we don't run into monsters."

Garron was impressed. Before the escape, Garron hadn't known Andros to plan… anything. Perhaps that had changed, in his years of training? But because of his cultivation rank, apparently Andros didn't need to sleep nearly as long as Garron did, so he had no idea how long his friend had been thinking about this. "Understood."

They walked through the fields behind the house, the sky slowly lightening even though the sun had yet to crest the horizon. Garron didn't feel much like talking, and it seemed Andros didn't either. The only sounds were the soft swish of the tall grass as they walked through it, the occasional cry of a morning bird, and the distant clatter of—

"Oh, abyss." Andros stopped in his tracks, whirling.

Garron whipped his head around an instant after Andros. They were still hidden by the grass, and neither of them could see the front of the farmhouse from their position. Even at this distance, it was easy to hear the grumbling chatter of perhaps a half dozen men and—even worse—the flickering light of a flame approaching the farmhouse.

Garron frowned, an uneasy feeling in his stomach. "People from the town? Or maybe… the Guild coming back to clear out monsters?"

Even as Garron whispered the words, he and Andros crept through the grass until the house stopped obscuring the view of the road. Sure enough, a group of men in familiar armor were jostling for position in front of the house. Two stood in front, a hulking man whose armor seemed barely large enough to fit him, and a slender figure dressed only in tunic and pants. The flickering light wasn't coming from a torch, though Garron hadn't really believed for an instant that it was.

Wreathed in fire, Jackson walked up to the farmhouse. Even from this distance, Garron could see the wisp of smoke rise into the air as he knocked, strangely polite.

CHAPTER EIGHT

"We should run." Andros sounded confident, but his expression betrayed both anxiety and uncertainty.

Garron looked back at the farmhouse. "But they—"

Andros laid his hand on Garron's shoulder. "We aren't *there*, are we? They should be alright. He's crazy, but he's not crazy enough to just randomly… They'll be okay."

The frail young man kept watching the farmhouse. Most of the guards were still standing outside the door. There were far, *far* too many people there for them to be able to fight off. Jackson alone would be too much to handle, from what Garron understood of cultivation ranks.

He gave a slow nod. "Alright, maybe we can—"

A flash of fire from inside the house interrupted him. It would have been impossible to hear from so far away, but Garron thought he could make out a frightened exclamation, and a scream.

Garron's stomach dropped. "Andy, we have to help them."

The young Noble looked at the farmhouse, where the firelight in the window seemed to be growing brighter by the moment, then back at him. "Run, Gar. Good luck."

Andros took off back across the field, running with all the speed his cultivation afforded him.

"You abyssal idiot!" Garron started after him, but Andros was already far, far away, almost to the house. Thankfully, he seemed to be headed towards one of the side doors of the house, so at least the guardsmen wouldn't be catching him right away. That just left Jackson; a man that Andros had no chance of taking on. Maybe—hopefully—he wasn't thinking of fighting.

Garron was careful not to create too much noise as he followed Andros to the farmhouse, but he couldn't help a mutter. "Did that moron actually think I would run?"

Thankfully, the semi-darkness, the grass, and the house itself provided plenty of cover, so he was able to move with relative speed. He was close enough to hear the crack as Andros broke through the wooden shutters of one of the windows and jumped inside. The orange light emanating from the house dimmed somewhat as Garron heard an indistinct shout.

Garron crept around the side of the house, careful to stay out of sight of the windows and the men in the front, until he reached the same one that Andros had broken through. Splinters of wood littered the ground, but Garron remained low, out of sight, and listened.

"So you decided to stop this foolishness then, boy? You've really done it now—even your father won't forgive stealing so heavily from the repository." Jackson's voice was quiet, pleasant and jovial even, but there was something ugly behind it. Garron could still see firelight flickering out of the window.

"Huh. That didn't seem to stop *you*, did it? The place was looking kind of... *empty* when I went there. He'll notice." Andros was trying to match Jackson's conversational tone, but he was doing a worse job of holding back his anger.

The fire cultivator gave a nasty laugh in reply. "I don't think he needs to hear about any of that, does he? It costs money to run an estate."

Andros' veneer of calm broke. "Not *that* much."

"Quiet, boy." The firelight flared. Garron heard a strangled exclamation from the other side of the room and breathed a quiet sigh of relief. The elderly couple were still alive, it seemed.

Jackson was nearly shouting now, whatever composure he'd had vanished. "Besides, it won't be me he'll blame. I have *plenty* of witnesses ready to swear how the little corruption-tainted servant boy manipulated you into letting him do it. Now I just need to carry out the penalty for theft from a Noble."

Abyss. Jackson had been stealing from Lord Tet? That had to be the stupidest thing Garron had ever heard of. Except that now, he was going to blame it on Garron. He had no idea if that was going to work, but it wouldn't matter much. He wouldn't be alive to find out. Without warning, Jackson was suddenly calm as a still lake, even as the flames burned around him. "So, boy, where is he?"

A pause. "I don't know."

Andros wouldn't be able to stall Jackson for long. They had to get out. Garron didn't have much to offer except for a surprise, and he couldn't even do that much without knowing what they were facing. Taking a deep breath, and praying that Jackson wasn't facing his way, he slowly peeked his head over the broken edge of the window.

As he looked into the room, his first reaction was relief. Andros had taken up a position in front of the couple, who seemed shaken but unharmed. Jackson was standing across from them, fire surrounding him, licking at the floor and ceiling even as he watched. The look on the slender man's face was terrifying for how calm it seemed, even as the flames emanated from him.

What could he do? Jackson was far, *far* too powerful for either of them to fight head on. Andros might have been able to get them away if he had a moment's head start, but what would stop Jackson from simply grabbing him as they tried to leave? He needed something to slow the man down. Think. The dancing flames, with their scorching heat, made it hard for him to focus. Garron was worried that the house would burn down if Jackson was in it much longer. The wood that made it up had been coated to hold off fire, but even now the floor around the man was warping and smoking, turning black as the heat began stripping away the wood's protection. Even the ceiling was—oh.

Garron ducked away from the window, backing up and looking wildly at the outside of the house. The tree next to his bedroom window was on this side of the house, thankfully. It was more difficult to climb than the one a few days ago, but now he wasn't wrestling against corruption in his Center to move, he managed to make it up the tree quickly at the cost of a few scrapes. Edging out on a particularly thick branch until he was almost to the window—still open, thankfully—he jumped.

The bedroom was still oddly serene, despite what Garron knew was happening downstairs. He ran out into the hallway, and immediately felt the temperature rising.

A muffled shout from the lower floor sent him running forward. "I told you I don't know where he—"

There. The floor in the master bedroom was blackened and twisted in a large circle, and the room was hot enough to make Garron begin to sweat. Now then, what to do? He could think of only one thing, and he retreated deep into his Center as the temperature continued to rise.

Water, water, *water*. Garron felt at his chi spiral, trying to sort out the different Essence types, trying to find what he needed. He remembered how the Essence had felt as he refined it only hours before, cool, soothing, somehow flowing. "*There.*"

Without thinking, Garron grabbed the power and let it push out of him, slamming into the floor below. He imagined that the Essence had splashed out in a wave, slamming into the already weakened wood of the floor, because there was a crack as it warped further, the beams below snapping and the blackened floor splintering.

He couldn't know for sure because his eyes were screwed up at the pain in his flesh where the Essence passed through. His hand suddenly felt as though he'd held it up to an open oven for hours, the uncomfortable dryness punctuated with a stabbing pain in his palm. Suddenly he remembered Andros' words. 'You shouldn't do that yet.' Now Garron understood why. He gasped and doubled over his hand even as the floor cracked beneath him.

He only had a moment to think, and he shouted even as hot air pushed up at him, the wood beneath him hitting a human head. "Andros!"

A moment before he hit the fiery floor, a force slammed into Garron. The wind rushed in his ears as the world blurred. For a split second, they paused, and Garron had time to appreciate the cool morning air on his scalded skin and desiccated hand, before the world sped up again in a horrible, if familiar rhythm. Oh, abyss.

More of this movement technique. He almost wished he'd just let Jackson capture him.

Well. Not really.

CHAPTER NINE

Aside from the pain of his ill-advised Essence blast, the accompanying weakness from the loss of cultivation, and of course the horrible nausea from the method of travel, the escape was surprisingly uneventful. Garron was sure that the guardsmen were on their tail, but he was also somewhat sure that they would be able to make it to some sort of cover before they were caught. With every momentary standstill as they continued forward, Garron fervently wished that they had gotten far enough, and the trip would be over.

In much less time than their first nightmare run, it was over. Andros dropped Garron to the ground without warning, though Garron had been ready for that from the moment they started. It still took a moment to reorient and, groaning, struggle to his feet, but when he did, Garron could see that Andros was still standing, and that they were in a forest.

The ground around Garron was coated in a layer of dead leaves, though there were fallen branches and small bushes all around. The air was thick with the smells of life, intermixed with the faint odors of animal excrement and the rot of decaying plant matter. The trees rose up as high as Garron could see, many branches already bare, though more held colorful fall leaves.

"I... took... a few... turns." Andros was breathing hard, his hands on his knees. Garron could feel him pulling in the Essence around them even as he spoke. "We should have... a little time at least."

Garron nodded sharply. "Good. Thanks, Andy."

His only response was a look, which Garron only answered with a snort. "Like I was going to let you turn yourself in to that psychopath."

Andros frowned, the wrinkles in his forehead making beads of sweat roll down his face. "What does that mean?"

"Eh. I read it somewhere. Means 'crazy person who steals from Nobles.'" Garron stepped up and put a hand on Andros' back. His friend didn't look very good.

"Oh. Anyway, that was dangerous." The young Noble stopped crouching over at Garron's touch, his strength clearly returning somewhat as he drew in Essence. There was quite a bit in this place, though not as much as a dungeon. "How did you even break the floor like that?"

"Blast of water Essence." Garron held up his hand, displaying the shriveled and flaking skin of his palm.

Andros winced. "Yeah, we have to have a talk about meridians sometime soon. Guess I should have told you a bit more about them earlier, but... well, I guess it worked out okay. Just *don't* do that again."

Garron flexed his hand. It felt strange, as though it didn't quite want to obey his commands. Though most of the pain had passed, it still wasn't pleasant, and he was glad he'd happened to direct the Essence through his left hand instead of his right. "Guess I can reschedule the excruciating pain to next week, if you insist."

Andros rolled his eyes and sighed. "Very funny."

"Thanks." Garron gave his friend a grin, glad his levity was returning.

"Anyway, we need to figure out what to do next. I say we get

Jackson alone and take him on." Andros stood a little straighter as he spoke, a note of steel determination in his voice.

Garron stared at his friend for a moment, waiting for him to start laughing at the joke, but his face remained as serious as it had ever been. "Did you hit your head or something?"

Andros frowned. "He's not going to stop chasing us now. My father will be back as soon as the Guild finishes clearing up all the rogue necromancers left after the war, and banishing all the demons and things they've summoned. If Jackson doesn't have me there waiting, Dad's going to be angry. The idiot will already have a tough time explaining where all the money from the repository's gone, but if he's trying to pin it on you, he needs to have you ready to show to Dad. Or, at least…"

His body. Garron felt a little band of fear tighten around his chest, but he was used to having certain death hanging over his head every day. He would take 'probably certain death' as an improvement. "What rank *is* Jackson, exactly?"

"Uh, he's almost at the C-ranks. D-rank eight or nine I think, and Lars is only a little behind him. He's been in charge of his little troop for years. They used to be dungeon divers. He was already in the higher D-ranks when he started working for Dad." An angry look crossed Andros' face, perhaps regret that his father had hired Jackson in the first place.

Garron could agree with that, but he was more focused on their present situation. "How about you?"

Andros snapped out of his brief reverie. "What?"

"What rank are you?" Garron demanded of his friend.

"D-rank zero." He muttered uncomfortably to the side.

Garron had already known that, but he wouldn't put it past Andros to somehow gain a few more with some special Noble magic thing. "So you've got as much chance of beating Jackson in a straight fight as I do taking you out, right?"

Andros let out a weak laugh. "Pretty much, I guess. Although you're pretty spindly. But I'm saying, if we—"

Garron put a hand up. "There's no way, Andy. You know he can't follow us forever. We can lose him in this forest, and then loop around to town. We… we might have to steal some money, but we can get a portal to a different city and blend in there."

Andros didn't look convinced. "You don't think he'll have someone waiting at the portal?"

"He probably will," Garron admitted. "But it'll still be easier than fighting him head-on. Besides, we don't have to keep running forever, do we? Once your father comes back, he'll sort everything out."

At that, Andros nodded, almost involuntarily it seemed. After another moment of consideration, his dark eyes scanning Garron, and the ground around them, he opened his mouth again. "You know, I could turn myself in."

"No. Not even just to buy us time. We're in this together." The response was almost visceral, but he stood by it. He knew just how much Andros hated Jackson, and he wasn't exactly sure what the man would do once he caught Andros in any case.

"Gar… just so you know. I'm sure he killed those farmers. They… heard too much." Silence filled the air as both of them thought about what had been said. Finally, Andros sighed. "We have to get moving."

Garron nodded, relieved that his friend hadn't put up a fight. He looked around at their surroundings, though it was impossible to see more than a few feet out in the dense vegetation. Even when Jackson's men began searching the forest, they would have the advantage in hiding. Hopefully Andros knew which way he'd gone using his movement technique, so that they could loop back around after slipping Jackson—if they could. That was a rather big 'if,' but Garron had confidence that they could at least…

A sound broke through the ordinary noise of the forest, a sound which set Garron's teeth on edge and had him crouched into a ready posture on pure instinct.

Snarling.

Garron could feel Andros tensing beside him, but they both

kept still. Garron felt at his Essence and was able to feel the different types in his Center. He could call on them if he wanted, and he might have to do so. One look at Andros, who was still pale, told him that his friend didn't have the Essence for another escape yet, but his friend still flashed him a smile. Garron felt a little bit of comfort at that; any normal animal wouldn't stand a chance against Andros, even in his weakened state.

It was hard to hold on to that sentiment when the source of the growling finally stepped out of cover, its brownish-gray fur blending into the forest but standing out against the more vibrant autumn colors. Garron stared indignantly at the creature before them. "*Another* wolf?"

The canine made the first move. Letting loose a growl, it lunged at Garron. Visceral fear surged through him, and he jumped backward as its gaping jaws drew closer.

Andros stepped smoothly between them and uppercut it with a meaty smack, following up with a kick and another punch as the creature crashed to the forest ground. He didn't let up as the animal let out another growl and snapped at him. Three more strikes landed as Garron scrambled to his feet, hands pushing against the cool forest ground as he stood. The wolf jumped with the beginnings of a whine in its throat.

"Oh, abyss." Andros breathed out, taking a step back as he stared at the creature hanging suspended in the air.

Garron counted the seconds. Five, six, seven. On eight, the wolf—the *Beast*—landed with a rush of wind, displacing a few of the dead leaves on the ground. It pivoted and jumped at Andros with unnatural speed, snarling even louder as dead leaves flew up beneath it.

Still cursing, Andros managed to dodge and land another attack, but the wolf twisted in the air, hanging for far too long as it reoriented itself to strike once again. But while Andros braced and Garron ran up beside him, the creature opened its mouth as it drifted towards the ground and let loose a howl so loud it hurt Garron's ears and forced him a step backwards.

More wolves answered the call, and they didn't sound far away.

"Gotta end this," Andros grunted, and Garron felt the air stir. The wolf lunged again, but Andros sidestepped with all of his grace, his foot shooting up into the air with the force of a storm wind behind it. The blow landed with a crack on the monster's neck, and it whimpered and went limp even as it flew past.

Andros sagged and fell to his knees. "We… have…"

"Yeah. This time, *I* got *you*." Garron grabbed his friend, pulling the other boy's arm over his shoulder and supporting as much of his weight as he could, and began running forward through the underbrush.

CHAPTER TEN

They hurried through the forest, though Andros was still leaning heavily on Garron. The extra weight slowed down the frail young man significantly. The downed wolf behind them let out one last howl; its voice growing weaker, but still far louder than normal. Its pack answered once more, filling the air with their voices. The sound was so loud that it almost made Garron clutch his ears.

He stopped dead, holding up his friend and resisting the urge to squeeze his eyes shut. He desperately began feeling at the Essence in his Center, though he doubted he had enough to take on even *one* of the monsters, let alone the five now stalking forward around trees and from behind bushes.

There was an instant when the pack looked at Garron and Andros warily, growling and baring their teeth… but refusing to move forward. Garron reflected that these were truly incredible creatures—even with their fur dirty and littered with twigs and leaves, they carried a sense of animalistic power about them. Or, maybe, that was just the air Essence swirling around them as they prepared to strike.

The first pushed off of the ground with a gust of wind,

shooting straight for them. Garron threw himself and Andros to the ground, feeling a rush of air and body heat as the monster's body flew over them. Garron held in a scream, and focused on his Center, scrabbling for threads of the Essence he needed. "Earth, come *on*."

A new sound split the forest air, a roar like the grinding of rock against rock, interrupting Garron's scrambling thoughts. Even the wolves grew quiet for a moment, before growing even angrier than before. Garron used the opportunity to pull himself and Andros to their feet, but his heart was already sinking. When he turned to look, it hit the bottom of his stomach and stayed there, beginning to beat faster and faster.

Garron had never seen anything like the creature before. More than anything, it resembled a great cat, though something about its golden fur, huge mane, and massive size made him think that it was unlikely to consent to being pet anytime soon. It took three graceful steps towards Garron, Andros, and the wolves; a bass snarl rumbling deep in its chest. The wolf which had first jumped at the boys gave an answering growl, and before long the other four were joining in, circling around them to face the newcomer. The wind started to pick up, and a wolf shot forward.

The creature's golden fur took on a slightly darker, almost metallic hue as Garron looked on, and the attacking wolf's teeth failed to break its skin. The monster cat shifted, fur lightening as it unfolded with feline grace towards its new opponent, and massive teeth scored the gray-brown hide before the wolf flew away with a gust of air and a yip of pain. Just before making contact with the wolf's hide, the teeth had turned the gray of stone and extended almost a hand's-width.

One of the first wolf's packmates took the opportunity to jump at the monster's flank, managing to get a slash in with its claws before the cat's fur darkened once again. The feline monster turned—noticeably slower—but moving with a terrifying weight. It slashed a claw—which also extended and morphed to stone—at the wolf, scoring its hide before it could back away.

With howls and yips, the wolves all blasted forward in a wind which filled the air with leaves. The lion *roared*, the sound carrying the grating of rock against rock, and began to fight in earnest, yellowing teeth biting down on the leg of an unlucky wolf and holding it there even as the others bounced uselessly off its dark hide. The creature shook its head savagely, drawing blood, and its fur lightened.

"Can't hold the transformation for long?" Garron made as many mental notes as he could, just in case he needed to fight this thing as well. Still, the feline hardly seemed inconvenienced as it took a cut to its hide in order to slash at another attacker. The wolves drew back in a gust of wind, but they seemed warier now.

"That's our cue." Once again, Garron pulled Andros along, his breath coming in ragged gasps and his heart hammering as he turned away from the ferocious battle. An angry yip made him whip his head around to see a wolf preparing to lunge at them, but in the next moment the golden cat-monster landed atop it with an earth-shaking thud, huge stone claws tearing into its prey even as the rest of the pack howled and ran to attack.

"Abyss," he and Andros both breathed as they turned and ran. They crashed through the underbrush with all of the stealth of an angry bull, but the sounds of fighting monsters died away by the time they reached a clearing and Andros sagged even further. "Have… to stop. Cultivate."

Garron agreed. He was feeling an enormous fatigue come over his body, along with a deep aching soreness that he suspected was from his earlier stunt with his Essence. "Okay. But keep an eye out."

Andros let out a weak laugh. "More… like ears."

Garron settled down, and Andros literally fell to the forest floor beside him. As Garron retreated halfway into his Center, still trying to keep himself as alert as possible, he felt the dense

Essence permeating the forest. Andros' cultivation was pulling in air Essence with such speed and force that Garron could feel the Essence shifting, but there was still enough air, as well as earth and water emanating from the ground, for Garron to add to his Center as well. No wonder there were so many monsters here.

Even as Garron began to pull the Essence toward his Center, his ears caught the sound of leaves and branches rustling. His eyes flew open. He looked over to Andros, who was already struggling to his feet, looking pale but at least not quite so weak as before. Garron wanted to speak, but he knew silence was their best defense against what he'd heard coming.

After his dash through the underbrush, it was easy to recognize the sounds of a human pushing through the trees.

"Stay calm." Right, calm. Garron remembered that feeling. Vaguely. He shot to his feet, managing to push away his fatigue once more. He hadn't worked himself nearly so hard as Andros, and besides, he was used to a body riddled with corruption. This much effort was nothing. Andros, on the other hand, had failed to stand all the way up by himself. Grabbing his friend, Garron pulled him out of the clearing, away from the sounds of the guardsman crashing through the underbrush.

As they moved away from the clearing at the best pace they could manage—a hobble which could charitably be called a walk—Garron thought as hard as he could about the situation. There was something to be said for staying put and trying to hide from the guard using the vegetation. The only problem was, the bushes in this area were all low-lying, too small to provide cover.

Garron glanced at the trees around them for a moment before dismissing the idea. Andros was having a difficult enough time *walking*, let alone climbing a tree, and they looked too sheer to be climbed in any case. The sounds of branches rustling grew closer, and Garron's chest tightened. The guardsman was gaining on them, and soon he would be close enough to see or hear them. They had to find a hiding spot before that happened.

Garron winced every time their footsteps crunched a fallen leaf or snapped a hidden dead branch, but he continued on, supporting Andros as best he could. Before long, the effort to take each step became monumental. Garron's awareness shrank to the ground in front of him and the faint sounds of the man behind. The brush on either side was too thick to traverse—the noise would give them away instantly—so they were stuck on the same path, trying to outpace the man closing in on them.

The roar of the feline monster from earlier suddenly shook Garron out of his focus; he couldn't tell how far away it was. The visceral terror filled him, mixing with his fear of the guard pursuing them and almost forcing his legs to give out beneath him. The ragged breaths of Andros in his ear quickened and, letting loose a quiet growl of his own, he picked up his pace. They had to escape. If only they could find somewhere to hide, he…

A glimmer of light in the corner of his vision caught his eye. A great tree was standing among an assortment of leaves, bushes, and even a few saplings on the forest floor. Could they climb it? No, too high for Andros, and its canopy grew thick too far in the air. Garron turned his attention back to his intended course, past a split pair of trunks, over a tiny hill, and hopefully to some sort of cover, but another glimmer directed his gaze towards the base of the tree.

There was a particularly dense collection of roots snaking across the forest floor, but beneath them he could see a patch of… darkness? Empty space? Hope gave him the strength to pull a faltering Andros towards the tree, stepping over and around the shrubbery with as much care as he could, but still making far too much noise. He was almost grateful to the monster's roar for covering the sound.

Garron tripped over a root near the patch of darkness, pulling Andros down beside him, but he hardly cared. His fingers scrabbled at the fine mesh of organic matter and found that he could easily push them aside—they were not anchored into the earth, but rather laid over it; covering a divot in the ground. It looked to be quite deep, an alcove sheltered and hidden by the roots. The perfect hiding spot. The grinding roar of the monster blasted over him again, and he could hear a gruff voice cursing through the trees, getting ever closer to catching them.

Pulling Andros, who was all but limp in his arms, Garron scrambled into the depression, tasting the loose dirt that he displaced in the process, and let the roots fall back over the opening above. Safe?

Andros' breathing calmed somewhat beside him, but his friend still didn't speak. Garron was focused on the sounds of the forest above. The roaring was getting louder, even in their little alcove, and the voice of the guardsman seemed to be getting more frantic. The sounds of stomping feet, crackling leaves and creaking tree branches grew so close that Garron held his breath. He imagined he could see the man's shadow passing over them, and could hear his muttering.

"… going to kill those stupid kids, and Lars too!"

The roar trumpeted out once more, then cut off abruptly. Garron could hear the familiar thud of the monster's footsteps on the forest floor. More loose dirt fell onto his face as the ground vibrated slightly from the weight. There was an indistinct shout, and the crashing sounds of a man running away. The monster snarled, and the pair moved away until they were out of earshot.

Garron let out a breath he hadn't realized he was holding. "That was close. I think we're clear now, you should start cultivating."

His only response was the quiet sound of Andros' breathing.

"Andros?" Garron shook his friend, but the other boy's lanky body was limp. He'd lost consciousness. Oh well. At least they were in a good hiding spot. There should be enough air Essence, even in this hole, to keep him alive and restore his consciousness in time. Speaking of which…

Garron looked around. He'd assumed that this was a simple furrow in the ground, perhaps some sort of abandoned animal den. But now that his focus was off of the guardsman and the monster in the forest above, he realized that there was quite a bit more space in here than he'd assumed. He could stretch all of his limbs out from his position and not touch a wall. The ground was sloped gently downwards, and he awkwardly scooted that way, trying to sit up. He found that he could, and with a frown, struggled to his feet. Celestial. This wasn't a den, it was a full-on cave, or perhaps a tunnel?

He walked forward, mindful of the slope, and confirmed that, indeed, it stretched further back and down into the earth. As he moved forward… was it getting brighter? A cold feeling came over Garron. He tried to cultivate, and bit back a curse. The Essence here was denser and purer than the forest above, water and earth permeating the air heavily enough that cultivating was as simple as breathing. He'd only felt Essence like this in one place before.

"This is a dungeon." Garron breathed out his fear with the words.

A tinkling laugh, feminine and completely unfamiliar, sounded in Garron's ear. "Sure is! We have an offer to make."

CHAPTER ELEVEN

Garron physically jumped, whirling a moment later and looking around wildly for the source of the strange words.

"Oh, I didn't mean to startle you, sorry." The voice sounded distinctly un-sorry, and Garron thought he detected another laugh at his expense. "I'm… representing the dungeon. You won't be able to see me, I'm afraid. But I'd like to make you an offer, and your sleeping friend there, as well."

Garron still looked around almost involuntarily, but even in the barely illuminated light of the cave—no, dungeon—he could tell there wasn't anybody close by who could be talking to him. It was an eerie experience, made worse by his realization that he could be about to fall prey to some mob or trap, leaving Andros alone and unconscious in a deathtrap.

But he couldn't see any threats nearby. Eventually, he answered the invisible voice. "Why?"

"Well, if you don't want to make a deal, I could go outside and start shouting about the two boys hiding underneath the big tree? Maybe they'd kill you in here, and the dungeon could grow from the Essence gain." The voice took on a vaguely threatening air, though honestly it wasn't all that effective. If this was an invisible person, Garron imagined they were only a few years older than himself, and they possessed a voice more suited to delivering choir performances than threats.

Still, the actual content of the words sent a cold shiver through Garron's spine. He was getting tired of those. He had little confidence in their ability to evade pursuers, or even just wild monsters, if the voice did as it threatened. With a defeated sigh, he walked over to Andros' form, and laboriously hauled his friend into a position where he could lift him up. "Fine, let's talk."

The darkness suddenly gave way to a surprisingly clear soft green light, emanating from down the sloping tunnel. Garron could see that the tunnel continued down through topsoil and dark earth for several meters before eventually turning out of view.

"Excellent! Come down, but stick to the sides of the tunnels. There are traps."

"Of course there are." Garron sighed and worked to lift Andros. The descent was nothing short of torture. Beyond the physical strain of carrying Andros across his shoulders, which necessitated several pauses, questions burned bright in his mind. It was too bad he didn't have the breath to ask them, and he doubted the voice would answer him in any case.

The winding tunnel leveled out after two turns, and after a while Garron started seeing the traps the voice had spoken of. They were not particularly inspired, just simple pits with spikes of stone formed at the bottom, but Garron still remained careful around them, skirting the visible ones and heeding the voice when it told him about any false floors.

The tunnel was quite long, but it had nothing in the way of monsters, more creative traps, or even a pleasing aesthetic. Packed dirt and soil seemed to be the main theme, though occasionally veins of rock or gravel broke the monotony. Finally, after another trip through a tunnel with only a narrow strip of safe ground, they reached the end: a relatively large, open space with a floor that was, as far as Garron could tell, clear of traps.

This room had more rock in the walls, but the effect wasn't uniform. It was surprisingly spacious, though it held little besides a pit of muddy ground near the back, sheltered under a lip of stone protruding from the wall. Garron thought he caught a glimmer of… something, before the voice spoke again.

"Just so you know, if you so much as *touch* the Core, I will go and lure the people chasing you here."

Garron frowned as he looked at the glimmer. Core? Yes, that was a stone there—it shone a cool turquoise, in between blue and green. He supposed it was a Beast Core, like the one that Andros had made him swallow to purify his Center, but what did that have to do with the dungeon? But whatever the voice was talking about, he had to forestall any suspicions. He held up his free hand. "I won't touch it. But, uh, what's going on? What is this?"

Despite his curiosity, he almost didn't want to hear it. In fact, he was sorely tempted to join Andros on the ground and take a nice nap. But he forced his eyes open with all the strength he could muster and stayed focused. He needed to sort this out, or they could both be in danger.

"Why are your eyes so wide? Don't worry, I'm not going to kill you now. I told you, I—the dungeon, I mean—has an offer."

Garron noted that she had said she wasn't going to kill them 'now,' but otherwise just tried to look attentive. Perhaps slightly less insane. He wasn't used to adjusting his eyelids like this.

"I couldn't help but notice that you're running away from some powerful people. I'm sure you noticed that this forest is full of strong monsters, too." The voice paused, clearly expectant, and Garron nodded. "How much do you know about how dungeons grow stronger?"

"Uh." Andros' memory stone hadn't really talked about dungeons, and the question hadn't come up. He did remember Andros mentioning the previous dungeon's rank, so maybe… "Do they cultivate, like humans?"

"Hardly." The voice sounded condescending, and Garron bristled a bit. This hadn't even mattered at all to him only days before. He thought he was doing well, all things considered. "Unlike humans, dungeons can get large amounts of Essence very quickly by having things die within them."

"That sounds… morbid." Honestly, it was extremely annoying not to have a face to watch as he listened, but that was the least of his concerns.

The voice seemed unconcerned, ignoring his interjection. "This dungeon is very young, and very weak. Just barely in the F-ranks. In the normal course of things, it would take years of cultivation to become strong enough to begin attracting and absorbing the monsters around this area, and only then would it be able to grow steadily in power."

Garron cleared his throat, interrupting the voice. "Um, why would its rank matter for getting monsters to come in and die here? I mean, it's not using techniques or anything, right?"

"*Right.*" She—he guessed—sounded annoyed at his interruption. "The amount of Essence a dungeon has determines everything it can do; how large it can grow, how many traps it can build, how many and how *powerful* its monsters are. *Ev-er-y-thing.*"

"Oh." Garron was still curious how traps factored into it, and suddenly wondered for the first time who exactly was building all of the ones he'd encountered in dungeons thus far. He decided that it was a question for later. If there was a later.

"Hm. In any case, the dungeon would like to grow as quickly as possible—which is where a pair of cultivators like yourselves come in. If you bring monsters into the dungeon and kill them there, the dungeon could do in *days* what would normally take years!" The voice sounded so excited that Garron wondered if its owner was bouncing up and down… wherever they were. He wasn't quite so enthused.

"Sounds great and everything, but why should we do it? I mean, we're not exactly here for tourism." Garron was proud of that word—he'd picked it up in a novel about a man who travelled around the world in one hundred days by flying on a magic cloud.

"I, uh…" The voice sounded confused, and Garron held back his smile. It seemed like the ghostly creature needed to do some more reading to expand its vo… vu… number of words it knew. "I know that you're in danger. This is an excellent hiding spot."

Garron frowned at that, furrowing his brow. "But you want us to go out into the forest and get monsters?"

"Well, yes—I'm sure you can stay undetected for that short amount of time, but you'll need a place to *stay*, won't you?"

"Actually, we were planning on leaving here as quickly as possible." Garron was looking around surreptitiously as he spoke, trying to see if any creatures were sneaking up on him while he spoke with the voice. He positioned himself close to Andros' form on the ground.

"Well, the dungeon can help you with that too. Especially if you make it stronger. You could have mobs fighting for you in here, the dungeon could create loot that would help you fight. If you haven't already noticed, the dungeon has a dual affinity for water and earth, which I see swirling all around your Center. If you help the dungeon get stronger, it will become the perfect training ground for you." The voice had an enticing note in *her* —this was most certainly a 'her,' Garron was sure now—tone.

Like a high-quality sword, she had a good point. Especially about the last bit. How many dungeons were out there with a dual affinity, and how many out of those would have the two strongest of his three? Even the dungeon Andros had taken them to before only had an earth affinity, though the underground river had provided a balance of water. That was… interesting, as were the other parts of the offer. "I—"

"Oh, would you look at that, there's someone near the entrance, and they don't seem too pleased. This is the perfect opportunity to show you what I mean! I'll be right back."

CHAPTER TWELVE

"Um, what?" Silence filled the room. A second too late, Garron blinked tiredly. When he received no reply, her words registered, and a cold feeling ran down his back. He turned and ran towards the tunnel entrance. He made it halfway to the next room before his chest began to burn and he stopped, gasping. Hands on his knees, he fought with all his will against his soreness and fatigue. His will lost, and he found himself lying on the floor.

But before he could fall into sleep, the voice sounded in his ear, startling him. "Why are you lying down on the floor over there? Anyway, I yelled down the tunnel at that man, and he took the bait. Now, once you kill him, the dungeon can get some real power and I can show you what I mean!"

"Are you *insane*?" Garron stared—at empty space. It was extraordinarily unsatisfying to yell at an invisible person.

"What's wrong?" The voice sounded entirely too innocent.

Garron rubbed the bridge of his nose. On top of everything else, he was developing an enormous headache. "Focus on the not-dying. Right. I don't have any weapons or anything! How exactly am I supposed to fight a guardsman?"

"Oh. Well, he's only F-rank five. That's the same as you, so—"

"Except that he's a trained adult who hasn't spent the past few hours running for his life. Also, he probably has a *sword*!"

"He does," the voice confirmed. "Looks good, too. Once he's dead, we can make it loot for the dungeon!"

Loot. Garron perked up, though only slightly. "Wait. You said the dungeon could help me fight. Can it make a weapon for me?"

There was a maddening moment of silence, and Garron tried to think how long it had been since the guardsman entered the dungeon. Surely not more than a minute or two. How long had it taken Garron to make it down this far? About ten. But he'd been carrying Andros. How long would it take an unencumbered man?

"Well?" Garron managed to keep from yelling again, but only because he was suddenly worried that the guardsman would hear him.

"If you… if you swear to help the dungeon become stronger, we can help you. Otherwise… no."

A large part of Garron wanted to say 'no' out of spite. This was blatant extortion! But his new motto flashed through his head again: not dying was good. "Fine. I… swear. It's a deal."

Part of Garron expected the words to echo through the tunnel, for the ambient soft blue light to flash, or to feel a sense of power flowing through him. Instead, he just felt sleepy. But the voice seemed satisfied. "Great!"

"Now, I need a sword, or maybe a spear." A spear would do better in a narrow space like this, wouldn't it? "Yeah, a spear."

"Hm, we could maybe do a spear. Or… no, we haven't managed to find any dead wood yet. Would just a spearhead work? A stone one, that is."

"What?" How long had it been now? Garron had lost count.

"Or wait! We could just make the whole thing out of stone! But that would be heavy, wouldn't it?"

Garron's anger mixed with a wave of confusion. What was she talking about? "You don't have a weapon for me?"

"Well, we can do rocks, and shift soil and ground a little. Not a lot, not unless you want to alert someone above ground to where we are."

Garron wondered if it was possible to strangle disembodied voices. "We'll talk about this later."

He tried to shake off the worry that he didn't have a moment to spare. What tools did he have? Well, apparently rocks. "Can you make a rock fall on his head?"

"No, his Aura would interfere. Can't collapse the ceiling of a tunnel over him either."

"Aura? Gah, useless. What else?" Well, he had perhaps one more blast of Essence in him before he passed out—not to mention whatever damage it would do to his body—but it wouldn't be enough to kill anyone. It had only worked so well before because the wood had already been warped and strained by the heat. He wished he could manufacture another situation like that, but this place just didn't have the right environment. "I have to adapt."

There wasn't much time, so he made the best decision he could. "I need a big rock. Something that I can hit someone with. Pointy on one end."

"Now *that*, we can do!"

Strangely, as the voice said the words, Garron suddenly felt confident. That lasted for all of a second, before the fear came back in force. He started off down the tunnel. He had to move fast. As he started his best approximation of a run, he noticed something on the ground ahead—a smooth brownish stone a little smaller than his head. He bent down and picked it up, hefting it as he continued on. "Perfect. Well, about as perfect as I can get."

The spot he was looking for was a sharp bend in the tunnel, which came right after a pit trap. The pit was open to the air, unfortunately, but there was only a narrow strip of a safe rock visible on its edge. If someone fell in… well, it was quite a drop, and the stone spikes on the bottom looked sharp. Even a solid breastplate would do little to prevent death.

"Can you weaken the ledge so he'll just fall in?"

"Hm. That's a little complicated. Make it weak enough not to bear weight, but still seem strong? Maybe if it was soil, but rock... it would take too much time."

Of course it would. Without much hope, he asked one more question, heart hammering. The guard had to be past the second room by now. Minutes away. "How about a hollow wall behind the ledge?"

"Hollow's easy but wall... oh, actually, I've got it! Step back a bit."

In seconds, Garron watched as the loose earth by the ledge compressed inward with a strange crunching noise, leaving a space just big enough for him to squeeze into with his rock.

"Okay, get in there."

Garron practically leapt into the space, clutching his rock and standing still. This was perfect—the false wall would make an ambush child's play. He was somewhat surprised that the dungeon was able to do it on such short notice, but then even just the appearance of the rock was somewhat amazing.

"Now, take a deep breath. He's almost here, so no more talking. Oh, and don't move or you might displace it." The last words were whispered, but the first gave him pause.

What? A strange anxiety, almost excitement, came over Garron, and soil the same color as the surrounding wall began piling up at his feet. But instead of only forming a narrow barrier to conceal him from his enemy, the stuff was stacking up around him. It took less than half a minute for him to be completely entombed—he barely managed to squeeze his eyes shut in time, and the dirt began finding its way into every open crevice of his clothes and body. It was... unpleasant.

"I'm going to find a way to make that voice suffer." But Garron still felt an odd satisfaction—he supposed this would work, and the plus side of being surrounded by earth was that it did feel a little easier to grab at the earth Essence in his Center, not that he would ever tell Andros. His preparations, few as they were, were complete. Now for the difficult part.

Luckily, it only took a half minute for the sound of cautious footsteps to come into Garron's range of hearing. He felt his heartbeat quickening, though from the tiny dirt-filled breaths he was forced to take or from the prospect of the upcoming fight he had no idea. He resisted the urge to move as he heard his target approaching, though he did grip his rock tighter.

"Stupid kids. Little servant's gonna die anyway, so why'd they have to go and make me…?"

The muttering grew louder and louder, and though Garron barely listened to the actual words, they still made him angry. Here was a grown man—a guardsman, no less—complaining about how annoying it was to kill one child and bring another back to his insane leader. Any qualms he had about what he planned vanished. When he heard boots stepping slowly on the stone ledge a bare hand-length away from him, he finally moved.

Soil fell away, spilling out over the ledge and into the pit below, but it barely hampered Garron's strike. His rock came swinging up and, a moment after he identified his target, made impact, slamming into the man's head with a thud. And a ring of metal. The helmet. Why didn't he think of the—

Garron saved his self-recrimination for later, swinging the rock again, but the guardsman had already managed to avoid falling by stumbling to the side, and the attack met empty air. Now Garron looked, and he saw the guard in full armor, wobbling slightly on the stone ledge but still standing. Then the man looked at him, and Garron saw recognition in his eyes. It was Joris, the man Garron had worked the pulley with only days ago.

He barely dodged the sword that came down at his head by ducking back into his alcove, but the move left him pinned as the guard clanked back toward him. The hulking form raised its sword, poised to strike. For an instant, Garron thought he might hesitate—after all, Garron had worked with Joris before, even if the man had never been remotely friendly. Then he pointed the sword at Garron, clearly about to thrust it forward.

With a shout, Garron let loose the best kick he could manage, pushing his back against the wall and compromising his balance in the process. The move was totally useless—alone. As he planted his foot on Joris' breastplate, he let loose the blast of the earth Essence he'd held ready in his Center. The armored form toppled backward, Essence impacting his armor with a dull crunch and forcing him into the waiting pit.

Garron's eyes screwed up as the pain hit, a searing stiffness and buzzing pressure which left him unable to control his muscles for a moment. His leg went numb, and he felt as though something was weighing it down, preventing him from moving it. He still heard Joris hit the spikes, the tearing clang as his armor was punctured by the stone, and the strangled cry of pain which mirrored his own.

The guard's yell ended in a gurgle, and Garron knew he'd won. A paradoxical wave of happiness washed over him, though it passed in a moment and left him with agony, fatigue, and vague disgust. He shuddered, and not from the pain still racking his body. What—Garron's head spun, and black spots began appearing in his vision.

He managed to crawl out of the alcove, past the pit, and halfway down the tunnel before he collapsed in a heap. The last words he heard, however, left a half-formed snarl on his face.

"Great job!"

CHAPTER THIRTEEN

"*Gar.*" Andros' whisper woke Garron from his unconscious state. He shot straight up off the floor, swinging his hands around wildly. He nearly fell as his leg gave out, still numb from the Essence blast, though it seemed better than earlier.

"Good. I need to move." He started grabbing at the Essence in his Center before his vision resolved itself. "What's going on?"

Could he get a weapon in time? He didn't have a sword, he had… "Where's my rock?"

"Calm down! What are you doing? Rock?" Andros' hand landed on Garron's shoulder, and the struggling teenager blinked. The blurry spots in his vision finally cleared as he looked around. They were in the large room at the end of the dungeon, though thankfully he was on the dry ground near the entrance rather than the pit of mud at the end. The soft blue light cast strange shadows around the corners of the roughly cubic space, but he had no trouble seeing Andros right in front of him.

"Is Jackson waiting at the entrance or something? Or is he

smoking us out?" Garron was frantic. Could the dungeon make them air vents?

Andros raised his hands before him in a calming gesture. "What? No! Calm down, Gar. You've just had a hard few hours and—"

"That's not it!" Garron shook his head violently, still looking around for the danger he was sure was about to sneak up on them. "This is your fault! Every time you wake me up like that, we end up almost dying a few minutes later."

"Oh." After a moment's pause, Andros started laughing, though he looked vaguely worried. "That… that's just a coincidence. Right?"

Garron shrugged, though he covertly tried to locate his rock. Surprising how comfortable a nice big rock could be. "What happened?"

Andros eyed Garron with a hopeful look. "You tell me! I woke up and you were just lying in that tunnel and… there was this voice. It said it talked to you?"

"Oh, yes. I talked to her. I'm going to talk to her again." Garron grit his teeth, partly at the soreness which hit him in a wave now that he was coming down from his excitement, and partly from his anger. "She almost got me killed by luring Joris in here, then extorted me into swearing an oath to help her stupid dungeon, she buried me alive, and—"

"What?" Andros shot to his feet, a wary look on his face.

"Oh, you're being *dramatic*. Everything worked out!" The smooth voice held a note of cheer which induced absolute rage in Garron as he whipped his head around to try and find the disembodied voice.

"You! What in the *abyss* were you thinking? I'm going to—"

"You look a little funny shaking your head around like that, you know. Hm… now that you've sworn an oath to help us, I guess you can see me." The voice chuckled and a strange ball of light appeared. Garron was ready to strangle the person who'd been responsible for his near death. But there was only this… ball?

"Is that... are you a *Dungeon Wisp?*" Andros' voice was filled with awe, but Garron still couldn't see who he was talking with.

"You know it!" came the perky voice.

Andros was looking up at the ceiling. Garron followed his gaze back to the ball of light. Was *this* what he'd been looking for? It was just a floating ball of salmon-colored light, bobbing slightly up and down in the air as words rang out. It was mesmerizing in an odd way that made Garron take an involuntary step forward before shaking his head and frowning.

"What are you?" Even as he said the words, he felt an odd surge of... pride? He supposed it was just the influence of her appearance, which he had to admit was quite beautiful. But in a moment his anger reasserted itself, and he frowned up at the creature.

"I'm a Dungeon Wisp! I'm like... a dungeon helper, I suppose, or a manager. I help the dungeon get stronger, and help it use its power to improve itself." The ball of light did a little circle in the air as she spoke.

Garron's eyebrows rose almost involuntarily. "So you're saying that you... what, direct the construction of the dungeon? How does that work?"

"Well, I don't exactly... I mean *yes*, that's basically right." The Wisp stopped her spinning. She had hesitated, Garron was pretty sure. It was surprisingly hard to tell without body language or facial expressions to accompany her voice.

"I can't *believe* you're real! I read about Dungeon Wisps in one of my dad's books when I was little, but it said they were a myth!" Andros gushed at the energy ball. "When he took me through my first few dungeons, I brought a little net so I could try and catch one! I never found one of you, obviously, but..."

Catching the Wisp didn't sound like a bad idea. Garron tried to shoot a meaningful look at Andros, but his friend was too focused on the floating creature.

"Well, we don't tend to show ourselves. Ever. You're probably the first humans at such a low rank to detect one of us." If the Wisp had a body, Garron got the impression that she would be preening. In fact, she was subtly shifting color towards a pale yellow. "Just another benefit of our partnership."

"Partnership?" Andros mumbled the question. He was staring at the Wisp dreamily, and Garron gave him a subtle nudge. The Noble shook himself, and asked in a stronger voice, "What partnership?"

"Well." Garron's voice held an edge of bitterness. "Let me tell you what it… she… the Wisp—"

"My *name* is Talia." She sounded affronted that Garron didn't even try to come up with a proper descriptor for her.

"Fine," Garron grunted. "What *Talia* did."

He told the story, though he felt he couldn't convey the madness of the whole ordeal properly. Towards the end, he managed to give Andros a meaningful look, indicating the Wisp. "They were trying to *catch* us, so I had to… kick him into the pit."

Andros seemed to understand what he was getting at, but he frowned and gave Garron a slight shake of his head. Garron managed to hold back a growl. "Why not, Andros?"

"Why not what?" Talia's suspicion was clear.

Was Andros saying it was impossible to capture the Wisp? It didn't seem particularly powerful. Or, more likely, he just didn't think it was 'the right thing to do.' From Garron's perspective, the ball of light had more than earned a solid capture for forcing him into a deathmatch with a cultivator, but Andros hadn't been awake for that. Garron flushed and he sat down heavily on the dirt floor, nearly giving into his impotent rage as he rubbed his wounds. His leg was getting better, but it still couldn't bear much weight.

When he finished the story with his collapse in the tunnel, Andros patted him sympathetically on the shoulder. "I'm sorry that happened, Gar. I didn't know—his body was gone by the time I woke up. Dungeons, you know."

"Right, the dungeon absorbed him! And let me tell you, all that Essence was *amazing* for its cultivation. It broke into F-rank one!" Talia bobbed excitedly as she said all of this.

Garron felt a strange satisfaction at the words, but he immediately rejected it with a shake of his head. What was *wrong* with him? He was *angry*, for celestial's sake, not proud or satisfied or… happy at what he'd done. The young cultivator shivered, thinking of Joris falling into the pit. He hadn't even said a word to the man before killing him.

The Wisp flew down to hover between Garron and Andros, casting a salmon tinge on the rock around them. "Now then, there's so much to do! When can you two go out and lure some monsters in here for us? We've got to work on expanding the dungeon, fixing up traps—we get to make *loot*! This is going to be amazing!"

As she said the words, Garron felt a sense of excitement and hunger intrude on him. Underneath it, his own annoyance was still there, but… Garron quested with his mind, retreating into himself as he did to cultivate. Yes, these weren't his emotions at all. Something was—confusion. An almost animal wariness, or… no, childlike. There, a hint of hurt pride.

"What is this? Am I…? I mean, what's going on? I keep feeling…" Garron paused and tried to collect his thoughts. "There! Why would I feel worried about what you're saying? Or, I mean, something's feeling that way, but I can *feel* it too."

Andros moved beside him, and put a hand on his shoulder. "Gar? Are you alright?"

"Yes. *Are* you alright?" Talia's voice was strained, and her color tinged slightly deeper as she spoke. A blush. "It seems like you might have hit your head while you were fighting or… or something."

It wasn't Talia herself, was it? Garron had no idea what Dungeon Wisps were capable of—perhaps they could project emotions? But he felt none of the embarrassment she was displaying, only a vague confusion, a hint of protective annoyance, and a deep, abiding *hunger*.

"What did you do to me?" Garron glared at the floating ball of light before him, heart beating a little faster. Fear and confusion warred within him—no, the confusion wasn't his own.

With an effort, he pushed the strange emotion down, and took a step back from the Wisp. "Stop it!"

"Gar!" Andros shot him a concerned look, but moved to interpose himself between him and Talia. Slowly, the young cultivator raised his fists toward the Dungeon Wisp. A surge of rage suffused Garron at his friend's actions, and he actually gasped; hunching over as he wrestled with the overpowering sensation. Out of the corner of his eye, Garron could see Andros step forward. "Stop whatever you're doing to him, *now*."

"I'm not doing anything!" The Wisp floated backwards, bobbing nervously.

More anger. It wasn't like anything Garron had ever felt before. Not just fierce, but murderous. He wanted to attack, kill, protect... *Talia?*

"Wait, Andy." Garron straightened, though he squinted as he held up a hand to his friend. He was beginning to get a pounding headache. "It's not her."

Andros looked between Garron and Talia for a moment. "Are you—"

"I'm sure." Garron kept his face as calm as he could manage, though that horrible animal anger was still roiling in his chest. Andros lowered his fists. Garron wasn't quite sure what he'd been planning to do with them, but the motion brought with it a surge of relief for Garron. Whoever's emotions Garron was feeling, they had truly been terrified that Andros would hurt Talia. There weren't any other living things in this place.

It was just Andros, Talia, and him. What would want to protect Talia so badly? Some kind of monster? That hunger... Garron took a sharp breath. "It's the dungeon!"

Silence. Talia only bobbed up and down worriedly, and Andros stared at Garron like he'd gone insane. But the surge of confused worry he felt confirmed it. He took a step towards Talia, frowning. "Abyss, it *is*. Why can I feel what it's feeling?"

Talia let out a defeated sigh—an incongruous sound for her

form, but clearly heartfelt. "I... I don't know. Your Aura should block any mindspeaking that he's doing."

"Wait, what?" Andros paused as he looked between the two. "Huh, I say that a lot, don't I? What are you talking about?"

"I'm feeling the emotions of the dungeon we're in, Andy. Not the Wisp, the actual *dungeon*." It felt strange to say, but the creature pressing on his mind was agreeing with his words even as he said them.

Andros, however, didn't have such confirmation. "Are you sure you're alright, Gar? Dungeons *aren't* alive. They can't 'feel' *anything*."

"No, Andy." Garron smacked his forehead. He really should have wondered a bit more about this after the first dungeon he'd been through. "Haven't you ever wondered what makes all of the traps and loot and monsters in dungeons?"

Andros appeared to consider it for a moment, but then he shrugged. "Not really."

Garron stared at his friend for a moment, then sighed. "The dungeons make the monsters and the traps. It's the only explanation. After all, you said before that dungeon we went to had a rank. What other thing that cultivates Essence isn't alive?"

"Oh. *Oh.*" Andros appeared to chew on Garron's pronouncement, then looked at Talia. "Is that true?"

The Wisp sighed again. "Yes. I was going to tell you, but... I didn't expect one of you to be able to hear him like this. He's young. Now that he's properly in the F-ranks, he can start to control what he sends out more... directly, but he's still stuck at emotions and images right now. Stronger dungeons *can* actually talk."

"'He'?" Andros still seemed in shock.

To tell the truth, so was Garron. However, he was also feeling the sort of embarrassment that came from a parent talking about you to other adults in front of you. It had been a long time since he'd felt that, and even though it wasn't truly his emotion, he felt himself flushing.

Talia seemed defensive. "Yes, *he*. His name is Typo."

Now it was Garron's turn to frown. "You named a rock? Why... 'Typo'?"

"Hey! He's a dungeon, not some rock." Talia whizzed forward, her light momentarily crowding Garron and forcing him to take a step back in surprise. She backed up, apparently satisfied with his reaction. "I don't know, it's just a nonsense word, but he seemed to like it."

The surge of pride confirmed that the dungeon—Typo—quite liked his name. Right. Because dungeons were 'alive.' It was still a bit strange to think about, but then he hadn't ever seen a dungeon before a few days ago, so it wasn't as much of a shock. To him. Andros was having a harder time processing the information, judging by the way he was muttering feverishly to himself.

"Living dungeons, making traps and monsters and... loot. Ooh, I'm going to go and find that one that gave me that potion and make it—hold on," he cut himself off, looking to Talia. "So how come Garron can hear it and I can't?"

The Wisp bobbed downward in a swift plunge, the motion somehow conveying confusion. "I told you already, I don't know. His Aura should block any interference from the dungeon. Right, Typo?"

Assurance, yet... curiosity. A moment later, something hit Garron on the head hard enough to make him rub it in pain. "Ow! What—"

A rock clattered to the floor, not big enough to cause real harm, thankfully, but enough to exacerbate Garron's existing headache further. A surge of amazement and excitement hit Garron, but he pushed it away with annoyance. Now that he knew the emotions weren't his, they were easy to compartmentalize.

"Wow!" Andros stared at the rock as if it might explode. "Where did that come from?"

"The dungeon, obviously," Garron growled, still rubbing his head. "I thought it couldn't do that?"

Talia made another circle in the air. "He can't. I mean,

normally he can't. You... your Aura must not impede him anymore? Because you swore an oath to him! This is *incredible!*"

Talia seemed as excited as the dungeon, which only soured Garron's mood further. However, Andros seemed to agree. "You're right! You said it would get smarter if it gets more Essence?"

"Yes!" Talia didn't pause her frenetic circling through the air.

Andros showed his devilishly charming smile. "You'll both help us with loot and creatures if we help you, right?"

"*Absolutely!*" Talia seemed hopeful at Andros' words, but Garron was resigned. He could see the light shining in Andros' eyes now.

The young Noble turned towards the dungeon's exit, a new spring in his step. "Then we should go and find some monsters!"

Talia fell into line behind him, bobbing up and down. "Great idea! You know, you could swear an oath too, and we—"

"No." Andros' reply was... harsher than Garron expected. As much as he hated to admit it, he agreed with both of them to some extent. He knew that Andros just wanted to see if they could talk to a dungeon, and they were both interested in the proposed help, yet it seemed that the young Noble knew something about oaths that Garron not did not.

He called out at Andros' back. "Fine, we can go get creatures. But how about food first? Maybe cultivating? Checking to see if the coast is clear?"

Andros' stomach rumbled, and he stopped in his tracks. "Huh. That's an even *better* idea."

Garron felt a small measure of vindictive satisfaction at the disappointment which radiated from the dungeon. "That's what you get for dropping a rock on my head, *Typo*."

He picked up the rock in question. It was a nice rock.

CHAPTER FOURTEEN

They decided to start with cultivation. Garron was still too exhausted and injured to want to move anywhere, and Andros was only in slightly better shape. They both simply dropped to the floor where they were and began drawing in Essence.

Garron was amazed. Even at the dungeon's low rank, there was still an abundance of mostly purified Essence permeating the room. There was both water and earth, which made cultivating those types almost as easy as breathing. Essence flowed into him with incredible speed, as though he was simply plucking it out of the air to add to his Center.

The only limiting factor was the air Essence, which surprisingly wasn't completely absent from the room, it just wasn't anywhere near the density and purity of Garron's other affinities. His affinity to air was his weakest by far, but he still needed to cultivate it at the same time as the other two types.

There was a problem with that.

"This isn't going to work, is it?" Andros' voice was resigned, and Garron felt a pang of guilt for his friend.

"I'm sorry, Andy." He shot the young air cultivator an apologetic look.

"Don't be." Andros struggled to his feet. "I probably already sucked most of the air Essence out of here while I was unconscious. You'll have to stop soon too, but you should get as much into your Center as you can before that happens. I'll go find us some food."

It was nice of Andros to afford him the opportunity to cultivate, but… "Are you sure you should be going out? We don't know where the guards are yet. Not to mention all the monsters?"

Andros laughed to ease his friend's tension, "The monsters shouldn't be an issue—even that lion wouldn't be able to catch me if my Center wasn't nearly depleted. Not saying I could kill it by myself, but I could run away!"

"Uh, sure, but what's a lion?" Garron had never heard that word before, even in the books he'd read.

Andros scratched his chin. "That big cat thing? I mean, it's not *just* a lion, not anymore, but before it started taking in earth Essence, that's what it would have been called. I saw one when my dad took me to a dungeon way out east of the estate, in this huge plain. No idea how one got here though. I guess a high Essence-density place like this attracts animals from all over, or there could be plains to the east that—"

"Sounds interesting," Garron lied quickly. It *was* interesting, but Andros could get a bit long winded if Garron didn't rein him in. "But even if you can get away from the, uh, lion, there's still the guards?"

Andros waved the concern away. "The forest's huge! Even the part we passed through already is more ground than they can cover. I'll bet you that by now they're going to be staying mostly near the edges, so they can catch us if we try to leave. Should be easy to avoid them—it isn't like they're Wood Elves or anything."

Garron pressed his lips together. "Don't ask, don't ask… okay, *fine*. Wood Elves?"

"Oh, you know how there's a bunch of different kinds of Elves? High Elves are the stuck-up ones, and then there's Dark

Elves, those are pretty much mercenaries and assassins. Sea Elves basically live on their ships, I always thought those were kind of boring. Wood Elves are really good at forest-craft though—if one of them were after us, they'd have caught us already." Andros snorted at that thought. "Of course, if a Wood Elf was out here, we'd have never made it this far."

Garron's stomach was protesting, but at this point he'd given up fighting his curiosity. Lord Tet was a senior member of the Guild, and apparently that meant Andros knew a lot. He was jealous. "Are they something we should look for?"

"Oh, no." Andros waved a nonchalant hand. "All of the Elves are cultivators. *All* of them. I don't really know how they manage it. But they don't let anyone out of their homelands if they aren't in the Mage ranks—even Dark Elves don't start working as mercenaries until then. Which means if you ever meet one, they're ridiculously strong, fast, and they can use Mana to blast you out of existence if they want."

Garron supposed that when your father was a Mage, and you were expected to become one as well, their power didn't shake you quite as badly. Andros held up a finger. "Oh! Unless it's a Wild Elf. Those are like outcasts, so they don't have that rule. Still dangerous though. My dad—"

That was enough. They would be here until they both starved to death if Garron just let Andros go on. "You know what? If you think you'll be safe, you should go cultivate in the forest."

Andros finally paused, though it looked like he'd been going a bit blue from lack of a breath anyway. A deep inhalation later, he nodded. "I'll see you soon!"

Once Andros had walked back out of the room and up the tunnel, Garron settled in again to cultivate. Thankfully, Talia didn't seem inclined to speak to him, which was definitely nice. He focused on refining Essence and adding it to his new chi spiral, the work quickly putting him into a meditative state. It was truly a joy to feel the energy flowing into him, feel how it purified his body and increased his strength. His fatigue and even some of his soreness faded as he cultivated the Essence. Slowly, feeling returned to his leg and hand, though the leg was still very sluggish.

Even his hand had almost returned to normal, though the skin of his palm was still dry and cracked. Unfortunately, he found it difficult to maintain his concentration after a few minutes of cultivation. With his head cleared by the Essence and his immediate concerns mostly addressed, his mind was wandering to an uncomfortable place.

Joris.

Garron had killed the man. He didn't feel bad about it—Joris had made his choice, and left Garron without one—but it felt strange. The thought of the silent guard falling into the pit left him… empty. The memory didn't feel quite real. A voice interrupted his introspection. "Now Typo, you're going to have to increase your influence, and make it denser in the area you already control."

<Confusion.> As time went on, Garron was finding it easier to think of the dungeon's projections as a sort of communication, but the mild feeling shook Garron out of his introspection, and he looked up at Talia. She was bobbing patiently in the air near the mud pit where the dungeon Core—Typo, he supposed —was situated.

"Remember how you pushed your Essence out into the soil, to make the tunnel and the traps?" The Wisp's voice had a lecturing quality, though given the youth evident in her voice, it sounded a little forced.

The dungeon was acting like an eager young student though, so he supposed it worked. <Confirmation.>

Talia bobbed in place. "You have more Essence now, so we should try to start hollowing out more area for you, and make the things you have stronger than they are now. It's easier than just making *more*."

<Cautious agreement. Embarrassment.> Garron got the sense that, though Typo remembered doing… whatever Talia was talking about, he didn't remember the specifics at all.

"Oh *no*," Talia muttered, though Garron didn't know why, since he and Typo could both still hear her. "It took him *months* the first time."

Garron winced at the thought of getting nothing done for months at a time. "What does he need to do?"

Talia gave a startled bob, then flashed a mild red that Garron took for annoyance. "He has to expand his influence. It's a dungeon ability."

Her tone was making it clear that she thought he should go back to cultivating and let her work, but Garron was actually interested. He wanted the dungeon to become stronger in as short a time as possible, if only so that he could fulfill his side of the oath. "How is he supposed to do it?"

"He... Typo needs to take his Essence and pump it out into the world around him. The problem is, even though he's in the F-ranks now, he hasn't had to do this for a while, so he's forgotten what it feels like." Talia described a strange pattern in the air, her tone slightly frustrated.

Hm. Garron gave a slow nod. "So it's as though he's turning the Essence into something like... air? Or a gas, I guess?"

"Yes, that's the idea. Now if only he understood what that meant properly." Talia's annoyance was seemingly forgotten as she floated closer to the dungeon Core. "Typo? You *need* to focus on this."

<Guilt. Eager attentiveness.> Garron got the impression that the dungeon's mind had been wandering as he and Talia spoke. Talia spent several minutes trying to coach the dungeon through the process of expanding its influence, even using Garron's analogy of Essence and air to no avail.

The problem, as Garron saw it, was that the first time they'd done this, the dungeon had no influence to begin with. Now, his job was to expand from what he already had, and into new areas, which meant he had to transmit Essence through his influence. Garron could visualize it in his mind, seeing the Essence as a bluish mist that grew brighter around the Core and diffused outward until it reached the target area, and from there pushed outwards. If only the dungeon could see that.

"Oh." Garron considered his connection with the dungeon. It was sending its thoughts to him, and apparently it could perceive him in return. Even now, he could feel a sort of low-level awareness of himself radiating from the dungeon, along with its other emotions. What would happen if he…?

<Hello?> Garron did his best to project the thought towards the presence in his mind, and immediately felt the dungeon's reaction.

<Surprise! Confusion… Cautious welcome?>

So it *was* possible. Garron felt a thrill of success, and decided to try something more complex. <My name is Garron. What's yours?>

The dungeon paused. <Welcome! *Identity*.>

Garron blinked at the feeling of self which the dungeon—no, his name was definitely Typo—sent towards him. That was more complex than a singular feeling, which was all he'd received from Typo thus far. Then again, children always learned their own names early on, didn't they?

<I want to help you learn.> Garron tried to imbue the words with a sense of 'teaching,' casting his mind back to the people who'd taught Andros and him in their childhoods.

<Shame. Hope. Invitation?> Garron felt a pang of sympathy. The dungeon truly wanted to do well, if only to please Talia, but he couldn't wrap his mind around her words.

"Are you listening to me?" Talia's half-shout startled both Garron and, he felt, Typo. He also felt a surge of childlike guilt from the dungeon, which he reacted to instinctively with the feeling of calm.

<Let her relax a bit.> Garron couldn't deny a bit of vindictive satisfaction at the Wisp's annoyance—after all, she deserved some retribution for what she'd done with Joris—but he kept it in check as best he could. He felt his headache returning. These mental gymnastics weren't easy.

After a moment of consideration, the dungeon projected a reply. <Cautious agreement. Interest. Query?>

Time for the important bit. Garron focused, fixing the image he needed in his head. <You need to do *this*.>

In Garron's mind, Essence, not just bluish light but the actual idea of the stuff, flowed out from Typo. He replayed the scene he'd constructed in his head, deciding to show the dungeon's influence spreading at a point he thought he remembered down several bends of the tunnel, near where it leveled out. He had to approximate exactly what the Essence spreading to the earth around the tunnel would look like, but he thought water seeping into soil would be somewhat close, so in his mind the gaseous Essence turned almost to liquid as it contacted the tunnel walls. Close enough.

He held the image for as long as he could, and he could feel intense scrutiny from Typo. Finally, however, he got the response he'd been hoping for.

<Understanding!>

"You better not be—hold on… That's *it*! Keep it up, Typo, you're doing it! Now, where do you want to—oh, you're just going, okay, I'm coming!" Talia, cut off mid-rant, zipped out of the room, and Garron felt the pride emanating from Typo. He felt some of his own as well, and couldn't hold back a grin.

<Good job!> He glanced at the turquoise Core still embedded in the mud nearby, but he could see no obvious sign of life.

Typo clearly appreciated the congratulations. <Pride. Gratitude!>

Smile still on his face, Garron settled down again. He could feel, in the back of his mind, Typo focusing on slowly pushing and condensing the soft earth of the tunnel to form a room. From Talia's shouts, he gathered it would take some time to complete, in order to avoid disturbing the ground around the dungeon and causing an earthquake. Still, he suspected that if there were no large veins of rock, the process couldn't take much more than a day. After all, it wasn't like the dungeon was burrowing through solid stone.

Garron felt his grin widen as he thought about what he'd just done in another way. He'd helped a dungeon change the very nature of the world around it—something he hadn't even known was possible even a week ago. He—

"I'm back! Do you know why Talia yelled at me when I came down the tunnel? She said something about my 'Aura interfering with the expansion.'" Andros' voice echoed slightly as he crossed the threshold into the room.

Garron stood quickly, surprised to see Andros carrying a rabbit in each hand. "That was fast. Don't worry about it, she's just excited."

"Yeah, well, I'm light on my feet." Andros preened, grinning as he swung one of the rabbits back and forth. "Besides, these weren't monsters, so it wasn't too tough. I don't think they've been alive long enough to absorb that much Essence."

Under different circumstances, Garron might have felt guilty about eating such young rabbits, but empty stomachs had a way of hardening hearts, so he just nodded. "Why don't I skin them while you get the fire going?"

Andros' grin froze on his face. "Uh, Gar? How do I…? Uh, I could use some help with that."

"Figure it out, Andy." Garron's voice was filled with a threat as he took the rabbits from Andros' hands. "Noble brat."

"Peasant swine."

"Layabout cultivator."

"Garron… I don't want to eat raw rabbit."

CHAPTER FIFTEEN

The next day, Garron was cultivating quietly in the dungeon. They had agreed that Andros should do his cultivation outside now that he was mostly back to full strength, in order to conserve the air Essence in the dungeon for Garron. The forest was incredibly Essence dense, so he should still be able to make some progress.

Garron had been focusing for what felt like hours, refining Essence and filling his Center, occasionally moving through the tunnel, when the Essence finally became depleted in the large room. In the process, he'd gotten to see the room Typo and Talia were working on. It was already beginning to take on larger dimensions, and as Garron passed by, he could hear the very faint crunching sound which signified the dirt and soil being compressed to open up the space.

From what Talia explained in the process of her endless cajoling, directing and, he felt, micromanaging of the process, they were rushing the expansion slightly. That would cause minor tremors in the earth, but the fact that Typo was moving only a small amount of loose earth, and the ground above was strongly anchored by an entire forest's worth of tree roots, hopefully meant he was able to remain undetectable.

When Garron had dared ask the reason for the rush, Talia scoffed. "When you two start earning your keep, we'll need to have some space to house dungeon monsters, as well as more area for traps to kill them in the first place."

Garron had refrained from pointing out that he and Andros had already contributed much more to Typo's growth than the dungeon had to their survival, and that Talia herself hadn't done anything at all to help them. He was curious to see exactly how Typo would go about creating monsters, but he was more interested at the moment in getting as strong as possible before he and Andros would have to face either monsters or Jackson's men.

The chi spiral in Garron's Center grew with each passing moment as he refined threads of Essence to add to his cultivation. This place had already done wonders for him, and he found himself drifting again as he sank into the cultivation trance. His body thrummed with energy, and he gloried in the purity of a Center which had once been rife with corruption.

"Gar!" The shout brought Garron to his feet instantly, he could practically feel that Andros had done something stupid. He began running up the tunnel, moving much more easily than he had even just the previous day.

"What did you *do*?" Garron would have held in the shout, but if Andros had yelled down from his position near the dungeon's entrance, he had to assume that the noise wouldn't matter. But what—

A grinding *roar* echoed down the tunnel. Even though Garron was hundreds of feet away from the dungeon entrance, he stumbled at the pure force of the sound. Recognizing it too well.

"Andros, you idiot." Garron stopped dead an instant before his friend's voice came down the tunnel.

"Don't come up here! I'm coming down! Get ready!"

"Right." Garron started backing up, thinking about the

plan. The 'lion' had been terrifyingly strong to Garron's eyes, but they had encountered it when Andros was almost completely depleted—he'd said that he didn't have anything to fear from the monster. But… he'd also said he couldn't kill it.

<Typo.> Garron imbued his call with a sense of urgency.

<Startlement. Query?>

Garron focused. He sent an image of the sword that Joris had been holding, wishing he'd thought to ask for a suit of armor earlier. No time to put it on now.

<Please make this for me.> After a moment, he hurried to add, <In front of me.>

He really didn't want a repeat of the rock incident with a piece of sharp steel.

<Consideration… Acceptance. Assurance.>

Almost immediately, a clump of grass and soil appeared on the ground before Garron. <What? No, a sword.>

<Shame.> Garron got the impression that Typo didn't know why he'd made the heap of grass, but immediately the dungeon was focused again. A moment later the clump of earth… decayed, falling apart before disappearing. Strange.

It took a minute of waiting awkwardly, but eventually a gleaming sword appeared on the ground before him, an exact replica of the one Joris held. Before cleansing his Center, Garron would have found lifting a weapon like this difficult—it was much heavier than the ones he'd used in that first dungeon —but now he was able to heft it easily enough. Hopefully the weight would be an advantage against the monster.

As another roar blasted down towards him, Garron had the feeling that, even if it was, it wouldn't be enough.

"Gar!" Garron turned to see Andros' pale face sprinting towards him with superhuman speed. "I saw a bunch of these deer monsters roaming around that kept tossing out air strikes with their antlers, but they didn't seem too dangerous, so I tried luring a few toward here and—"

Another roar split the air. With a chill, Garron realized that this one sounded different than the first, higher pitched and painful to hear. He thought he could hear scraping. Were the monsters entering the dungeon?

Andros seemed unfazed by the sound. "So anyway, on the way I ran into the lions and—"

"How many?" Garron's sharp tone centered Andros; it wasn't the time to let the man ramble.

"Two. They live in groups. I forgot. They're really not so bad, we can probably deal with them."

"Do they *both* have the stone hide? Stone claws and such?" Garron was already trying to formulate a plan.

Andros coughed into a closed fist. "Uh… yeah. Nearly broke my foot kicking the second one. On the bright side, it's weaker than the first. Still mean, though."

"*Wonderful.*" Another roar. Yes, the monsters had definitely found their way into the dungeon.

<Query?> Typo had picked up on the creatures' entrance as well. <Excitement!>

<Monsters.> Garron didn't have the attention to tell the dungeon more. "Andy, let's get behind the pits."

A dubious look crossed the young Noble's face. "I, uh, think they can jump over those."

"Andros…" Garron stared at him, then shook his head. "We still need the choke point."

They ran back down the tunnel, the lions' roaring coming up behind them, closer and *closer*. Thankfully, the monsters were still wild animals. They weren't rushing down the tunnel like humans might, and were probably wary in the unfamiliar environment. Perhaps they'd even decide to leave… but Garron wasn't counting on it.

They made it past the soon-to-be room, and further down until they hit the traps. Garron was forced to skirt them as quickly as possible, though Andros demonstrated why they were so ineffective. He waited until he'd passed, then hopped each with a gust of air, wanting to avoid crowding Garron on the narrow safe paths. Finally, they got to the first pit with a false floor.

"Hey, maybe this will do it! Can't jump over it if you don't know it's there." Andros seemed annoyingly unconcerned to Garron, but his words brought a measure of hope.

Still, Garron only nodded in acknowledgement, eyes focused down the tunnel, glancing down at the patch of ground concealing the pit trap. "Fine. Let's… let's get ready."

Andros gave an infuriatingly carefree laugh. "Right! Don't worry, Gar, they're only in the F-ranks. They're more bark than bite. Roar than bite?"

Garron just shook his head. Andros was sometimes very, *very* bad at planning for the worst-case scenario. The roars continued to get louder before suddenly stopping, and Garron's grip on his sword tightened. Finally, he glimpsed yellow fur as the monsters rounded the corner.

<Warning.> Suddenly, an image of the two creatures flashed before his eyes, as though he were standing directly in front of them. The first one was the monster that had fought the pack of wolves earlier—it had several fresh scars in its hide, but it still moved with the same grace and majesty as before, along with undertones of the solid strength of the earth.

The second looked much like the first, save that it was larger and lacked a mane. When twin fangs of stone suddenly protruded out of its mouth and it gave that high-pitched keening roar again, Garron didn't think the lack of hair made it any less intimidating.

<Thanks Typo, but not now.> He sent the message out of pure startlement, nearly staggering backward at the sudden shift in his vision.

<Concern. Apology.> Typo withdrew, shrinking back like a scolded child.

Garron was touched by the dungeon's attempt to help, but by the time he reoriented himself, the two monsters were bounding up the tunnel, bestial rage in their eyes. The maneless lion's hide darkened, but its momentum carried it forward beside the first. "Please fall into the pit. Please fall into the—"

The ground fell away silently from beneath the snarling

monster, and it scrabbled at the air for a moment before falling into the pit with a surprised hiss. There was a sound of stone slamming against stone, and Garron felt the ground shake. High-pitched screeches continued to emanate upwards from the pit, and dust flew everywhere as the monster thrashed below, but he hardly paid attention. The spikes should take care of it, which left just one for them to deal with.

The second lion let out a snarl of its own, its fangs withdrawing into its mouth, and leapt over the pit at them. Garron stumbled back, holding out his sword weakly in front of him. Abyss. Only the fact that Andros was already moving saved him. The air cultivator attacked with Essence-enhanced speed, slipping around the monster's claw swipe and—twisting his body with effort—slamming his heel into the monster's flank, where its hind leg joined the torso. The creature's hide darkened, but the kick still landed with a solid thunk and made the monster let out a roar.

"*Ow!*" Andros accompanied the exclamation with a perfectly timed sidestep as the lion whirled and swept a claw at him. He made the creature look slow and ponderous, but Garron remembered the last time he'd seen Andros fight like this. For as little of a threat the lion posed to Andros, it would still be deadly to Garron. But his friend would still need Garron's help to finish it.

The young man took a deep breath to banish his fear, and stepped forward with his sword leading. The lion had turned almost completely around to attack a dodging Andros, and he used its preoccupation to close the distance without being attacked. He raised his sword and… stopped. The creature's hide was still dark, its skin too hard to take any damage from Andros, let alone *him*. Abyss, the first lion was still alive despite falling a dozen feet onto stone spikes. Its thrashes were shaking the ground all along the tunnel. His job was to wait until—

<Danger!>

The force of emotion and impression of urgency behind the message sent Garron backwards, almost tripping in his haste. In the same instant, the monster whirled, its skin suddenly bright gold once more as it swept an elongated claw through the air.

"Watch out!" The roars still echoing upwards from the pit made the shout barely audible, but Garron saw Andros easily enough when he vaulted over the roaring monster and sent another kick down on its mane. Then he landed with an easy grace as the creature's hide turned dark to weather the strike, though only for an instant.

"It's getting weaker!" Garron shouted towards his leaping friend, letting his hope seep into his voice. "To the next pit!"

Without waiting for a response, he began backing up rapidly, not able to bring himself to turn away from the monster. That gave him a clear view of Andros fighting the huge feline, dodging easily as it swept claws and snapped at him, and even managing an Essence-enhanced kick to the flank which landed without issue.

As the monster hissed in pain and fury, Andros vaulted backwards, coming level with Garron. "Hold on!"

Arms wrapped around Garron and the wind rushed as his friend bore him into the air; not fast enough to be the terrible movement technique, but still faster than he could manage on his own. His vision filled momentarily with the dirt ceiling of the tunnel, inches away from his face, but his heart lifted. The next pit was also covered, and it should be child's play to lure the monster forward, trap it, and kill it at their leisure.

Andros suddenly took a sharp breath. "Celestial feces—how did *that* happen?"

"What? Oh." Garron knew it couldn't end easily. When he reoriented himself, he looked in front to see that the pit's covering had cracked, much of it fallen down into the trap below. Even as he watched, another huge section of dirt fell away, making the trap obvious even to a monster.

The lion in the pit. It was still roaring, still smashing against the sides of its container, still shaking the ground all along the tunnel. Enough, apparently, to damage the next trap. A quick look down the hall showed that the last pit's covering had also broken. They needed a new plan.

The two lions roared together, the cries of the trapped one seeming to enrage the second even further. It bounded forward again, and Garron backed up. "Hold it off, Andy!"

"What was that you said? Infernal *roaring*!" The lion leapt, and Andros went to meet it, wind swirling around him. Garron shrugged.

<Typo.> He sent the thought with as much urgency as he could manage. It wasn't difficult.

He'd felt the dungeon's rapt attention throughout the fight, and now Typo responded eagerly. <Eagerness. Query?>

Garron took a deep breath. The dungeon was limited, but it could still do some things very well. He sent the most detailed image he could manage to the waiting consciousness.

Typo considered. <Confusion…? Realization! Determination. Assurance.>

Andros leapt backward again, and Garron saw with a flash of fear that he had a thin line of red across his chest. Even more concerning, his face was getting slightly pale again. For all his skill, Andros' endurance had a limit, and he clearly wasn't as recovered as he'd claimed.

The deep roar of the lion told Garron that the creature was preparing to rush in again, but another sound behind them told him that they needed more time. Garron shouted for all he was worth, screaming over the lion's roar. "Let's go!"

Garron still let Andros lead the way—he wasn't stupid—but as the other boy engaged the creature, forcing it to stop and chase him around the tight confines of the tunnel, he interjected stabs at the creature's flank. They never did much damage before its stone hide kicked in, but each strike was leeching more of its power.

The blows also drew the monster's attention to Garron. Only for a brief moment, but that was almost enough to make him break and run. Up close, he could smell the stink of its hot breath, see the rage in its golden eyes, and feel its near-constant roar vibrate in his chest. His general strategy whenever that happened was to jump back and let *Andros* make it mad instead.

<Satisfaction. Assurance.>

"Get back! Trap behind us!" Garron turned and ran, looking up to see if what he'd asked for was there, and a moment later Andros was beside him.

"Where?" The young Noble was pale and shaking, and only lightly bleeding. Garron pointed while running, nearly tripping over his own feet in the process. When the monster came running up towards them again, a blast of air was enough to break the little space in the ceiling that was already falling apart since Andros' Aura prevented Typo from supporting it directly.

Condensed earth, dirt, and rocks all tumbled down on the lion, which never saw the debris coming: even now, his death-stare was still locked on Andros. Down the tunnel, the other lion's cries were growing hoarser and quieter, but Garron just stood there, panting. Then he rounded on Andros. "How in the *abyss* do you go out to cultivate and end up bringing two lions back with you? *Two lions?*"

Andros sat down on the spot, clearly exhausted, but he gave Garron an apologetic look. "I'm—"

"However you managed it, please do it again!" Talia—who'd been noticeably absent while they were actually fighting—chimed in enthusiastically, flying in from down the tunnel. The sight of her stoked Garron's rage further; this was the second time he'd been forced to fight for his life in this place, and he still hadn't forgiven the first time.

<Enthusiastic agreement!> Typo was responding to Talia's words, but the projection only irritated Garron further.

<Anger.> Garron snapped back at the dungeon, though it had already sensed his mood, and was currently feeling somewhat apologetic in addition to its excitement.

"Now then, the other one's almost dead from the spikes, and *wow* is that a lot of Essence! We have reno~*vations* to do!" Talia whizzed around in a circle around them, nearly breaking into song as she did.

"Congratulations." Garron injected as much sarcasm into his voice as he could, but he was already more focused on Andros. The other boy had fewer wounds than Garron, but he was clearly tired once again from the fight. "Andy, you need to cultivate again, don't you?"

"I… Yeah. A… little." Andros' labored breathing as he said the words sealed it for Garron. His friend wasn't as bad as he'd been the day before, but if he kept this up, he would be.

"Why don't you *both* leave for a while? There aren't guards around here, are there, Andros? It will make things smoother for everyone if you're outside for a little bit." Talia's voice betrayed her obvious excitement, her voice setting Garron's teeth on edge.

"That's… probably a good idea. Gar?" Andros sounded like he thought it was a very good idea. He probably wanted the company as he recovered from the fight, and Garron couldn't blame him.

<Regret.> The dungeon's message was coupled once more with his abiding excitement, and Garron growled.

"Fine. But if we run into another monster, I'm going to see if it can eat Wisps." He punctuated the words with a glare, but Talia seemed unaffected.

"Hah! Good luck with *that*!" The Wisp flew down the tunnel towards Typo's Core, vanishing from sight before she was even halfway out of the area. "Can't hit what you can't see!"

Skirting the pit where the maneless lion had bled out, Garron and Andros helped each other out of the tunnel and into the forest above.

CHAPTER SIXTEEN

The crisp, calm, slightly chilly air of the forest seemed strange after what had just transpired in the dungeon. The fight with the lions had gone well. Andros' skill, as well as the advantage of the fighting ground, had made victory more a matter of time and care. Still, it was hard to reconcile the idea that the huge, terrifying monsters with powers of stone were *substantially* weaker than Garron's lanky friend. It was also difficult to shake the thrill of the conflict, but the peaceful surroundings helped with that right away.

"Let's go walking. I'll be fine in a few minutes." Andros' voice already sounded stronger, though to Garron's eye he still seemed a bit pale. He started off without waiting for a response, heading east of the dungeon entrance.

Garron hurried to catch up, moving with much less grace than his friend, and wincing a little at the noise of crackling leaves and branches underfoot. "Wait! Are you sure? I mean, I know they weren't here before, but those lions were *loud*. Do you think the guardsmen might have heard it?"

Andros let out a little chuckle, patting Garron on the back as he continued to set a hard pace through the trees. "Those things were roaring like that when I was out here before too. They do it when they fight other predators, I guess. I don't think the guards would notice. Besides, I'll notice them even if they're only close enough to hear them."

Garron frowned at the certainty in his friend's voice. "Why?"

"Oh, right! We needed to talk about this anyway." Andros turned to look at him as they walked, and Garron was glad to see that most of the color had returned to his face. He still had a strange look in his eyes, but it faded as he focused on Garron. "Meridians."

Garron grinned. "Manda—"

Andros rolled his eyes. "You can stop, Gar, I know you know what I'm saying."

"Couldn't help myself." They both smiled, but Andros' lasted only for a moment before a serious expression reasserted itself.

"So, meridians are basically pathways for Essence to run through, in and out of your body. There's twelve, and they all have names that I can't remember, but the basics of it is that meridians reinforce your body with Essence, give more pathways for it to enter your body, and provide a way to control your Essence. If you try to push Essence out of your body without a meridian…"

"It hurts," Garron supplied, hopping over a fallen log. He was hardly paying attention to where they were going now, too engrossed in Andros' words. "That sounds useful."

"They are *so* useful!" Andros demonstrated the point by vaulting several feet into the air to clear a large rock in their path.

Garron went around the rock somewhat grumpily. "So what does that have to do with you seeing the guards?"

"What?" Andros turned and focused on Garron. "Oh. One of the things you can do with open meridians is cycle Essence to your eyes, so you can see Essence sources in the world around you. Pretty much all of Jackson's crew are cultivators. They have really pure Centers, and I'd be able to see them coming from a long way off."

"Oh." Garron supposed that made sense. "So all cultivators open their meridians?"

Andros nodded easily. "Yeah, at least a few by the time they're in the D-ranks. My dad wanted me to start early, and I had lots of Essence to spare, so I've nearly got all of mine open now."

It didn't surprise Garron that Andros was ahead of the curve, but his answer still raised a question. "So wouldn't all of the stronger guards be able to see us too?"

Joris had, apparently, been in the F-ranks, but he was also the most junior member of Jackson's 'inner circle.' Guards like Lars spent the entire day cultivating and bossing their inferiors around, and Garron would be shocked if a good portion of the remaining hunters weren't in the D-ranks.

Andros gave a bitter laugh. "That's why you shouldn't join up with people like Jackson. He 'helps' his crew members become cultivators if they stick around long enough, but he still keeps them under his thumb. He tells them how to open their meridians, but he never teaches them how to actually *use* their Essence for anything. They only get the physical benefits, while he and Lars can scare them with their Essence techniques! Well, the ones they managed to pick up over the years, anyway."

"Huh." That was just like Jackson. It also made Garron just a little bit more afraid of the slender cultivator and his bulky lieutenant. Both of them had all of Andros' capabilities and higher ranks to boot. Still, it left one very important question. "So, when can I open a meridian?"

Andros laughed, looking over at him again. "You're at F-rank five now, which is great! But… you still need more Essence in your Center before we can open one. Once it's in a meridian, it's not in your Center, so you need to make sure you have enough available to keep you alive."

"Right. Not dying always comes first." They continued walking, though Garron wasn't certain where they were going.

Luckily, they hadn't been forced to deviate from their course, so once they turned back, they would only need to walk due west until they reached the dungeon entrance.

That was fortunate, because this forest was much wilder than the small woods on the Tet estate, and full of a vibrant sort of life. Through the trees, Garron thought he spotted a rabbit running away from them, and as they continued on, he saw a badger among the bushes. Even as Garron watched it scrabble away at the earth, it let out a little stream of liquid from its mouth, and a wisp of smoke rose up from the ground.

Garron edged away from the creature, and a flash of movement higher up in the trees caught his attention. There was a squirrel drifting slowly down from the air, holding an acorn between its paws. It seemed as though it were being lowered by an invisible string, but the rustling of a localized wind as it passed through the trees showed the truth.

"There are so many monsters in this place." Garron was eyeing the surroundings warily, waiting for another one to show itself, but most seemed scared of something. Andros, probably.

"Yeah, it's got really high Essence-density, so regular animals become monsters pretty quick. That's kind of how it works. It's nice for me though, I've already managed to climb back to D-rank one!"

"What? So soon?" Garron eyed his friend with surprise, nearly tripping over a root.

Andros let out an embarrassed cough as he skirted a patch of bushes. "I think it's a little easier the second time around. Also, well, you know my cultivation technique is really good, right? Father 'echoed' it into me and everything. I pull in Essence so fast that I have to work my body to keep it from doing… bad things to me."

"Right." Garron did remember most of that, but it still seemed just a little unfair. At the moment, his Center was only a spiral, but he somehow doubted that even when he hit the D-ranks he would have a technique like Andros' available to him. Although Garron considered himself lucky enough already: he was alive instead of dying from a corrupted Center. Before he could ask more about different cultivation techniques, Andros stopped without warning.

"Hey Gar." Andros' voice was uncharacteristically serious. "Do you think you're up to leaving here?"

Garron blinked at the sudden change in topic. "What, now?"

"Yeah. I… well, I know you made a promise and everything, but it seems like we can get out this way, and we did kill some monsters for the dungeon." Andros looked at him guiltily, and Garron raised his eyebrows. "That means you kept your promise, right?"

"Ah. So that's why you wanted me to come with you? For you, that's pretty sneaky." Garron kept the smile on his face, he was once again impressed. Andros really had grown up since his Jackson had taken over the estate, it seemed.

But Garron's friend was still ridiculously… nice. He cast his eyes downward, genuinely ashamed at his trick. "I'm sorry, I wasn't even sure if we'd be able to get out from this side of the forest—there's a huge river to the south and it seems like the northern tree line curves around a lot, so we'd probably end up getting spotted."

Now Garron was even more surprised. Andros had been scouting? Not that Garron minded, but he could have been caught without anyone else knowing about it. "You should really tell me about stuff like that before you do it."

"Sorry." Andros' expression grew even more downcast. "I, uh, well, you made a promise, and I didn't really know how Talia would react and—"

"It's okay." Andros had good reasons for doing what he did, and Garron wholeheartedly agreed with the sentiment. "You don't have to keep apologizing, you know. Thanks for doing it."

Andros sighed, obviously relieved. It seemed this had really been bothering him, and Garron almost regretted his mild admonishment. It wasn't Andros' fault they hadn't had time to talk since escaping the farmhouse.

"So, do you want to try leaving?" Andros looked to him hopefully. Garron considered the question. His promise to Typo and Talia was not an issue—he didn't consider an oath extracted under duress binding, and even if he did, what they'd already done more than repaid Typo for his 'aid.'

Still, the dungeon himself was… surprisingly friendly. Garron had no issues with helping him grow, even if he found the way Talia had acted thus far unacceptable. Not to mention that every day Garron spent in the dungeon would do wonders for his cultivation. He hadn't forgotten what Andros had said about meridians. How much time would he save in accumulating the necessary Essence to open one if he cultivated in Typo's tunnels instead of the outside world?

Even so… none of that was worth risking capture. Not for him, and especially not for Andros, who was enjoying none of the benefits that Garron was from their 'partnership' with Typo. Mind made up, he nodded. "Let's go."

Andros smiled. "Alright! So we'll just keep heading this way, I guess. Keep your eyes open for anything I miss."

They kept walking in a straight line for over an hour. For all of Andros' assurances, Garron couldn't help but try his best to remain quiet—a feat which Andros himself was managing with unconscious ease. The forest grew slightly chillier as time went on, the sun began descending in the horizon, and Garron began wishing they'd thought to pause for food. He'd eaten in the morning—apparently Andros hadn't needed to eat much because of his cultivation, so there was plenty of rabbit left for Garron. Still, they both needed to eat more than once per day.

The image of Jackson striding through the forest, emanating fire, flashed through Garron's mind. Maybe they could figure out food *after* they'd left the forest.

However, he was still tempted as they passed by a small creek and he got to see some of the deer Andros had mentioned. Their bodies seemed smaller than normal, and they moved with a sort of jumpy speed which Garron associated with air Essence. Even as he watched, a stag swept his antlers before him, and leaves flew away in a flurry, revealing grass beneath. Before Garron could decide whether they should retreat, a chorus of howls split the air far away in the forest and the deer scattered; bounding away with speed and grace augmented by Essence.

"Must be another wolf pack moving into the old one's territory, now that the lions are dead too," Andros muttered while making sure Garron didn't fall too far behind. After they'd passed the creek and moved into a sparser section of the woods however, a slight frown appeared on his face. Garron couldn't see any reason for it, as there didn't seem to be any monsters in this area that Garron could see; though admittedly there was less and less life of any kind.

The soil seemed to be getting closer to gravel as they continued, which probably explained the lack of trees, but perhaps that meant they were getting near the end of the forest? The ground was beginning to slope upwards as well, but that probably just meant they were on a hill. Still, Andros' frown continued to deepen as their feet began crunching slightly on the rocky soil, so Garron finally broke the silence.

"What happened?" Somehow, the sound of his voice felt wrong, as though it didn't belong in the silence of the—well, it was more of a gravel slope than a forest, but the point stood.

Andros shrugged at him. "The Essence around here's thinner than back in the forest."

"Hm?" Garron felt at the Essence in the air—it was much less dense than what he'd become used to in the past two days, but his sense of the ambient Essence still wasn't fully integrated into his awareness yet. For all that had happened, he was still very new at this. "Is that because we're leaving the forest? It's not usually that dense, is it?"

It certainly hadn't been anywhere near as dense at the Tet estate, nor at the farm outside the forest. Andros nodded slowly, but the tension didn't leave his face. "Could be. Essence density is basically random, but it also has to do with the amount of life in a place. As more things pull in Essence, the concentration decreases. The forest's not going to stay as rich as it is for all that long, as long as the concentration of Essence doesn't increase for some other reason, but…"

"Wait." Garron's feet crunched on the rocky soil as he looked around. He couldn't see a plant or animal in sight ahead of them, though to be fair the slope was becoming quite steep, blocking much of his view forward. "If more living things means less Essence, then shouldn't this place be denser than the forest?"

"More living things, or stronger ones," Andros corrected, looking around warily. "Be ready to—"

Andros stood still for a moment, ear cocked, before beginning to back slowly down the slope. Then his eyes widened, and he grabbed Garron's shoulder. "Monsters ahead… *someone* ahead. We have to check on this."

With that, he pulled Garron into a run up the gravel. Rocks rolled down the slope beneath their feet as they scrambled up the ever-steepening incline. Garron wanted to protest, but as they continued up the slope, Garron began to make out the sound Andros was talking about. It sounded like shrieking, almost like the call of a crow, but far deeper. "What is that?"

They crested the slope, and for a moment it was all Garron could do to admire the scene before them. The first thing that caught his eye was the rocky slope in the distance, the foot of a mountain high enough to obscure the view of anything past it for as far as Garron could see to either side. But the space between the mountain and their position was what dropped his jaw: a field of rocks, strewn across the ground as though some giant had smashed a second mountain to pieces there.

At Garron's feet, the gravel soil gradually became larger and larger, until closer to the mountain there were veritable boulders forming solid—albeit cracked and clearly treacherous—ground. The larger stones rested atop more gravel soil, though in places water seemed to seep up between the cracks.

A single man stood among the rocks, his face in profile to Garron's eyes, though he wasn't all that far away across the field. He was familiar, but his face held an ugly bruise, his clothes were dirty, and his hands were shaking as they held his sword. Garron had never seen him actually draw the thing before. When Garron saw the source of the shrieking still echoing in the stone field, he didn't blame the poor young guardsman.

"Ulysses!" Garron's shout rang out across the open field, and he regretted it immediately. He didn't want to draw the attention of the creature before the guardsman. The monstrous bird before Ulysses snapped its gleaming beak shut. Above, a haunting cry still echoed over the field, and with a shock Garron realized there were two of them. He and Andros looked at each other for a moment, then back at the scene before him.

They turned and started running to save the man without another word.

CHAPTER SEVENTEEN

As they ran, trying desperately not to trip as the footing across the rocks worsened, Garron appraised their opponents. He wasn't surprised that he'd missed the still figure in the air, its massive wings spread without flapping. It should have blotted out the sky above—just one of its wings was long enough to dwarf Garron—but it seemed to shimmer as it hung in the air, and Garron swore that he could see through its white feathers to the sky above.

Its body seemed wreathed in a haze of smoke, droplets of condensation falling below it onto the rocks, and its beak—nearly translucent and longer than both of Garron's arms—was spewing forth a white cloud even as it cried. The image was almost haunting, the perfectly still creature hanging motionless in the air, its body so hazy and insubstantial that it hardly seemed real.

The second was just as unbelievable. It was the same size as the first, its torso twice as large as the lion's had been, its wings folded tight to its body. But while the first seemed like a painting, ethereal and almost dreamlike, this one was a statue cast in steel. Each metal feather glimmered in the light, the effect made even more stunning as its fellow's mist drifted down and condensed on its plumage. The rest of its body seemed to be made of the same metallic substance—its two legs gleamed and its talons were cutting furrows into the rock it perched on. Its beak was so straight and sharp that it seemed almost like a spear. Its eyes… were fixed on poor Ulysses.

"What are we doing? What are we *doing*? Andy, get him out of there!" They were close enough now for Andros to use his movement technique. He shot forward, slamming into Ulysses and pausing only to grab the guardsman before shooting back toward Garron. As Andros came back toward him, Garron could see the lad visibly slowing. Ulysses was heavy in his armor, and Andros could only do so much with his technique. In three jumps, the two were beside Garron. Thankfully, the metallic bird hadn't reacted much to the maneuver, only letting out a cry and tensing where it stood. Garron could see its metallic legs bending like boughs of springy wood, but at least it hadn't tried to attack Andros.

"What—" Ulysses seemed startled by the sudden save. They tensed and he fell silent as white mist was falling around them, and as one they looked up to see a translucent white body hanging above them, merely a few feet away.

"*Abyss!*" There was a gust of wind as Andros attempted to push away the mists surrounding them, but even though the air cleared for a moment, more was spewing forth from the creature's beak.

Ulysses laughed frantically. "That's not so bad, at least. It's just limiting visibility, that's not—"

Andros suddenly pulled the guard and Garron forward with superhuman speed, almost tossing them across the rocks before landing with a thunk beside him. Behind, Garron could hear the screech of shearing rock, but when he looked back the mist obscured what had happened. He had a feeling that, whatever the bird had done, he was *very* glad that Andros had pulled him away.

The mist around them cleared in a gust of wind, revealing

Andros' worried face as well as Ulysses' battered one. Behind them, there was now a mass of white mist like a cloud coiling around on the rocks. Garron still couldn't see the white bird, but even as he watched, Andros gestured towards the cloud of mist. There was a dull thud, a puff of mist exploding outwards, and the ethereal cries paused for a moment before returning, sounding angrier. The mist seemed to thicken and Garron thought he could see… *something* forming in the swirls of white.

"Move!" Andros grabbed Ulysses and turned to run, followed by Garron. Wisps of smoke ran along their feet, but the cries of the white bird had begun mingling with those of its fellow. Even from this distance, Garron could feel the wind stirring as the second monster took flight as well.

They were less than a hundred feet from the tree line as the cries of both birds drew too close to ignore. Ulysses was slowing down, unable to keep up with them in his armor. If Andros used his movement technique again, they could be there in seconds, but he couldn't take both Garron and Ulysses at once.

"Andy, take Ulysses!" Garron saw his friend's dilemma and scooped up a rock from the ground as he ran, then whirled. It wasn't difficult to miss the monsters now winging after them—the white one was ahead, now wreathed in mist that formed a rough outline of an even larger bird, giving the impression of a phantasm as it flew toward them.

Andros hadn't moved, looking at Garron in confusion. "Gar, what are you—"

"*Go!*" Garron threw the rock with all his strength. With a flash of pride, he saw it hit center mass.

The rock clattered to the ground without ever impacting flesh, passing through the white bird as though the monster was no more substantial than its mist. "Oh. Well, it wasn't like I was going to kill the thing with a rock."

He seemed to have gotten the monster's attention though, and he desperately hoped that Andros would hurry up. He turned and started running as the bird's haunting cries turned piercing, mist beginning to fall down around him again as the bird caught up. On instinct, he jerked to the side, and managed to avoid… something. Had that been the creature's talon, or the mist formed into a cutting edge? Garron didn't want to find out.

He continued to run, heart hammering as the steel bird's cries became nearly as loud as the closer mist bird. The fog was only around his feet now, it seemed the white bird had slowed down when it went for the strike, yet Garron could feel the wind rushing as it climbed back into the air. He felt a rush of relief at the sight of his friend at the edge of the slope, the top of Ulysses' head disappearing beneath the summit as Andros turned back to face him.

"*Move*, Gar!"

Without hesitation, Garron jumped forward as far as he could, bunching up to land painfully on the rocky ground. He felt a searing, almost *cold* line of pain on the back of his left leg, but he scrambled to his feet, hardly pausing his run. It took him a moment to get his bearings, but suddenly his vision was filled with Andros' form, and he felt lanky arms wrap around him. There was a surge, and a moment of vertigo as he felt the lack of ground under their feet. They'd made it to the slope… then their feet touched the ground, and they went tumbling down.

Garron hardly cared about the pain. Most of the rocks were small, so it was more a *dizzying* experience than anything. The monsters were still crying out behind them, so Andros pulled Garron to his feet again and forced him to run as they landed. What felt like a moment later, they were standing beside a startled-looking Ulysses.

Now they were in a slightly more forested area, and the shrieks of the monstrous birds were being blocked by the acoustics of the landscape again. As soon as Garron got over his vertigo, he whirled on the spot, surveying the slope behind them. There were stray wisps of mist falling down over the edge, but the monsters hadn't followed them further. "Thank the celestials."

He collapsed to the rocky ground, and twin thuds to either side told him that Ulysses and Andros had followed suit. They spent several minutes lying there, taking heaving breaths in the rocky soil. Finally, Andros rolled over towards Garron and hit him on the arm. "You idiot. What was the point of doing that?"

"Wanted to make sure it wouldn't get you two while you were busy with him." Garron was a little embarrassed, but at least the exchange had worked out. He had no idea if the mist-bird-monster had even noticed his rock-throwing, but at least he'd bought enough time for Andros to get Ulysses away without getting killed. "What were those things?"

"Too strong for us—guess you'd call them Direbirds? Uh… Direbird Mistraven and Direbird Steelraven if you want to get technical, I guess. But they were almost *Beasts*. Lucky they were only protecting territory instead of hunting for food." Andros seemed too tired to berate Garron for his idiocy further, but his voice held a sort of dull appreciation for the two monsters they had just escaped. "Abyss, I'm glad only one of them got to us—I have no idea what we would've done if that steel one started shooting feathers."

Garron felt his eyes widen. "Shooting *feathers*?"

"Usually that's what happens with the steel-feathered birds. But they aren't usually that big. Or mean. The Mistraven was… dangerous. Don't know what we could do to even hurt it." Garron could hear the shiver in Andros' voice, and he frowned. It seemed as though they wouldn't be getting out of the forest in this direction after all, if those things considered the stone field their territory.

"Ulysses, are you… healthy?" As he said the words, Garron began to sit up slowly, wincing at the pain along his side where he'd landed on the rocks. Andros was also sitting up, but Ulysses seemed content to lay there, staring into the sky.

"Yes. Thank you two. I… I don't think I would've… Thank you." He still seemed stunned by the experience. His voice was distracted, and a slight quiver in his lips showed as he spoke.

Andros reached over slowly and patted the guardsman on the shoulder. "Don't worry about it. Why were you even there in the first place?"

Even from his position on the ground, Ulysses winced visibly. "Jackson has... been getting worse. He's blamed me for—well, in any case, I was told to scout out the other borders of the forest or face..."

The guardsman seemed unwilling to finish the words, and Garron felt a pang of guilt. This is because of what they did when they escaped. For all that Andros' disabling Ulysses hadn't hurt the man physically, they should have known how Jackson would react. Garron cleared his throat, suddenly awkward. "We're so—"

"No, *no*!" Ulysses finally struggled into a sitting position as well, shaking his head vehemently. "I *refuse* to let you two apologize, especially after saving my life! Celestial knows, I can see why you'd run away from a man like that."

Andros laughed, laying a hand on the guardsman's back. "You know, you don't have to stay either. If you come with us, we can all try to escape together!"

Ulysses' face shifted into an uncomfortable, apologetic look, and Garron sighed. "He has a family back at the estate, Andy. He can't put them in danger like that."

Andros winced at the reminder. "Oh, right. Sorry, Ulysses."

The guardsman shook his head. "I'm the one who should be sorry, I—"

Suddenly a fearful look crossed his face, and he looked down by his belt. His hands scrabbled at the soil for a moment before he breathed a relieved sigh. He was holding a slim cylinder of some sort of powder wrapped in red paper. It had a long black string protruding from one end, almost like the wick of a candle, and what looked like a miniscule firestarter strapped to its side.

"What's that?" Garron eyed the object curiously.

As he carefully placed the object back on an appropriate spot on his belt, Ulysses replied absently, "Jackson called it a 'flare.' He handed them out this morning after Joris never reported back. Apparently, it will signal him to come find us."

"Hah! That's alchemy, then—it must be from the repository

if he had it with him. Hold on." Andros mirth faded into a thoughtful expression. "If that's all they've got, I bet we can just grab it off one of the weaker guards before they can use it and get out without Jackson knowing!"

Huh. It almost seemed too simple, but knowing about these 'flares' was a large advantage—they knew what to target now, so they could... Garron narrowed his eyes. "Ulysses, where is Jackson staying?"

Ulysses was already shaking his head at Andros' proposal. "He's at the western tree line. Either he or Lars is always watching, and it's all open ground from there to most of the northern border—except where it intersects this place. He has sharp eyes. I saw the southern border yesterday, as well, it's—"

"A big river, yeah," Andros cut in gloomily. "Seemed like it had plenty of monsters swimming around it too. East's out now too, if those birds don't want us going through their territory."

Garron didn't say what both of them were thinking: they were *trapped*. A weight settled in his stomach as he considered their situation. It hadn't seemed so bad before, when they'd had an entire forest to lose themselves in, and Jackson was unable to pinpoint them directly. If they couldn't leave, it was only a matter of time before they were caught.

"Thanks for the tip, Ulysses." Andros' smile seemed a little forced, but that was still better than what Garron could manage at the moment. "You should get back before Jackson throws a fit. You can handle getting through the forest, right? If you head straight west, you shouldn't hit any dangerous territory."

"Thank you, milord. Thank you as well, Garron. I... Good luck. You seem healthier than before." Ulysses' face held a sad look, but he smiled back at Andros as he struggled to his feet. With that, the battered guardsman walked off into the woods. As Garron watched him, he felt the stone of worry grow heavier in his stomach. Ulysses was in a predicament of his own, but they weren't in any position to help him... or make it out of this forest at all.

"We'll survive. Don't worry." Andros kept his voice low, but

Garron found himself smiling at the steely determination under the pronouncement. As long as they were together, they had a chance.

Garron rubbed his stomach. "The only thing I'm worried about is starving to death. How likely is it that we catch a deer on the way back?"

CHAPTER EIGHTEEN

Andros' abilities made catching rabbits easy as they walked back, but Garron wanted a little more time in the woods. Part of it was relief after their escape from the two monster birds. He wanted nothing so much as to have a moment of peace, and Andros' strength seemed to keep away most of the predators in this part of the forest, now that the pack of wolves and the lions had both been killed.

But even though Garron enjoyed the silence of their walk, there were still questions burning in his mind, and he couldn't help asking them as they went back towards the dungeon, Andros leading with a rabbit in each hand. "Andy, how did those things—I mean, it didn't seem like they were using any of the normal affinities. What were they?"

Andros chuckled at his ex-servant's words. "It's kind of funny that you don't know, considering how many affinities you have."

"Well, my teacher's a little dim, sorry." Garron gave a smile of his own, hopping over a root. Out of the corner of his eye, he could see another squirrel shooting through the canopies like a furry-tailed bird. "They had multiple affinities? But wouldn't that just mean they can use abilities from different types of Essence?"

"Ah... there's only so much I can do to help a terrible student." Andros bumped into Garron's shoulder without pausing his stride. "But yeah, normally Essence sort of... mixes together when you have multiple affinities. It can make all sorts of different things, depending on how much of each you have. Like take your earth and water affinities: those can make mud Essence, or wood, or flesh, or a bunch of other stuff. With a little air, you could get something even better! Probably. I know earth and air does lightning, but with water... maybe plant stuff?"

"Huh." Tossing lightning around sounded considerably more interesting than growing plants, but from what Andros was saying, more affinities meant more possible combinations. What other types of Essence could he cultivate, with his three affinities? That brought his mind back to the birds. "Those things were what, metal and mist? What combinations are those?"

Andros shrugged. "Metal is earth and fire, I think—you see those in some of the older volcano dungeons. Mist is probably air and water, but that thing was *scary*. Did you see it use that mist-slash thing? It seemed sort of... not all there, you know? I'm just glad I was able to drop it from the sky for a bit."

The worst thing was, the monsters hadn't seemed to be trying particularly hard to kill them, just run them off, but just one of them had almost been too much to handle. Garron was lucky he hadn't sustained a serious injury. "Oh... hold on."

As his feet crunched forward on the leaves, he felt at the back of his leg, and winced at the ripped cloth of his trousers, as well as the wetness of blood. Andros turned around and walked back toward where Garron was lagging behind. "What are you doing? Is that *blood*?"

"Looks like the white bird got me with that last slash. I barely felt it after we got away." Garron was getting a little worried. He and Andros had accumulated a host of minor cuts and bruises, and the more they got, the more likely it was that rot would infect one. Or at least, that was the case for Garron. Andros probably had less of a chance of that happening due to his open meridians.

Andros was now examining the wound, sucking in a breath between his teeth. "It's not *too* bad, but it's wide enough that it might not close on its own. We should bind it."

Garron shook his head vehemently. "We don't have the cloth to spare. Besides, I wouldn't want your disgusting rags over it anyway."

Andros looked down at the sweat stained, dirty, and extremely smelly shirt he'd been about to tear apart for a bandage. "Huh. Good point, but what'll we do about the cut then?"

"Just leave it. It'll stop bleeding eventually." It wasn't the best option, but there really wasn't all that much they could do about it. Without clean cloth or something else to make bandages, it wasn't worth the risk of hurrying the rot to slow down the minor bleeding.

Andros snapped his fingers. "Wait, can't the dungeon make more clothes for us? Bandages?"

"That wouldn't—" Garron stopped walking and started staring at Andros. There was no reason that *wouldn't* work, as far as he could tell. He gave his friend a proud grin. "Let's get back quick then. I really want clean clothes, and I don't want any monsters to get the wrong idea with me dripping blood all over the place."

<Excitement!> As Garron entered the dungeon, he nearly fell over as an image blasted into his mind. It was from the room where Typo's Core was situated, but Garron only caught a flash of turquoise before he instinctively pushed the image away.

<Calm down!> Garron snapped at the dungeon.

Typo withdrew. <Confusion?>

Right. Can't tell him to calm down and project annoyance. <Calm. We're coming, Typo.>

Garron still wasn't sure whether the dungeon was actually

comprehending his words, or just the feeling associated with them, but either way, Typo refrained from sending him any more images as Andros dropped down beside him and they began heading down the tunnel.

"Huh. Not bad, I guess. We can have our own rooms now!" Andros looked around appreciatively at the first room they passed, where Garron had first shown Typo how to extend his influence properly. It was now a proper chamber, large enough to hold perhaps a dozen people and leave room to fight.

Garron was impressed—the room had been less than half this size when they'd left, though of course there was no telling how much of the work Typo and Talia were doing had been visible before. "That's true, but where are the monsters? The traps?"

Typo was apparently still listening. <Slight embarrassment. Eagerness!>

Garron shook his head, mostly for Andros' benefit. "Never mind. I guess we'll see."

The rest of the tunnels were the same, somewhat to Garron's disappointment, but at least the pit traps had been reset, and a few more had been covered. Garron wasn't clear on why any of the pits were uncovered, but he supposed it must be difficult for Typo to do.

Finally, they made it to the end of the tunnels. Andros let out a little whistle, though he cut it off in embarrassment when Garron looked at him. "This is nice! Little bit more room, you know?"

<Pride!> Garron got the impression that the dungeon would be grinning if he could.

Indeed, the room was much bigger, slightly larger even than the first one they had passed. It was still composed mostly of bare compressed dirt, but now instead of transitioning into a muddy pit in the back half of the room, the mud was contained within a small semicircle of stone, which was further covered with the same gray rock. A small bubble of rock protruded from the smooth surface of the covering, giving an indication as to the location of Typo's Core, but Garron could no longer directly see the glint of the blue-brown stone. Not bad. Still, the room itself was hardly the most noticeable change—that distinction went to the creature currently growling quietly at them.

"Isn't he adorable?" Talia's voice edged into a squeal as she bobbed up and down, but a moment later she appeared to forcibly still herself. "Ahem. I mean, he's already getting much bigger."

Something in the back of Garron's head wondered why exactly the Wisp had cleared her throat, considering she had no windpipe to begin with, and another part of him was busy agreeing with her first sentiment.

It was clearly of the same species as the lions he and Andros had killed, but this creature hardly came up past his knee. It was a pale yellow in color, its fur thick and exceedingly fuzzy, though Garron thought he could see a faint dark spot on its flank as it turned towards Andros, baring tiny fangs and growling. Its eyes were a startling deep blue, and its black nose was wet.

<Excitement. Pride. Affection.> Garron smiled as the dungeon's feelings washed over him, but the last didn't seem as directed at him as the others did.

The tiny creature padded up toward him hesitantly, and Garron thought he could detect a little wobble in each step, as though it wasn't quite capable of supporting its weight fully yet. Garron knelt slowly as it came closer, trying to look as welcoming as possible. Warm breath washed over his face, the smell surprisingly neutral, and as he reached out a hand, a pink tongue lashed out at him, rasping at his skin, but Garron continued on without hesitation, laying a hand on the creature's head.

The fur was as soft as it looked, and the little cat purred as he began to pet it gently. Andros stepped up beside Garron, looking down at them. "Oh wow, a lion cub, huh? So the dungeon couldn't make the full mob?"

"Aww, look at him—what? Oh, actually, Typo didn't make

him at all." Talia sounded distracted as she once again bobbed closer to Garron and the cub.

At Talia's statement, Garron felt Typo's excitement pull back slightly. <Slight embarrassment.>

"What?" Garron didn't look away from the cub, which had now bent its front paws downward as it purred louder.

"The uh, lioness, the one in the pit, was pregnant. Two babies, almost ready to go into labor." Talia made a lazy circle around Garron and the cub, voice drifting off for a moment before she snapped back into focus. "When Typo showed me, we decided it would be a good idea to save them and raise them up as dungeon born creatures. He... messed up the first one."

<Regret.> Garron got a vague impression of a creature encased in stone.

Talia bobbed upward, voice brightening. "But he managed to get the second one!"

Andros had crouched down next to Garron, and though the cub was leaning into Garron's leg, it still accepted his petting. But as Talia said the words, he looked up at her with an eyebrow raised. "What does 'dungeon born' mean? This doesn't look like a newborn animal to me."

"Hah! I almost forgot you two don't know *anything*." She moved in a strange pattern in the air which seemed somehow dismissive to Garron. "Dungeon born monsters are ones that a dungeon gives life to... more *indirectly*. Usually, they're born when two dungeon monsters mate, but miracle babies count. The biggest factor is that the dungeon provides Essence to the monster, which is why this little cutie is already so big!"

She seemed to have completely given up on hiding her adoration for the little cub, and she swirled around it as it purred, causing it to paw at the air.

Hm. As cute as the lion cub was, Garron was still interested in how they could use it to help them in future fights. "So it's going to get the stone-hide and the claws? How long will it take until it's fully grown?"

<Embarrassment.>

Talia let out another coughing sound. "Uh, well, you see, Typo's still young, and he was having trouble understanding what I wanted him to do so… he didn't give Cutie earth Essence."

Andros laughed. "Cutie? That's *not* going to be his name."

<Increasing embarrassment.>

Garron looked at the lion he was petting more carefully. "If Typo didn't feed it earth Essence—"

"Water," Talia sighed the answer to the unspoken question. "But at least it didn't turn into a stone statue like the first baby!"

<Confirmation.> Garron received another image of the misshapen statue. He gave an involuntary shudder, pushing the image away, though he noted that Typo was getting better at sending complex thoughts than he had been even earlier today. He'd never sent a memory before, and now he'd done it twice. A result of his increased rank?

"Water?" Garron let his thoughts be voiced. That was Typo's other affinity, and Garron's other major affinity as well. "That doesn't sound so bad. What's its ability?"

Talia seemed as worried as a new mother as she swirled around the cub. "He doesn't have one. *Yet*. At least, I don't think so. Typo can't absorb him to see, and he's not showing anything yet. Water Essence doesn't usually do much on land… but he's a lion. I don't know if he'll be comfortable in water."

Andros reached down and pet the little lion, which flinched away for a moment before calming. Typo's influence, no doubt. "Hah! That's no good, but at least we'll have a lion! Can't be worth *nothing*, and the Essence will make him stronger than a normal animal, just like it did for his parents."

"I hope so," Talia grumbled.

Andros seemed more amused by the error than anything. "Hey, if we manage to get it into the D-ranks and fully grown, it can probably handle another Essence type, and then it'll have an ability for sure!"

"Right." Garron would have preferred the magic powers

now, but that was good to hear. "What about more lions? Can Typo make them?"

<Hunger.> Garron absently rubbed at his own stomach. The dungeon's hunger was something that always pressed at his mind, but when Typo projected it, the feeling was *many* times worse.

Talia whizzed around in another dizzying pattern, salmon color tinging more toward red. "He's too low on Essence. He could make a few in the low F-ranks with no abilities, but what's the point? We focused hard on the renovations, and there wouldn't have been enough space for lions in here before."

She sounded defensive, but Garron agreed as he thought through their situation. Though he couldn't help but wish for full-grown lions in place of the larger space in the dungeon, the lions wouldn't have been able to do much for them. If nothing else, a pair of gigantic lion monsters would have done wonders for his confidence.

The cub purred as he continued to rub it, and Talia finally moved away, beginning to talk with Typo about adding in new traps. Garron listened with interest, but she appeared to only be able to get him to form more pits, as well as a few of the rockfall ceiling traps like the one that had killed the lion.

He watched as the new traps formed, cleaning the rabbits as Andros went to collect firewood. It seemed like they would be in here for at least a little longer, and Garron wasn't sure he minded.

<Typo?> Garron felt the dungeon's attention shift towards him. He formed an image in his head—his own clothes, clean and dry, sitting next to a set of plain bandages. <Can you make these for me?>

The dungeon appeared to consider for a moment. <Assurance.>

Garron suddenly felt an unexpected draft. He looked down to see that his clothes had vanished. "What the abyss?"

"Yuck! Cover yourself, why don't you?" Talia flew away

from him, though she was already halfway across the room, but Garron thought he could hear a laugh in her voice.

Garron looked wildly around, projecting his urgency at Typo as powerfully as he could. <I need my clothes!>

<Startlement!> In the next moment, a little bundle of herbs appeared on the ground before Garron. He stared at it. "Are those *cloves*? I need *clothes*."

<Error. Apology.> Garron got the impression that Typo was shaking his head, embarrassed at his inability to distinguish words.

"Typo, I told you to take your time and not make mistakes with the patterns! I still don't understand how you make random things like that!" Even as Talia scolded the dungeon, the herbs… fell apart before him. Not quite how Typo absorbed objects, but as though they were somehow unstable.

It took a moment before a set of new clothes appeared near him, next to the bandages. Hurriedly, he pulled on the undergarments, breathing a sigh of relief. But before he could reach for the bandages, Typo sent him a flash of concern.

<Query?> Garron got a close-up view of the back of his own leg. It was disconcerting to say the least, but it was also a relief to see that the cut hadn't gone too deep or wide. The blood had slowed to a trickle, but there were still bits of dirt around the wound, and he winced to see them.

Then a strange itching sensation overcame him. He reached to scratch at the cut, but stopped. Typo seemed… focused. Intent on something. It took several minutes before the dungeon's focus relaxed and the itching finally abated. Garron's mouth opened, and he felt at the back of his own leg. Sure enough, there was nothing there but smooth skin. <How did you do that?>

<Confusion.> Along with the emotion, Garron got a confusing jumble of thoughts, something like… a diagram? A pattern? Talia had mentioned 'patterns' when she was scolding him. Was that how the dungeon created things? Well, it could make monsters, so why wouldn't be able to fix a little cut? Still,

Garron felt a lingering trace of shock at the sensation of having the wound simply vanish.

"Garron?" Andros stood at the entrance to the room with a bundle of firewood in his arms, a strange look on his face. He seemed to be looking a little past Garron, but his eyes kept flicking back towards him. Suddenly Garron realized that he was standing in the middle of the room with nothing on but his underwear. "Should I... give you some privacy?"

"*Typo*...!"

CHAPTER NINETEEN

"Let's go over the plan." Garron paced back and forth in the Core room, hand on his chin.

Andros, leaning on the wall with drooping eyelids, whined at him. "*Again*? Gar, at this point we're just stalling."

Garron shot a glare at the young Noble. "I'm still not clear on why we have to do this now, but if we *are*, we should do it right."

Andros yawned and waved at Garron. "*Fine*. You'll lure the wolves into the entrance, I'll be waiting inside to slap a few around as they come in. You run down the tunnel to the first stretch, then when all of them are in the dungeon, I pull them further in and cut off the exit. You lure them through the traps. I still don't like *that* part, by the way."

"It's the best way." Garron kept his voice firm.

Andros shook his head absently. "Not arguing about it again. Anyway, whatever's left, I pick off in here. You keep Cutie close to you, just in case."

Garron nodded, but a grimace passed over his face. "We're *not* calling him Cutie."

The young monster in question had already grown half-again his original size—his fangs had come in, though they weren't as long as those of its parents had been, and Garron had seen him flex sharp claws when playing with Talia in the morning. The cub still hadn't displayed any abilities, but he was still moving with the speed of a much older animal, and startling flexibility.

Even as Garron pet him, he purred and stood in a lithe motion that reminded Garron of flowing water. He tried to reach up to Garron but appeared to change his mind halfway through, and bent over nearly backwards before twisting back onto his feet and beginning to pad around the room. "We really have to think of a name for him."

"I still like 'Cutie'!" Talia cut into their conversation, though Garron hadn't seen her before. She was bobbing up and down excitedly, looking like a child excited for gifts on their birthday.

"Just be happy we're doing this." Garron knew he sounded like a grouchy old man, but he was thinking about what he was about to do—and remembering that Talia had done less than nothing to deserve this favor.

The Wisp was unperturbed. "Well, you *did* promise! Besides, those wolves sound perfect for making real defenders in here! You should probably get going now, you know. I would hate if you missed them."

<Excitement, agreement!> At least Typo deserved the help, the only reason Garron relented. It had taken some time to find what they were looking for. Luckily, the wolves had decided that the territory near Typo's entrance was better suited to them than wherever they'd been before. Andros had gone out and located the creatures skirting around the edge of a clearing with a small pond, presumably waiting for prey to come and drink.

He'd confirmed that they were in the mid F-ranks, and that there were eight of them. A large pack, and they had more varied abilities than the first ones Andros and Garron had faced, but they should have enough of an advantage in the dungeon to overcome the uneven numbers. Still, as Talia stated, they should get going now, or else the monsters might leave the clearing. Garron wouldn't feel comfortable trying to bait them much farther away from the dungeon.

"Let's go." Garron's voice was thin, shaking with nerves as he imagined what they were about to do. The first large room of the dungeon was still devoid of traps, but as they moved into the tunnel, they began skirting pit traps spaced perhaps a dozen feet apart. There were occasional rockfall traps laid into the ceiling, and Garron had familiarized himself with their locations as well. They were held in place by a shell of hardened earth which had been made to break inward. Garron had tested one himself, and throwing a rock at it had been enough to trigger the trap.

Once they had made it past four pits—three of which were now covered—and one rockfall, Garron slowed for a moment. He had a few supplies laid out to retrieve once he made it this far. His sword, a chainmail shirt patterned after Joris', and a few rocks. Couldn't go wrong with chucking rocks at things.

Andros tapped him on the shoulder. "Hey, will Cutie be able to get here by himself? I mean, the traps wouldn't get him, right?"

"We're *not* calling him that! Yes, Typo can just direct him past them. He's already pretty used to them." Garron had spent a bit too much time playing with the lion cub in between his cultivation sessions last evening. It turned out that Typo could directly order the mob to do things, though with the dungeon's own… underdeveloped mind, that was of limited use.

Past his supply point were three more covered pit traps, one rockfall trap, and an open pit. These were much closer together, because Garron had asked Typo to create one more in the space. He wanted to thin the pack as much as possible before he had to bring the wolves down the second tunnel.

Finally, they made it to the entrance, which Typo had hollowed out considerably. Andros needed the space to fight, but there only so much the dungeon could do so close to the surface; it still wasn't as big as the other rooms in the dungeon. They both clambered out and began walking towards the clearing, Andros behind Garron and watching for danger. They still hadn't run into any guards, but they were in the interior of the forest, and presumably Jackson had most of his guards near the edge.

When they began to approach the clearing, Andros put a hand on his shoulder. "Are you sure about this, Gar?"

Garron sighed. "Do you think they'll follow if they see *you*?"

Andros chewed at his lip. "They *should*—"

"But you're not sure. You're in the D-ranks, and they might decide not to chase you. They'll come after me for *sure*. Besides, you'll be watching, and it's not like I'm an invalid. Not anymore." Garron drew in a deep breath, partly out of nerves and partly to prove his point. "I can do this."

After a long moment, Andros nodded unhappily. "I'll be in the canopy. You know what to do… Just make sure to keep close to the trees. I'll slow a few down before I head into the dungeon, so they won't trap you. Be careful."

Garron nodded, and his friend began ascending a tree like one of the giant flying squirrels in the area. Garron kept going, and in a few moments entered a clearing with a large pond of clear water. Even though he knew not to drink the still water, the pond was beautiful in its own way, the light shooting through it to land on the rock and mud below, a faint reflection of the cloudy sky rippling on its surface.

He felt the air stirring, saw a flash of gray fur, and that was enough to start running. Garron was surprised to find the wolves were almost completely silent as they chased him. For a good few seconds, he wasn't sure if they'd taken his bait, until he looked over his shoulder. He was back among the trees now, trying very hard not to trip over a stray branch or root, but behind him, wolves were threading through the forest with all the grace of true predators. It looked as though they had been surprised by his sudden appearance, because most were just now emerging from behind the bushes, fallen logs, and trees they were using as cover.

However, there was a pair of wolves running disturbingly

close to him, picking up speed as they hopped over a large rock, the wind playing around them as they ran. Even as Garron watched, they slowed, pushed back by a blast of air from above, and Garron turned his attention back to running.

Branch, root, bush, rock. The trick to running like this was to be looking slightly ahead, but not so much that he forgot what was on the ground in front of him. He nearly stumbled a few times—the leaves carpeting the ground covered a few hazards, though they often made the run smoother. His chest was already burning, but running from predators like this convinced him to push his body in a way nothing else could.

They weren't far from the dungeon at all. Still, the wolves were faster than him. He felt something heavy shake the ground behind, heard the angry rustling of leaves flying as Andros shot more blasts of air, saw the flashes of gray fur getting closer and closer over his shoulder.

There. It was a rather innocuous tree in a forest like this, its most distinguishing feature being the mess of visible roots at its base, but when Garron saw it, a rush of relief surged through him. Then just more fear. There was another angry rustle as another blast of air came down from Andros, but as he continued to run towards the dungeon entrance, he saw Andros fall to the ground before it; entering the hole at the base. He had to complete the last stretch alone, and he could practically feel teeth closing on his limbs.

Garron pumped his arms as he ran, pushing himself to his limit. Even as the dungeon entrance got closer, he could feel wind stirring at his back. On instinct, he jerked to the side, nearly tripping over a root, and continued running. He managed to catch the thin rent in the ground from whatever had been aimed for him, and pushed himself even harder. For the last few steps he slowed, and he heard a snarl right behind him as he dove into the dungeon's entrance. There was a dull **thunk**, and pieces of tree bark fell down into the hole beside him.

"*Move*, Gar!" Andros' voice held a trace of relief along with urgency, and Garron picked himself back up with a wrenching pull from his friend. Without pausing to inspect the situation, he ran down the tunnel, deeper in the dungeon.

Typo perked up as Garron entered his influence. <Greeting. Much excitement!>

Garron sent his own greeting as he moved down the tunnel, finally slowing as he reached the first stretch of traps. He skirted around the open pit and the three covered ones until he reached the first bend where he'd placed his armor, sword, and rocks. As he struggled with the chainmail shirt, he sent a request to Typo.

<Please send the cub to me.> Garron sent a rough image of the lion cub walking up the tunnel behind Garron, skirting the traps. They'd practiced this already, so Typo understood immediately.

<Confirmation.>

Garron sent his gratitude and, after a moment to let the dungeon focus, decided to try for one more favor. <Please show me the dungeon entrance.>

Typo paused. <Confusion?>

Garron sighed, but he sent another image of the entrance as he imagined it, and after a few more tries, the dungeon finally understood. Andros was standing by the entrance with a wolf lying at his feet, its body barely twitching. A moment later, another came through the hole in a flurry of wind, setting down with impossible grace before attempting to run down the tunnel. Andros moved in a blur, sending a powerful kick at the creature's leg, but the monster jerked to the side at the last moment, feet lifting off the ground as it turned, snarling.

It seemed more in line with the first wolf pack's abilities: floating, then shooting forward to attack in bursts. Andros dodged easily, landing a punch and a kick on the monster's flank before it even touched the ground again. He moved in to strike, and another wolf jumped down the hole into the dungeon.

Andros didn't even seem tired yet as he landed another punch on the floating wolf, then skipped to the side as the second snapped at him. This one wasn't exhibiting any of the air abilities of the first two—it almost seemed like a normal animal until Andros threw a kick and it twisted unnaturally to move out of the way, its body contorting into a horseshoe before snapping back to place as it attempted another bite at Andros. It seemed as though the creature was imbued with water Essence, the same as Cutie. Garron shook himself. "Abyss! I'm *not* calling him that."

When Andros dodged, the water-wolf moved forward in a motion that seemed almost like a slither until it was coming at his flank, and the wind-wolf on his other side lunged at the same time. He skipped backwards, but his back came up against the wall of the narrow confines. He let out a blast of air at the wind-wolf, and it was pushed away as it scrabbled at the air. Andros turned his attention to its lunging companion, landing a kick on the creature's belly as he ducked around its strike.

Instead of jumping back into the fray with Andros however, the wind-wolf seemed to lose interest, turning and sprinting into the tunnel. Behind it, another lithe water-wolf jumped down, and a moment later, there was a heavy thud as a wolf with stone teeth and a glimmering coat landed in the dungeon. Garron felt a flash of recognition as he remembered the much larger stone wolf in the other dungeon. The water-wolf joined its fellow in engaging Andros, but the stone monster seemed focused. It followed the wind-wolf deeper into the dungeon.

Right toward Garron.

CHAPTER TWENTY

As Garron finally pushed the image away, he felt something against his leg. He looked down to see that the lion cub had indeed made it to his position and was now rubbing against him affectionately. As the snarls of the wolves began echoing down the tunnel, the cub stretched and came around Garron, twisting farther than any normal animal his size would be able to, baring his teeth towards the sounds. Garron smiled in spite of himself, patting the little monster on the head as he considered the tunnel.

The first wind-wolf came rushing down, gray coat shaking with every bounding step, teeth bared as it stared into Garron's eyes. At the first pit, the monster leapt without pause, clearing it with ease and remaining in the air as it continued down the tunnel, snarling.

"Abyss." Garron watched as the wolf floated over the first covered pit without ever noticing it was there. It touched down after that, continuing to run, and Garron held his breath. There were two more pits here, with one of the rockfall traps in between. When the wolf bounded forward onto the first covered pit, Garron clenched his fist in triumph. But as the stone crumbled away and the wolf let out a surprised yip, Garron saw dust kick up around the trap. A moment later, the snarling creature was flying out of the dust cloud toward him.

"Fine." He'd been hoping to wait for this but… he scooped up a rock and tossed it at the ceiling as the wolf passed under the rockfall trap. The stone hit with a dull thud, and cracks appeared along the ceiling. A moment later, the collection of heavy rocks, compressed earth, and random chunks of sharp metal that Typo had sprinkled in fell with a crash over the wolf. It barely whimpered before all sound was cut off.

Garron could feel Typo's muted satisfaction as Essence drifted into it. Garron took a deep breath, but his relief was cut short by the howl of another wolf down the tunnel. He could hear the thudding as it plodded forward, and as it rounded the bend, the stone monster broke into a strange, slow bound. It skirted the first pit easily enough, but a few moments after that, a step punched through the earth, and the creature fell precipitously into the pit with a heavy thud and a deep whine echoing up from the ground. He pumped his fist.

<Excitement, satisfaction!> The dungeon gave a feeling of intense happiness as it collected the monster's earth Essence.

Garron smiled, but the expression faded a moment later as more howls and whining echoed down the tunnel, and the moment after that, a faint shout. That probably meant the wolves were all in the dungeon, and Andros was herding them down the tunnel. Garron tensed and settled in.

Two gray-furred monsters bounded around the bend in the tunnel, both snarling and yipping. One was kicking up a cloud of swirling dust as it ran, while the second was one of the waterwolves Andros had been fighting. Garron was pleased to see that this creature was falling behind its fellows, mostly due to a limp in its hind leg. "Nice, Andros."

This wolf jumped over the first pit as well, though it didn't stay in the air like the other one had. It continued forward, letting loose a howl, before slashing a claw in the air. Dust kicked up down the tunnel, and Garron could feel stray breezes even at a distance. The lion cub snarled and began pacing in front of Garron, but he was more focused on the wolf. Would it also be able to escape the pit trap?

As the dust settled, Garron could see the wolf was still bounding forward. Behind it, there were thin furrows in the ground, as though someone had cut into it shallowly with a sword. The creature made the same motion, and Garron's eyes widened. Dust kicked up, but he already knew what would have happened. This creature's ability would reveal the pit, ruining the trap.

Garron rapidly considered his options. The wolves would be there in moments—should he retreat to the next tunnel, as they'd planned? But then this monster would reveal the other pits, and there was only one more rockfall. He needed to kill it, but how to protect against its air slash?

<Typo, I need a shield!> Garron accompanied the message with an image of himself, holding a simple circle of metal strapped to his arm. He cursed himself for not thinking of it sooner.

The wolf emerged from the dust, snarling, and leapt at Garron with unnatural speed, slashing at the air. Garron jumped backwards and to the side. Even though he'd dodged, he felt something impact his mail-clad shoulder.

<Confusion.> Garron got a feeling in reply that Typo had no idea how to make a shield, as it had never absorbed one before.

"I didn't know that was a requirement!" By the time he'd reoriented, the monster was upon him. He attacked with all the ferocity he could muster, sword slashing down at the wolf's hide, but the creature jerked out of the way with the speed of the wind.

Then the lion cub sank his teeth into the monster's flank. The wolf let out a yip of pain—despite his size, the cub's fangs were long enough to pierce the hide. Garron grinned, preparing a second swing at the wolf, which was even now trying to shake the cub away. The little lion was being whipped around like a rag doll, but he didn't seem to be affected—at least, not so much as the wolf, which snarled as the cub's teeth tore through flesh, ripping new wounds in its hide with each motion.

It didn't even notice as Garron's sword came down on its neck.

The cub didn't want to let go of his prey—Garron supposed this was his first kill—but Garron managed to pull the little monster away, still wriggling and growling at the dead wolf, and after a moment in his arms he calmed somewhat. He still didn't put the cub down as he turned and ran, though he noticed that he wouldn't be able to lift him for much longer at the rate he was growing. He'd caught the sight of another glimmering stone wolf running heavily down the tunnel, almost to the last pit trap, as well as the two water-wolves and one which was probably another air-type, though it was lagging as Andros pressed it forward.

Garron wove his way around the traps, hearing the water wolves howling behind him as they overtook the stone.

"Woah! Be careful, Gar, this one's—" Andros' voice became too faint to hear. Garron's fists clenched, and he almost went back. If he could keep the wolves chasing after him, they wouldn't be fighting Andros. He had to keep going.

He finally made it to the end of the traps, then nearly smacked himself. <Typo, I need rocks.>

<Confirmation!>

A moment later, a pile of socks appeared by his feet. Garron almost shouted, but then noticed they were all made of stone. "Good enough."

He sent his gratitude, dropped his sword, and picked up a rock; watching the tunnel's bend in anticipation. The snarling drew closer, and a moment later the two water-wolves bounded out, the limping one slightly behind its fellow. As expected, they both skirted the first visible pit with ease, but as the one in front ran across the false ground of the second trap and felt the ground fall away beneath its front legs… it *twisted*, writhing in a way no normal animal could manage until it got one paw on the ground beside it.

The part of Garron that wasn't panicked had to appreciate the incredible litheness of these creatures. The rest of him focused on the fact that the two wolves were now carefully skirting the pit, testing the ground beneath them before moving forward. Smart. But then, this wasn't so far removed from the behavior of a hunting animal, was it? Surely these creatures had dealt with treacherous ground before.

Wait for it. Garron watched worriedly as the two wolves approached, and a moment later, the glimmering coat of a third appeared, barreling down the tunnel. Garron hoped for a moment that it would be unable to arrest its momentum in time, or that it would be too stupid to notice what its fellows were doing, but he was disappointed on both counts.

Now a chorus of growls—two high, one low—started up as the wolves slowly crept towards him, testing their weight with every step, all bunched up in a line. Perfect. He waited until they were midway between the second and third pits, and threw his rock.

It bounced off the ceiling, leaving a crack but not triggering the trap. Garron stared at it in disbelief for a moment. "Abyss."

He bent and hurriedly scooped up another rock, but the two water-wolves had spooked at the rock's motion, and were already past the rockfall trap's area of effect. Cursing, he threw the second rock and the trap finally triggered, dropping its contents on the stone wolf with an audible crack of stone shattering.

The two water wolves spooked even further at the dropping rocks, and jumped again, landing inches away from the edge of the last pit trap.

"Hold on…!" Garron scooped up another rock, lifting up and tossing it at the ceiling above the wolves. The one without the limp jumped forward again, yelping at the motion, but the second was sluggish. The first landed directly in the middle of the pit trap, and fell through before it realized it had been tricked. Garron could hear the howl of pain as it landed.

Just two more remained. Andros' opponent, and Garron's. He needed to hurry. The lame wolf was growling, but it seemed unwilling to move forward for a moment. The only thing separating them now was the single pit, and as Garron considered, an idea struck him.

He picked up another rock and threw it. The creature dodged with its strange grace, growling more fiercely at Garron, but he just threw another rock. It dodged again, then snarled. <More rocks please, Typo.>

It took four throws to enrage the monster enough to attempt to cross the pit towards Garron, to which he responded by scooping up rocks in both hands. He pelted the monster as it edged along the narrow patch of trustworthy earth, and after the first two struck its shoulder and flank with twin *thunks*, the monster tried to dodge the third. Two legs dangled above the pit as it skipped away, and Garron *focused*.

The last rock took it in the foreleg, destroying its footing and sending it tumbling into the pit with a howl to match its packmate's.

<Excitement!> Typo's satisfaction radiated across their bond.

Garron smiled, and the cub purred at his feet, but his triumph vanished in an instant. Andros. He ran forward as quickly as he could, though he was careful not to share the same fate as the wolves he'd killed. He rounded the bend in time to see Andros jumping away from a slash, and his eyes went wide. Fire curled around the gray wolf's claws, and Garron could see orange light emanating from its mouth as it snarled.

There was a black mark on one of Andros' legs.

Garron was forward in an instant, but after a moment's consideration, he changed his mind. Andros was currently dodging the monster with ease, and a feel at the air told him he was trying to put together a technique. Garron tensed, and *threw* his weapon. "Andy, sword!"

His friend looked over for an instant and nodded, then turned back to the wolf and released a blast of air which pushed the creature back, streaks of fire flowing along with the wind. Garron winced as the blade did a half turn, pointing straight at Andros, but his friend sidestepped and caught the hilt without issue. "Used up all of my good throws on the sock-rocks."

As soon as the sword was in Andros' hand, the air cultivator shot forward, stabbing the wolf's shoulder and ending the fight with a cut to the neck. Garron noticed that, at each strike, sparks flared up around the wolf's coat, clearly the reason he couldn't kill it faster.

<Excitement, slight disappointment.> Garron knew that the dungeon was disappointed that the monster wasn't dead yet, but he barely paid attention.

Talia appeared in the air between Andros and Garron as the wolf breathed its last, bobbing up and down. "Excellent job as usual! Oooh, I'm so excited, we're going to make actual dungeon monsters! Do you know how hard it usually is to lure this many pred—"

"Andy, how's your leg?" Garron's teeth were grit as he ran over to his friend, who was still heaving from the fight. It was a burn, that was certain—the skin was reddened in a patch the size of Garron's palm, the cloth of the pants blackened around it.

"It's alright, don't worry, Gar." As he said the words, Andros leaned down to examine the wound himself, and Garron could see the slight wince. "You should see the other guy. Still, didn't expect the thing to have fire Essence, but that's my own fault. Should've checked. You sounded like you were doing alright, so I decided to wear it out a bit."

Talia whizzed around for a moment, still clearly excited. "Ah, it's unfortunate but at least the rest of the plan—"

"Stop *talking*!" Garron knew his voice had edged into a shout, and he controlled himself as he continued. "The plan didn't work, and now Andy's injured. What did *you* do to help us?"

The Wisp stopped bobbing. "Well, Typo—"

"I'm not talking about him. I'm talking about *you*." Garron could feel Typo's shock at his words, at the anger he knew was transmitting across their connection. "The first time I met you, you extorted me into promising to help Typo. Fine—he's your charge or whatever, I don't mind helping him. But you promised help in return. You said 'we' would help. Where's *your* contribution? You've been whizzing around, playing and telling us what to do! You even needed *my* help to do *your* actual *job*!"

The silence rang in the air for a moment after Garron stopped shouting at her. The Wisp was motionless, slowly turning a pale blue. "The traps—"

"Were made by Typo, and *if* the traps had worked like they were supposed to, that pack would have been dead before reaching the second tunnel! I could have gone to help Andy sooner!" Garron lashed his hand out to point at Andros' leg. "That might not have happened!"

"Gar, I'm not saying you're wrong, but it's my fault I didn't check the wolf." Andros laid a hand on his shoulder, but the furious young man shrugged it off.

"It doesn't change the fact that all *she's* done is hurt us and our chances of survival." Garron didn't look at Talia as he said the words. "Are you trying to feed us to Typo?"

A wave of anger slammed into Garron, and he staggered backwards, gasping. No, anger wasn't the right word; it was more. Protective rage, hurt, and fear. Not fear for survival, but the fear of being alone. Of not knowing what to do to move forward, fear of making a mistake and hurting a partner.

<Plea.>

Garron stared at Talia. She was all blue now, drifting slowly down to the ground. When she spoke, her voice was small, and though it shouldn't have been possible, it sounded like she was choking back tears. "You're right, I'm sorry. I'm useless to everyone. I should go back to Kant—"

"Stop!" Garron shouted. He didn't know if he—or Typo—could bear hearing her finish the sentence. "Don't say that. I… You probably shouldn't be luring random people in here."

"I'm sorry about that. I-I didn't know what to do." She sounded sincere, and Garron felt a rush of sympathy. Some of it was from Typo, but some was his own. After all, he and Andros had been adrift since they'd left the estate. How long had Talia struggled to make Typo stronger?

"No one is useless, Talia. We both have a long way to go, but we can do it." Garron gave her a weak smile. Though she could be a bit grating, she meant well. He hoped. He decided he could give her a fresh chance, or at least not be so negative toward her. "Now, why don't we get Andros' leg cleaned and get started on those… what does Andros call them? Mobs?"

Typo's storm of emotion withdrew in an instant, shifting in an almost childlike way. <Extreme *excitement*!>

CHAPTER TWENTY-ONE

"You're sure the sunlight isn't burning you or anything, *ri~ght?*" Andros glanced at Garron, a sly grin playing at the corners of his lips.

Garron frowned doing his best not to squint as they passed through a patch of light filtering through the trees. "Celestial, I do need to do this. Every day you spend out here alone, your sense of humor gets worse."

"I'm just *surprised* is all—don't you have more cultivation to be doing? You've only been working since dawn! If you don't get a little more in, you might fall behind your imaginary opponent." Andros put a hand to his forehead as though he might swoon, grinning. He *should* have tripped over the bush in front of him, but of course he just unconsciously hopped it.

Garron regretfully shrugged and waved back toward the dungeon. "Only so much free Essence in there."

"Believe me, I know," Andros mock-grumbled at him. "You think *that's* bad, try *not* having a dungeon with your major affinities all to yourself for a few days. Not to mention, I only have *one*. You're so lucky it's painful."

Garron tilted his head. "I've had five days in a dungeon. How many *years* have you had that cultivation technique?"

Andros pouted and gave a slight nod to concede the point. "You're nearly to the next rank in the F series, you know. Your work is paying off. At this rate, you'll hit the D series in a few years, which is fantastic. Maybe we should come back here after we shake Jackson off!"

Garron smiled to show his agreement, but privately he felt the seed of worry in his stomach grow a little. It had been two days since the fight with the wolves, and three since they'd saved Ulysses. In that time, they'd been… relaxing. Typo and Talia had worked on forming the new mobs—a process which Garron had found extremely entertaining—while Garron and Andros had focused on their cultivation a little. There wasn't much else to do, and Jackson hadn't made a move. Garron was beginning to wonder if they should just stay hidden in the dungeon for a few years.

"Huh. Looks like there's a few monsters heading our way. Can't tell at this distance, but it seems like they're in the high F-ranks? Only three or four of them." Andros scratched at his chin with a relaxed posture.

Garron cocked his head. "What do you think?"

"I'm thinking I want to see the wolves in action." Andros was grinning with excitement, but Garron tried to remain level-headed and calm as he considered.

"How strong are they?" He really needed to get Essence-sight as fast as possible—he hated having to rely on Andros for all of this information.

Andros was still staring into the forest. "They're coming this way. Uh, definitely high F-ranks, one looks like it might have broken into the D-ranks though. Still, if we lure them to Typo, it should be pretty easy to handle that many."

Garron thought for a few more moments. "Fine. I'm going to start running. If they're that strong, I can't outrun them if we just wait here, and they should still chase you."

Andros nodded, gaze still fixed in the distance, looking at

something through the trees. "Wait… it seems like they're curving away a bit. Let's make a little noise?"

"You sure?" After the Noble nodded, Garron walked over to a nearby set of bushes and shook it violently, then snapped a few tree branches lying on the ground, producing cracks of noise. Certainly enough to alert the monsters, but not give them away to someone outside Andros' field of vision. "Is that good?"

"Abyss." Without warning, Garron was pulled away from where he'd been standing over a broken branch.

"What?" Garron felt a cold sweat breaking out at Andros' tone. "What's wrong?"

"*Quiet*!" Andros' voice was barely audible as he steered Garron away from where he'd been standing. "One of them broke away to head towards us. The D-ranker. Not a monster. It's a human."

Garron's eyes went wide, and he struggled against Andros' grip. "Stop! We have to stop him! The flare!"

Andros paused for a bare moment before he let go of Garron. An instant later, his form blurred as he shot through the air in the opposite direction. He had to take short steps, deep in the forest as they were, but apparently it wasn't far. In seconds, heart hammering, Garron heard a startled yell from the direction Andros had disappeared, and without thinking he ran up around the huge tree to see what was happening.

They were far enough away that Garron had trouble making out details, especially through the foliage, but it was easy enough to know that the form blurring back towards him was Andros, and the red stick in his hand sent a wave of relief washing over Garron. But the man Andros was running from was still in sight, and he broke into a flat sprint which was more than Garron could hope to manage.

Andros was back in moments, though he seemed out of breath. With a smooth motion, he took the flare and smashed it underfoot, grinding the powder into the dirt. Garron approved. If the guard managed to get hold of it again and alert Jackson, they were finished. "I... can get us back, but we'll still be in sight."

Garron was already shoving his panic away, though most of his mind was screaming that he should be running in the other direction as fast as possible. *Think.* "Let him think you're running out of Essence. Stay with me. If he gets too close, get us a lead. We have to get him back to Typo."

Andros frowned, seeming like he was going to argue, but instead he just grabbed Garron and started running through the trees and the underbrush, stealth forgotten.

"This is the only way." The thought was small comfort to Garron as he sprinted alongside Andros, doing his best to keep up with his far more capable friend. They were already in a bad enough position for alerting the guardsman to their rough location, but if he reported back to Jackson now, they would be caught in days, even hours, and Andros wouldn't be able to finish off a D-ranker alone. They needed him to think they were easy prey, and fight him on favorable ground.

The run was worse than luring the wolves, both because it was longer and because he didn't have Andros to slow down the pursuit. They ran together, and soon the crashing sounds of the guardsman running behind them were easy even for him to hear.

Far too much time later, they came to a part of the forest Garron easily recognized. He passed a split tree to his left and a great mossy rock a moment later to his right. His chest burned a bit too much to speak, but as the tree which guarded Typo's entrance came into view, he grabbed Andros' elbow, coming to a stop.

Garron wanted badly to sit down, take a few heaving breaths, and possibly vomit a little, but he restricted himself to catching his breath for a second while Andros pulled at his arm in confusion, then gasping as loudly as he could. "It's no... use, Andy. We have... to fight him or... he'll trap us."

Thankfully, Andros seemed to understand because he stopped pulling at Garron's arm and gave him a determined nod. The man was unlikely to just follow them into the dungeon if he thought they knew where they were going. They needed to engage him, at least a little.

Garron let go of Andros' arm, then straightened, turned… and winced. Running toward them was a short man in chainmail with a simple helmet left on, exposing a heavily scarred, perpetually angry face. Hal was one of Jackson's senior guards—Garron had never seen him do an hour of work on the estate, but he had heard the other servants talk about what he'd done before joining with Jackson. If the kingdom hadn't been crumbling from The Necromancer's War, the man would be in prison.

"Well, it looks like I win, boy." The man's face broke out into a grin, and he was looking directly at Andros. "Come quietly, and I won't hurt *you*."

"No." Andros' reply was short, clipped. Garron could feel him shifting his balance, preparing for the fight, but Hal seemed infuriated.

"You—you know what? It's easier to bring you in with a broken leg… or two. And don't think I forgot about you, *fishie*." The guard was sneering as he looked to Garron. "I'm going to—"

He attacked mid-sentence, pulling his sword out with unnatural speed and lunging at Andros, but the air cultivator was ready before the sword cleared the sheath. He sidestepped, letting the blade whisper past him, then snapped a perfect kick at the other man's ribs. It impacted with a dull jingle of mail, a puff of air escaping from the short guardsman, but he was already turning to deliver a slash. Not at Andros, but Garron.

The young man was ready, but the sword still came startlingly close as he threw himself to the side, the flashing steel obscuring his vision for a moment as it came for his neck. He managed to remember his plan, and launched himself to his left, landing with a painful thud on the mess of roots near Typo's entrance.

Andros had already shot forward at Hal, somehow pressing

the attack despite the laughable difference in their armaments. He crowded the swordsman, delivering elbows and knees at every possible opening. Garron caught the glance sent his way and gave a nod.

Andros began to slow slightly, a change Garron wouldn't have noticed even days before. Meanwhile, Garron made a show of scrabbling around the roots for a moment, just in case Hal was watching. Between a grunt from Andros and a shout of rage from Hal, he yelled, "*Here*, Andy! There's a hole!"

He desperately hoped Hal wouldn't question why they would willingly close themselves into a tighter space, presumably without escape. It was a good bet—as Andros came 'stumbling' rapidly towards Garron, who was now holding open the roots over Typo's entrance, Hal shouted after them. "You're not getting away, boy! You hear me?"

Andros jumped in, and Garron followed him a moment later. They immediately began running down the tunnel, and sure enough, a thud behind signaled that Hal was following.

Typo had finally gotten enough time to cover the first pit trap in the tunnel, and Garron grinned savagely as he and Andros skirted it. They continued running, Andros pulling Garron along as he slowed, skirting another trap, but he still looked over his shoulder as the mail-clad guardsman rounded the bend. He sprinted forward, sword out, and a few steps carried him into the traps area. The ground crumbled beneath his foot—Garron felt a surge of triumph, and began to slow.

In a flash, the short man's sword slammed into the earth by his side, and he heaved backwards.

Garron's mouth fell open. In a maneuver that any normal human would have been utterly incapable of managing, the guardsman arrested his momentum, pulling himself out of the trap with a grunt and a curse.

"Oh, you sneaky little...! I'm going to—" Hal didn't finish the threat. Instead, he just swept his sword before him in a rapid arc, clearing away the false ground with ease, then taking the narrow strip of ground before him in a run. He continued in a low crouch as he cleared the pit, sword in front of him, plowing a furrow in the ground as he continued forward. He found the next pit and cleared it in moments, beginning to skirt it when Garron threw his first rock.

Hal let out a breathless, ugly laugh. "I'm coming for you, *fishie.*"

Garron threw another rock. The man didn't bother to do more than duck the ones aimed at his head. The projectiles bounced off his armor, and even Andros' blast of wind produced nothing more than a quick snort as he continued to skirt the pit.

Finally, there was only one more pit between the man and where Garron and Andros were standing next to a fresh pile of rocks. With a growl, the guardsman ran forward, eyes already locked on the stretch of ground Andros and Garron had run on to avoid the third pit trap.

Garron screamed out. "Now!"

Andros' blast of wind was even more effective at triggering the rockfall than Garron's rock, but Hal reacted with disturbing speed, lunging forward and towards the strip of safe ground. A single stone caught him in the back and he stumbled, but wasn't enough to disrupt his footing.

Andros and Garron ran.

The second tunnel barely managed to slow Hal. He managed to round the bend in time to see the path they took through it, and simply followed. When Andros triggered the second rockfall, he got away cleanly; the physical gifts of his rank were too much for the simple trap to handle. The entire time, the scarred guardsman shouted invectives at the pair, promising revenge. Garron, on the other hand, was focused. The traps weren't having an effect. They would have to finish him off personally.

<Typo?>
<Query?>
<I need some help.> When they finally ran out into the first large room, they both stopped running and turned to face the

entrance. In moments, Hal ran out into the open room, sword raised, snarling.

A mass of sparkling gray fur rushed at him from the side, slamming into him with a snarl of its own. The guardsman let out a startled shout before leaping away. "What the...?"

He was cut off by a trio of howls, joined a moment later by a snarl. From behind the humans, a pair of lithe, impossibly flexible monsters bounded up, followed by a feline one. The heavy gait of the third wolf joined its fellows, and in seconds there were four wolves and a young lion attacking Hal.

Andros had named the stone wolves Crystalfurs, and Garron had decided to call the water-wolves Riverdancers. They had both made fun of each other, but they'd been too excited by the creatures to worry much. Even as they watched, the two Riverdancers came running up to nip at Hal's sides, one twisting around his sword while the other harried his legs. The young lion—now more than half the size of an adult with claws and fangs to match—pounced on the man as he turned to deal with the second Riverdancer.

The Crystalfurs came up from behind, ponderous in comparison to their lithe counterparts, and while Hal was trying to deal with the three water monsters twisting around his attacks, each swept a stone claw at him. Both strikes connected with a sound of tearing metal, and Hal screamed. Garron saw when the man's mind turned from anger into blind rage.

Moving in a blur, the guardsman kicked one Crystalfur in the side as he continued swiping his sword at the Riverdancers and lion. The strike connected with a resounding crack, and the stone wolf whimpered as its protective coat shattered. Hal let out a howl of his own, but the pain of the strike seemed to spur him forward. His next swing was so fast that even the Riverdancer couldn't dodge in time. The sword pressed deep into the monster's flesh before finally breaking skin, but the fountain of red sent the creature down instantly.

"I'm going to help." Andros let out a dismayed snort of breath. The young Noble sprinted forward with the wind playing around him, and joined the wolves in attacking Hal. It took but a moment to occupy the man's full attention, barely even trying to land hits as he dodged around Hal's strikes. Whenever the man tried to focus on a wolf, Andros was there with a kick or a punch, letting Cutie and the remaining Riverdancer swipe claws at the man's legs.

"You *brat*! You're not—" Hal's shout ended in another scream, and Garron smiled like a proud older brother. The lion had managed to ravage the guard's boots enough to sink his teeth into the back of the guard's foot. The monster went flying a moment later as Hal kicked it with savage strength, but it landed on its feet, absorbing the impact with its elastic muscles.

The damage to Hal was already done. He swept a sword at the Riverdancer going for his calf and the monster twisted away like a snake. Andros kicked him square in the chest, a blast of air accompanying the move, and without the use of his foot, the guard finally went down. The last Crystalfur snarled as its stone claws ripped through the chainmail and it exacted revenge for its injured fellow.

<Mmm.> Garron could feel the intense satisfaction emanating from the dungeon as it absorbed the massive amounts of earth Essence in the man's Center. Faintly, he could hear a squeal from Talia as she zipped toward Typo's Core. As Garron plopped down to the floor, breathing heavily, he sent a thought to the dungeon.

<Typo, after you finish processing that Essence, let Talia know that we're going to sit down and make some new traps for this place.>

Though the dungeon was distracted as he attempted to process the Essence he was receiving, Garron still felt, <Confirmation.>

Good. In the next second, he joined Andros on the floor, heaving deep breaths as the lion-they-definitely-weren't-naming-Cutie came over and rubbed his face, purring.

CHAPTER TWENTY-TWO

Garron watched carefully as the wary pair of wolves moved down the tunnel. One was a Riverdancer and the other a Crystalfur, and both had been instructed by Typo to simply move through the dungeon. They were as wary as any animal would be in unfamiliar territory, and they were right to feel that way.

The Riverdancer took a cautious step forward, and Garron held his breath. Nothing happened. In a smooth, lithe gait, the creature continued forward, completely unharmed. Garron let out a disappointed sigh, but a moment after, the Crystalfur stepped into the same space.

With a grinding hiss, a set of stone spikes shot out of the wall, slamming into the wolf's glittering coat. Ahead, the Riverdancer instantly flattened against the ground, managing to avoid being hit. The stone wolf behind it weathered the strikes, none of the spikes managing to actually hurt it.

<Excitement!>

"Wow! I mean, I know you said that would happen, but still! How'd you do it?" Andros gave him an enthusiastic pat on the back.

Garron gave a small smile of his own. "There's a stone plate with a little blade on the bottom resting just above a string. The string runs into the wall and holds up another plate that blocks the spikes from escaping. When someone steps on the first plate, the blade cuts the string and the barrier falls, so the spikes can shoot out."

"How do you make the spikes go flying out like that, sir engineer?" Andros gave a little chuckle.

"Springs in the walls. There's a few holding up the plate too." That had actually taken the most time, because Typo hadn't understood the concept of a coiled, compressible piece of metal. Truth be told, Garron barely understood it either—he hadn't seen them more than once or twice in the engineer's devices—but once he'd gotten Typo to start making models, they'd quickly settled on the appropriate design.

Andros gave a low whistle, then another laugh. "I don't know, Gar, it sounds a little too simple to me. Where's the army of ants to haul up the plate when it's done?"

Garron let out a huff that could faintly be considered a laugh. "Maybe next time."

"Garron…"

Garron eyed his grinning friend… the smile was just a little too wide. For a moment, the expression froze on his face, then dropped.

"Are you okay? I mean, you're a little… subdued."

Garron let out a little laugh. "Big word."

"You swine…" Andros gave him a reproachful look.

"I'm fine. It's just… we just killed somebody in here yesterday, you know?" Garron ran a hand through his hair in consternation.

Andros' face said he'd already known what Garron would say. "Did you ever hear what Hal did before he joined up with Jackson? He killed a man, Gar. We aren't talking about self-defense. He stole the poor man's stuff and left. The only reason he joined with Jackson was because the kingdom couldn't enforce its laws on Noble estates anymore."

Garron nodded, subdued. "I know. I… don't feel *bad* about

it. Not the killing, I mean. But it's—I can't *not* feel something. I just wish we didn't have to do it like this. Don't tell me you're not the same, at least a little."

Andros let out a much more genuine smile. "A few laughs help, you know."

"Good point. Guess I should find someone funny to talk with." Garron gave his friend's arm a light punch, receiving a mock scowl in return. "I'll be fine. But let's try and be a little… kinder next time."

Andros eyed him quizzically. "I mean, we can try, but I don't think Jackson is going to give us much of a chance for mercy."

Garron grinned and watched his friend out of the corner of his eye. "Do you want to see the cages?"

Andros threw up his hands. "Celestial, I'll be in here all day. Let me try to get us some food, yeah?"

Garron's stomach felt like it was trying to eat itself and succeeding. "Can't say no to that, but be careful. Don't assume everything's a monster again."

"Yeah, yeah. I know, I know." Andros waved a hand irritably. With that, his friend started off down the tunnel, skirting the two wolves who were still growling sullenly and waiting for Garron to move down and let them continue the tests.

"So, do you want to get back to work then, or do you have a few more *feelings* to let out first?" Talia didn't sound in a much better mood than the wolves. She'd taken his 'interference' in Typo's trap designing a little personally, but Garron was making a real effort to include her in the work.

"Right, sorry. So, what did you think?" He kept his voice open and interested. He really was curious what the Wisp would say. She'd been very helpful designing the concept of the trap, though Garron was responsible for the finer details.

"Well, the mechanism needs to be more sensitive, *clearly*. I think the wall springs could be heavier as well—the Crystalfur wasn't even injured. The Riverdancer dodged the spikes, so maybe they could be lower." As they began discussing the trap, her voice became progressively more enthusiastic.

<Confused agreement!>

Garron smiled at Typo's overenthusiasm. "Hm, I definitely agree on the sensitivity—we can make the plate heavier, so it takes less weight to cut the string. We can try the stronger springs, but I'm worried about them just pushing the plate out of the wall. And I'd love for the spikes to be lower—after all, people have to step on the plate for it to work, so legs are the best target—but we don't have enough room for the plate to drop down if the spikes are too close to the floor."

Talia thought for a moment. "Typo can just hollow out space beneath the floor level, can't he?"

Garron smacked his forehead, having forgotten the dungeon's capabilities. "That's right! Let's try it, then."

They started with lowering the spikes because it was by far the easiest. It only took a few mental images for Garron to convey the right meaning to the dungeon, and soon the holes in the ground had shifted with various grinding, crunching, and popping noises.

<Congratulations!> Garron had gotten better at projecting emotions the more time he spent in the dungeon.

Typo basked in his praise like a proud student. <Pride! Excitement!>

The next two changes were more *frustrating* than anything else. Typo could understand changing the weight of the trigger plate easily enough, but that didn't mean they instantly got the mechanism to the correct sensitivity. It took several more attempts, a few more tests by the Riverdancer, and a minor argument between Garron and Talia to iron out the design.

"Why shouldn't the trap be as sensitive as possible? What if it's an air cultivator or monster?" Talia was vehement, but already she sounded less annoyed at Garron's 'intrusion' on Typo's development.

Garron considered the point. "If I were trying to clear this place, I would just throw a rock on the plate. It needs to tolerate some weight, or it would be too easy to clear."

"Hm... Why don't we make some more sensitive than others? That might trick some cleverpants like you into stepping on a live plate."

Garron gave an involuntary grimace. "You're evil."

"Thank you!" Talia's coloration shifted to a cheerful yellow.

Once they had settled on three appropriate weights, they moved on to the springs in the wall. Unfortunately, as Garron had predicted, the wall itself could only tolerate so much force before collapsing outwards. Still, at Talia's suggestion, they reduced the number of spikes from six to four, which allowed them to increase the force of each spring by a considerable amount.

Talia let out a raspberry-like sound, which should have been blatantly impossible. "Phew! That was tough!"

Garron didn't know if he agreed. Yes, they had been forced to work for a few hours the previous day, and this fine-tuning had taken another, but that was still incredible. He shuddered to think how long this would have taken without Typo to instantly modify the design and perform difficult maneuvers like threading a string through the earth, loading the springs, and placing the pressure plate.

Still, he gave the Wisp a satisfied smile. "Great job. If it's alright, I'll do some cultivation and then we can try out the cage droppers?"

Talia let out a mock sigh. "Alright. Go do your silly human cultivation."

"Doesn't Typo cultivate as well? Then feed you the Essence?" Garron eyed the Wisp skeptically.

"I don't see you *cultivating*!" Talia turned pink as she snapped at him, making Garron laugh as he went to the big room.

He spent a full hour drawing in Essence, refining it, and adding it to his chi spiral. The death of the air-wolves a few days ago had left a good deal of air Essence in the dungeon, which Typo had moved to the big room at Garron's request. He found it very interesting that, even though the dungeon couldn't actually draw in Essence types outside of its affinities, he could still manipulate them somewhat and keep them within his influence or use them to craft things. Still, using that Essence for cultivation was certainly the best thing to do at the moment.

He was progressing quickly thanks to the uninterrupted time in the dungeon, as Andros had noted, only limited by the amount of Essence available to him. Garron was determined to abuse his good fortune as much as possible. "It's about time I get some 'easy' in my life."

Once he had all but depleted the room's Essence, he went back to an impatient Talia, who bobbed up and down when he entered the tunnel. "*Finally*! Okay, let's try your silly cage."

<Agreement.> Typo focused, commanding the wolves as Garron had prepared him to do. Some of the command bled into their connection, and the human felt a minor urge to begin walking toward it himself. Strange, but easy to ignore.

The haggard pair of wolves paced forward and into the big room. It took some effort to lead them to the correct spot, especially since Garron didn't want to be anywhere near the trap when it triggered, but eventually the Riverdancer in front stepped onto the pressure plate, and a huge cage of stone dropped down from the ceiling with a thunderous crash, the stone spikes at its base piercing deep into the earth as it enclosed the yelping monster.

Garron winced. The Riverdancer had tried to jump out of the way, and with its Essence-enhanced speed had actually gotten a leg beyond the cage's bounds. The leg was still beyond the cage, and the rest of the wolf was rolling around on the ground in the cage, whimpering.

<Typo, please absorb it and make a new one.> Garron stepped forward and rammed his sword into the animal's skull.

<Agreement.> The poor wolf vanished, and in moments another was pacing into the room from beyond the tunnel. There was very little in the way of Essence loss when doing things like that, a concept which Garron found fascinating. He

would have expected the dungeon to lose something in the process, but if it did, it was too small to notice.

Talia bobbed impatiently again. "Well, the cage worked. *Yay*! Now about that giant crossbow…?"

Garron shook his head. "Hold on, it still took a while to fall. Someone could escape in that amount of time."

Talia sighed. "So what? Who ever heard of a dungeon with a cage trap? I mean, if that happens it's usually a test, but there's no test here!"

She hadn't liked quite a few of his trap designs, even the lethal ones, because she claimed they were 'unfair.' Apparently, dungeons with a reputation for traps that couldn't be circumvented had trouble getting people to challenge them. It had taken longer than it should have to convince her that, just for now, they shouldn't worry about that. She'd liked the traps which were clearly designed to help Andros and Garron if another human came into the dungeon even less, but had grudgingly allowed them. After all, Typo had reached F-rank eight with the death of Hal.

"We're in a unique situation, remember?" Garron reminded her once again. "Anyway, I think we should just add a few heavy springs to the cage's loading mechanism so it falls faster."

An irritated circle. "Fine. But why not just make the cage heavier?"

Garron chuckled as he remembered asking that same question once upon a time. The engineer had *loved* to demonstrate that one. In fact, though he'd only known the man for a few weeks, Garron had to have seen him drop a small stone and a large stone together a dozen times. He kept ones especially for that purpose in his pouch. "Heavier things don't fall faster than lighter ones—unless there's Essence or something involved, I guess. I've seen some raccoons…"

Talia scoffed. "You do know that *I'm* the will-of-the Wisp here, right? I've got fairy tales covered, thank you very—"

"Gar!" Andros ran into the room a second after his shout

reached Garron's ears. He was emptyhanded, Garron noticed, and his stomach grumbled in complaint.

"What happened?" Garron looked at his friend in concern. He seemed... anxious. Not quite as though they were in danger, but certainly not carefree.

"Ran into a pair of guards." Garron's heart froze, but the tension eased as his friend continued. "I stayed out of their way, but... they're closer than they used to be. There's no animals left close to here, like they've been spooked off."

The chill came back. They knew. Not where they were *exactly*, thank celestial, but enough to make venturing outside at any point a gamble. What if they were caught leaving the dungeon? Moreover, if the guardsmen were spooking wild game from this area, what would they eat?

"Trapped," Garron muttered, though he regretted it as a shadow passed over Andros' face.

"We have to *do* something! Gar, I know you don't want to do it, but I think it might be time to try to make a break for it. If we're careful, we can still get past anyone besides Lars or Jackson. Then we've only got to..." Andros' voice cut off, though Garron was concerned at the note of hysteria in it.

"It won't work. Even if we managed to leave the forest entirely, there's just one way out, and Jackson was standing right on top of it, between us and freedom." They needed to get past him somehow, but Garron was convinced that simply making a break for it would get them captured in moments.

After a long breath of silence, he felt his expression harden. "Typo, I have some questions. Talia, Andros, come here. We need to make a plan."

CHAPTER TWENTY-THREE

Garron was tired, but he hardly cared. It was time for something *exciting*.

Andros' voice was quiet, though a smile could still be heard in it. "Okay. So, you need to feel your Center. Really get *in* there and feel how the Essence is, you know... spinning."

He tried his best to follow the instruction, retreating deep into himself, envisioning the swirling mass of energy at his Center. Once this had been a foul tainted pit, but now it felt... beautiful. Not that he would ever say it out loud.

Andros let out a little breath after a few minutes had passed. "You got it? Alright, now you should be able to feel the boundaries of your Essence, the wall that keeps your spiral in place."

That was easy enough. As soon as he thought about it, it entered his awareness. Almost like thinking about his breathing. *Abyss.* Now he was thinking about his breathing. "*Focus.*"

A moment later, Andros spoke again, "Okay, now you just find the holes in the wall. Should be easy. Found them?"

Garron took a moment, but Andros was already continuing. Still, he quickly located what seemed like empty spaces randomly arranged throughout the borders of his Center.

"Now, you need to pick one. Considering what we're doing, it should be... heart? Maybe the periwinkle one?"

For the first time, Andros' quiet voice sounded uncertain.

Periwinkle? What in the abyss is he—

"Okay, Gar, we've got a choice here. There's a bunch of different meridians to choose from. You want to start with the ones that lead to your hands, but even then there's options." Andros paused, gathering his thoughts. "If you choose the, uh, the peric—the heart meridian, you'll be able to get by on a whole lot less sleep. If you choose the heart, you'll have more endurance and your healing speed will increase. The lower intestine one improves sight and hearing, and the upper one does... I don't know, it goes to your head, so maybe your mind?"

"*What?*" Garron left his trance abruptly, glaring at Andros in annoyance. "First of all, why in the abyss didn't you ask me this *before* I started meditating? Second... what was the first one again?"

Andros laughed easily. "I forgot. When it comes down to it, no offense Gar, but you're kind of weak, physically. So you should open either the heart or periwinkle—whatever it's called. Better endurance or less sleep?"

Garron thought for a moment. In the end, his aching hands provided the answer. "Endurance."

"Good answer! Now—oh yeah, hey, Typo!" Andros shouted, though Garron knew the dungeon could hear even a whisper in his influence. "I need you to be ready to start Garron's heart, just in case!"

Typo seemed startled that Andros had addressed him directly, but he still answered. <Confused... assurance?>

Garron glared. "What the abyss are you planning—"

"Back to your Center! Come on, we're wasting time!" Andros clapped his hands.

It took much less time for Garron to retreat into his Center and find the holes again. Andros guided him to an opening indistinguishable from the rest, and directed him to feed

Essence into it. After his attempts at using Essence blasts, grabbing the Essence in his Center wasn't difficult. However, he'd never needed precision before, so he struggled for a moment with feeding a thread of Essence into the hole. When he finally managed it, he jerked in shock.

The Essence sped along a path Garron hadn't ever noticed in his body, and *impacted* his heart like a sledgehammer. For a moment, Garron felt as if it *had* stopped, but as the Essence looped and burrowed through every part of his heart and continued onwards, he felt it starting to beat normally. He let out a breath he didn't remember holding as the thread of Essence continued to speed down to his upper intestine, looping around in a small pattern before moving on… and picking up speed.

Then the Essence hit his lungs.

Garron felt a flash of pain, and *coughed*. He could feel the black substance from his purification briefly filling his mouth with bitterness before slipping out in a clump. The Essence continued to weave around his lungs, forming the same pattern it had on his heart, but Garron began shaking. He couldn't *breathe*!

The Essence thread continued onwards, and the resistance in his lungs vanished. Garron heaved a breath, losing track of the Essence thread as he focused on feeling air rush into his lungs, smooth, easy and… strong. Even stronger than after he'd purified his Center. He took a deep breath, deeper than he'd ever taken before.

It was wonderful.

Then he started coughing out huge gobs of black phlegm.

"There you go! No heart-starting needed!" Andros' hand pounding his back hardly distracted him from simply *breathing*, but his friend's voice brought a smile to his face even as more and more chunks of *stuff* shot out of his mouth. "Now you won't have to go through the whole 'excruciating pain' thing if you need to do an Essence blast. Oh! Try taking some Essence from the meridian to your eyes."

He waited until he wasn't spewing filth, and though he was still taking huge breaths, glorying in the simple feeling of power suffusing his body, Garron followed the instructions. "*Celestials.*"

For all that Garron found his own chi spiral a massive improvement over the corrupted Center he'd once held, it was still a candle flame next to the sun of Andros' cultivation. His friend's Center was like a swirling storm, howling as it strained to pull Essence deep into itself, and as Garron stared at it, the pattern seemed to shift in three dimensions, revealing progressively smaller and smaller twisters within itself until it disappeared—not because there wasn't more there, but because Garron had reached the limits of his perception.

Garron wondered what it would look like to see Andros actually *cultivate*. That technique seemed to want to pull in Essence the same way a starving man wanted to eat food.

He found that he could even discern his friend's rank. "D-rank two? So fast?"

Andros grinned, though Garron could barely catch the expression, so focused was he on the marvel before him. "Yeah, it's basically straight Essence-accumulation from here 'til rank five. I've already held D-rank two before, so it was easier to get there again. My technique also makes it a little easier than it is for most people."

"Huh." Garron had no doubt that was true. He finally tore his eyes away from Andros' Center, and looked around. The air swirled, thick with Essence, beautiful in its purity. Garron felt as if an entire world had opened up to him as he stared at the energy of the world itself surrounding him. "Andy, thank you. I can't ever thank you enough. Because of you, I'm—"

"No, Gar." The mirth faded from Andros' voice, and he looked seriously into Garron's eyes. "*You* earned this. Not me. *You've* helped *me*, every step of the way. Without you, I'd have been caught a week ago, or died while I was escaping. We're in this together."

Garron considered his friend for a long moment. Finally, he let out a little laugh, gripping his shoulder with a hand that felt stronger than it ever had before. "Alright then. Time to dig together."

While it had been a good break, they still needed to get back to work. Stepping past the area where messy piles of dirt had rested only minutes before, they moved into the side tunnel set into the first big room. Garron ventured into the cramped tunnel until he reached the spot where he'd left his crude spade... then set to digging.

It had seemed like a simple plan when he'd proposed it: use Typo to burrow underneath Jackson. If they continued far enough, they would be able to escape without alerting Jackson to the fact. He would still be searching for them in the forest while they made their escape.

Yet, Garron hadn't realized just how restricted Typo was when it came to manipulating the earth. Yes, he *could* burrow down *slowly* to create a large tunnel system, and he could modify the earth close to his influence to hollow out a few rooms, create traps and the like. But he couldn't extend his influence so quickly *and* compress earth, even *soft* earth, without causing very noticeable seismic activity, as well as cave-ins.

Unfortunately for them, it was still a good idea. Typo couldn't do the digging, but he could support a tunnel that they dug themselves, and help a bit by softening the earth as they moved forward. Which meant there was a *lot* of boring, monotonous work to be done. Work that required lots of *endurance*.

For a solid half hour, Garron didn't mind the constant routine of digging his stone spade into the earth, turning and dumping it behind him, all while Andros moved the dirt away and patted down the sides of the wall as they went. He was too focused on the easy strength he moved with, on the lack of strain he felt as he picked up his pace, and most of all, on the deep, powerful, *easy* breaths he could take in despite the hard work.

Soon, the digging became so second-nature that it was almost a form of meditation, and Garron found it easy to retreat inside himself and examine his meridians. The path looped through his heart, upper intestine, and lungs, as he'd seen, but from there it continued down to his little finger before looping back into his Center. Essence seemed to flow continuously through the channel like a river. Garron thought of the pain he'd experienced before, trying to force Essence directly through his skin. That wouldn't be an issue anymore, and he was grateful for it.

His newfound endurance meant that he and Andros were able to work for hours without rest. His body, especially his arms, was noticeably stronger now as well, and as a result he was able to come closer to matching Andros' pace as they continued.

There was something oddly satisfying about the process, despite how boring it was. The hole in the distance which marked the end of the tunnel grew smaller and smaller as they burrowed forward, until they were finally forced to create a bend in order to avoid a large vein of rock. Luckily, it didn't run too far to the side, so they were able to maintain a relatively straight path west after skirting it.

Typo's help was invaluable—not having to worry about supporting the tunnel saved incalculable hours, and just as importantly, the dungeon made sure their course remained straight.

<Warning. Hunger. Regret.>

With the projection, Garron sighed. "Andy, Typo's too low on Essence to keep going."

"Phew! I could use a break anyway." Andros sounded relieved, but Garron was still worried. They still had a long way to go, and there was only so much Essence Typo could cultivate from their surroundings. Would they be able to make it?

They walked down the narrow tunnel single file. Garron was gratified at how far they'd managed to dig in just the last afternoon and this morning. But now that the novelty of his meridian was fading, he was feeling his own source of discomfort—*hunger*. Essence mitigated the feeling somewhat, but without more meridians open, it wasn't nearly enough. Typo had made them food the previous day, but there was only so much he could spare because creating the food for consumption was extremely Essence-inefficient, and he needed every scrap to extend his influence as far as he was.

They finally exited the tunnel, finding themselves back in Typo's Core room. But before Garron could turn to Andros to ask about food, another sight stopped him in his tracks.

"*Finally.* Taking so long after I go and do all of this... *scouting* for you. No manners." Talia's voice was grumpy, but Garron could still hear a trace of excitement in it. Privately, he thought the Wisp was enjoying her new assignment more than she let on.

Still, he put on a grateful expression. "We're sorry. But what did you find?"

The Wisp huffed. At this point, he'd stopped wondering about the anatomical impossibilities of most noises she made. "Using my incredible talents in *stealth*—"

"You mean turning invisible?" Andros was less than impressed. He'd been slightly miffed at Garron's suggestion that they use the Wisp to scout out their surroundings.

Talia sent a sneering retort, "Can *you* turn invisible? No? Then maybe you should just stay quiet and listen."

They waited for a moment. Finally, Garron prompted her. "Go ahead."

The Wisp zipped around in a circle. "*Well,* there are guards patrolling nearby in shifts, but there's usually only one group in the area at a time. All of the patrols are in pairs, except for one very large man who stomped around for a while by himself and then left. He was a very strong earth cultivator."

"Lars," Andros cut in again. Garron punched his arm.

"Obviously. Keep going, Talia." Garron looked eagerly at her.

She waited a moment, and Garron silently cursed Andros' rudeness as well as the Wisp's sensitivity, but eventually she went on. "Well, none of them said much interesting, mostly complaining about wearing full armor all the time, having to carry the… 'flares,' I think they called them, and saying impolite things about Andros which I thought were *hilarious*."

Andros opened his mouth to cut in, but Garron gave him a warning look.

Talia went on. "But one pair—one was very short and skinny, and the other was almost as big as the earth cultivator—they were talking about something Lars had told them. Apparently, Jackson has hired local mercenaries from the wildlands to the north and south to come and provide reinforcements. Cultivators, they said."

"There's reinforcements coming. Why wouldn't there be?" Garron grumbled ineffectively. It didn't change all that much, but more cultivators—presumably ones stronger than Andros—would just mean they had less time before discovery.

"We need to move faster, Gar." Andros had that slightly panicked look on his face, but in a moment it vanished again.

"I wish we could, but there's only so much Essence Typo has to work with, and we already used a lot of the strength from Hal to make all the new traps and get as far as we have."

<Regret. Apology.>

Garron sent his assurance to the dungeon. In truth, it was his own fault. He hadn't realized how much Essence this tunnel would take, and he'd thought that better traps would be an investment that could easily repay itself in monsters killed. But then they'd been effectively starved of fodder by the guards spooking away all the monsters.

"So we need more Essence. There's all these guards coming around here now…" Andros let his voice trail off meaningfully, but Garron gave a stern look.

"Andy, Hal was one thing, but most of the others aren't that much worse than Ulysses. Luring them in here to kill them isn't the same as—"

"Lars," Andros cut in again.

Garron stared at his friend, working his jaw in an attempt to say the words he was thinking. "Are you *insane?*"

Andros shrugged. "I know he's strong, but how much worse is he than *two* guards? We'll have a much better chance of luring him in here, and I'll bet you twelve Beast Cores he doesn't carry one of those flares. Besides, he's an earth cultivator, and he actually knows techniques. He'd have a *way* better chance of sniffing us out than anyone else."

Garron blinked. "That's... Are you okay, Andy? That made *sense*."

Andros punched him in the arm.

"Ow! You do realize you're stronger than most *bears*, right?" Garron rubbed his arm absently, but he was already thinking. "Fine. But luring him here won't work if we do it like we did with Hal. I want to confirm the flare thing. Talia..."

Garron paused as an idea struck him. "Talia, I have a job for you."

The Wisp sighed.

"How in the *abyss* do you manage to sigh without lungs?"

CHAPTER TWENTY-FOUR

Garron fervently wished he'd chosen to open the meridian that reduced his need for sleep. He would still be exhausted, but at least his eyelids wouldn't be so heavy as well. As he stared at the patch of ground before him, the young cultivator tried to detect anything that would distinguish it from the rest of the forest. He spread the leaves over it, a branch or two as well, but that was all the weight it could take before crumbling.

A whisper at his side interrupted his examination. "Come *on*, Gar, they'll be here soon."

"One more test?" Garron knew his voice was one step from an insane mutter, but he was too focused on the trap before him to care.

Andros grabbed his shoulder and pulled. "You've already done that a dozen times! Listen, it's incredible. He won't be able to avoid it even if Talia *doesn't* mesmerize him perfectly."

Garron gave an involuntary shiver. That was the other major variable in the plan. Well, *one* of the other variables. He'd lost count several hours ago. Still, Andros was right, and he let out a deep breath, nodding. They'd worked through the night to set this up, Typo pushing to extend his influence this far with the dregs of Essence he had left.

Garron had thought of the pit design as a way to prevent what had happened last time with Hal, when the man had realized he was standing on a trap and managed to save himself.

Instead of thin false ground covering the entire hole, they'd made the earth get progressively thinner toward the Center of the pit, so that when the person fell through, the ground around them would fall as well. That way, even Essence-enhanced reflexes couldn't let the target anchor themselves and escape.

That was how it was *supposed* to work, and the last three times he tested it, that was how it *had* worked. But what if the fourth was the time it would fail? Garron meant to start moving, but his feet hadn't actually taken him anywhere.

"*Move*, Gar." Andros finally managed to pull him back, and they walked to the big rock near the dungeon entrance.

"I'm still not sure about this." Garron shot a glance back toward the trap again.

"Calm down. Odds are, the trap will finish him by itself, and we won't need to do anything." Andros pat his jumpy friend on the shoulders, trying to get him to calm down. "I mean, they probably won't kill him, but they'll still injure him enough that he can't fight us."

Garron rolled his eyes at his friend. "I thought you said you were *sure* the spikes wouldn't be enough to kill him?"

He had wanted to give Lars a chance to surrender, so the pitfall terminated in a metal cage Typo had already made for another trap. But Andros had convinced him to place spikes at the bottom, in case the earth cultivator was able to break free—with his durability, even that wouldn't do more than injure him. Given their limited ability to make a stronger nonlethal trap, Garron had reluctantly agreed.

They waited behind the rock for far too long, Garron staring into the little clearing where the trap was set, as though he could *will* it to work better. They'd chosen the spot so they would have a good view of the situation, and the foliage between them and the clearing would obscure them from view, but it quickly strained his neck to continue peering past the bushes and trees to stare at the innocuous patch of ground. Garron hated doing things like this outside of the dungeon; in there, Typo would tell him exactly what was going on all the time.

Andros took in a sharp breath, and Garron's heart froze.

The faint sounds of a man crashing through the forest finally reached his ears. Fear let him ignore his exhaustion for the moment, and he fixed his eyes on the direction of the sounds, past the clearing and into the dense trees beyond. With the forest obscuring his sight, it still took nearly another minute before he saw anything.

Talia came bobbing through the trees first, her light twinkling faintly as it wove around the foliage. Garron stared at her for a moment, then another. He felt his mouth open slightly, and shook his head violently, breaking eye contact with the Wisp. Even from this distance, with all of the plant life obscuring her, she had a certain mesmerizing quality which disrupted his focus. He'd worried that it wouldn't be enough to deal with Lars, despite her claims, but there was little else they could count on.

Soon enough, Garron could catch glimpses of a huge armored figure lumbering through the trees, shoulders slumped forward slightly as it followed the Wisp. Any time it encountered an obstacle smaller than a tree, the giant simply crushed it underfoot—Garron could faintly see the trail of broken branches, crushed leaves, and squashed bushes behind the man as he continued forward. *Perfect.* Garron watched with bated breath as Lars wove around the trees, following Talia's bobbing light, though a large part of him wanted to duck behind the rock they were hiding behind and simply leave it to the Wisp.

As they got closer to the clearing, some of Garron's fear began to fade. It seemed as though this part of the plan would work, at least. Now what? If the pit trap malfunctioned somehow, they would simply abandon the attempt. That would be a disaster, giving away their position to the enemy, but there would be no other way—they couldn't face the man on open ground. But Garron *had* tested the trap as many times as Typo's Essence reserves would allow, so celestial willing, they could count on it functioning properly.

What else? Once Lars was in the dungeon, it should be as simple as demanding his surrender. If he refused, Garron could have Typo release the second trap they'd prepared, and that would be it. If the spikes didn't finish him first. But what if—

Andros' second intake of breath made Garron's eyes snap back into focus, and he looked around wildly. Talia was in the clearing now, bobbing in her hypnotic pattern, but beyond her the armored form was standing still, and as the image resolved itself, Garron took a breath of his own.

Lars was pushing a leafy branch away from his face, shaking his head as he did so. He'd broken the eye contact, and now he was close enough for Garron to see as he took a clanking step backward.

"*Abyss.* No… Calm down," Garron whispered, hardly making a sound. It was bad, but this wasn't the worst outcome. Hopefully, the guardsman wouldn't even realize what had happened properly. As long as he didn't suspect how close he was to their hiding place, they could always try again. Still, it was a blow. They didn't have all that much time before the mercenaries came. A breeze washed over their rock, kicking up some twigs and loose leaves and making Garron blink. He swiped at his eyes and refocused on Lars. Maybe Talia could…

He blinked his eyes rapidly. Maybe it *was* better this way—he clearly needed some sleep. Garron could have sworn he'd just seen a slender, black-haired figure shooting toward the clearing at top speed. Now the figure was slowing as it approached the clearing, making no effort to remain quiet as it entered the open air.

Garron knew he should just look to his side, just to make sure, but he couldn't bear to do it. First, he pinched himself. *Ow.* So, not a nightmare. Then he reached a shaking hand out to the side to grab Andros. His hand closed on open air, and he let out a sigh at his friend's rash actions.

"Hey, *Lar-ge!*" The taunt was almost loud enough to be a shout. A spike of fear pierced Garron directly through the heart. Andros was standing a dozen feet away from Lars, arms crossed, tapping his abyssal *foot*. Garron sincerely wished his friend was still next to him, so he could try strangling the idiot.

The giant guardsman gave an almost comical start of surprise, but almost instantly he focused on Andros with a snarl. "You! What the aby—"

"You know, sometimes it's funny to hear you talk. I mean, you've opened your meridians, right? Isn't that supposed to make you smarter?" Garron could see the mock shudder even from so far away. "I wonder what you were like before you started licking Jackson's boots for a living."

Garron started thinking *very* quickly. Lars would have to be a moron to fall for Andros taunting, but at the least the guard would be distracted for a few moments. How could he use that to his advantage?

"You *brat!*" Lars ran forward in a straight line toward Andros like a charging bull, picking up speed until his form blurred slightly. A blast of Essence preceded him, flying at Andros' stomach, but the young cultivator dodged it with contemptuous ease, a mocking smile on his face. Lars roared, not even noticing when a step cracked the ground beneath him. He *did* figure it out when ground fell away beneath him and the earth in a five-foot radius around him collapsed inward.

The huge man dropped through the hole in the ground in an instant, the surrounding earth covering the opening and muffling his yell.

"*Huh.*" Garron supposed that for all his power, Lars *was* a moron.

"Hey, Gar! Did you hear me call him '*Lar*-ge'? Do you know how long I've wanted to do that?" Andros' breathless laughter broke the sudden silence in the forest. He sprinted back toward

Garron as he shouted the words, but the stoic young man ignored his friend; they had an objective to complete.

As his friend hopped clear over the mossy rock, coming to rest beside him with a wild grin on his face, Garron stood. "Come on."

The mirth fell away from Andros' face, and he gave a hard nod. They turned and ran for the dungeon.

CHAPTER TWENTY-FIVE

<Greeting! Excitement! *Hunger.*>

As he ran into the tunnels, Andros at his side, Garron sent a greeting of his own. Then he returned to business. <How is he?>

He almost stumbled as the dungeon sent him an image of Lars howling as he smashed away at the interlocked bars of metal they'd used for his cage. His greaves had been sheared open in several spots, and Garron could see blood dripping down over them, but at his feet were a trio of shattered stone spikes. The trap hadn't killed or even crippled him, it seemed. Andros grabbed his shoulder, pulling him to a sudden stop. "Gar, focus!"

Reality reasserted itself. They were at the pit traps. "Sorry. He's alive. Still in the cage, still standing, and *furious.*"

<Typo, is *everything* in position?> With the word *everything*, he sent images of the traps he'd prepared, the wolves, and Cutie. "Abyss, even I'm calling him that now."

<Confirmation.> Along with the projection, Garron felt an undercurrent of fear emanating from the dungeon. Or... was that his own?

Garron wanted a moment to take a deep breath and steel his nerves, but Andros was already running toward the tunnel's exit. With a sigh, Garron followed, pausing only to pick up the sword he'd left at the edge of the tunnel. They'd been severely limited in options for where to have the trap deposit Lars. Garron and Andros had been forced to do a good bit of the digging themselves, with Talia standing as lookout through the night, and they'd needed a spot with the fewest obstructions—stone, groundwater, extensive tree roots—as possible. Since Garron insisted they at least *try* to trap the guardsman, they'd needed the space for a cage.

That left the first room as the only option, but they'd been forced to position the cage in an awkward spot, off in a corner out of view of the entrance. Which meant that as they ran out into the room, Garron had a moment of panic as he tried to find Lars. When he finally located the man, he wasn't sure whether to laugh or cry.

Unlike the massive stone affair which was set to drop down from the sky at the pressure plate's trigger, Garron had modeled the steel cages after those used to hold Lord Tet's birds. Typo had taken the material from the three cages he'd made for another trap, and formed a dozen pillars of steel anchored deep into the floor and ceiling, crisscrossed by wide, flat bands of metal; which left the man only partly visible.

All Garron could see now was a single, bloodshot eye. Lars' voice was already hoarse from shouting. "You… I'm going to *kill* you two!"

"Oh no, I'm so scared of the moron in the cage!" Andros was gleeful as he considered Jackson's lieutenant. "I can't believe how easy it was to trick you, *Lar*—"

"We have you trapped," Garron interjected with as much strength as he could muster, though his voice still sounded small to his ears. "Surrender, give up as much Essence as you can without dying, and we'll let you live."

There was a moment of ringing silence. Then Lars let out a

brutal laugh of his own. "Was that *you*, fishy? Oh, I see your Center doesn't look like a latrine pit anymore."

Garron ignored the jab, but he didn't like the savage note in the guard lieutenant's voice. <Typo, get ready to trigger the trap.>

<Confirmation.> Typo was more focused than he'd ever been, perhaps because of Garron's own urgency.

Through another hole in the cage, Garron could see a flash of white teeth. "Doesn't matter. *You* don't matter. Jackson wants you dead, so I guess… You know what? *Sure*. You can have some of my *Essence*."

"*Down!*" Andros grabbed Garron, throwing both of them to the floor in an instant.

<Now, Typo!>

In a moment, there was a rumble and a deep, sustained *crash* as all of the rocks and earth Typo had been able to muster and store above the cage hit the ground. Garron could hear the ringing as the bars were struck, the yell as the rocks buried the guardsman, and a wave of guilty relief washed over him. It was replaced by panic when a powerful *shove* sent him rolling away from his position, and he heard another brutal, breathless laugh.

"You… really thought that… little thing would stop me?"

From beside Garron, Andros shouted. "Sounding a bit tired there. You want to take a nap before we start?"

The wordless snarl shook Garron out of his momentary paralysis. Scrambling to his feet, he took stock of the situation. The cage had a hole torn in its side, a mess of dirt and rocks spilling out of it into the room. Lars was standing among twisted shards of broken metal, apparently unharmed aside from the wounds in his legs. Even as Garron watched, Lars grabbed a warhammer that had been mostly buried and rushed at the waiting Andros with impossible speed.

<Typo! Send in the mobs!>

<Assurance.>

Andros ducked a wide swing, raising a hand. For a moment,

Lars' eyes bulged through under his helmet. As he jumped away, there was a *pop* and the technique vanished. Andros had apparently planned for that, because he was already lifting the other hand. Garron could almost *see* the blast of wind shooting toward Lars. But even that was a feint. As the Essence broke against the guardsman's armor, Andros shot diagonally across the guardsman, blasted into the air, then his foot was in Lars' face, kicking with the force of a hurricane.

A giant hand grabbed the outstretched leg.

Garron drew in a sharp breath, but his friend was already twisting as if he wasn't midair, wrapping his other leg around the huge man's neck and swinging around it, folding his knee to minimize the effect of Lars' grip. The guardsman growled, hauling on the leg, clearly intending to pull Andros off of him.

The first Riverdancer chose that moment to shoot forward and sink its teeth into the open wound on Lars' leg. In a moment, the second joined it on the other side. A golden-furred streak leapt up, scrabbling past Andros and clawing for the lieutenant's eyes.

Hope rose in Garron's chest. For a moment, the guardsman seemed as though he might just topple from the weight of the attacks. Then, with a muffled scream, Lars shook his legs in turn, sending the Riverdancers flying. Dropping his hammer, he reached for his face and tossed Cutie away like a toy. He grabbed Andros and threw him to the ground, where the young Noble bounced and let free a gout of blood. Then he raised a hand and pointed it at the downed teen.

"Not enough time." Garron was already running forward, and he found his step matched by a pair of Crystalfurs beside him, and raised his own hand. "*Earth.*"

The blast of Essence slowed him for a moment, but he managed to direct it at Lars' outstretched hand. The strike felt pitiful compared to what he'd just seen Andros do, but it was enough to knock Lars' hand to the side an instant before the guard let out another roar and Essence of his own blasted outwards.

Garron was still several feet away, but he had to cover his eyes as the chips of stone went flying. By the time he looked back, Andros was on his feet, panting, and Lars was picking up his hammer. "Brat. All that training, all that *money*, and you're still this weak."

Andros grinned, teeth stained red from a split lip. "Still strong enough to beat *you*."

Lars was on Andros in a blink, hammer swinging down as if it weighed nothing, but the air cultivator danced to the side, then whipped another kick at the guardsman's face. An armored hand shot up again to grab the leg, but something *shot* through Andros' shoe before he could, blasting the leather apart and throwing Lars' head back. It wasn't enough to put the D-ranker out of the fight, but he was distracted for an instant as his balance was thrown.

That was when the Crystalfurs finally joined the brawl, Garron a few steps behind them. The stone monsters' claws punched through armor, leaving huge rents running down the breastplate as they moved to take bites at Lars' greaves. Garron took the opportunity to stab at exposed flesh. To his relief, his sword managed to slide between metal, and he pushed forward with all his might.

"Defense technique?" He couldn't pierce Lars' skin, so Garron had a moment to stare in shock as Lars recovered his balance. One hand swept a Crystalfur away—though the monster's feet were anchored in the stone—and then a hammer was descending on Garron's face. Despite Lars' loss in speed, the blow still came too fast for Garron to register anything but dull metal filling his vision.

Something slammed into him from the side, and wind rushed around him. Garron stumbled, looking around wildly. They were across the room, and Andros was already turning to shoot back toward Lars.

"Andy, get him to the—" Before he could finish the sentence, Andros had already shot away, kicking up a cloud of dust in his wake. Garron sighed, though part of him was still shaking at the memory of that hammer, inches away from crushing his face. <Typo, the bolt trap is ready?>

Typo jerked his attention away from the fight. <Confirmation.>

Garron exhaled slowly. Now he just had to get the man in position, and hope that the trap would work like they'd intended. He ran over to the spot in question, a pressure plate set into the middle of the room, and turned to locate Lars.

It was like watching a whirlwind assault a mountain. Andros moved with an insane speed, each move enhanced with a burst of wind, every attack explosive and infinitely graceful. Lars had no chance of blocking every punch, kick, elbow, and knee that the young Noble threw at him. Dents were appearing in his armor as strike after strike landed; all while the guardsman furiously tried to pin down his prey. Stone claws were tearing into him, Riverdancers were worrying at his wounds, and a snarling young lion was leaping for his neck, teeth bared.

The problem was, it just wasn't *enough*. As Cutie tried to sink his teeth into exposed flesh, Garron could see—almost *feel*—the Essence emanating from Lars when he engaged his defensive technique. The young lion's teeth failed to pierce flesh, and Lars attempted to backhand the creature while swinging a slow hammer at Andros' flickering form.

That hand swept through empty air as the water monster twisted, landing on his feet and pouncing for the guardsman's legs. At the same time, Andros flowed around Lars in a blink, rounding the man and lifting a leg straight into the air. His foot slammed down on the back of the guard's helmeted head, and even with his technique active, the man's head snapped forward.

Garron focused inwards. <Typo.>

Lars whirled, speed restored as he abandoned his defense, hammer catching Cutie as he brought it around.

<Query?>

Andros skipped back smoothly, and the hammer blurred through empty air.

"Stay calm," Garron whispered to himself, before focusing on Typo again. <I need a—>

Lars' hand came up, and an arc of force caught Andros in the stomach. With a grunt, the young Noble went flying, landing across the room with a dull *thud*. Lars tensed, ready to bound after his prey. Without looking, he threw a kick at a Crystalfur which leapt for his side, then raised his hammer at Andros.

Garron threw the rock Typo had deposited in his hands. The stone hit the guard's helmet with all the force Garron could muster—and pinged off without leaving a dent. But the huge man's head whipped around, and a snarl to match the lion's tore out of him. Instead of jumping at Andros, the man turned, and shot for Garron with a blast of force destroying the ground he had stood on.

The young cultivator stumbled back frantically, and whipped another rock forward. Not at the armored giant slamming into the floor before him, but at an innocuous patch of ground behind the man which concealed a stone plate. Garron threw himself to the side, blessing Talia for convincing him to make this trigger *hyper*-sensitive.

Garron could hear the muffled *crack* that split the air. Not the *thrum* of a giant crossbow firing its bolt, or the *thump* as the bolt slammed into the target. The sound of wood splintering and string snapping. The trap had failed.

"Feces, abyss, abyssal *feces!*" A shiver ran down his spine, and without looking, he knew there would be a huge man standing above him, hammer raised. He rolled to the side, but it wouldn't be enough. Not with Lars' power.

A snarling hiss filled his ears. He felt something jump over him, and a moment later, an incoherent roar of rage came from where Lars was standing. Garron struggled to his feet, feeling flashes of pain all along his side where he'd hit the ground, but he was already looking around. The first thing he saw was Andros. His friend was on all fours now, breathing heavily and clearly trying to stand. Garron couldn't see any visible injury on his friend, and a flash of relief passed over him. His eyes locked on Lars.

The man was screaming, hammer smashing down again and again onto the earth as he tried to hit the mass of yellow fur before him. Cutie twisted and leapt, moving like flowing water, and each strike missed. As the lion sidestepped another blow and Lars turned, Garron could see that there was blood dripping down his face, and his left eye was a mess of red.

Lars raised a hand toward the snarling lion and a blast of Essence ploughed a furrow in the earth. The cat was already leaping backwards, but the shockwave still caught him, sending him flying even further.

Garron's eyes widened. <Typo, make Cutie stay *right* there!> <Confirmation!>

Garron turned and ran for the lion, feeling from the shaking of the earth that Lars was doing the same. The man bellowed—promising death for the cat—just as Garron dove forward, feeling chips of earth shower him as he scrambled to his feet and kept running. He spared a look over his shoulder in time to see Lars slam his hammer on a Crystalfur in passing, smashing through the creature's armor in an instant. "Keep running!"

The young cultivator reached the spot where the lion was waiting, still snarling in Lars' direction but remaining still. Carefully, he stepped around the creature, turning to face the giant running toward him.

Blood was dripping onto the ground with every step the massive earth cultivator took. He limped slightly, armor dented where it wasn't ripped apart, and his one working eye was fixed on Garron and his companion. He screamed, hammer raised and ready to slam down on them. Garron watched intently.

Something flashed in the corner of his eye, and his gaze flicked to see Andros standing on shaky legs in the corner of the room. Garron raised a hand as his friend shot forward. Lars was feet away. "*Air*."

A blast of wind hit Andros midair, an instant before his foot contacted Lars' head. Garron's Essence was too weak to send his friend flying, but the blast nudged Andros past the guardsman, and he kept going to land among the loose earth spilling out of Lars' cage. The lumbering guardsman didn't appear to notice through his charge at Garron, his lips pulled back to reveal bloodstained teeth.

Garron stepped forward and stomped. It took precious instants for anything to happen, and Lars kept running as loose earth fell around him, drawing back for the strike.

The falling stone cage's edge caught him on the shoulders, slamming into him with the force of a rockslide. His hammer tumbled to the ground beside him as the abyssal cultivator *finally* fell with a cry. The cage had gone tumbling backwards at the impact, landing with a great *thud* on its side behind Garron. "Yes!"

Lars' arms twitched. The man's armor had been smashed against his skin, and both of his arms were splayed at odd angles, his shoulders clearly dislocated. He shouldn't have been able to move, but he still raised his head, and Garron could *feel* the last of his Essence gathering.

Cutie pounced forward until he was face-to-face with Lars. The young monster was beginning to lose his black spots, and the beginnings of a mane were forming around his neck. As Garron stumbled to the side, trying to avoid Lars' last strike, he could see the monster's yellow eyes staring the guardsman down. Cutie opened his mouth, and roared for the first time.

The sound had all of the bestial majesty Garron remembered, but instead of the grinding of stone, it contained the crash of a waterfall. In shock, Garron watched as water *shot* out of the lion's mouth, focused and sped by Essence, directly at Lars' face.

Garron hadn't realized how deeply pressurized water could cut. The blast lasted for an instant, and he got the impression it wouldn't have worked from much farther away, but weakened as the guardsman was, it was enough. It took moments for Typo to absorb the giant earth cultivator's body.

<Satisfaction.> That was all Garron got from Typo, before

the dungeon's attention was overwhelmed by the flood of Essence, and a wash of relief swept over him.

"Garron!" Andros was on his feet again, though he swayed slightly. His shirt was torn across the middle, and Garron could see dark, bruised skin, but otherwise his friend looked unharmed. Cultivation, food, and a little rest would fix him up. Apparently he agreed, because he quietly laid down, and Garron could feel him drawing in what air Essence was left in the room with the force of a twister.

"*Hate* fighting earth cultivators," was all Andros mumbled before closing his eyes.

Garron sat down with a thump, leaning against the toppled stone cage behind him. Cutie came stalking over and laid a wet head in his lap, purring.

Garron stroked the cat's fur slowly, taking heaving breaths. "Typo… had better… hurry up and process… that Essence. He needs to make me some abyssal… *food.*"

CHAPTER TWENTY-SIX

When he awoke the following morning, Garron felt like a new person. It was amazing what food and sleep could do to someone who'd been without either.

Andros was once again his old self, bragging about the previous day's battle. "I still can't believe he fell for that! Remember when I called him *Lar-ge?*"

"I remember." Garron tossed a shovelful of dirt over his shoulder. "I remember that defensive technique he used too. It was... familiar."

"*Yeah.*" Andros moved the dirt down the tunnel with a growl. His weakness yesterday had stemmed from rapid Essence loss, Garron had been relieved to find out. While Garron slept, Andros had absorbed all of the air Essence left in the dungeon, then went out and cultivated in the trees for hours. "He stole that technique from the repository. It was in the memory stone I gave you."

Garron had already shoveled out two more spadefuls by the time Andros returned, and he dumped a third onto the pile as he considered. With Typo's help, he felt more like he was moving earth out of his way than digging, but over time it added up. "I heard you talking to Jackson about it, but... how much did they take?"

Andros let out a bitter laugh. "Jackson took pretty much every fire technique in there, and he must have given Lars that one as well. No way he's managed to actually *learn* all of them. Then there's the Beast Cores—there's barely two dozen left— the alchemical stock, the gold and silver... Abyss, Lars raided the *wine cellar* down to nothing!"

Garron frowned as Andros went to transfer the dirt. Typo was being strategic with extending his influence, which meant they had to move dirt out of their way and far back enough for Typo to absorb it to move as fast as possible. When Andros returned, one question was filling Garron's mind. "How much worse would a fight with Jackson be?"

They both paused for a moment, looking at each other. Andros touched his midsection, where Garron knew there was still heavy bruising. Typo had wiped away most of Garron's own minor injuries, though he seemed better at cuts and the like than blunt-force injuries. He'd even offered to replace the blood Garron had lost from injuries in the past few days, but Garron declined. He remembered too well how the failed attempts at making monsters went; he wasn't going to let the dungeon alter him without *much* finer control.

"I'm not so good against earth cultivators like Lars—they counter my fighting style. Jackson could beat Lars in a fight with one hand tied behind his back so... it'd go a lot worse."

Garron shivered at the memory of Andros being brought to his knees by the fight with Lars. He'd been doing incredibly well considering the difference in rank, but if Jackson was *that* much stronger... Garron was glad they'd thought of a way to get out without fighting him.

Andros grinned at him, showing a streak of dirt where he had wiped away some sweat. "Then again, now that Typo upgraded the mobs, maybe it *wouldn't* be that bad!"

"Hm, maybe. I just want to see what he'll be like once he hits the D-ranks." Garron was skeptical; even that advancement wouldn't be enough to give them the edge against Jackson, but it would certainly be a boon.

Andros gave a noncommittal shrug, grabbing another pile of earth. "Well, Talia said he was right on the edge. Still, breaking into the D series can take days, so maybe it's better if he holds off until we're out of here."

Garron sighed, and felt a thread of sadness extending across the link to Typo. The dungeon was at the brink of breaking through, but he was also expending Essence to help them. Part of him wondered if the sadness had more to do with the fact that they'd be leaving soon… but Garron couldn't help but be proud of their progress. He looked back down the darkness of the tunnel. "We've gotten pretty far. How much longer before we start slanting it up again?"

Andros paused, looking back at Garron with a speculative look. "If we keep our pace, we'll hit the tree line in… maybe a day and a half? But we should probably try to take another day after that. We really want to get as far out as we can."

Garron shrugged and kept working. That would be acceptable, especially with Lars out of the picture. It would be *that* much more difficult for Jackson to find them. The further out they surfaced, the less likely that they would still be spotted by Jackson—a prospect which still worried Garron. "Well, *I* say we take a break."

"Again? Is this just so you can work on that trap again?" Andros was already several meters down the tunnel, and he didn't look back to Garron.

"I'm *tired*!" Garron called the words to his friend's back, receiving a snort in reply.

"We opened your heart meridian. Superhuman endurance, remember?"

"I'm… still getting used to it!" Garron lied with a smile on his face.

Andros blew out a mock sigh. "Take fifteen minutes to play. Then we're working for a few *hours*."

"Fifteen minutes?" Garron dropped the spade eagerly. "It'll take me that long to get to the end of the tunnel!"

"*Fine.* One hour, but I get a break after you. It still doesn't feel like we put in those ventilation shafts." Andros wiped ineffectually at his face again, worsening the mud.

It did take Garron a full fifteen minutes to jog down the tunnel. With his newfound endurance, he guessed that meant the tunnel was a full two miles long now, and that was with only two days of work put into it! Garron knew almost nothing about digging, but he had a feeling that any excavator would sell his soul to the abyss for production speed like that.

As he got closer to the dungeon, he sent out a message. <Typo.>

<Greetings! Query?> Garron smiled at the increased complexity of the dungeon's emotional projection. From his 'query,' Garron got the sense the dungeon was asking 'is it playtime?'

Garron tipped his head forward conspiratorially. <Yes, but don't let Andros hear that.>

<Agreement.> Garron got the feeling that, if the dungeon had a head, it would be nodding seriously in return. First, they ran through all of the traps they had set. They'd finally gotten around to installing the springs in the stone cage trap, so now it would shoot downwards much faster. Still not a perfect solution, but better than before at least. But there were other traps that needed more drastic improvements.

Garron frowned as he looked at their current project. <It didn't break yet?>

<Confirmation.> The dungeon's cautious optimism radiated through their connection.

Garron tossed a rock onto a patch of earth. There was a momentary *hiss* as a string released, and then...

Crack.

"Celestial Feces!" Garron stared daggers at the hole in the wall through which a huge crossbow bolt should be flying out. They'd tried reinforcing the wood with bands of metal, replacing the braided gut-string with wire, even reducing the draw weight. None of it had *worked*!

When he had thought of other ways to use the pulley system the engineer made to lift heavy objects into the air, drawing back a string on a crossbow had seemed like an easy prospect. The system—which he'd actually managed to make *correctly*, anchoring the drawstring directly to a pulley just as the engineer's system had been designed—allowed them to hold a powerful crossbow in tension for long periods of time. Except, apparently over those long periods, the wood of the bow just warped, and when the tension was removed, the entire structure snapped.

"Is it just a problem of material?" Garron had realized during the night of preparation for battle with Lars that he quite liked muttering to himself. "Hm, maybe if we anchor the —no, at this point we should just get it loaded as the —hold on."

<Typo, I need you to make *this*.>

Once Garron had figured out how to use the pulleys properly, a world of possibilities had opened up to him. The smaller cage traps—now dotted all around the tunnels in place of many of the pits—used counterweights hooked up to pulley systems in order to operate. When triggered, twin weights behind either wall fell down, and pulleys redirected their force into cords running through the floors. The cages were laid in two sections under the ground, and each piece was anchored so that it functioned as a lever. When the cords pulled on the 'levers,' the sections sprung out of the ground like claws closing in on a victim from below.

That one had been a *little* complicated, but with Typo's help, the execution hadn't taken that much time. He'd regretted it after they'd begun running out of Essence, however. Still, the same system could be added to the crossbow, so that instead of remaining drawn at all times, the pressure plate would release counterweights which would draw the bow and release it immediately.

Typo processed the images Garron sent his way. <Confused agreement? Confirmation.>

Garron wondered if Typo would have been able to do this before absorbing Lars' Essence. There was only so much imagining he could do, especially considering how much of this was impossible for Garron to see, but the dungeon was beginning to grasp Garron's intentions on a deeper level the more they worked.

Several minutes passed as Garron wandered around the dungeon, passing mobs and petting Cu—*the lion*.

Before long, Typo's awareness returned. <Triumph! Readiness.>

Garron blinked. That had been fast. <Good job! Alright, let's—>

"Garron! Andros! Get out here! You need to see this." Talia's voice preceded her as she whizzed into the room, bobbing up and down in agitation. Garron raised an eyebrow. Every time she'd reported back from scouting, she'd at least *pretended* to be disinterested in what she'd found. What was going on?

Garron ran over to the tunnel, calling down as loudly as he could, "Andy! Come over here! Talia wants to tell us something!"

He was almost certain that Andros could hear him—his friend's ears were incredibly sharp, and sound carried far in the tunnel—so he just waited, shooting glances at Talia. Part of him wanted to ask what had the Wisp bobbing impatiently up and down even as she asked Typo about the traps they'd worked on, but that wouldn't be fair to Andros.

In almost half the time it had taken Garron, Andros' slender form came running up the tunnel, his face growing brighter as he reached the downward slope toward the exit. "What's going on?"

Talia was still talking with Typo, but the moment Andros appeared, she cut herself off and whizzed over. "You two, come up outside for a minute. There's something you'll want to see."

Garron thought she sounded a little worried, and he began to frown. "Is it safe?"

"It was the last time I checked, but... I'll go first. Just come up. Hurry." The Wisp flew away, turning invisible before she left the room. Garron exchanged a worried glance with Andros, but there wasn't much to say.

"So dramatic. Why can't she just tell us?" Andros wasn't breathing hard, but his face was flushed from his run. He frowned with irritation at the entrance Talia had disappeared through.

Garron started walking, resigned to just going along with this. "Let's just go see."

The tunnels were even more crammed with traps after their renovations, but Garron was intimately familiar with their layout, and Andros still found it simple to just hop over most everything. They were up in minutes, though Andros poked his head outside cautiously before they left the dungeon entirely.

Talia was waiting for them, still bobbing, but she gave them a moment to take in the surroundings. It wasn't hard to see why she'd called them out. A haze of smoke hung in the air, and the scent of burning wood filled Garron's nostrils. It was the middle of the day, so he couldn't locate the fire by light alone, but he had a good idea where to look. All he could see was the thick plume of heavy, dark smoke rising into the air, twisting and whirling as the wind caught it. West. Their exit, and the place where Jackson had made his camp.

"They just started, maybe an hour ago? A tall, thin fire cultivator, and he's having the guardsman chop down anything that won't burn. He seemed... I don't know, calm, but like he might blow any second."

"That sounds like him," Andros muttered, but he was staring at the fire. "How long do you think he'll take to get here?"

"He was using a powerful technique, but he *is* only in the D-ranks, and it's not summer. It depends upon how much the fire spreads by itself, but... maybe a day and a half? If he works through the night and he's lucky, it could reach here by tomorrow afternoon. That could change depending on how he decides to spread it, but then the more area he covers, the likelier he'll get it to catch properly." Talia sounded surprisingly certain. Garron wondered just how long she'd spent in this forest. Had she witnessed a wildfire before?

Andros winced. "That's..."

"*Dangerous.*" Garron finished the thought heavily. They had to assume the worst. Even Talia's more conservative estimate meant they wouldn't be able to get their tunnel past the tree line in time. Of course, the fire reaching them wouldn't do much on its own, but it *would* clear the ground for a search, and narrow the area for Jackson. Once the cultivator had a clear field to see, Typo's influence would make him stand out like a beacon. Not to mention the mercenaries on their way. They were running out of time on every front.

"I mean, we could just carry on like we've been doing. If he's shrinking the tree line, the tunnel will be shorter, won't it?" Andros' voice had a note of forced cheer.

"It'll still be open ground, and he'll have watchers. I bet he isn't just standing in the middle of the fire all the time, is he, Talia?" Garron looked over at the bright mote of light hanging in the air.

The Wisp shook in the negative. "No. He only went out to stoke the fires when they started dying."

"Celestial. I mean, if we really push it, and Typo helps a bit more, we can get the tunnel out past the old tree line by tomorrow morning, I think. But then he'll just catch us, or one of his guards will light a flare and then he'll just be chasing us again." Now even the false cheer was gone from Andros' tone as he considered the rising smoke.

"Flare?" Garron whipped his head around. "Talia, are guards still doing patrols outside of the fire?"

The Wisp bobbed in a strangely good approximation of a nod. "They're heavy to the north and south, to try to box you in, I suppose."

"Are they still in pairs?" Garron impatiently waited for the answer.

After an anxiety-inducing moment, the Wisp answered. "No, but they're much closer together now. Shouting distance, almost. I don't think you'd be able to kill one without alerting the others."

Garron bared his teeth in a wicked smile. "I need you to find me a guardsman and ask him a favor."

The Wisp huffed. "You do *know* I'm a Dungeon Wisp, right? Dungeon Wisp. As in, I should be *in* a dungeon. Why not do it yourself?"

He clenched his fist. "We're going to be busy digging. We're getting out of here tonight."

CHAPTER TWENTY-SEVEN

Ulysses was wondering if there was a way he could beat Jackson back to the estate, grab Mylena and Myra, and get the abyss *out* before the madman found them.

"A forest fire to drive them out." He muttered the words, looking around warily. Not for the boys, but for any guardsmen who might report him to Jackson. "They're abyssal *children*."

The 'man' terrified Ulysses; he rarely went anywhere without a corona of fire dancing around him, and he would fly into uncontrollable rages at random moments. Ulysses was certain that Jackson wouldn't let him leave. He was relieved the madman had let him *live*. Walking aimlessly around the stretch of forest he was meant to patrol, Ulysses was thankful that the wildlife was scared off by the other guards. He was supposed to be looking for the boys, but he wasn't trying.

They'd been in the camp at the edge of the tree line. Ulysses had been standing by Franklin and Geran; both relatively low-ranked men who'd begun getting the same hunted look in their eyes that Ulysses knew he had. Jackson had been standing at the edge of the tree line for a solid hour, and they'd all known that he was waiting for Lars. The flames grew larger with every minute he waited, until Ulysses couldn't even see the man underneath.

Jackson kicked down a tree at the start of the second hour. He screamed something incoherent about children and weaklings, the flames rising around him as he spoke. Ulysses had grown sick watching it. There was something… *wrong* about the way the fire moved, swirling, spreading like it was alive and hungry. But then, perhaps that was just Jackson's rage coloring his perception.

Despite the heat, he'd shivered at the look in Jackson's eye when the flames spread to the underbrush. Even now, every few steps Ulysses took his gaze flicked west and south, where the haze of smoke was the worst. He couldn't help but imagine poor Garron, with his illness, trying to deal with the smoke-filled air, or even Andros running to escape the flames and being spotted. He'd understood going out to catch the boys—apparently, they'd even been stealing from the Lord's vault—but this was too far. *Beyond* too far, to tell the truth. How could he participate in this… *hunt?*

"Should have listened to Mylena." He tramped through the underbrush, wincing at the crackle of every leaf. Not because of the noise, but because it meant that they were dry. How easily would this underbrush go up in flames? "No Lord hires math tutors from his *guard*."

Truth be told, Ulysses didn't have nearly the skill with numbers he'd imagined when he left the village with Mylena, seeking a Noble who might want a teacher for their child. In fact, Jackson, who managed the estate in the Lord's absence, had more mathematical knowledge than he did. He still wished he could have spoken to the Lord at least once, or even just *seen* the man. But the war raged on, and it was only thanks to Ulysses' own weakness that he hadn't already fought and died in it.

Privately, Ulysses held out hope that Lord Tet would finish his work for the Guild and finally return home. *He* could put a stop to Jackson's madness, perhaps in time to save the boys. Perhaps.

At the least, he preferred this simple patrolling duty to what he'd been assigned the first days in the forest. Scouting the tree line—and finding how open it was to sight from their camp—had been easy enough. But once he ventured into the forest, he'd seen more horrors than he could have imagined. Wolves that shot through the air like arrows, badgers that smashed the ground with incredible force, even the abyssal *deer* nearly took his arm off with their invisible slashes of air.

It had been harrowing enough to reach the southern river, and before he'd gotten within a foot of the water, he'd seen a massive shadow pass downstream. A spout of frothing white water at least a dozen feet in height had bloomed out of nowhere, following the river's current until it was out of sight. His single glance at the other side of the river had sent him running back, certain that *no one* would be escaping over it.

But the *east*.

Ulysses still had nightmares about a spear-like beak, dead black eyes, a body cast in steel. The shrieking had filled his ears, and he'd *known* that his first move would earn him a talon to the neck. He'd been moments away from the end, he was sure, when the boys had swooped in to save him. Even Garron had been running, shouting, fighting with Andros. When the mist bird began chasing them, he had done more to aid their escape than Ulysses himself.

The two teenagers had worked together better than any two guardsmen in Jackson's company, and when they'd finally escaped and spoken, both of them had shown an intelligence and drive that had astounded him. Garron, especially, seemed radically different than he'd been before running away. He'd never seen the boy so happy and healthy before, even hunted as he was.

"Um, excuse me?"

Ulysses nearly jumped out of his own skin. In a flash, his hand went for his sword, and he drew out—a handkerchief.

Fumbling, he dropped the little square of cloth and reached for his sword again, more carefully. All the while, he looked around for the source of the voice. It had been female… there were no women in Jackson's guard, so what was a random civilian doing out here?

He'd done a full circle, checking high and low, and he hadn't seen anyone. Suddenly, a snigger sounded next to his ear. "I'm sorry, this is just *so* funny. You're Ulysses, right?"

Whipping his head around, he still found… nothing. The trees in this section of the forest showed more green than the one further south, but the ground was still carpeted in the detritus of autumn. The branches swayed above Ulysses' head, and he could only see for a dozen feet in any direction through the foliage, but the voice had sounded in his ear. "Abyss. He's driving me insane too."

Ulysses rubbed furiously at his eyes. The smoke was thinner here, but maybe there was something in it?

Then the voice called out again. "I know you probably think you're going insane. Actually, you might be, I have no idea. But *I'm* real. I just need to know you won't yell or anything when I reveal myself."

A salmon-colored ball of light materialized in front of him. Ulysses stared at the floating ball of light, then choked for a moment as unswallowed drool trickled into his windpipe.

"Now, stay quiet." The voice from earlier was definitely coming from the ball. But how was it speaking?

Ulysses sputtered. "What…?"

"I'm going to stop you before you say something rude. You shouldn't be asking '*what*,' you should be asking '*who*.'" The ball was… spinning now, bobbing up and down expressively in a way that made Ulysses think it—she—was annoyed. It was so mesmerizing, it took Ulysses a moment to gather himself.

"What *are* you?" Ulysses knew his mouth was hanging open, but he couldn't bring himself to care. The ball sighed. *Sighed*. How in the abyss did *that* work?

"I'm a Wisp. My *name* is Talia. Wow, Garron said you were

nicer than the other guards, but none of them have been *this* rude to me. I mean, none of them have talked to me, but still." She bobbed once again.

"Garron?" Ulysses eyed the ball. "You know Garron?"

"*Yes.*" The creature suddenly flew in a dizzying pattern. "I tell you, all I wanted was an unfailingly loyal servant to bring power and glory to my dungeon, but *no*, the kid has to have *plans* and *goals* and a *brain.*"

The last word was said in such a tone of disgust that Ulysses found himself smiling slightly. "That he does."

He was a good boy—nearly a man now, Ulysses supposed. No parents since he was little, from what Ulysses had gathered, and no friends since Jackson separated him from Andros, but he'd done his best to help around the house, and he was friendlier than most of Ulysses' fellow guards.

The Wisp seemed to take his comment as agreement, and she let out a **hmpf**. "Horrible. Anyway, the faster we get this over with the better. I need you to follow me. Garron said to tell you, 'this won't put you or your family in danger, as long as no one sees you while you're gone.'"

Ulysses tensed, but at the Wisp's words some of it eased. Still, even he'd heard stories about strange creatures luring men to their death, and this abyssal forest *would* have some sort of ghost ball monster that would lead him to its den and devour him. "Follow you? Where? This is to help the boys?"

"No, they just want me to take you on a tour of the forest. The plume of black smoke is especially beautiful this time of year, you know, and the wildfire's supposed to really stand out at this time of day." Another pattern, this one subtly different.

Ulysses gave her a quizzical look.

The creature—Talia, she'd called herself—sighed again. "*Yes*, of course it's to help them."

Sarcasm. Some of Ulysses' fear about this being some sort of evil apparition faded, and his fists clenched. It was a risk still, for all that he didn't think a ghost would sound and act like a particularly acerbic teenage girl, but it was an acceptable risk.

Even if the boys hadn't saved his life, he would do what he could to help them. "Fine. Lead on, Talia."

They walked—well, *he* walked and she floated—through the trees for long enough to make Ulysses nervous. He wasn't meant to report in for hours yet, and honestly the other guards hardly cared about him, but if one found him so far from his posting, there would be consequences. One look at the haze of smoke to the west was enough to sharpen his resolve. "I have to help them."

As they continued through the trees, Ulysses considered the Wisp. He had to look away after a few moments, as the creature's light became mesmerizing, but he still spoke, trying to keep his uncertainty out of his voice. "So then, how did you meet Garron? Andros as well, I assume?"

The Wisp didn't bother lying. "Hah! Lured them into my dungeon while your friends were chasing them around and trying to kill them."

He frowned. "Friends?"

"You know, the people who wear the same uniforms as you, work for the same guy, and keep trying and failing to kill a pair of teenagers?" The Wisp's voice was cheery, but Ulysses thought he could detect a bite in the words. Certainly, he felt the mark they left on his pride… what was left of it.

"I couldn't… do anything to help them. I couldn't even leave." Ulysses kept his voice quiet, measured, not even sure why he was trying to explain himself to a ball of light. "My family…"

"It's funny, I would have said that the *teenagers* are the ones who can't defy a group of armed and armored cultivators by themselves." Yes, there was acid in the Wisp's tone. "But then I'm just a Will o' the Wisp, aren't I? Maybe humans are different, but grown wolves protect their pups. So do bears. Oh, hold on! Some of the insects eat their young—are you like them, then?"

The Wisp's words cut Ulysses deeply, and he found himself growing angry. "What exactly should I do? This is the *second* time I've risked my life for them, and I would do it again. But I *cannot* put the lives of my wife and my daughter in the hands of a madman!"

There was silence for a moment, and Ulysses looked around, wondering if he'd been too loud. Finally, the Wisp broke the silence. "Don't worry, nobody's close enough to witness you bravely risking your life."

Shame crept over Ulysses, though it would be more accurate to say that it grew stronger in his heart. He opened his mouth, then closed it, saying nothing.

"To be fair, I'm probably not the one to be throwing stones. Both because I don't have hands and because I didn't really care much about the two of them when I found them. I... made some mistakes, to tell the truth." The Wisp's voice grew quiet, for a moment, almost... younger. Ulysses looked up at her. Had she tinged blue? "They're not my biggest priority, but they're not supposed to be. It'd be nice if one of you 'humans' could have some decency and look after your young properly, so I can look after mine."

There was a moment of silence before the Wisp added hurriedly, "I mean, my dungeon's not really *my* young per se, the relationship is a little more complicated, and honestly now that I said that it sounds a bit... creepy, I think. But it sounded good so why don't we pretend it made sense?"

Ulysses stared at the ground before him. You needed to do that, in the forest, or else you risked tripping and falling. They continued for long, silent minutes before the Wisp stopped.

"Alright, we're here!" They were at an unremarkable stretch of land, standing in front of a great tree with a huge mess of roots at its base. "Now, I have a simple job for you. That flare at your belt. Just put it down *here*."

Ulysses frowned. The Wisp was hovering above—was that a space beneath the roots? His hand went to his flare, but he hesitated. "Jackson checks the flares. He'll know if I—"

The Wisp flew in his face, making him blink and take a step

back. "Don't worry about that, *brave warrior*, you'll get it back. Just put it in there for a minute."

He thought about debating further, but his shame was already overwhelming him. He put the flare beneath the roots, and waited. In less than a minute, a flash of red popped back out, and he grabbed it immediately.

"Great! Now go away." The Wisp retreated, floating away from the clearing.

"That's… it?" Ulysses frowned at the ball of light, which had almost disappeared under the roots. "Can I see…?"

"Sorry, they're busy. Being hunted like wild rabbits, you know." Was that red tinging the Wisp's color?

Ulysses winced and felt his eyes dry too far. "Wish them… luck. Please. Thank you for helping them, Talia."

He sighed as the Wisp vanished, turning back to his patrol. "I wish I could be so brave."

CHAPTER TWENTY-EIGHT

Garron stared at the red paper-wrapped cylinder before him with bloodshot eyes. He'd set it in a little shelter against the wind, and thankfully Typo had been able to make the fuse much longer, but he worried. His test indicated that this would take a full half-hour to ignite. That would give them the time to get to the end of what they had dug and finish the tunnel.

"What are you waiting for? It's already almost morning, you know. What happened to 'we're escaping tonight'?" Talia bobbed next to him, though he saw her through the slight haze of smoke which still permeated the air.

They were standing in a clearing surrounded by dense foliage on every side. Talia had confirmed there were no guards anywhere near them now. Jackson had given up locating them directly. He wanted to squeeze the forest until there was nowhere left to hide.

Garron shook his head at her words. "It's still dangerous. What if...?"

"That's why *I'm* here, silly. I'll tell Typo when Jackson's on his way. Now *go*." The Wisp put a threat in her voice.

He was still worried about other guards, but there shouldn't be more than one or two there, and Andros would be stronger than anyone except Jackson. Talia would make sure Jackson had taken the bait, and she could get to Typo fast enough that they would have plenty of time before he realized what happened. They could do this. If they were lucky.

Garron *hated* relying on luck. Still, he looked to the Wisp floating beside him. "Thank you, Talia. For everything."

The Wisp huffed. "You did an *okay* job, I suppose. I'll have to figure out how to make all those stupid cages lethal somehow, but… maybe you can come back to help, sometime."

He smiled weakly. "I'll try. But I'm excited to see what you'll think of, too."

The fuse lit.

They'd put it far enough from Typo to not give the dungeon away, but as Garron ran back to the dungeon entrance, he was met by Andros running the opposite way. "Gar! Is it done?"

"Fuse is lit. We have a half-hour to get in position." Garron rubbed at bloodshot, stinging eyes as he said the words.

"Time to start moving." Andros' face didn't betray quite as much exhaustion as Garron felt, but his smile was still tired. They sped through the trees, and too soon they'd reached the dungeon and rushed down the tunnels.

<Greetings.> Garron could feel the sadness tinging the dungeon's projection even more clearly now.

Still, he felt a twinge of joy at the familiar presence. <Hello, Typo. Thank you again for your help.>

<Gratitude… Affection.>

Garron could feel a sad smile stretching his own face, even as the wind rushed in his ears. They'd already said goodbye to Cutie, in the scant minutes they'd had between frantic digging, rigging the fuse, and the collection of what supplies they could carry. But they would be with Typo until they left the tunnel—his influence was all that was keeping its haphazard structure stable.

They were in the tunnel now, and by continuing at full speed they were soon past the long stretches and into the more winding paths forced by the presence of several deep root systems and veins of rock. Neither of them said a word as they ran. The tunnel shifted, the floor becoming dirtier with every step and the walls turning from hard-packed earth to churned-up soil.

Garron still wasn't sure how they'd managed to finish the tunnel. One of them had been digging at all times, and he had pushed himself to the limits of his Essence-enhanced body. Though he recovered quickly, the fatigue and exhaustion seemed to build up behind his eyes with every passing hour.

When the ground finally began to slope upwards again, Garron's heart sang with relief. He'd been afraid they would reach it too late after the flare was lit, but it appeared they were early. They finally reached the little circle of hollowed-out earth that would be only feet away from the surface. Garron heaved in great breaths—even with the ventilation shafts Typo had made periodically down the tunnel, it had felt difficult to sustain his breath as they ran down the hot, cramped spaces. More air filtered down now that they were closer to the surface, and his breathing was noticeably easier.

<Typo?>

<Sadness.> The full weight of the dungeon's emotion hit him—and Garron felt the loss of a child losing a close friend. The pain brought him back to a time he had trouble remembering clearly. Except for the tears, and the loneliness, all brought on by the loss of two parents. Andros had been there for him that time, though they were both too young to really understand what happened.

The feeling withdrew in an instant, as if the dungeon hadn't meant to project it. <Query?>

Garron tried to hold his emotions in check. <We'll try to come back someday, Typo. But if we stay now, we'll be *taken* away.>

A pause. <Confirmation. Query?>

<You'll tell us when Talia comes back?> Garron shifted guiltily at asking the dungeon for yet another favor.

<Assurance...>

Garron sat on the ground, Andros standing behind him. They'd left their tools here, and they were close enough to the surface that it would take moments to break through, with Typo's help.

Andros locked eyes with him. "Are you ready?"

Garron hesitated a moment before answering. "We've got to keep running."

Behind him, Andros let out a long breath. "I know. We've just got to hold out until Dad gets back. Maybe... we can try finding him?"

Garron considered that option. The Guild was still busy with cleaning up after the war. Their kingdom had all but fallen, and it wasn't the only one. Andros' father ranked high among them, and Andros was a Noble heir. They'd worried about the Guild simply turning them over to Jackson, Andros' guardian, but if they could somehow prove the man's theft, or even his maliciousness, maybe...?

<Urgency! Confirmation, assurance, sadness, farewell.> The flood of impressions and emotions from Typo hit Garron with almost physical weight.

<Thank you, Typo. Goodbye.> Garron scrambled to his feet. Out loud this time, he spoke somberly, "It's time to go, Andy."

"Yeah, I kind of figured." Andros had the spade in his hand, and was poking at the earth above them, but the ground was shifting without their interference, loose earth falling around them. Garron covered his eyes, squinting slightly, but it only took moments for him to feel the cool touch of the night air.

"Come on." Andros spoke in a whisper, even as he grabbed Garron and jumped in a gust of wind. They settled gently on the grass. Before Garron was a massive open plain. There was grass nearly up to his chest everywhere here, though he could see several paths crisscrossing the field to either side. That was easy enough, because the field was lit in the flickering orange of the blaze behind them, and instinctively Garron turned.

The fire was still blazing in places at the edges of the tree line, only a dozen feet or so away from them, and indeed the grass behind them had been reduced to ash. But the fire was truly roaring further into the forest. Past the blackened and glowing husks of the trees, it was easy to see the hungry orange flames devouring the leaves on the ground, the underbrush, even the trees. As Garron watched, he saw the dark form of a tall tree outlined in flame fall, smashing to pieces in a shower of sparks. The heat, smoke, and dry air washed over him, and he instinctively closed his eyes.

Andros gripped his shoulder. "Let's get moving."

Garron didn't bother speaking. He gave one last look at the blaze, then another at the hole of churned earth still open to the air. Then he nodded to his friend, who grasped him and launched them away.

Something slammed into Garron's chest just after they started, separating him from Andros, and he fell to the ground, his vision blurring slightly with pain and vertigo. A small hand hauled him up with impossible strength before he could even think to struggle, and something cold pressed into his neck. Garron blinked several times, clearing the haze away from his vision, and took a sharp breath.

Andros was standing a dozen feet away, looking at him in horror, his face cast in odd shadows by the light of the fire. Between them was a short, gruff looking man in a leather vest, and as the light flickered, Garron could see that his ears were pointed. He was holding a flare in his left hand, a firestarter in his right, and a bow was slung across his shoulders.

"Silverwood's mercy, boy, you are fast. Thought that fire-blooded moron was just being a pansy but… abyss. Good thing you saw them, Illana."

Garron could feel hot breath in his ear as the person holding him replied in a cold, professional voice, "Al arsantha, sir. It is my job, though we would have caught them regardless."

"Right, right. Now, let me get this abyssal thing lit." The man—Elf—began fumbling with the firestarter. For a moment, Garron's heart squeezed in fear. The mercenaries. They were Elves. Andros had said all Elves outside their own lands were Mages—if their captors were in the B-ranks, they might as well give up then and beg for mercy.

He cycled Essence to his eyes, looking at the man, and a little of the pressure eased. He was in the mid D-ranks, a little stronger than Andros but certainly not a Mage. What had Andros said? If you see an Elf, they're a Mage. Except for the… wild ones?

"Hold on." Garron's voice was trembling, but he was leery of swallowing. The knife was pressed tight. "You don't need to do that."

"Boy, I'm sure you had a good reason for running away, but you're not convincing me to let you two go without a mountain of silver. You got that on you?" The man waited for a bare moment, then nodded. "Didn't think so."

"Wait!" Now Andros ran up to them, though he didn't come within more than a few feet of the short man. "I'm a Noble, I can pay."

The Elf held up his hand. "Yeah, I'm thinking I'll stick with the guy who has the key to your vault, lad. But we can talk, just as soon as I…"

Silence fell for a moment as the man fumbled with the flare and the firestarter. Garron's eyes flicked around wildly, but there was nothing. Just the grass of the field, gently swaying in the breeze, the smoke from the flames drifting out and casting a haze over everything. Andros seemed frozen in horror, staring between Garron, whoever was over his shoulder, and the Elf trying to light the flare.

Finally, the short Elf just gave a sigh of exasperation and stomped the ground. A spout of water shot up and the man vanished, shooting past Garron at a speed that almost rivaled Andros' technique. He was heading toward the edge of the blaze.

The woman holding Garron gave a sigh of her own. "Don't move, or I'll kill him."

Andros seemed terrified as he looked at whoever was holding him, but after a minute, his face fell even further. Without needing to look back, he knew the flare had been lit. He was already captured, and now Jackson was coming.

CHAPTER TWENTY-NINE

There was dead silence for a few moments. Andros seemed to have taken the Elf's pronouncement to heart, because Garron didn't see him move a muscle. The knife was pressing harder into Garron's throat now, and he could feel a line of white pain along its edge. At the rough sound of a cough from behind, he twitched, and his throat flashed in pain.

The short Elf rounded Garron and his captor, walking as though he was on an evening stroll, and as he turned his head, Garron could see he had an easy smile on his face. He turned it on Andros.

"I've got to say, from what he told me about chasing you, my technique doesn't have anything on yours, boy. Can't sustain it that long, you see? Though it looked like you were dropping bits of your cultivation so... I'm not complaining." The Elf gave a short laugh, looking expectantly at Andros.

"Let my friend go." Andros' voice was tight, thin. He sounded... scared.

The Elf scratched his ear. "Why would I do that, exactly? What do you have to offer me in exchange for letting him go?"

Andros almost seemed surprised, as though he hadn't

expected the mercenary to even acknowledge his words. Garron was surprised as well, and a thread of hope rose in his chest. But when Andros spoke his voice had constricted further, so that Garron had to strain to hear him. "Wh-what do you want? I'll pay anything."

The Elf shifted, turning back to Garron—no, to the person holding him hostage. "Illana, what's our job?"

Another expelled breath by Garron's ear. "Capture the No—"

"No, *no*, what's our *job*? Not our task, our job? Celestial, girl, I ask you this every single mission!" The older Elf had an exasperated note to his voice that reminded Garron of Hila lecturing her cooking staff about proper procedure.

When the voice responded, it sounded sullen. "Make the most money for the least effort and the fewest chances to die."

"Right, right. Don't work, don't die, get paid." The Elf turned while nodding. There was a bit of sweat on the back of his stubby neck, and it shone in the firelight. "So, my young lord, what are you going to offer us? More money? Less work? Don't think I could be further from dying, to tell you the truth."

Silence. The person holding Garron drew in a breath as if to speak, but her partner beat her to it, sounding annoyed. "Well? Tell you what you can start with, a few words!"

Andros opened his mouth, but Garron could see the look in his friend's eyes. He was frozen. He would want to move, to attack or run, but the knife at Garron's throat was stopping him from acting.

Garron cleared his throat and spoke as loudly as he could, acutely aware of the pain at his neck. "If you kill me, he runs. You'll end up chasing him. That's effort."

The grip pinning his arm to his sides tightened, and Garron could feel a breath drawn in behind him. "Be quiet, boy."

But the short Elf had turned, his dark eyes fixing on Garron. The firelight was directly on his face, and in its shifting shadows Garron couldn't quite make out his expression. "Now

Illana, we're mercenaries, not my old dad. We can listen to the boy talk."

A huff, and silence.

Garron drew in a pained breath. "If you kill me, he runs. If you hold me until Jackson gets here, then he'll kill me, and Andros still runs. If you let me go…"

The Elf scratched at his ears, looking consideringly at Garron, then back to Andros. "You got a smart friend there, boy. Don't know if he's worth all this trouble, but he's smart, at least."

Andros looked to be standing slightly easier now, and as the mercenary spoke, he gave a slight nod. The Elf finally finished scratching his ears, examining his finger as he spoke.

"You know what? I don't really feel like chasing you from here to El'Landrissa. If you come quietly, we'll let your friend go. Don't really like killing kids anyway."

"You're a Wild Elf." The words seemed to fall out of Andros' mouth before he realized he'd said them, still in that same tight, constricted voice. Almost immediately, a horrified look overcame his face and he paled. Garron cursed quietly to himself.

"He's a nervous snarker. Of course he's an abyssal nervous snarker."

The short Elf had bristled at Andros' comment, but in an almost comfortable way, like an old man complaining about the ways of young people. "Did you see me tossing hellfire or summoning demons? Celestial, the Dark Elves do this stuff all the time and people just think it's 'mysterious,' but—"

"Sir." The cold voice behind Garron's ear sounded frustrated, but Garron was just relieved the man hadn't taken more offense. That was about the only thing that eased him about the situation. Notwithstanding the knife at his throat, how much more time before Jackson arrived? The man had to be at least as fast as the Elf. Had he made it all the way to Garron's bait before the second flare went up? If he was only halfway through the forest, it could be minutes.

"Right, calm down, Illana. Not like they're getting away here." The Elf patted his bow. "Might not be able to run quite as fast as you boy, but I can still shoot your friend before you reach him, and I've got great aim. Not to mention I can still shoot you on this ground. Might not put you down, but running's no fun with an arrow sticking out of your leg."

Andros looked torn as he considered Garron. "I... I don't believe you. If I come to you, how do I know you won't just...?"

"What, eat him?" The old man gave a short laugh, nocked an arrow on his bowstring, and pointed it down at the ground. The message was clear: he didn't want to fire, but if anything happened, he was ready. "Fine. Illana. Let him loose a little."

Silence for a moment. Then the voice responded with heat infecting her tone. "Sir, this—"

"Look, Illana, it isn't like our job is to torture these kids, is it? That's effort for no money and the same danger. You already cut him! Leave off. He's not even in the D-ranks." As the Elf considered Garron, he gave a low whistle. "Abyss, kid. Rare to see three natural affinities like that. Too bad you're so weak."

The Elf rubbed his ears again, then shot a hard look over Garron's shoulder. With a huff, he was pushed away, and he heaved a relieved sigh, feeling at his throat. It came back wet, but he could still breathe and the blood wasn't gushing. He had much bigger concerns.

He turned to consider the mercenary behind him. She was still only inches away from him, and Garron could see she was still pointing a long, wavy-bladed knife at him, hand on the other one at her belt. She was dressed in a leather tunic identical to her partner's, but she was a good foot taller. Her face looked as though it had been drawn with a straight-edge—every line was sharply defined, and the fire behind her cast deep shadows down her cheeks. In his Essence sight, she shone like Andros—she was an air cultivator in the lower D-ranks.

The short Elf was still talking behind Garron's back, though from the sound of his voice he had turned away again. "We mean well, boy. But if the fireblood gets here, I won't have much of a choice in the matter. So what'll it be?"

Garron looked over his shoulder in time to see Andros open his mouth. For an instant, his hope grew, but then he saw Andros' eyes. Sorrow. Loss. Resignation. And determination. He was going back to his cage, under the thumb of a man he hated and a life he'd run away from, for Garron's sake.

Garron couldn't allow it. Andros had a clear line to him, but even if the short Elf wasn't as fast or accurate as he claimed, his partner could stab Garron in a blink. What could they do? The mercenaries knew about Andros' movement technique, and they'd still let Garron go. But the man had said that was because he had a clear shot on this ground, no matter where they ran. Garron believed him, but that didn't mean he and Andros couldn't escape.

"Wait!" Garron turned back to face the woman Elf. Her hard face looked ominous in the shadows, her eyes almost seeming to glow in contrast. She was weathered slightly by the elements but still young, maybe even within a decade of Andros and Garron. *What in the abyss am I doing?* But Andros hadn't spoken. "I have a question."

The Elf considered him coldly, which he took as a signal to continue. He took a deep breath, tasting the smoke in the air. "How do you say 'Cutie' in Elvish?"

She stared at him, lifting the dagger menacingly with her lips pressed tight, but the one behind him gave a startled laugh which carried across the few feet of distance. "Abyss, boy, that takes some... She's a little old for you, isn't she?"

Garron flushed and asked himself again: what in the *abyss* he was doing? "No, I was just curious for... I mean—"

"Raiki for a girl, Raike for a boy." The short Elf interrupted him, a smile in his voice. "Doesn't sound so sweet, I know."

Garron brought his hand up and snapped his fingers exaggeratedly, giving his best smile. "Raike. Rai. I'll take it."

Andros finally spoke, voice almost normal in its annoyed confusion. "Gar, what are you—"

"We'll have to tell Rai his name, Andy." As the female Elf stared daggers at him, glancing down at the blade in her hand as though she longed to shove it forward, Garron scratched his chest with the hand he'd raised for his snap. A breeze passed over them all, sending a shiver through Garron when it cooled the blood at his neck. He felt the balance of the nature around him, the earth at his feet, the water even further down and drifting in the wind.

Behind him, the older Elf let out another bark of laughter. When he spoke, he sounded genuinely curious. "Who do you know named *Cutie*?"

Garron's hand shifted, and he pulled at his Center faster than he ever had before. "Please work."

Earth and water Essence blasted out of him in equal measure, as much as he could push into a single strike, and shot at the Elf before him at point blank range. She twisted with all the grace of an air cultivator, but she couldn't move fast enough. The Essence of mud blasted toward her, knocking her back and weighing her down. The knife just managed to prick his skin before it went flying with the rest of her.

He dove to the side the instant the blast left him, but he still heard the *thrum* of a bowstring, and pain shot across his side. "Feces."

A force slammed into him from behind. They paused for a bare instant, enough for Garron to recognize Andros' familiar grip. He heard a shout and felt a gust of wind wash over him, but his friend was already moving. In a rush of air, they shot away. Not into the field, where they'd be easy targets, nor into the blazing fire behind.

They stopped over open air and Andros threw him down, twisting as another *thrum* filled the air. A moment later, Andros landed beside him, and they began sprinting back down the tunnel.

<Greeting! Excitement!>

CHAPTER THIRTY

<Typo, collapse the tunnel behind us!> Garron pumped his arms as he ran. His side burned like it was on fire, and his throat wasn't much better, but that didn't matter. All that mattered was making it around the next corner, and the sound of shouting behind them as the mercenaries dropped into the hole.

<Confirmation.> Garron could feel the unrestrained joy emanating from the dungeon as it jumped to follow his command. It felt wildly incongruous with the situation, but he paid it no mind.

Andros grabbed his arm, and they shot forward before hitting something with a thud and a cry. Abyss. The tunnel wound in a series of jagged turns at this section, and Andros' technique could only take them in straight lines.

The blow pushed the air out of Garron's lungs, but there was no time to be winded. He kept running on his friend's heels. Behind them, he could hear the rumble of collapsing earth. They were far enough underground that the weight should at least pin the mercenaries. They could…?

"Gah! *Faster*, Illana!" An uncomfortably close voice.

The mercenaries had outpaced the falling earth. <More, Typo!>

<Regret. Warning.>

Garron would have cursed if he'd had he breath. They were too close. The mercenaries' Auras interfered with Typo's fine control, and if he simply withdrew his influence, they would all be buried.

Garron forced out a shout as he ran. "Andy, we need to gain a lead!"

From behind, the Elf yelled at the same time. "Illana, *now!*"

Andros grabbed his arm as they rounded the next corner, but an instant before the rush of air filled his ears again, he heard a howl of wind and the sound of rushing water.

Garron groaned, the pain in his side flashing again, but Andros was already pulling him forward. <Now?>

<Denial. Frustration.>

A bowstring thrummed, but Garron was already being swung forward by the arm. He ducked instinctively, and heard the thunk of the arrow hitting earth.

"*Move*, Gar!" Now Andros was pushing him, one hand on the small of his back as they sprinted through the cramped tunnel. Garron was gasping, feeling his strength slip away, but a spike of fear shot through him. If he was too slow, the Elves would catch Andros. Behind, the tunnel was still falling slowly, but the mercenaries were still too close, and Andros couldn't use his movement technique properly in the small spaces.

They were still running at top speed, and Garron could feel the blood leaking from his side. Andros' voice sounded behind him. "I'm going to try something, hold on."

Hands wrapped around him, and the wind rushed, though it was much softer than before. They hit the next corner with a thump, but Andros didn't let go. Instead, he just shot them forward again into the next wall. In between the rushes of wind, the flashes of pain as they slammed into wall after wall, and the internal cursing, Garron managed to catch a glimpse behind. He didn't know whether to laugh or cry.

The short Elf had grabbed the female by her leather vest, and dirt was kicking up in clouds behind them. Spouts of water propelled the two forward, each jump much smaller than those from Andros' technique. In these spaces that was an advantage, but it also meant that the female was being dragged along like a sail in the wind, knocking into walls at every turn.

Soon the world melded into earth flying by, and flashes of intense pain as they slammed into wall after wall. Garron's side flared at each hit, but the pain was… dampening as time went on. He began feeling cold at his fingertips, and his head spun more than the impacts could account for.

<Warning!> The projection lanced through the haze of his thoughts, giving Garron sudden insight.

"Blood. I'm losing blood." *Slam*. There wasn't much he could do about it. *Slam*. They had to keep running. *Slam*.

The next rush went on for much longer than the last, and Garron's eyes snapped open.

<Now Typo!> If he could scream his thoughts, he would.

<Assurance.> There was a deep, sustained rumble as Typo's support vanished from the long stretch of tunnel they'd passed. As they took another jump, Garron could hear a faint yell.

"Stop, Andy." Garron knew his voice was weak, too thin for his friend to hear, but Andros still slowed, lowering Garron gently to the ground, cursing softly.

"Abyss, abyss, *abyss*." Something pressed into his side. Garron expected pain, but all he felt was a slight pressure. "Come on, Gar, it's just an infernal *cut*. Stop being a baby and—"

"Move back, Andy." Garron's tongue felt heavy in his mouth, and shimmering black was closing around the edges of his vision. "Typo has me."

Garron saw his friend's eyes widen in sudden hope, and he jumped backwards in a rush of air.

<Worry. Assurance.> Garron could feel the dungeon working, and his side flared in sudden agony. He didn't have the

breath to scream, so he flopped a little on the ground. An image filled his mind: himself, covered in dirt and blood, his tunic torn on wide open on his right side, revealing new skin. The cut on his throat had closed as well, though the blood had dried down his front so his skin looked flaky and almost black below his neck.

The fog over his thoughts settled back, heavier than ever. His heart was hammering—not from fear, but as though it was struggling to get his blood around his body—and his breaths were coming too fast. <Blood, Typo.>

<Determination… Concern.> Garron chose to ignore the undercurrent of uncertainty coloring the dungeon's projection. This wasn't as simple as replacing a bit of lost fluid like the dungeon had offered before, but Garron still wished he'd let the dungeon do it, if only for practice.

The cold pressed on him, traveling up his limbs and bringing a deep ache with it. Garron focused on his breathing, but it was getting harder and harder. The darkness closed in… and stopped. He could feel himself shivering, but slowly it got easier to draw in each breath, and the darkness began to retreat. The cold remained, and the pain, but it moved no further up his limbs, and slowly his heartbeat began to settle.

"Gar? Are you… alright?" Andros' voice, quiet and uncertain. "Alive?"

"I'm just wondering…" Garron let out a wordless groan, but he sat up. The cold in his limbs was retreating somewhat, but it felt as though it was getting hotter all around. Sweat beaded on his forehead, dripping down into his eyes as he looked to Andros.

"Is it getting hot in here, Andy?" His tongue still felt heavy and his limbs weak. Still, he was getting stronger by the second. He suspected that had to do with his heart meridian, but he wasn't going to question the gift.

Andros was grinning at Garron, surveying him as though checking to make sure a new wound wouldn't suddenly appear on his body. "I guess we're under the fire. So you're okay? No missing parts or—"

"It wasn't hot on the way here, Andy. We're too far down for a fire to make it this hot." Indeed, it was getting almost uncomfortable in the cramped tunnel, to the point that Garron was having trouble drawing in breath.

Andros' eyes widened and he looked up. He reached a hand up and touched the tunnel ceiling, then jerked it back.

"Jackson." He ran forward, scooping Garron up in his arms and tensing. They sped forward, moving in more sustained bursts down the longer stretches of tunnel, and thankfully no longer hitting walls with every turn. As much as Garron wanted to simply drift off and let Andros bring them back to the dungeon, he couldn't.

<Typo, we need you to fill in the tunnel behind us. Then you can withdraw your influence.>

<Tension. Confirmation.>

Garron breathed a sigh as Andros continued to bear them forward, then hurriedly shut his mouth as a surge of nausea overwhelmed him. It would cost Typo Essence to make earth to fill in the tunnel, but there was really nothing else to be done. Simply collapsing the tunnel would leave a trail of disturbed earth straight to Typo, and leaving the tunnel open would be worse.

He tapped Andros, signaling that his friend could slow down, but he could already feel the technique faltering. They guttered to a stop, still in the tunnel, and a moment later both were on the floor, heaving out the contents of their stomachs.

"What's... got... you... sick?" Garron recovered first, wiping his mouth.

Andros barely had anything in his stomach, but he was still dry heaving on the tunnel floor. "Rapid... Essence loss—*hurk*—took... too much in... and got rid of it—*hurk*—too fast."

Huh. Andros had done a lot of jumping around just now. Garron supposed it made sense that there would be some ill effects to using that much of his cultivation up so fast, even if he wasn't lacking Essence in his Center.

Come to think of it, Garron himself wasn't feeling very good either. That Essence blast had been stronger than the ones he'd used against Lars—perhaps because he'd used two affinities—and though it was nothing to Andros' expenditure, he was still feeling the loss as his body struggled to recover from its ordeal. His limbs shook as he stood, his breathing was heavy, and his body alternated between flashes of heat and cold.

Garron waited patiently for several minutes as his friend heaved, and once that had stopped, simply breathed, splayed out on the floor. He felt the Essence in the room shift as Andros gathered all of the available air Essence into his Center, but that still wasn't much.

"Come on Andy, Typo's caught up to us now with filling in the tunnel. The faster we move, the less likely Jackson will be able to follow us here." Garron reached a hand down, and his friend took it.

"Thanks." Andros whispered the word, still looking at the ground, and Garron winced as he helped his friend up. *He doesn't sound good at all.* When Andros was on his feet, Garron bore as much of the weight as he could, though he was swaying a little himself. Together, they began stumbling down the final stretches of tunnel before them in silence.

CHAPTER THIRTY-ONE

<Greeting!>

"When I said to come back, I didn't mean this soon."

Purr.

As they left the tunnel, Garron couldn't help the smile that broke out on his face. Typo's joy was infectious, if misplaced, and it bled into Cuti—Rai's behavior as well. As they stepped into the dungeon proper, the young lion—now sporting a half-grown mane and the golden fur of its parents—bounded up to them like a dog, stretching up and laying huge paws on Garron. Garron nearly stumbled, but Andros slipped off to the side, taking his own weight and removing much of the burden from Garron.

Even Talia whizzed around their heads once, flashing a bright yellow before returning to her normal color. Before anything else, Garron sent the sincerest projection he could to Typo. <Gratitude, pride. You saved my life, Typo. You were amazing!>

<Mild embarrassment. Pride. Affection.> Typo's response was muted, as though the dungeon was holding himself back.

Garron's smile widened at the dungeon's response, and he petted Rai as the lion began to purr louder against his chest.

Then Talia cleared her throat, and Garron finally let out the words he'd been practically choking on. "Alright, that's *it*. How in the abyss do you clear your throat? Do I even call it that? You don't have a throat! What's the point?"

"Oh, calm down. I'm just messing with you." Talia did another circuit around Garron's head, then one around Andros. "But you'd better get explaining right now what happened. Typo isn't very good at story time yet."

Garron let out a long sigh, and told the story. "Then I asked her the Elvish word for—anyway, Cutie's name is Rai now."

He pet the young lion as Talia whizzed around. "Rai? Wow, that actually isn't terrible! Okay, go on."

Giving a tired nod, he kept going. "I was really close, so I shot a blast of Essence at her."

"What in the abyss were you *thinking*?" Everything froze. Talia, who'd been spinning around their heads as she listened, hung in the air. Rai stopped purring, and soundlessly put his paws on the ground. Garron could sense Typo's shock, which mirrored his own. He realized suddenly that Andros hadn't said a word since they entered the dungeon.

His friend was sitting, leaning his back against the wall next to the dungeon entrance, his hair, though cut shorter than usual, was still long enough to hang down and nearly cover his eyes. He was covered in dirt and sweat had run down his face, so it was cast in stripes of light and dark as he looked at Garron. *Glared* at Garron.

"Andy?" Garron's voice came out scratchy.

"Why did you do that? He was going to let you go, it was *perfect*! You would have been safe!" Andros looked down. Were those tears? "Now you're going to die so that Jackson has a scapegoat."

Garron found himself resting his head on Rai's stomach, and now his eyes were beginning to blur. In an instant, the faint good cheer from surviving the ordeal vanished. Looking at his friend's agonized face, all he could feel was guilt. "I'm sorry, Andy. You've been keeping me alive this whole time, and I keep pulling you ba—"

Something hit Garron's head, igniting a brief flash of pain, and clattered to the ground. He looked down. It was a smooth stone about the size of his fist.

<Annoyance.> Garron get the distinct impression that Typo—a barely sentient rock—was calling him stupid, but he was still staring dumbly down at the stone on the ground.

"Stop being idiots." Talia was suddenly crowding his eyes, forcing him to jerk his head back and blink. A moment later, she did the same to Andros, who looked at her as though he'd been the one that was hit over the head, not Garron.

"What?" The young Noble blinked at the Wisp.

Talia whizzed back and up, so that she hovered above them like a miniature sun. "I mean, it's not complicated. Typo can see the answer, and he has trouble understanding the difference between night and day."

<Slightly indignant confirmation.>

"You're both trying to save the other person. Stop it. Neither of you can even save yourself at this moment, which means we're on a schedule here, so skip past all the emotional stuff and get some sleep so we can get back to work." Talia whizzed around in a dizzying pattern, before flying to hover near Rai's head.

Talia floated upwards threateningly. "I'll count to three, and you'd better be shaking hands or sleeping!"

Rai lifted his head from Garron's shoulder, and let out a light growl, as if agreeing with Talia. Garron glanced at the lion. "Talia, what—"

"One…" The Wisp tinged red.

Garron took a long, shuddering breath, and expelled the air in a huff. Then he took another, and another. He could remember a time not even a month ago when doing that much had seemed impossible. Andros had made his dream reality, and he kept letting him down.

<Annoyance.> An image flashed through Garron's mind: himself, stumbling down a tunnel with Andros draped across his shoulders, looking around in suspicion as he followed an invisible voice into a dungeon. In an instant, the memory was replaced by one of himself standing before Lars' twisted body, while Andros struggled to rise. Then himself walking into the room, covered in dirt and dried blood, all but carrying Andros on his shoulders.

<But those things were all my fault, Typo!> Garron knew the dungeon couldn't truly understand him, not yet, but he couldn't help protesting. <If he hadn't run away to help me, he wouldn't have...>

Andros' face bloomed in Garron's mind, smiling, laughing. His friend looked so happy, Garron could feel the corners of his own lips stretching upwards. Andros was free, and whatever he said, that meant something to him.

"Two..."

Garron didn't feel much like standing, so he scooted over awkwardly toward Andros, displacing a yowling Rai from his lap, and threw an arm around his friend's shoulders. He coughed awkwardly. "I, uh, don't know many teenagers who can save their dying friend and keep them away from a company of bloodthirsty cultivators, Andy. I think you might be setting your standards a little high, and that's a jerk move."

Andros laughed, shaking his head slightly. "I don't know many people who go from barely surviving corruption-sickness to beating D-rankers and teaching dungeons to make traps in half a month. Everybody starts from somewhere. I'd say you've already made it pretty far, but you'll get even... farther."

The Noble cocked his head, and a laugh escaped his throat. "That sounded better in my head. Guess I've got to work on my aphorisms too."

Garron nodded sagely. "Big word. Expected for someone that likes to hear themselves talk."

They both smiled. Talia let out an exasperated... breath. Of course she did. "Gah, that barely saved any time! I didn't realize they could do it out of order like that!"

<Confused agreement!>

Rai purred, then came over and laid himself across both of them. Garron laughed, and began stroking the giant cat's fur. "Greedy."

"No, his name's Rai. I like it, by the way. It'll confuse any Elves he meets, that's for sure." Andros joined him, ruffling the lion's mane.

"Yes, yes, Rai is very cute. Now decide what to do next! You know that there's a wildfire coming straight for us, right?" Talia was clearly agitated, bobbing up and down and doing occasional circuits around their heads.

Garron frowned as he remembered the situation. For all of Talia's shouting, nothing had really changed. They were stuck in the same position they'd been in before digging the tunnel—much worse, in fact.

"Don't think we're getting out west or north." Andros' voice had a resigned note to it. "Not unless we go through Jackson. So… there's east or south."

Garron shook his head. "East would be worse. South—"

Andros stopped him there. "The river's got monsters as strong as the birds. They just like the water."

They had both known that already, but it was still disheartening. "So there's no options."

Suddenly Typo's consciousness crashed into Garron. <Hunger. Rage. Hunger.>

Garron grabbed his stomach on reflex, but that wasn't what Typo was projecting. It was the hunger of a predator, of chasing down prey, of destroying threats, of *hunting*.

"I mean, I wish he cultivated earth or water, but I guess it'll do." Talia's voice had a savage edge to it, like she was sharing Typo's emotions. "Let's get him!"

Garron frowned. "Who, Jackson?"

<Hunger.>

Some deep part of Garron found itself agreeing with the

dungeon. Not that he wanted to eat the fire cultivator, but he did want to stop letting the man chase Andros and him down like wild game. He wanted to turn around, and do the hunting. He looked to Andros. Even though his friend couldn't feel the dungeon, his expression mirrored Garron's own.

"I'm just about finished running from that guy." Andros rolled his neck around, stretching with a lithe grace to match Rai. "I still can't beat him alone, but we've got a secret weapon."

Garron looked at him, suddenly hopeful. Andros sighed and gestured at his healthy friend. "*You*, idiot."

"Oh. Well, I have a secret weapon too." Garron grinned, scrambling back to his feet and picking up the rock Typo had dropped on his head. He looked around for a moment, aimed, and threw. The rock hit the floor with a dull thud. There was a second of silence, and another, more muffled sound came from across the room. In a flash of gray and brown, something erupted out of the far wall, impacting the opposite side in a shower of broken earth. A giant crossbow bolt, its head buried in the wall, its shaft still quivering slightly. "My secret weapon is a secret weapon."

Andros whistled. "Can we trade?"

Talia made a sound that somehow made Garron think that she wanted to roll her eyes. "Wildfire. Evil crazy cultivator. Dozens of guards. *Move*."

Garron gave a sharp nod. "Typo, we have traps to get ready. Andy, I'm sorry but you need to get in fighting shape… fast. We don't have too much time."

"I'll be fine! Honestly, I'm not worse than I was before—it was just too much, too fast. I even ended up with a little more Essence in my Center than when I started!" Andros gave a thumbs-up.

Garron eyed him skeptically, but eventually he just nodded. "Good. We're going to need it soon."

CHAPTER THIRTY-TWO

Garron threw a rock, truly enjoying the feel of it. He'd decided he was done using dungeon mobs as test subjects, despite the fact that they weren't quite 'alive' in the way normal animals were. The accident with the stone cage had demonstrated that there was still significant danger that the wolves would be hurt —too much for him to be comfortable using them.

The stone he threw was much heavier than he preferred, intended to simulate the impact of a human footfall. When it landed with a thump and a puff of dust down the tunnel, there was an instant of silence before the ground shifted. Out of nowhere, half-domes of crisscrossing metal bands sprang up out of the dirt, nearly occluding passage in the tunnel, and snapped together with a crash.

Garron smiled; the action had worked perfectly. If he'd been forced to create this trap himself, it would have been all but impossible just to line the domes up properly. Having a dungeon to do the actual construction made being an 'engineer' so much easier.

He walked up, leery of the disturbed earth but knowing that it would be safe to walk. He grabbed hold of the half-dome closest to him, just barely managing to get his fingers in between the steel hatch-lines, and pulled. Nothing happened. He made sure to give it every ounce of strength he could, but the dome didn't budge. He tried pulling sideways, and then pushing up and down. The dome remained firm.

<Triumph!>

Garron grinned, sharing the same emotion back to the dungeon. He still found the pulleys incredible. He didn't quite understand how it worked, but by continually connecting the rope to other pulleys, so that the entire system would move together, he could multiply the force of his counterweights, so that a two hundred-pound-stone would require four times that force to displace. The cages also used a lever to further multiply their force to truly drastic levels.

When he and Typo had first tested the system, he'd noticed that each pulley increased how much distance his weight needed to move. That was the major limit on the strength of the trap, and with Typo running low on Essence, there was only so much space he could hollow out for the weights themselves. If they'd had more space, perhaps they could have made the cages strong enough to stymie even Jackson, but for now, they would only work for any other guards who happened to find Typo.

<Okay, now let's go to the spikes.> Garron looked down the hallway. He'd set up only three types of traps in the tunnels: cages, spikes, and a few of the improved pits. They tested the spikes, which now shot out much faster and slightly lower. They had swapped the dulled spikes they'd used when the mobs were testing it for sharp stone, but Garron still thought of the trap as more of an impediment than anything—the spikes were set so low on the wall that any human who triggered the trap likely wouldn't die from it. Immediately.

The pits were of the type they'd set up above ground in the little clearing a few dozen feet from the dungeon entrance to trap Lars. They had reduced the number to only one per stretch of tunnel, but now each one would not give itself away on the first step, instead only collapsing inwards when the target reached its center. He'd removed the spikes, these were more side projects and amusements than anything, but if their plan went wrong and other guards found the dungeon, he was determined to give all of them a chance at life.

Jackson may have lost that chance, but the rest hadn't.

<Good. Let's get to the big room, then.> Garron began walking down the tunnel.

<Agreement.>

As Garron entered the large space, his spirits fell slightly, tension returning to his shoulders. The room was now dominated by the pillar of metal and stone they'd set up around the drop point of their pit trap. Looking at it, Garron couldn't believe that Jackson would be able to escape like Lars had, and the fire cultivator's abilities shouldn't even be as well suited to breaking out of confinement as Lars' earth was.

Still, they'd set up as much of an impediment as they could without absolutely bankrupting Typo. The same rockfall trap and sharpened stone spikes had been replaced and reset within the confinement area, and just in case, a pair of the giant crossbows had been set up and aimed at the center of the pillar, linked to a pressure plate Garron could activate at will with a rock.

The sight reminded Garron of what they were about to do, but he shook it off and tried to enjoy himself checking the room's few other traps.

The effort of making the trap for Jackson had taken a good deal of Essence, and Talia had insisted they save a large portion of what was left for some reason, but Garron hadn't wanted to do more in any case. The same falling cage trap was still set in the ceiling, and the first crossbow was still functional. He didn't know how effective any of those would be in dealing with a powerful cultivator like Jackson, but it would have to be enough.

"Hmpf. Are you done checking out my dungeon?" Talia's voice came up from the tunnel leading down to the Core room. "I'm still annoyed about the trap you put in Typo's room, you know."

Garron had made everything in the Core room except for the dungeon Core's little mud well into a giant pit, as deep as Typo could hollow out on short notice. He'd put spikes in that one—after all, no guardsmen should be moving that deep into the dungeon.

As the Wisp floated into the room, Garron addressed her directly. "Well, do you want Jackson to come in here and just grab Typo's Core?"

Typo's consciousness recoiled. <Fear.>

"No, but... whoever heard of the boss room of a proper dungeon being a giant pit?"

Garron sighed. "The boss room is where the boss is. Typo's Core room doesn't qualify. Actually, this one doesn't either—does Typo have a boss?"

Inexplicably, Talia brightened. "No! And that's going to change right now."

Garron raised an eyebrow, but the surge of excitement from the dungeon sparked his own interest. "Go on, but hurry. We only have a few more minutes here before we should be heading out."

The Wisp bobbed. "Typo, call all the mobs here please."

<Excited agreement!> A moment later, five creatures came bounding from both entrances to the room, coming to a stop one after another. The first was Rai, his half-mane shaking as he ran with silent grace toward them. He laid himself at Garron's feet, purring, as a pair of Riverdancers bounded up behind him. The sleek wolf mobs waited with rigid attention, facing Talia almost like statues. It took almost another minute before the two Crystalfurs came to a grinding halt beside the Riverdancers, their coats gleaming, eyes fixed on Talia.

Talia made a slow circle around the mobs. "So, Typo, you don't have all that much Essence left, but you should be able to make one of these into your boss monster."

<Enthusiasm.>

The four wolves all twitched, spasming slightly, and Talia

whizzed around in agitation. "No! Listen. You can only have one boss, and we have to make sure we choose carefully!"

Discreetly, Garron sent an image of one of the wolves growing larger and stronger while the others stayed the same, along with the feeling of patience and respect.

Typo radiated sudden understanding. <Guilty gratitude.>

"Are you listening, Typo?" Talia's voice took on an authoritative tone. "We need to choose which monster to make your boss! The wolves are all at F-rank six, so whichever you pick will become a lot stronger."

Garron raised a hand. "What about Rai?"

Talia bobbed, snapping, "What? Oh, he's higher. F-rank seven. But he's a dungeon born mob; Typo can't control him directly! Who ever heard of making a dungeon born into a boss?"

He nodded, though he hadn't followed most of it. "Sorry I asked."

"It's okay," the Wisp replied magnanimously. "Anyway, Typo, we should decide whether we want a Riverdancer or a Crystalfur. Do you have a preference?"

The dungeon seemed to pick up the intent of Talia's words, but even Garron could feel its projection. <Dissatisfaction.>

Talia seemed exasperated, her voice startlingly similar to Hila the cook's. "What's wrong?"

Garron's head filled with an image of Rai. The lion stood, then suddenly grew to several times his size. The proportions were wildly off, the head many times larger than the rest of the body, the nose too small, the limbs too thick with muscle. When he roared, a blast of blue liquid which looked more like blueberry juice than water issued forth from his mouth.

Garron didn't know whether to laugh or scream in horror at the ridiculous image filling his mind's eye. He settled on a cough. "Ahem. I, uh, think he wants Rai to be the boss."

"What? We don't have time for this, Typo! Rai is too young to accept that much Essence anyway! You might kill him."

Typo sent an impression Garron could only describe as a foot stomp. <Dissatisfaction.>

Talia was right that they were running out of time. They'd given themselves four hours—enough time for a modicum of sleep and food, as well as for Andros to fully recover and for Garron to review Typo's traps—but now that time was almost up. Garron tried to make a deal. <Typo, why not make one of the Riverdancers the boss? It would have the same abilities as Rai.>

<Curiosity. Query?> A truly awful image of a grotesque, vaguely wolfish creature spewing blue liquid from its mouth filled Garron's mind. Typo wasn't very good at creating hypothetical images.

Garron was confused for a moment, but Talia spoke up, sounding even more annoyed. "It might not have the same powers as Rai, and it definitely won't be shooting blueberry juice anywhere. Especially since you're feeding it Essence. It doesn't have to evolve in the same way it would normally."

Something about that idea sparked Garron's interest. "So if Typo just gave a regular wolf water Essence, he might not get a Riverdancer?"

"No, it could be anything, really. Probably still flexible and all, but it might have an ability other than its 'Malleable' thing."

Garron rolled his eyes; of course there were actual names for all of the monster's abilities. He'd thought saying the lions had 'stone hide' was just a description, but now he wondered if the trait were somehow imprinted on the creature's souls. "Hold on. If he wants a lion so bad, why not make his own?"

"Because that would take too much—oh, right, the weaker mobs won't help against Jackson anyway." Talia made a quick circle. "Fine! Let's just get this over with."

While Talia instructed Typo, Garron sent images to speed along the dungeon's understanding. Garron drew his sword and slew two of the monsters in the room with him, a Crystalfur and a Riverdancer, and Typo retrieved their Essence along with what little they'd cultivated during their short lives. Then he formed the basic pattern for a lion—this was difficult, as apparently the influence of earth Essence had fundamentally altered the two they'd killed before. But because Typo had absorbed the body of Rai's sibling, he still had something to work from. From there, he just fed it earth Essence—earth, because Rai was already a water monster and Garron was incredibly curious.

In the first few moments, Typo produced a strange, misshapen creature with feathers peeking out where it wasn't encased in stone, but before Garron could examine it closely, the creature fell apart. "Was that a *loon*? We need a *lion*."

"Typo! Be careful!" Talia shouted, whizzing around in exasperation. Once the dungeon had calmed down, it focused once again. The whole process took minutes with Garron's help, and before his eyes, a shimmering light formed into a lion cub, even smaller than Rai had been when Garron had first seen him.

It grew rapidly as Essence flowed into its Center, a process which Garron could actually observe with his Essence sight. The power of earth entered the young lion without resistance, and before Garron's eyes, the creature began to grow, its form twisting and warping. The earth around it began to crack, and suddenly flew toward it. For a moment it was covered in earth, until suddenly it shook itself, clearing much of the brown grime away.

Garron took an involuntary step backward. The monster before him dwarfed Rai, coming up to Garron's shoulders, though thankfully its proportions matched its height. Its coat had gone from black-spotted gold to the deep brown of freshly turned soil, and its mane had taken on a hard, frozen look not unlike that of the Crystalfurs. Its teeth had turned to stone, and as it shifted, raising a paw above the ground, Garron could see that each of its motions was ponderous, slower even than the Crystalfurs.

Slowly, but still with the lazy grace of a cat, it walked toward Garron. No, toward Rai. The other lion was on his feet, fangs out and snarling, but with the defensive posture of a predator that knew it was overmatched. When the huge creature came close, its smaller counterpart leapt at it.

Garron sent a sharp thought. <Typo, tell him to calm down.>

<Excitement!> The dungeon barely seemed to acknowledge Garron's instruction.

Before Garron could say more, Rai had already tried to swipe his claw at the huge brown lion. The blow landed, surprisingly, and after Garron was done glancing away in horror, he saw that the monster had sustained a cut along its side. The wound was thin, small, and the huge lion hadn't appeared to notice it. So it didn't have 'Stone Hide'?

Then Rai roared, and there was a rushing sound as a blast of concentrated water issued from his mouth, hitting the huge lion from point-blank range. This time, the boss monster twitched, glancing down at Rai and shaking its coat. When it turned back, Garron could see that Rai's blast had left a wide, shallow wound in its coat, but Typo was already healing the damage.

The lion looked back at Garron, then past him, and he felt his heart squeeze in fear. The creature had dark eyes to match the rest of its coloring, but they almost seemed to glow. It opened its mouth wide and roared, a sound so deep that it rumbled in Garron's chest and set the floor vibrating. Or no, the floor was… rippling?

Garron almost panicked—the effect could easily disrupt their traps and destroy hours of work—but it seemed to be highly localized. He did panic when the rolling floor beneath him sent him to the ground, unable to stand, but the effect faded, and the lion settled down, still rumbling slightly.

"Wow. I leave you alone for one minute and boom—giant lion." A cheery, though somewhat strained voice called across the room. "Is it a boy or a girl? What's its name?"

Talia responded almost immediately. "Girl! I'm so excited, I've been so lonely! But what should we…?"

Garron thought back to what the Elf had told them, Raike for boys, Raiki for girls. So… "Aiki."

Andros groaned, but Talia whizzed around the earth lion's head excitedly. "I *love* it! Wow, all of a sudden you really got good at giving names, Garron!"

Struggling to his feet, Garron gave a short laugh. "Time to go, Andy?"

His friend rounded the still form of Aiki, eyeing her deep brown hide and crystalline mane warily. "Yeah, the fire's pretty close, and the sun's up, so the guards should be on patrol unless something changed."

"You checked the trap?"

The young cultivator rolled his eyes. "Yes, I'm not an idiot. I sat there staring at it so long that I named it."

Garron raised an eyebrow as Andros cheerfully told him. "Pittney!"

<Typo, I need a flare.> If they stayed there any longer, Garron might have to feed himself to Aiki just to escape Andros' humor.

As the red-wrapped cylinder fell into his hand, Talia stopped whizzing around Aiki. "Okay then, time to go! Don't worry, I'll protect you. As long as nothing dangerous comes our way."

"Terrible." Garron's left eye twitched. "Let's go."

As they walked out of the dungeon, Garron felt the weight he'd managed to lift from his chest for a few hours settle back. For all that they were the ones with the lions, he felt as if he was running into one's den and poking it with a very short stick.

CHAPTER THIRTY-THREE

The smoky haze was much, much thicker than it had been before. Talia had spent some time of her own scouting before letting them leave the dungeon, noting that she couldn't find Jackson nearby. At this point, the blaze spanned most of the width of the forest, so that was no surprise.

They moved in silence, Talia only occasionally visible as she continuously shimmered away and went to scout. They'd decided to place the bait northwest, far enough away that Jackson would reach it before anyone else could. The downside was that it was also a long run to their trap site, and a long walk from the dungeon. As they moved through the trees, Garron reflected how much their presence had changed this place. Smoke drifted through the trees, and the sounds of wildlife had faded completely. Andros speculated that they had migrated south and east.

He found it difficult to walk in the haze, his feet tripping over roots and branches, but he still found it easier to keep up than he had before opening his meridians. Wind still rustled the trees, but in the short time they'd been in the forest, it had turned further away from summer and closer to winter. Few branches bore any leaves, so that it was barely possible to tell that the trees were alive. With the smoke drifting around them, curling around every twig and hugging each branch, it almost looked like the great plants were choking to death.

"Remember, I don't know if luring him will work. There's a lot of smoke in the air, and it doesn't always work as well on crazy people. For all I know, the lights he sees in his head are much prettier than me." Talia whispered the words as she drifted forward. The smoke was blowing in the opposite direction, so the effect was almost eerie.

Garron gave a sharp nod. "It's only the first option. That's why we're here, remember?"

They made it to the spot a few minutes later, and Garron set down the flare carefully. Andros handed him the firestarter, and he lit the fuse.

"Come *on*." Andros' whisper was nearly drowned out by the crackle of the flame eating at the fuse.

Garron and Andros hurried away through the trees, heading toward the clearing where they'd reset the pit trap for Jackson. They wouldn't go all the way there, but Jackson could use Essence sight, so being anywhere near him when he was moving to the flare would be a disaster. He was most likely west or north, so moving southeast should keep them in the clear and still put them in a position to step in if the cultivator didn't fall for Talia's mesmerization.

Garron wished he could have had more time to make a better plan. As they moved around the foliage—quick, quiet, and careful—he went over every possible failure. They would stop at the edge of Andros' Essence sight; in the dense Essence of the forest, that wasn't too far. Hopefully in the distance they would be nondescript enough to be unnoticeable, but, what if Jackson approached the clearing from an unexpected angle? What if he waited, and had his guards surround them on all sides so that luring him away would be impossible? What if…

A hand slapping Garron's chest stopped him in his tracks. "What's wrong?"

"Cultivator out that way, heading toward us." Andros hissed as he pointed out in the direction they were headed. Garron squinted, but he couldn't make anything out through the trees and the smoke.

"Jackson?" They were already moving to the side, trying to get past the person's sight. Garron looked up for a moment. Through the bare branches, he could see the red light of the flare hanging in the sky.

Andros shook his head. "I... abyss, it's a water cultivator."

They moved even faster, Garron cursing silently. Perhaps there were other guards with water affinities, but the description instantly made him think of the Elvish mercenary, the short man with the bow and the water-based movement technique.

Was he checking the flare instead of Jackson? They had both discounted the possibility; Jackson was faster, and he would certainly want to catch them himself. Was he just in the area? It was strange that the Elf was coming from the southwest. Jackson's men seemed concentrated at the tree line and in the northern part of the forest. Perhaps he'd been checking something, maybe even the site of their first flare, and noticed the light?

Garron stepped quietly over a fallen branch, eyes on Andros' back as his friend moved, continually looking over his shoulder and into the trees, but they were beginning to slow. They were far out of position now, but as long as the Elf didn't notice them, that was worth it.

If the Elf had come by coincidence, then the operation was somewhat salvageable. Jackson might still arrive, and there was no reason Talia couldn't lure both man and Elf into the trap together. It was far from perfect, but it was possible. Even in the event that they had to move into the open and draw the two back to the trap, Jackson's speed would be the determining factor.

Garron cycled Essence to his own eyes. He wasn't nearly as proficient at blocking out the sensory noise that came with using the sight as Andros was, but he hated not being able to see what was going on. Andros had almost stopped, so there was little chance he would trip over anything.

The world lit up in a fog of colors, thicker even than the smoke which covered the real world. The balance of air, earth, and water had been disrupted by fire, even so far away from the blaze, and corruption hung thicker than it should have as the smoke tainted the air.

The moment he opened his Essence sight, he saw the twinkle of pure light. Andros put a hand on his chest again, but Garron knew before the whisper left his mouth. "Air cultivator. Heading toward us."

He was already a little dizzy from using the Essence sight like this, but Garron spared a look behind. A dot coming at their flank popped into his vision, growing larger as it approached. "Closing in on us."

Andros took a sharp breath. "We need to move."

The air cultivator was coming at them from the northwest, and now the water was coming from the west. There was only one way to go. They began moving east, some silence lost to urgency as they ran. Garron had to dismiss his Essence sight, but Andros still periodically looked over his shoulder, managing somehow to remain on his feet with ease despite barely checking the ground before him.

Then Andros slowed. "Abyss. They've moved. They're coming at our flanks."

Garron stopped running. Andros, with his heightened senses and reflexes, whirled almost immediately, an angry, almost wild look on his face. "They're herding us. We're being pushed toward the fire."

Andros looked at him for a bare moment, clearly thinking. Without warning, he slammed into Garron, grabbing him and rushing through the trees with as much speed as he could manage in the tight confines. Garron settled in, fear and nausea mixing in his stomach. The Elves had gone for a two-pronged attack, trusting the fire as the anvil to their hammer, but if

Andros could shoot out from between them, they might be able to escape.

The Noble changed directions with a jerk and a curse. The motion almost had Garron vomiting onto his friend's tunic, but he managed to just barely hold it in. The implication had him swallowing, in any case. The Elves must have closed in too fast for Andros to break through.

They turned twice more, and each time Garron's throat closed a little tighter. The forest wasn't as bad as the tunnels, but he could feel that each jump his friend took was shorter. Were the Elves outmaneuvering him? When they stopped, Andros whirled almost immediately before setting Garron on his feet.

Garron knew the answer by the heat at his back, and the gleaming arrowhead pointed at his chest.

"Hello *again*, boys." The short Elf sounded considerably less amiable this time around. His tall, severe partner looked even colder than before beside him, holding twin knives in each hand. "I tell you, I'm starting to see what has the fireblood hopping. Lordling, you have three seconds to walk over to Illana there, and let us hobble you. Otherwise your friend dies in front of you."

Garron swallowed, his throat incredibly dry from breathing the scorched air of the fire as well as from staring down the arrow pointed straight at him. When he spoke, he tried to keep his voice confident. "If you kill me, he'll just—"

The Elf bared his teeth. "Two."

"How much money did you want again?" Andros sounded desperate. Afraid.

"One mountain of silver." The Elf paused, his gaze becoming businesslike instead of angry. "Got that? Give it to me in… oh, one second."

"I…" Andros clenched his fists beside Garron, taking a shaky step forward. Garron wanted to grab his friend, but he was pinned in place by the arrow pointing at his heart. "I'm comin—"

Garron almost missed it. The short Elf's head jerked back

and his bow went wild, the arrow shooting wide off target. Wide enough that Garron's quick dive to the side saved him. A light had appeared directly in the Elf's face, crowding his field of vision, startling him, giving them a chance.

Talia.

Andros was above Garron in an instant, picking him up and shooting away in a burst of power. But Garron took a sharp breath as he felt the air around himself. Andros hadn't chosen to try to make it past the two cultivators, or even just dash south and escape.

When Garron took his first scorching, smoke-filled half breath, he knew that they were dashing into the flames.

CHAPTER THIRTY-FOUR

Andros dropped Garron the moment the first jump ended. He would have questioned why if it weren't obvious: the air Garron breathed in was cool, clean. He wasn't burning to death. And the wind was stirring around them in a circle, the smoke forming a translucent barrier between them and the rest of the world.

"Can't... hold for long. Not... practiced. Stay close." Andros' teeth were gritted, and he grabbed Garron's arm as they ran. Garron was more than willing to sprint for all he was worth, clinging so close to Andros that he nearly stepped on his friend's boots, but he couldn't help looking around.

The smoke had said little about the fire itself. Only twice had he been close enough to actually see the blaze, though not so close as to be in danger, and both times he'd been in too much mortal danger to pay attention. He probably still was, but he couldn't help noticing the way the flames had eaten at the ground. Only in a few patches, where perhaps a tree or heavy branch had fallen, were flames blazing. The rest was all blackened ash, a landscape completely unrecognizable as the leaf-strewn earth they'd walked days before.

Each tree was its own separate inferno, huge black figures outlined in red and orange, and even as they ran, limbs fell in showers of sparks. One dropped close enough that pieces of burning wood flew toward them, and Andros jerked Garron to the side. It appeared his barrier wouldn't work against the flames themselves, only their heat and smoke. A single spark landed on Garron's skin, earning a wince and a lancing pain to the side.

They were still on the edge of the true fire. Past where they ran, flames roared so high and so hot that Garron couldn't tell each apart by source—some almost seemed to float in the air, waiting for something to pass through and provide them with food. There was no way, even with Andros' technique, that they were getting through *that*.

Andros' strained voice broke into Garron's awareness. "Watch… behind."

Garron glanced behind him, trusting Andros to guide him past the flames. There was a half dome of smoke speeding through the blackened landscape, much faster than them. "They're behind us. Catching up soon."

His friend didn't speak, but they changed course slightly, angling out of the flames. He was going to try to outlast them? Garron sincerely hoped Andros could manage it, but he was also glad that escape would be near if he couldn't.

Garron was still focused behind, though he had to jerk his eyes back constantly to avoid tripping, stumbling, or falling prey to a stray breath of flame. Andros did most of the work, pulling him along and jerking him side to side to avoid obstacles, but it was still deadly terrain.

The ball of smoke was catching up, not moving with quite the speed the Elves had shown in the tunnels, but still fast enough to make escaping all but impossible. As they drew closer, Garron began to catch glimpses through the haze surrounding the two Elves. The air cultivator was in front, her face strained in an expression almost identical to Andros'. Garron could faintly make out pulses of steam jetting out behind her, and the edges of the other mercenary's tunic. He must have been using his movement technique, but something was wrong. The ball of smoke shot forward in fitful jerks, weaker but also less controlled than Garron seen from the short Elf before.

Suddenly Garron's eyes widened and he slowed a fraction. The ball of smoke was getting very close now, and in its uncontrolled rush forward it had paused beneath a great burning tree, feet away from the blaze. That was far enough not to be dangerous alone, but there was a long branch burning directly above them. Before he'd even fully registered the fact, his hand was extended toward the branch, and he had gathered the Essence in his Center.

"I have them." It would take a split second for their next jump—Garron was faster. He could drop the flaming branch atop them. His hand was beginning to scorch as it passed through Andros' defense, but it would be worth it. The perfect shot. A frozen moment.

He dropped his hand and ran, catching back up to Andros and rubbing the red skin.

Part of Garron felt slightly numb, but he couldn't bring himself to regret his decision. Mostly. Seeing the ball of smoke jerk fitfully, catching a glimpse of the rage on the tall Elf's face, and dodging away from a patch of still burning earth gave him some pause. "They're almost on us, Andy."

"We... can..." Andros didn't finish the thought. Instead, he just grabbed Garron's hand and ran even faster, feet blurring across the blackened ground.

It was all Garron could do to keep his balance and stay within the bubble of safety. They began drifting back toward the blaze at the center of the burned ground. No matter how far they ran, Garron could not see an end to the flames. It almost seemed like Jackson had erected a wall of pure fire across the forest line, though that would be far beyond even him.

Garron spared one last glance backwards as they skirted a

branch burning on the ground, and then a bush still smoldering with a dull glow and a shimmer of heat. The ball was… slowing? Could they outlast the Elves? They would be able to strafe the blaze, exiting at their will, and so long as they were careful, they could escape the two mercenaries.

Andros' bubble popped.

Heat rushed over Garron in a wave, a near-physical force that threatened to send him to his knees. He wanted to draw in a breath, but in the moment Andros' technique failed, he whirled, clapping a hand over Garron's face hard enough to leave him momentarily stunned. In a burst of wind, a shower of sparks, and a scorching pain, they blasted away from the burning ground.

It took moments for cool air to replace the scorching heat rushing across Garron, and finally Andros' hand lifted. Garron drew in a single shuddering breath, but it puffed out immediately as Andros dropped him on the leaf-strewn ground of the forest, his grip failing.

"Phew! Sorry, Gar, never thought I'd need to use that technique like that. That's supposed to choke people, you know." Andros sounded tired, but not nearly exhausted as he had been in the past. He hadn't collapsed either, which was an enormous relief.

Still, Garron could feel the Essence in the air shift as the young Noble's cultivation technique drew it in greedily. He himself was still weak after what he'd used to blast the tall Elf before, but most of that had been restored while he'd been working with Typo. That was the least of his concerns now.

Garron looked around the forest warily. "They saw us. We have to get moving now."

Andros nodded over Garron, then scooped him up in both arms. "Right. Let's move."

"I really need to learn a movement technique." Now Garron was lying across Andros' shoulder, head nearly bouncing off the ground. Actually, he did know one, almost. The basics of the technique were in his head, planted by

Andros' memory stone, but he wouldn't be able to actually execute it without a great deal of practice. Still, if that was what it took to get Andros to stop carrying him around like a rag doll, he would take it.

The trees behind them rustled, and Garron distinctly saw a brown streak tipped with silver flashing in the sunlight, shooting straight for them in the instant before Andros took off. "Focus on not dying. Right."

The surging movement was even worse for Garron while he was upside down, but it afforded him a decent view of what was behind them. As much as he wanted to close his eyes as nausea overcame him, he kept his eyes wide open. The two Elves were shooting through the trees. The short one was once again moving on spouts of water, mobility and control apparently restored now that they were out of the burned area. The taller Elf was keeping pace, but instead of jerky bursts of motions, she appeared to almost dance through the air, each movement launching her into the air longer and faster than should have been possible, each landing lasting for a bare moment and resulting in a swirl of leaves on the ground.

Andros' superior speed should have been enough, but once again his maneuverability presented an issue. Each tree trunk, rock, or steep slope hindered the escape. Several times he broke into different modes of transport, jumping on gusts of air like the tall Elf, though he seemed less proficient than her at it, even simply running with the speed of the wind coating him, each change in direction accompanied by a gust of air.

Perhaps that would have let them escape, but even as Garron watched the two Elves round a particularly large trunk, they split, the short Elf shooting diagonally to head off Andros' path as the other continued to give chase from behind. Garron couldn't hear Andros cursing over the howling of the wind in his ears, but his friend did pause for a moment before reorienting and shooting off in another direction.

It happened again too many times for Garron to keep track of, and he soon lost sight of the tall Elf. The sky and branches blurred into a mess of blue and white and brown and blinding white in his vision, and only one that filled him. "We're heading southeast."

If they could make it to Typo, they could try to capture these mercenaries, maybe even convince them somehow to fight against Jackson. It wasn't what they'd hoped, but perhaps it could work. When they jumped past the large mossy rock, and Garron caught a glimpse of the split tree, bare branches blurring together in the speed of their passing, his heart rose. "Made it."

He looked around as best he could, his vision swimming slightly from the constant motion. As he moved his head, everything devolved into smears of color, but a lighter brown patch moving backwards much slower than the rest of the surroundings still stood out. The tall Elf. A moment later, a second patch joined her, though this one's jerkier motion made it more difficult to pick out. The mercenaries had joined back together, apparently giving up on trying to block Andros' way, but now they were falling behind as Andros navigated more familiar terrain with ease. Soon, they disappeared from sight.

Garron felt a flood of relief as they began to slow. If the Elves had known where they were headed, they could have tried herding Andros away, but they'd been lucky. Now, once they got into Typo's tunnels, even the two D-rankers would hopefully have difficulty succeeding against the traps and monsters set against them. Andros slowed down, and Garron prepared himself for the disorientation of stopping. His friend set him down gently this time, but he still nearly went to his knees as the world spun.

His vision took moments to sort itself out, but he was still confused. He could hear Andros cursing softly behind him, panting. "Why aren't we running to Typo? Weren't we right by the dungeon's entrance?"

Garron's heart sank. They were standing before Typo's tree, recognizable by its size and the shape of its branches swaying in the breeze. Its most distinguishing feature, the mess of roots at its base, was hidden from Garron's view by the boots of a half-dozen guardsmen. As he stared, confused, at the stony faces, his attention was drawn away as flames bursting into being directly before them.

A slender figure, outlined in fire, stepped forward, and Garron shivered at the look on his face. "Hello, brat. Time to stop playing and come home."

CHAPTER THIRTY-FIVE

For a single moment, Garron stared at Jackson's face. There was something terrifying about the flame-wreathed man, his eyes cold but full of controlled rage. No, not controlled... chained. He wondered what would happen when those chains broke.

Behind him were six men. Five of them, Garron barely recognized. They were technically senior members of the guard, but none were low enough to work much on the estate, nor high enough to be memorable. The sixth was Ulysses, a strange cast to his eyes as he looked to Garron, then Andros.

Then a hand snapped out and grabbed his arm. Andros. His friend was tensing, not even bothering to speak to Jackson, just getting ready to shoot away again. Garron jerked out of his stupor. Focus. They needed to cover their escape. He began to gather Essence, pulling it through his meridian. He could—

"Wouldn't run if I were you, boy. I've got a clear shot." Garron didn't have to turn to recognize the voice. The short Elf. Could he really shoot them if Andros started moving immediately? He'd claimed to be able to do it before, but Garron had never been able to find out. Certainly, he wanted to avoid another arrow wound if possible. He was wearing a light chainmail shirt, but he didn't think that would protect him from a cultivator's bow.

Andros seemed calculating, eyes hard and flicking between Jackson, the guards, and the Elves behind. Garron could see from his stance that he was still thinking of a way to fight, and apparently Jackson could too. The fire cultivator raised a threatening hand. "Not a chance, brat. I could take you by myself, and you don't—"

"Two minutes." A whisper, so quiet Garron thought it might have been his imagination, sounded in his ear. It was Talia. Typo was *right there*. Garron dared to hope as he listened to Jackson speak.

"Maybe a year ago, I would have been impressed. Killing Lars? How *did* you manage that?" The man's words were soft, a strange smile twisting his face, but the flames blazed up around him. The leaves at his feet had already burned away, but the flames weren't spreading. "I suppose you lured him into that little dungeon?"

Garron almost choked, and Andros had a similar reaction beside him, but Jackson only gave them a tight-lipped smile. "Oh, you don't think I can spot a dungeon when I see one? No, I'm not stupid enough to go inside without proper scouting. Once you're all wrapped up, I'll let my men take a look. Might be worth something. Anyway, Lars. I was angry at first, but now, I'm just... *disappointed*. I really thought the weakling was fit to be my second. Thank you for showing me otherwise."

The tight-lipped smile split into a wide, manic grin and the flames burned higher. His gaze was locked on Andros, ignoring Garron as if he wasn't even there. That was fine with him. Two minutes. How long had it been now? Ten seconds? Cursing himself for not doing it immediately, he started counting. Eleven, twelve.

But Jackson spoke again, his voice almost playful, and Garron lost the count. "You know what? This has almost been fun. Good training for you, spoiled Noble brat. With every advantage the world could offer, you still can't measure up to me. You never will. Because you're *weak*."

Garron wondered if Andros had heard Talia's message. There was no way to tell. But he seemed incline to stall for time anyway, his fists clenched, eyes darting all around the forest before settling back on Jackson.

"I don't know. Give me a year or two, I'm pretty sure I could take you." The words were short, clipped, almost thrown away. Andros wasn't focused on Jackson at all.

The flames rose, and Garron felt their heat wash over him. "What, another year of using that *wasteful* technique of yours? Of throwing away my time with your idiocy at every turn? They call you a *genius*, boy. Spoiled is what you are. What *all* of you are. If I had a year in your skin, I would be knocking on the doors of the B-ranks, and your darling father would be bowing to me in two!"

At that, Andros appeared stunned. He stared at Jackson, some of the tension dropping from his shoulders. Then he laughed in the man's fiery face.

"That's the stupidest thing I've ever heard. Did you hear that?" He tossed the words over his shoulder, clearly directing them to the mercenaries behind them. "He thinks he can reach *Mage* in just two years!"

Garron didn't know if this was the best move on Andros' part. How long? One minute? A minute and a half? Jackson's face was twisted in rage, and the flames surrounding him began to writhe, intensifying with each breath.

"You worthless child! Do you know what it is to claw for every advantage by yourself? To bow to weaklings because they had the money and time to surpass you? If I could strip away your cultivation and force you to start as I did, I would. If I could show you what a real cultivator could do with the power your family passes down like bloody jewels. I would. I *will*."

Andros had a real smile on his face now, though Garron could see that it was more a release of his tension than anything. "Oh, so now you're going to steal my father's cultivation technique as well? He's going to love that, Jackson. I actually *want* to see you try it."

The manic grin was back on Jackson's face again, the flames high enough to scorch the lowest branches of Typo's tree. "You'll see, boy. It may take a while, but you will."

Where was Talia's help? What was she…? A flash of gold caught the corner of his eye, and it took all of his effort not to jerk his head past Jackson and to the roots of Typo's tree. That color was instantly recognizable to him, though it looked a little different in the light of the day and Jackson's flames than in Typo's Essence-light.

Andros was saying something, but Jackson cut him off with a scream. "That's it! Grab him now and tie him up!"

"Hey! You pathetic excuse for a cultivator!" Garron's voice rang out, loud with fear and real anger. "You're done showing us how incredibly weak you are already?"

Silence, but for the crackling of the flames. The branches above Jackson were truly aflame now, turning black and releasing smoke into the air above them. The men behind Jackson, all save Ulysses, had begun moving but stopped at his words. Beside him, Andros stiffened, and Garron thought he might have caught the barest whisper of Talia's voice.

"Weak? You worthless piece of… you *fishy*. No, you're worse than that. Taint doesn't wash away with a Beast Core, boy, whatever your Center shows." The man laughed, and for a moment he seemed to be breathing the flames like some demon. "You'll always be a weak little servant, leeching off your Noble friend to stay alive. To think, that fool of a Lord was going to… You didn't *deserve* it."

Garron let the words wash over him, feeling his anger grow. "Where did you start, Jackson? You might be right—whatever taint you had before you got lucky and found a Beast Core, it's still right at the surface, almost as ugly as your face."

"Twenty." Talia's voice sounded in his ear, making him shiver. The look on Jackson's face made the effect worse; he'd gone completely calm again, cold, and the flames retreated around him. The branches above still burned. Twenty seconds.

"You're too stupid to understand, boy, but I am *different* than you." The manic gleam was back in Jackson's eyes, though it was difficult to see through the flames. "I am meant to be great, and you should have died a long time ago. Kill hi—"

Not enough time.

"Sir! You *agreed*!" Garron's head jerked over to Ulysses, and he caught another flash of gold to the side. It vanished a moment later, and he focused on the face of the young guardsman. It was drawn in horror, staring pleadingly at Jackson as if he were the one about to be killed. "You said if I... that you would let him go."

"He gave us away." Garron felt a flash of anger, but he didn't let it interrupt his count. Two, three, four... Ulysses had known from when he'd given them the flare where they were. Perhaps he told Jackson that he'd seen them leaving the place?

Jackson barked out a laugh. "Oh, that's right. The other fishy wanted to save his friend. Take your own life as payment and be quiet."

Eleven, twelve, thirteen... so he'd bargained for Garron's life, then? Hadn't he known that wouldn't work? Why would he? Nineteen. In the next second, several things happened.

The first was that Garron and Ulysses raised their hands at the same time. Ulysses in a warding gesture, Garron for a very different reason. Two sounds split the air in the next moment: Talia's voice ringing from across the clearing, and Rai's own declaration of war.

"Now!"

Roar.

The next instant, a jet of water blasted from between Ulysses and the guard next to him, barely visible before a cloud of steam erupted around Jackson with a great hiss, obscuring the man from sight. Garron blasted Essence from his Center for all he was worth, and then jumped to the side as a startled grunt reached his ears, along with the deep *thrum* of a bow releasing an arrow.

In the final moment, Andros grabbed his arm, wind swirling around him, and the burning branch Garron had aimed for fell down into the cloud of steam with a crash and an enraged scream.

Then they were running.

CHAPTER THIRTY-SIX

Garron was getting very tired of being dragged along by Andros' movement technique, but this particular instance had the distinct honor of being the worst by far. Well, the one in the tunnel hadn't been fun, but the point stood: he was in a bad mood.

Andros had his arm in an iron grip, and Garron was in turn grabbing his friend's forearm for all he was worth. He was also exercising some of the arm strength he'd acquired in opening his heart meridian to keep each surge of Andros' technique from tearing his shoulder out of its socket. He was successful, but only in the sense that his joint remained in place. Each burst of motion was a searing pain along his entire arm, and he could feel whatever was holding his shoulder together begin to tear slowly.

Andros didn't slow to readjust his grip, however, and Garron didn't blame him. After all, Jackson was shooting after them on a blazing trail of fire, screaming as he wove around the trees in a constant stream of accelerated movement which didn't seem to end. "That's just unfair."

Luckily, for all the constant speed the technique appeared to provide, it wasn't as fast as Andros. Unluckily, it did do better in the rough terrain of the forest, so that the flame-wreathed man followed only a few dozen feet away from them as Andros surged through the forest, Garron flapping like an extremely unhappy banner loosely attached to its pole.

"Focus." His shoulder did hurt very, very much. No, focus on not dying. "Right."

Garron tried to move his other arm, the one not currently being torn slowly off by his sadistic friend. He found it surprisingly easy. In each surge, the flapping motion of his body actually stabilized, and he had a solid moment of viewing the world as blurs of colors instead of chaotic, incomprehensible swirls. He had to use that moment. He gathered water Essence, and at the next opportunity shot it toward Jackson's blazing light.

It missed.

"Huh. I probably should have expected that." Garron was still trying to think of a way to use his position to their advantage when he noticed something. Despite everything that had happened, it was still just past midday, and whenever the sun made it through the branches, it shone directly in his eyes. He decided to save his Essence. If he was right about where Andros was taking them, they would need it.

Apparently, like Andros, Jackson couldn't use two techniques at once, because he didn't even attempt a ranged assault as he sped toward them. Garron could still hear his screaming occasionally over the rush of air, but he concentrated on simply holding on to Andros. Every surge brought tears of pain to his eyes, but they were whipped away by the wind. Could he call it wind, if they were the ones moving, and the air itself was still?

Just as there was a moment when everything was whipped into tension by the force of Andros' technique, there was a moment of total slack. Garron had considered it just another form of pain, because each time his feet would smack the ground for an instant before being borne aloft again, but it was also an opportunity. If he could get his other arm on Andros, he could support himself far better. But would it overbalance his friend?

"Please. Do it. Please." Garron had never heard of someone's shoulder talking to them, but he swore he could hear its voice in the wind, tortured and pleading. Garron needed to sleep. Badly.

It took three tries. Three incredibly painful attempts as he twisted in Andros' grip, pulling his body toward his friend, only to have it whipped back with extra force on the next surge. Garron didn't know if Andros even noticed his distress. He didn't want to tell his friend. Jackson was too close. Finally, as they nearly crashed into a particularly dense patch of underbrush and Andros was forced to finally use his jumping technique to maneuver around it, Garron managed to get his other arm on Andros' shoulder.

"Thank you." Not the time, shoulder.

Garron decided to wonder about his mental state after he and Andros had escaped the psychotic murderer, but he was starting to get a little worried. It was more than offset by the blessed relief of relieving the pressure on his shoulder, though he knew that now he must look like a particularly strange cape flapping behind Andros.

His worry intensified as the trees became sparser around them, and the soil became visibly more granulated. In two more jumps, they were at the slope, and Garron's heart was squeezing in fear.

As Andros set him down, and Garron finally felt the pain in his arm fade, except for occasional flashes, he spoke, his throat dry from the trip. "Andy, is this a good idea?"

Andros ignored his words, already looking over his shoulder, and Garron followed suit. Jackson would close in moments. "Come... on."

Garron scrambled up the slope with him, though he heard Jackson's screaming behind, and halfway up, Andros took hold once more and jumped, sending them cresting over the hill. Garron felt the pressure of the wind pushing him from below, and only just managed to keep from flailing in Andros' grip. They ascended in a scream of wind, but by the time they reached the zenith, Garron had recovered enough to get his bearings. Already startled by the sudden ascent, his heart squeezed further. A wash of flame was dissipating on the rocky slope, and another was heading directly toward…!

He held out a hand, and let loose the water Essence he'd gathered. Floating in the air as they were, he could aim far better, and his blast impacted the flame midair. The effect was less impressive than he'd hoped. The Essence did do a little to dissipate the fire, but Jackson had let loose the flames as part of a technique, not a raw blast of Essence, so they didn't interact strongly with Garron's blast.

It was still enough to break the technique before it reached them. Garron supposed it had already weakened, traveling over such a long distance. Another flame wave was coming, but before Garron could answer it, or even look around from the new vantage, Andros had sent them rocketing toward the ground with a blast of wind.

There was a unique terror in seeing the ground rush upward, unable to do anything to prevent the impact. Garron knew that Andros would slow down their fall before they landed, but he couldn't help the fear.

They touched down softly, and for a moment Garron just looked around warily. The field of stones was familiar, though they were still standing on what amounted to gravel, but something was distinctly missing. Two somethings, with huge wings and wicked beaks.

"They're coming." Andros muttered the words, eyes on the mountain slope.

Garron thought about summoning his Essence sight, but he trusted his friend. Instead, he looked around. "Move!"

He had another blast of Essence shooting out of his Center before the words even left his mouth, but he still dove to the side, certain it wouldn't be enough. He heard the light clicking of gravel next to him, and knew that Andros had landed beside him. Then the roar of the flame drowned out all noise, and he felt the air pulled out of his lungs, heat washing over him where he lay.

It passed a moment later, and Garron struggled to his feet. Jackson was at the summit of the slope leading to the field, though in the next breath he was streaking toward them on a trail of blazing fire. When Andros was jumping away from the man, he had seemed slow gliding along his flames. He wasn't. It took moments for the fire cultivator to cross the dozen feet to where they had landed. Andros was there to meet him, wind swirling and displacing some of the rocks at his feet.

Garron was forced to back away when Andros' sweep kicked up a cloud of rocks, and sent the flames in Jackson's wake licking up at the air around. The kick did little else, because Jackson hopped it with a smooth ease, converting the momentum of his forward rush into a blazing strike at Andros' head. Garron's friend ducked lower, the flames pushed away from his skin by a blast of wind, so that for a moment it seemed his hair erupted into a plume of flame.

When Jackson landed, the fire sheathing his body had returned, tongues of red and orange accompanying his every move. Andros responded by refusing to touch the man. Every attempted blow met empty air and a whisper of wind. When he threw his next kick at Jackson's side, leg blurring with the speed of the motion, wind pushed at the flames again, sending a wash of hungry orange shooting away from Jackson's other side.

Jackson skipped back from the blow, and his flames surged toward Andros in a solid column, his best ranged technique. Andros jumped to the side with the wind's grace, touching the ground so lightly that not a single rock moved.

Garron shot Essence of earth, water, and air at Jackson's side. The man's head was turned, the flames surrounding him gone for a moment. The Essence left Garron's hand with enough force to send him reeling slightly, the earth imparting weight, the air speed, and the water a flowing elasticity. The Essence whipped out in an arc, catching Jackson hard in his ribs and pushing the man back a step. Garron sagged, feeling the drain on his Center.

He still saw Jackson's head whip around, rage blazing in his wide eyes, apparently unaffected by the blast. He lifted a hand of his own at Garron, snarling, and Garron prepared tired legs to dive away.

Andros' foot made a ripple in the man's skin an instant before it smashed into his face. Even exhausted, terrified, and desperate as he was, Garron's heart soared at the perfect image: Jackson's hand pointing toward Garron, shoulders turned to the side, and Andros' foot planted in his cheek, the Noble's heel, knee, hip, and shoulder all aligned in the air to deliver the blow.

Jackson was sent reeling, and Andros landed in a flurry of wind, knees bent to give chase. Instead he hopped to the side as another jet of flame came for him.

"You *brat*—" Jackson's scream cut off, his feet finding purchase on the rocky ground, then hopping away in a flash.

In the same instant, the rocks at his feet shot up in a small shower and a *crack*. Garron thought it must have been the force of Jackson's leap, but the glint among the rocks told him that wasn't the case. He didn't need to hear the shrieking, painful cry descending toward them to know where the steel feather came from.

CHAPTER THIRTY-SEVEN

Andros was by his side in a rush of wind, a shower of rock preceding him, but Garron was looking at the sky. He had never seen the steel bird in flight. It seemed an impossible sight: metal wings blotted out the sun, cast in shadow so that they seemed almost black from below. The long, spear-like beak jutted out, open to deliver the monster's challenge.

Garron knew his mouth was hanging open slightly. It just didn't seem possible that such a large, dense creature could possibly fly, even if it appeared to be descending in a slow glide, wings remaining still in the air, the creature almost seeming a statue rather than a monster. Then its wings twitched, and Andros pulled Garron away in a burst of air. He heard the crack of another steel feather slamming into stone, and his wits returned in a cold rush.

Andros had set them both down a dozen feet along the field, but no farther from the gravel slope back to the forest. Garron could see Jackson across the rocks, easy to make out by the flames climbing into the sky around him. The man appeared crouched, looking up at the massive bird and across at them. He clearly knew what was going on; Ulysses must have reported back to him after returning from this place, but he wasn't running yet. Rage was warring with caution.

"Abyss, I really hope he doesn't decide to run away." Andros kept his eyes on the scene across the stone field, even as he prepared for another jump.

"Yup, we'd be bird food." A column of flame streaked toward them, and Jackson followed it with blinding speed. Andros bore them to the side, closer to the mountain, and set them down gently on the rocks.

The young Noble gave a nod as they landed. "Good. Now we just have to get him tangled up in—"

The rush forward cut short as another flashing piece of steel interrupted Jackson's path. Then the metal bird landed with a clanging thud that echoed around the field. Jackson's scream of rage answered it, and red flame washed over the bird in a great wave.

Andros let out a short laugh. "Easier to read than my first book."

"Your first book had six words in it." Garron was only half listening to his friend.

"Did I stutter?"

Jackson had apparently looked at the mass of perfect, gleaming steel, the beak made to pierce flesh, the legs like springs ready to coil and pounce after prey, the talons so sharp they sheared through the very rock they stood on… and decided to attack it head on.

Flame impacted steel with almost physical force, the heat prompting gouts of smoke and steam from the water beneath the rocks, each blow accompanied with a rush of air that could be heard even from so far away. The bird had ceased its cry, and was instead ducking its head, letting the flames wash over it without any sign of discomfort. It tensed its legs, and shot forward, a motion that put Andros' speed to shame, talons out and ready to tear into flesh.

Instead, they cut into rock, kicking up a plume of gravel and a few droplets of water. That water turned to steam as another column of flame blasted over the steel bird, and then Jackson shot toward the beast, his flames wrapped around him, attacking with a fury and rage that Garron could almost feel. He wanted to see more, but the flying rocks, the steam of the water below colliding with flame, and sheer volume of fire Jackson was calling made it all but impossible.

"Celestial. I still don't get why he's not in the C-ranks. He even works on his Aura. It's like… he's holding himself back or something." Andros was quiet, as focused on the fighting as Garron was, but his voice still carried a measure of grudging respect, and plenty of fear.

"Let's go." Garron pulled at his friend's arm, looking around nervously. He hadn't heard the haunting call of the other bird yet, and he had no desire to receive another cut from claws of mist. They were still only feet away from the edge of the slope. Andros nodded, and they began to run back toward the forest.

"I see you, brats!" The scream was so loud that Garron heard it over the roar of the flames and crashes of rock against steel. He looked over his shoulder in time to see Jackson shooting away from the great cloud across the field, and hear the shrieking as the great steel bird expressed its own rage.

"Andy!" Garron shouted over the deafening noise, and sure enough, Andros was already turning, gathering him up and tensing. They streaked forward, straight to the summit, gravel flying up in their passing. After landing, they found Jackson before them, rage in his eyes, fire gathering around him once more.

Garron lost sight of the man as the steel bird came crashing down between them, metal body once again ringing as it struck the rock, kicking up a shower of gravel and a few drops of water. It appeared the bird's body had heated from its combat, because the water turned immediately to steam, rising…

No, it was falling. Garron's head snapped upwards, and he felt Andros tense beside him. Barely visible, more like a cloud than a monster, was the white bird. It was silent, but mist poured from its open beak, shrouding them all in white. For a moment, the mist faded away as Andros pushed at it with his own Essence. Jackson let out another scream, flames shooting upwards to impact the white beast, burning away the mist.

The bird was coated in mist so thick that it almost seemed like a cloud, thick enough that the flames disappeared into it, with no sign that they did anything. Mist poured downwards, but Andros kept it away with bursts of wind. Garron felt glued to the spot, only feet away from the colossal steel monster now nearly hidden in the mist, and standing beneath the white cloud he knew contained another monster. The mist glowed as more flames shot at the white bird, and then rippled. He heard the crack of stone slicing, and another yell, before a gout of flame billowed up from outside the mist cloud, just barely visible around the mass of white.

Jackson had dodged, it seemed, but he was still trying to fight the monsters. Andros pulled Garron back as a steel feather shot out of the cloud, kicking up stones at their feet, then there was a rumbling sound as something huge shot away, and more ripples in the mist cloud made their way to the light of the flame, drawing farther and farther away from Andros and Garron.

Andros staggered for a moment, clearly exhausted, but he steadied himself on Garron's shoulder. Before Garron could speak, he shook his head. "Let's go."

They ran, though Garron did his best to stay silent as they scrambled down the gravel slope, rocks sliding down before them until they reached the bottom. They didn't speak as they sprinted back toward the trees, though Garron felt his heart grow lighter as the sounds of Jackson's yelling and the cracks of stone shattering faded.

Garron glanced at Andros as they ran before returning his attention to the terrain. "Do you think he beat them?"

"Not a chance. If we got away, he can too. We've got a few minutes." Andros sped up, and Garron pushed himself to keep pace. They stopped when the trees grew thicker, and Garron could feel Andros pulling in the air Essence all around with blistering speed. He wished he could follow suit, but there was hardly any water Essence in this place, and it was hardly worth the effort with his cultivation technique.

"What should we do?" Garron looked around nervously, waiting for something to pop out of the trees and attack them, or for Jackson to come roaring at them, flames ablaze.

"You think. I'll get ready." Andros began dancing around. His motions were almost mechanically swift, Essence drawn in with all the speed his cultivation technique afforded him.

Garron thought hard. Escape. They had minutes of respite from Jackson. They needed to use it. "Hold on. If Jackson was still on the plateau, then… Andy, can you get us *over* the wildfire with your flying technique?"

Andros paused his dance, a light appearing in his eyes as he considered. "I… don't know. Hot air rises, and I can't do two things at once. If we go over that… I couldn't see how wide it was. Maybe?"

The flames had been too high and too hot for Garron to examine. He thought about sticking his hand out in that air, his skin burning and blistering immediately. It would be many times worse to go over the flame, where the heat was concentrated. But was it their best chance? He shook his head. "It's either that, or we try to get to Typo. He has mobs and traps. We might not be able to get Jackson in the cage, but… it's our best shot. If we can push through them."

Andros paused again in his cultivation, though Garron could feel that what air Essence there was had already been drawn into his Center. He looked for a long moment at Garron, considering. His eyes looked more thoughtful than Garron had ever seen them, brow furrowed, though the edges of his bangs had been seared away by Jackson's flames, and droplets of condensed mist coated his hair so that it looked nearly gray.

Finally, the young Lord spoke, eyes determined. "Those Elves are tricky. I'll have to maneuver around them, so you'll have to be ready to take an opening to get to Typo. I can keep the guards off, too, but they're strong enough to give me a little trouble. You have enough Essence for a few more blasts, right? Maybe Rai will help a bit, if we're lucky."

Garron looked at him, and felt a smile tug at the corners of his mouth. "We're not running?"

Andros grinned. "Abyss, no. Even if we wouldn't die for sure going over that fire, I'm done with running away. Besides, I really, *really* want to see Aiki fight."

CHAPTER THIRTY-EIGHT

They shot through the trees in intermittent bursts of Essence-enhanced speed punctuated by full sprints. Andros wanted to conserve his Essence, a sentiment with which Garron couldn't help but agree. There was only so much in the other boy's Center, though apparently their time in the forest had increased his capacity a great deal, and they would need every scrap of Essence Andros could muster to break through to Typo, and even more to make it through the fight to follow.

As they ran, Garron tried his best to silence the screaming voice in the back of his head calling him foolish. Yes, the only other option was a mad dash to the tree line and a jump over a blazing wildfire that would likely get them killed, but he was running toward a fight with a half dozen guardsmen, a pair of Wild Elf mercenaries and, eventually, Jackson.

He had a grin on his face that put Andros' to shame. They made it to Typo's part of the forest with a trio of bursts from Andros' technique, but before Garron could continue running with his friend, he felt a hand on his shoulder. "We have to move fast. *You* have to move fast. I'll get us close, but they'll be after me, and there's a lot of them you will need to push through, got it?"

Garron frowned and swatted at the hand gripping him, "We're both pushing through. *Together*. We can do this, Andy."

Andros let go of his shoulder, smiling. "Course. Let's move."

They shot through the trees once more, and passed into the clearing where they had set the trap for Jackson. Garron sincerely regretted setting spikes and rockfalls to trigger with the trap, or they could have simply entered through there. Andros slowed and pointed. "Hey look, it's Pittney!"

"You sound as tired as I feel." Garron rolled his eyes as he ran. "Keep moving."

Two more jumps, and Typo's tree came into sight. Andros shoved Garron away from him with a blast of wind to send him flying. For a short few seconds, the world was a jumble of colors, then his backside hit the ground with a painful *smack*. He still heard the sound of a bowstring vibrating, and of an arrow slamming into earth.

Garron got to his feet, looking around. They were in the patch of woods near Typo's tree. He was off to the side, launched into a patch of underbrush by the throw. He could just make out the dungeon entrance around another ancient trunk, but his gaze was quickly captured by the sight across from the dungeon, past another set of bushes but otherwise in clear view from his position.

Andros was engaged with the tall Elf, the air cultivator. They were trading blows that howled through the air, moving with impossible speed, so closely intertwined that—the Noble ducked, and an arrow streaked above his head. He landed a kick on the tall Elf's side, then ducked under a blast of Essence from her.

A voice rang out across the forest. "Don't move or I'll—"

Andros moved.

Garron had rarely seen the other boy use his movement technique without being along for the ride, but it was truly something. His form blurred, streaking over the forest floor like an arrow. Garron's eyes could barely follow his friend's path, but it ended beside the split trees across from Typo's entrance, where the short Elf in his leather tunic perched. The mercenary was holding a black bow with an arrow nocked and half-drawn, pointed at Garron.

Andros kicked the bow, knocking it aside before he even landed, and grabbed for the weapon. The Elf had a tight grip, and for a moment they wrestled silently over it, before the Elf snarled.

"I'm not that old yet, boy!" A blast of raw Essence accompanied the words, and Andros released his grip on the bow to dodge to the side. The Essence splashed to the ground, plowing a furrow in it.

"You idiots, hurry and help!" The other Elf screamed the words, already moving to her partner with her jumping technique.

"Gar, get—gah! Moving!" Andros grunted the words out as he wove around the short Elf's strikes, each of his motions a puff of air to the fluid stream of the Elf's attacks. It was strange to see such a short, squat man move with such grace—every punch flowed into the next, and though he rarely displayed acrobatics like Andros', his kicks were perfectly timed, yet short and brutal.

Andros ducked another punch, threw one of his own, and screamed. "*Move!*"

Garron started. The word had come from two mouths at the same time, and as he looked away from watching Andros fight, he saw that Typo's tree was still being blocked by a half dozen guardsmen. Four of them, large men in full armor who Garron vaguely thought were in the upper F-ranks, were beginning to move, but two remained. Better than all of them.

Garron ran forward, pulling at the Essence in his Center in desperation, wincing at the lack of power there. He had probably lost a rank at this point, but that was better than his life. As he approached, coming into full view of everyone else in the area, he heard another shout from behind.

"You two! Don't let him—" The voice cut off, but the two guards in front of the entrance had heard. The one to Garron's left had raised a long sword and eyes fixed on him, though his cap had a faceguard which concealed his expression.

The second man was Ulysses.

Garron didn't hesitate, letting loose the earth Essence he'd gathered straight at the first guard's head. From this distance, his aim was perfect, and the man hadn't seen his attack coming. His head jerked back and he stumbled. Garron ran up and ripped the sword from limp fingers.

Without pause, he turned the weapon in his grip, and let loose with a vicious blow to the guardsman's head, then another. The flat of his blade struck over the guard's ear twice, the man apparently too stunned to do anything. In the back of his mind, Garron wondered if the guard had opened any meridians yet. Even if he had, he'd reacted too slowly.

As the tall guardsman fell, bludgeoned into unconsciousness, Garron looked to the second. Ulysses had pulled his sword out, but it was pointed at the ground to the side. His cap didn't cover his face, so Garron could see the fear and consternation on it without issue. Ulysses looked back at him, then down at his sword, clearly torn. He took a step forward, raising a hand as if to grab Garron's arm.

The younger man focused, and smashed the flat of his blade into the side of Ulysses' head with the force of his entire body. An almost comical look of surprise crossed the guardsman's face an instant before his knees buckled.

"Serves him right." Garron immediately regretted the mean-spirited thought, but not the blow. It would save the man a beating, or worse, after the battle, if he was seen to have taken an injury doing his duty. The man had given up their location, whatever the reason.

"Andy, let's—" Garron looked over his shoulder, and the

breath froze in his chest. Andros was being swarmed by six combatants, weaving around sword strokes and kicks and blasts of Essence, doing everything he could to keep free of the attacks.

The two Elves had moved to flank him, one with her knife and the second with his bow slung across his shoulders, kicking and punching and throwing the occasional technique. Four armored guards were crowding the young Noble so hard that he could do little but dodge. Even as Garron watched, the flat of a blade intended for his head struck a shoulder, and a blast of water Essence caught the other. Andros leapt away, but the monster was on him as he fled.

That was, until the tall Elf noticed Garron standing in front of the dungeon entrance, the two guardsmen stirring weakly at his feet but unmoving. "*Fools*! The boy! Sir!"

The short Elf paused his assault on Andros, looking over with an eerie calm. He glanced back at Andros, now engaged with just the four guardsman and still having a tough time staying away as the attacks became more vicious. "We get the boy, we win. You bucketheads, keep the little Lord away from the entrance."

The Elf tensed, and his companion on the other side of the fighting did the same. One of the guards grunted an affirmative, and the steel-clad men closed ranks, cutting Andros off from Garron's view. But his voice still carried. "*Go*, Gar!"

The Elves were on the move, their movement techniques making the distance trivial, and Andros was boxed in. Garron only had a breath to think.

"Pittney in two hundred!" He dove into the hole at the roots, stripping away the covering with practiced ease and landing with a dull thud.

<Concerned greeting!> Garron could feel the dungeon's worry. He must have heard much of what happened from Talia already.

"One... two... three." Garron carefully kept count as he

moved. <Listen carefully, Typo. We have some guests coming. I need you to help me with the welcome.>

Almost instantly, the dungeon responded. <Excited agreement!>

"Five, six, seven." As Garron ran down the tunnel, he heard the Elves land behind him in pursuit.

CHAPTER THIRTY-NINE

They were behind him, and that meant he was in trouble.

<Typo, here's what I need.> Garron sent images along with the words, all the while keeping a desperate count. "Ten, eleven…"

<Confusion? Acceptance.>

"Stop running, boy! Make this easy and I won't have to hurt you!" The voice sounded tired, reasonable even; but it pushed Garron faster as he skirted trap after trap down the tunnel. He could hear the sound of rushing water behind him, then the *thrum* of springs uncoiling, and a curse. Garron risked a glance behind, though he was careful with his steps down the tunnel.

The Elf was touching his leg, a trio of spikes around him, two embedded in the wall and one lying to the side. Garron thought there was red running to the ground, but it was hard to tell at such a distance against the brown of the mercenary's clothes. A shudder passed through the man's body, and he stood, shaking the leg.

Garron's heart soared for a moment as the short Elf stayed still, looking down the tunnel, then back at the wall with a wary look on his face, and he himself slowed. Would he just wait there, content to hold Garron in? Then his partner landed beside him in a gust of air, and Garron breathed out a curse.

He turned back as the tall Elf grabbed her partner and began jumping quickly and quietly along, the Elf shooting water at every landing spot, just to be certain.

The short Elf's voice echoed down the tunnel. "Last chance you get, boy!"

"Eighteen, nineteen..." Garron ran faster down the first stretch of tunnel before the Elves could catch up, and Typo sent him a tense projection.

Garron could sense him bending all of his new mental faculties on the task Garron had set him. <Focus. Partial confirmation.>

The human almost smiled. <Good, keep going. Send Rai.>

There was one more long stretch of tunnel before the first room. Garron knew it contained a single pit, two cages, and a spike trap. Of all of those, the only one which might work was the pit. If he was lucky, the Elves would miss the cracking earth of his modified trap and—

"Abyss! Jump, Illana! It's a pitfall! Why didn't it show when I...? Jump, girl!" The short Elf screamed behind him.

Now Garron grinned. There was one in the first stretch, too. <Typo, reset any traps you can once they're through!>

<Distracted confirmation.> There were more, so many more things the dungeon should be doing, but Garron kept their link clear. Typo was already stretched to the limit of his attention and ability, and Garron couldn't afford to have him mess up his current task.

"Thirty-six, thirty-seven..."

"Stay still, sir. Be ready to move us." Now Garron could hear the other Elf's voice, quiet and focused. They were getting closer. They just skipped all of the cage traps, too. Not fair.

Garron was midway through the final stretch of tunnel. He could see Rai coming up toward him, and the exit into the big room beyond. He couldn't let the Elves in the room yet—their

Auras would be strong enough to cause serious interference with Typo's work. As the young lion approached on silent feet, navigating the traps as though they were each marked with a signpost, Garron turned, sending a 'quiet' request to Typo for a pile of rocks. The dungeon didn't bother replying, but the stones appeared beside him.

Rai came up beside him, purring gently, just as the Elves rounded the bend. The short one was being hoisted into the air by his armpit, the image comically absurd as the Elves flew into the air once more. When they caught sight of Garron, standing with a stone in his hand next to Rai, they landed immediately. The short Elf had an easy smile on his face.

"Not a bad place. Like the water Essence quite a bit." He scratched his ears, the motion jostling his partner somewhat. "Decided to come with us?"

Garron took a deep breath, and threw a rock at him.

The tall Elf dodged with an easy grace, and her companion swayed along with her, his smile turning rueful. "Good, solid answer. Something about a nice rock that you just can't get across when flapping your lips, isn't there, boy?"

Garron threw another rock. It bounced off the short Elf's leg, as the pair jerked to the side, prompting a wince, and a scowl. "Let's end this, Illana."

The pair started jumping forward, a long, slow arc that had them floating far too long. It was further slowed as the short Elf raised his hand, Essence twisting around him, and water gathered from the walls, floor, and air before discharging in a short burst at the ground. The blast left a small furrow, but revealed no traps. Those came later in the tunnel.

Garron managed to hit the Elf in the face with the next throw. "Forty-five, forty-six…"

The Elf growled at him as he rubbed his sore nose. "Oh, just you wait, boy. I'm going to—"

"Sir. We will get the boy faster if you focus." The tall Elf sounded the same as the first time Garron had met her. The voice reminded him of a line of fire at his throat, and black creeping in at the edges of his vision... so he threw a rock at her.

"Sixty-five, sixty-seven," Garron breathed. Only a minute, so far, and he needed more than three.

"Ooh, how'd that one feel, Illana? That's what you get for mouthing off so much." The older Elf had a rough laugh in his voice, but it had a savage cast. Another blast of water hit the floor and they landed again, having skipped over the spike trap.

<Typo, how's it going?>

<Distracted *irritation*.>

Garron took that to mean 'almost finished.' The Elves were in the air again, perhaps a quarter way down the stretch of tunnel. Garron waited and threw a rock. Both the Elves flinched in the air, but the rock was low, just barely missing their feet. It hit the ground with a dull *thunk*.

The one disadvantage to the counterweight systems, beside the space required, was the speed the trap engaged. Garron had tried to mitigate it somewhat with springs, but it still took a moment for the weights to fall far enough. Luckily, Garron knew exactly how long that moment was.

Even as they sailed through the air, the twin domes of the trap snapped up with several hundred pounds of force guiding their motion. By the time the dome closest to Garron hit the Elves midair, it was moving fast enough to be a blur. They saw it coming in time for the short Elf to slam his blast of water at the edge of the steel dome, and for the taller one to let loose a blast of air which Garron felt down the tunnel, pushing them up enough so that the cage's edge only clipped them with a hard ring of steel.

"Ow! Infernal lakes of fire, that—" Garron managed two throws in quick succession before the Elves could touch down. When they did, the short Elf was snarling, and even his partner seemed mildly annoyed.

"One hundred."

"That's *enough*, boy!" The mercenary raised a hand, and his companion stuck hers out from beneath his armpit.

"Rai!" Garron dove back as twin blasts of Essence shot toward him, and all sound was drowned out as Rai let out a roar like a rushing waterfall. A sound like a crashing wave followed it, and Garron felt a fine mist spray over him, Rai's water blown back by the force of the twin blasts. A moment later, the remaining force of the blasts hit him, like heavy thumps of a weighted pillow that carried him back over the ground. "Hundred-ten."

The Elf let out a grunt of resignation. "I'm done with this. I can cultivate a few extra days if it means doing this faster. Come on, Illana."

"Let's move, Rai!" Garron grabbed a rock and started sprinting down the hall, leaping over traps and zigzagging as best he could.

Twice more, Rai turned beside him and roared, but the Elves apparently found it easy to dodge, because blasts of Essence followed him down the tunnel, slamming into the floor behind him with enough force to leave crevices in the ground. He managed to avoid the blows, though he kept throwing looks over his shoulder.

The world flashed white, and Garron pitched forward, spilling onto the floor just as he exited the tunnel. He could hear a high-pitched ringing, but everything else was silent for a moment. Serene. It had been so long since he was truly alone. Even when Andros wasn't there now, he still had Typo in his mind.

<Fear, concern, warning, urgency, *frustration*!> The emotions washed over Garron in a wave that forced a convulsion through his body. What?

"Oh, looks like he's waking up." A hand closed on his wrist. Garron's eyes flew open, and he pulled sharply against the grip, trying desperately to get to his feet and shake the hand free at the same time. He succeeded at the first, but the second...

"Not so easy when you're up close and personal, is it boy?" The Elf held his arm almost casually, his hand a little sweaty against Garron's wrist. But the grip was so tight that Garron could feel everything compressing, and he knew that if he moved the wrong way, his wrist would snap like a twig.

A snarl drew his attention to the side, where Rai was slipping away from a kick aimed by the other Elf. She stepped forward, pivoting to deliver another kick, but Rai was already moving, shooting to the Elf's blind side before letting loose a roar. Water shot forward in a concentrated stream, focused enough, Garron knew, to cut through flesh and leave marks in bone even at a foot's range.

The tall Elf sidestepped easily, moving in to attack again.

Maintaining his grip on Garron's wrist, the short Elf grunted. "Careful there, Illana. That's a crafty one, you know. Water monsters are tricky, remember. Don't commit too hard to any—"

Was the Elf teaching the air cultivator? Now? His eyes weren't even on Garron anymore, his head turned as he called advice and suggestions to his partner. She didn't appear to listen to a single word, though she seemed to be doing fine to Garron's eyes. Speaking of which…

Garron looked around the room. Only clear space to the naked eye, though large enough to provide plenty of space for a fight. <Good job, Typo.>

<Pride.>

Now he only had to… drat, he'd lost the count. The short Elf was turning. <Aiki. Send in—>

His thoughts scrambled as the Elf's grip tightened further and his bones creaked. A slight twist, and he was on his knees. A little more, and he was choking back a scream. This was the same arm that had nearly been torn off during his escape with Andros, and his shoulder was loudly announcing its displeasure.

"Sorry, boy, but I'm no saint." The Elf still looked calm, though the fighting raging behind him, punctuated by snarls as Rai dodged attack after attack, gave his serenity an almost eerie cast. "You throw rocks at a fellow, you can't complain if he gets a little upset. Not to mention that cage thing. How long have you been in here, anyway? Pretty advanced traps for a place this weak."

Garron opened his mouth to reply, but his wrist was still flaring in pain, forcing him to bend awkwardly to keep it from snapping, and his shoulder screamed as he twisted it further. For a moment, he couldn't so much as draw breath.

<Warning.>

"Get her, Rai!" He shouted the words desperately, his eyes half closed and forced to the ground. *Please* look away. He looked up awkwardly to see the short Elf turning his head back to his companion.

"What in the—"

He almost wished the Essence leaving his Center would hurt. Instead, it just left behind a horrible emptiness, a weakness that told him how close he was to running out. But the blast of his combined affinities still blasted out, shooting at the man's chest.

Where the two D-rankers' Essence blasts could send him sprawling if they so much as clipped him, Garron's own didn't pack much more power than a particularly large rock. But a particularly large rock shoved in someone's chest from point blank range when they weren't expecting it was enough to stagger them. That was enough for Garron to rip his arm away with all the strength he could muster, both wrist and shoulder flaring in agony.

He scrambled back with all the speed he could manage, but the short Elf was already moving, motions fluid, taking two light steps toward him. On the ground, still backing away furiously, Garron looked up at the mercenary's calm, professional face. The mercenary looked down at him in turn, until something behind Garron caught his eye.

"Second mob, Illana! It's a mean one!" The easy tone had vanished, replaced with a hard bark, a practiced shout that carried even as a deep snarl carried across the room, setting Garron's chest rumbling.

Two roars filled the room at once, making a strange

harmony of bass to baritone, the sounds blending together so that Garron couldn't tell which was which. From the fine mist washing over him, he supposed that Rai had managed to break away from his fight long enough for a strike at the short Elf, and from the lack of shaking in the ground, that Aiki was still across the room, too far for her ability to affect him.

The mercenary was letting out a shout and a curse, so Garron took the opportunity to scramble to his feet. Rai was leaping for the air cultivator again, but Garron could see the lion's chest heaving in the moments between blows, and the Elf hardly looked tired. Her partner was turning back, an expression of *supreme* annoyance on his face, and Garron could see pale red dripping around his neck. How many seconds? The last count he remembered was a hundred and ten. Had it been a minute since? More?

He hoped so. He couldn't stay away from the Elf for more than a moment, so he used it. The thudding footsteps of a huge lion behind him, he cut across the short Elf in front and ran for a corner of the room with all the speed he could muster. The Elf seemed surprised at his sudden move, or perhaps still preoccupied with Aiki lumbering toward him, because Garron managed to make it four steps before something tripped his leg, sending him sprawling an arm's length away from the wall. How long? One-eighty? One-ninety?

"You're a tricky one, boy. Forgot you fishies can still pack a punch, but that's on me." A hand like iron grabbed at his arm, and Garron scrambled to stand as his shoulder made its displeasure known. The Elf turned from looking at Aiki's slow charge, and Garron could see calculation, annoyance, and a very slight trace of worry in his dark eyes. "Be better for us if you took a little nap, I think."

A hand raised, pulled back, ready to strike.

One-ninety? Or two—

A breath of wind was his only warning, but Garron threw himself backward as the Elf's hand blurred through the air. He felt the grip on his arm tighten, then heard a meaty thunk as flesh impacted flesh. The grip broke, and he stumbled back.

Andros, panting but otherwise unharmed, was standing before him, a shower of earth falling around him. Typo had taken a while to remove the cage, disable the traps, and clear any trace of the opening in the ceiling, but he'd done a good job —the Elf was taken completely off-guard.

Aiki let out another roar, and Garron could feel the ground tremble. Rai snarled, and Garron could hear the howls of wolves coming up the tunnel. Everything seemed frozen for an instant as Garron and the mercenary stared on opposite sides of the lanky young man.

Then Andros kicked the short Elf in the knee.

<Excitement!>

CHAPTER FORTY

Andros' leg blurred and a small cloud of dust puffed up in its wake, the motion so incredibly swift that even the other D-ranker was a hair too slow to dodge. The Elf let out a short scream as he collapsed, clutching the limb. Before Garron could even draw in a tight breath, Andros had taken a short step forward, seized the bow slung around the man's shoulders, and snapped it across his leg in a shower of splinters. The Elf raised a shaking hand, but Andros knocked it aside, reaching across the man's back in the same motion and pulling an arrow out of his quiver, putting a knee hard on his stomach, and pointing the arrowhead directly at the man's throat.

"Stop!"

The hard shout shook Garron out of his paralysis. How long had that taken? He didn't think he'd had the time to draw a single breath since Andros dropped down into the dungeon, and now he was kneeling atop the short mercenary, a blade pointed at the man's throat.

Garron's eyes widened. <Typo, tell Rai to back away, and Aiki to stop moving.>

The dungeon only paused a moment in reluctance. <Confirmation.>

"Kyliar! Don't kill him!" The tall Elf had turned at Andros' shout, staring at the scene only feet away from where she'd been fighting Rai. The young lion, now retreating, was limping slightly, and his chest was heaving with each breath. The Elf hardly seemed to care as she took a step toward Andros, raising a hand.

"Don't move!" Andros' voice was still hard, as cold as any word out of the tall Elf's mouth, and he pressed the arrowhead against the Elf's skin. Garron walked around the side in time to see his friend glance down at the Elf beneath him. "You too. I've got Essence sight. I'll see if you try anything."

The short Elf nodded, breath coming in short gasps. The other Elf still had her hand raised. Her voice, though a slightly softer than before, still had a cold edge. "Please, don't—"

Andros snarled. "Hand down, now!"

The Elf dropped her hand, though her eyes still flicked around the room, calculating.

"Gar?" Andros looked at him expectantly, still panting, a frantic light in his eyes. For all the hard focus and competency he'd just displayed in the past few moments, it was clear he'd done it all on instinct and battle-fever. Garron owed it to his friend to give him a moment to breathe.

"Drop the knives. Walk over there." Garron directed the tall Elf tiredly, rubbing at his arm. He could still move both, but the pain of his shoulder had not left like it had before. It still throbbed gently, reminding him what would happen if he abused it again.

At his instruction, the tall Elf dropped the knife in her hand, unbolting the sheaths at her waist. She made her way past Aiki, who sat perfectly still, watching her, and stood by the exit to the room.

"What… do… you… want?" The Elf beneath Andros appeared to have recovered some of his wits, though he still sounded pained with every word.

Garron glanced at him. "I want to hold you two without killing you. Will you agree to that?"

A wheezing laugh. "Of... course. Still... get paid. Let... me heal... my leg?"

"Sir. We cannot just submit to them! We were bound to capture the boy! We were paid, and *they* offered us nothing!" The tall Elf had to nearly shout the words from her position across the room, but she sounded almost frustrated. Her face showed real concern mixed with annoyance. The ice was giving way to heat, but the cause confused Garron. She didn't even seem angry that her partner had been crippled and captured, so much that they were surrendering so easily.

The short Elf, in contrast, had a smile on his face, despite the grimace trying to fight its way free around the corners of his mouth. "Not... Huine anymore, Il-an-ayla. No honor... to protect."

The other Elf—Garron had thought her name was Illana, but apparently it was something more complicated—opened her mouth at her partner's words, then snapped them shut.

The short mercenary turned back to Garron. "Can... I heal... leg?"

Garron considered. "What's your name?"

The Elf let out a breath. "Cayar."

"Hurry up, Gar, we don't have that much time." Andros was looking nervously down at the entrance leading out of the dungeon, clearly expecting Jackson to appear at any moment. The hand holding the arrow didn't waver a bit.

<Hunger.> Typo wanted him to let Andros finish the job, he knew. A powerful water cultivator would do a great deal for his growth, and he'd used a huge amount of Essence recently in creating Aiki, and more in modifying the traps in the room around them.

Garron back to Cayar. "What rank are you?"

The short Elf took a long moment to answer, his breath coming in short gasps. "D-... five. Please... let me—"

"Drop two ranks. Push the Essence out of your aura, toward the door. Then you can heal your leg."

The grimace on the Elf's face deepened. When he spoke, confusion and reluctance warred with pain in his voice. "Why? You can't… cultivate it… before he comes."

<Hunger.>

Garron gave the man a hard look. "Do it."

Andros punctuated Garron's command by pressing the arrowhead down slightly harder, so that beads of red welled up around the blade. Garron would have scolded his friend, but he could remember Cayan's partner doing the same thing to him.

The Elf spent another moment considering, chest heaving, arms clenching and unclenching by his side with every second, but before the first drop of blood hit the ground, he let out a long, shuddering breath, and purified Essence flowed out of him, spreading through the air, drifting away in a cloud of power even as its owner shuddered at the sudden loss. The moment it got far enough away, Typo absorbed it greedily, and Garron could feel his satisfaction echo through their link.

"Good." Garron nodded. That would weaken the mercenary as well, which would make holding him easier. In fact…

"You. Illana, right? Drop down to D-zero. Now." Garron knew his voice was harsh, cold. Cruel, even. It reminded him of the Elf he was addressing. He didn't feel particularly bad about it.

A look with Essence sight told Garron that the air cultivator was in the lower D-series, perhaps two or three. He wasn't experienced enough to tell, but either way, the already-purified Essence in her Center should give Andros something to work with. He would just have to be quick to convince her.

The tall Elf sagged, Essence drifting out of her from across the room, enough to be noticeable even in the dense earth and water of Typo's influence. Garron's eyebrows went up even as she went to her knees, chest heaving, mouth pressed closed, eyes as hard as ever.

"Uh, thanks. Okay, now just walk down that tunnel there,

straight down the middle. Don't worry, the first trap is a cage, so just stay there." Garron felt more than a little awkward, giving directions to the Elf across the room while his friend held a blade to her partner's throat. Still, she got to her feet, swaying slightly, turned, and staggered into the far tunnel. The sharp clang told Garron the cage trap had triggered.

<Typo?>

The dungeon sent him an image of the Elf, seated cross-legged in the cage, eyes closed, a thin sheen of sweat on her face. Good. She hadn't tried tricking them somehow.

Cayar coughed. "Can... I... heal?"

The short Elf seemed to be getting weaker over time, but Garron wasn't particularly sympathetic. His side tingled where an arrow had ripped across it, and his heart pumped louder in his ears, as if to remind him of when it had almost failed to keep him alive. But he couldn't help looking at the Elf's knee and wincing.

He walked to where Illana had dropped her knives, picking one up. The long, wavy-bladed weapon felt too heavy for a knife, though with Garron's newfound strength, he found lifting swords only moderately difficult now.

Garron shivered slightly, looking at the sharp steel and remembering it cut him, but his grip firmed after a moment, and he walked back to Andros. "Andy, can you lift him?"

"I mean, he's on the heavy side, but sure." Andros flashed a tired grin, and below Cayar let out a breath that might have been a laugh. Carefully, the air cultivator eased his knee off the Elf's stomach, lifting the arrow from his throat when Garron replaced it with his new knife. With his Essence-enhanced strength, Andros lifted the Elf under the armpits, Garron to the side with a knife pressed awkwardly into skin.

Garron gestured to the exit. "Come on."

Together, they shuffled to the other side of the room, Andros doing his best to keep the ruined leg off the floor in the process. It took much longer than it should have, and only the fact that Garron could feel Typo working to reset traps, strengthen mobs, and generally prepare for the coming fight with his new Essence kept him from hurrying the process along. That, and the pain he could see lingering around the edges of Cayar's expression as they moved him, leg swinging, into the far tunnel.

Once they'd passed a still seated Illana, skirting wide around her cage, Andros finally set the short Elf down as gently as possible. The man still shuddered involuntarily at the pain, but he didn't let out more than a grunt.

"Crawl over there. You can heal your leg once you're in the cage." Garron indicated the spot only inches away from the Elf's position as he and Andros backed away. The cage's sides would snap them up if they were too close.

The Elf spent a moment with his mouth pressed into a thin line, chest heaving. When he spoke, Garron could hear a real note of pleading in his voice. "Please. Push my leg… straight. Can't heal… properly. Won't be able… to walk."

Garron snarled; they didn't have time for this. He felt an itch at his back every second it was turned away from the dungeon entrance, and Andros was even jumpier beside him. "You have to be in the cage. We can't—"

"Please. I won't fight you. I swear."

Garron lifted his knife, stepping toward the fallen mercenary. Suppressing his revulsion, he looked down at the injury—the knee was bent sideways, grotesque in its deformity. Garron didn't need the Elf to tell him that he wouldn't be able to heal it as it was. He'd seen bones set before, even had his own arm pulled into alignment once when he was little.

He stretched the knife toward the Elf for a moment, then pulled away. "Hold this, Andy."

His friend shot him a puzzled look. "Come on, Gar. Let him do it himself. He can go to a Flesh Mage when he gets out of here."

The Elf let out another almost-laugh. "No… money. Can't afford."

Andros looked startled at that, as if he hadn't considered the possibility, but his face hardened as he looked at the man on the ground. "He almost killed you, Gar. He's not going to—"

"Hold the knife, Andy." Andros had that wild look in his eyes again, but for the first time Garron felt real concern for his friend. For all his talent and skill, Andros wasn't vindictive. The pressure was getting to him. "Take a deep breath. I know you're getting ready for the fight, but you're no good like this."

It took a long moment, Andros looking past Garron to the Elf on the ground, then over his shoulder as if expecting to see Jackson running in, but he took the knife and stowed it at his belt, the blade pointing backwards so that it wouldn't interfere with his movements.

"Thank… you." Cayar exhaled.

Garron looked down at the Elf. Andros' words had ignited a small fire in his own heart, and though he'd resolved to help Cayar, the sight of his face brought a frown to Garron's own. "You almost killed me. Just remember how I'm paying you back."

Eyes closed, the Elf nodded, breath coming in tight gasps. Preparing.

Garron knelt. "Tell me when."

Silence, but for tight breaths. Garron stared down at the broken bone, envisioning how it would realign. He would have to manipulate it with his hands, not just pull the leg into place. Which meant they couldn't shake. He took a long breath of his own, and braced himself, settling his hands on either side of the leg.

The Elf tensed. "Now."

Garron pushed, then pushed *harder*. Somewhere in the back of his mind, he'd expected the bone to pop into place at the slightest pressure. It didn't. It took all of his Essence-enhanced strength to force the bone to shift, and he could feel a terrible grinding with every inch. As he moved it, the displaced knee twisted slowly back into the correct configuration, until it was as close as Garron could make it. Under his fingers, bone, blood, and flesh all rippled, the sight of the knee shifting bringing with it a terrible feeling of wrongness.

The entire process took perhaps ten seconds. Ten seconds of screaming from the short Elf, his other leg kicking wildly, his hands smashing into the floor. Garron felt his bile rise, and as Essence began rushing down the Elf's leg, he backed away and vomited.

He was still vomiting when a clang told him that the cage had snapped shut. He looked up to see that Cayar was curled in on himself, save for his injured leg. A look with Essence sight showed that the man was still healing the injury, but the slight bend in the joint told Garron that something had been fixed.

Nodding to himself even as he wiped away the bile, Garron remembered what it was to be helpless, trapped by his own body. He couldn't wish it on anyone, even a man who'd nearly killed him. He was free now, and while he would hold who he needed to, he wouldn't consign anyone else to his own cage.

Andros was cultivating in the big room, drawing in the Essence Illana had expelled. Garron felt at his connection with Typo.

<Confirmation.>

Everything was set. Even as he directed the mobs to appropriate places, walking back into the large room beside a pair of wolves, Garron felt his fists clench. The Elves were neutralized. Lars was gone. Of the remaining guards, none were powerful enough to be a real danger, and he had traps for them. There was one man left to face.

Jackson was coming.

CHAPTER FORTY-ONE

Garron looked over to Andros, and with his Essence sight still active, noted that his friend had already absorbed a great deal of the Essence Illana expelled. He thought that maybe it was like cultivating in an air affinity dungeon, since the Essence required little in the way of purification? It seemed the only limit was the actual speed of Essence accumulation, and Andros' was many times faster than an ordinary cultivator's.

They locked eyes, and Garron could tell that nothing about this process was good for the young Noble. Andros was pale, a thin sheen of sweat covering his skin, and just looking at him made Garron want to shiver. "You alright?"

Andros turned his head to the side and vomited. "Too much. There's a… it's a lot. I'm sorry. Going to need to get rid of this soon. Body can't handle the strain. Messed with my head a little."

Garron felt his concern deepen. "Andy…"

A flash of annoyance crossed his friend's face, but it was gone in an instant, replaced by chagrin. "Sorry, Garron. It's my cultivation technique. It… remember I told you I need to exercise a lot to process the Essence I gather? It wasn't as bad because I was recovering what I lost, and I kept expelling a bunch, but I'm not perfect at it. My father echoed this onto me, and he's a Mage. His level of understanding with it is so much higher than mine that… Just make sure I don't cultivate later without pushing my body."

While he was still concerned about how far Andros seemed to be pushing himself, it would be over soon one way or another. Typo's consciousness pressed on Garron's. <Warning!>

Fear shot up his spine, and Garron forced himself to take a deep, calming breath. "He's here. Andy, I… However this goes, thank you."

Andros smirked at him, "Thank *you*, Gar. I'll say it again after we feed this fool to the dungeon. Come on."

They ran together for the entrance tunnels. <Typo. Can you show me?>

Jackson was standing down in the entrance space, flames blazing high enough that the entire little room was filled. He looked into the room, and Garron could see a long line of blackened flesh running down from the corner of his lip, across his chin, and along one side of his neck. He wondered if mist or steel was responsible for the cut, which was deep enough that it had forced Jackson to cauterize it.

Garron suspected the hole in the back of the man's tunic was from a steel feather, but he was somewhat disappointed the fire cultivator hadn't taken more severe wounds. Currently the black scar was standing out against the skin of Jackson's neck as he looked upwards, outside of the dungeon. It twisted as the fire cultivator snarled, face contorting into a mask of rage and flames blazing hot enough to cause damage to the surrounding earth.

In an instant, his anger calmed and the flames dropped back to a simple sheath coating the fire cultivator. Four large men in armor dropped down into the dungeon, one after the other. With a brief nod, Jackson began walking into the tunnel, the guardsmen trailing him.

Garron's words felt oddly disconnected as he focused on the mental image. "He's in the tunnel."

Andros' hand on his shoulder stopped him from walking forward. Garron opened his eyes and looked at his friend, who now seemed calculating rather than ill. Andros leaned in, whispering. "Let me go in first, so I can get him fighting me. You handle the guards."

Garron considered their options. Jackson wouldn't be likely to fall to any of the traps he'd set in these tunnels. None of them could best his raw power or reflexes, but they would be more than enough to handle four lumbering guardsmen. He recognized immediately why Andros would have to move in first; Jackson's flames would roast Garron alive, and unless Andros could occupy the man, Garron might as well wait in the big room with the mobs.

"This is dangerous, Andy. Are you sure you can handle him *here*? There's not a lot of space to move." Garron looked at the young Noble, letting his concern show in his expression.

Andros flexed his knees and jumped, clearing much of the first stretch in a burst of power. Garron smiled in spite of the danger. He supposed that was as clear of a 'yes' as he could have hoped for.

The Noble young man rounded the bend, and Garron turned half of his attention back to Typo's projection as he began picking his way much more slowly through the traps. Jackson was striding down the tunnel with relative caution—Garron was somewhat surprised the man wasn't shooting toward them on a blazing trail of fire, but he supposed even a mad cultivator knew to be careful in an unfamiliar dungeon.

He stepped onto the first pressure plate, the one that triggered a spike trap, and immediately shot backwards, nearly barreling over a few of his guards in the process. Spikes slammed into the wall in front of him, sending chips of earth flying. Garron was impressed despite himself; the traps were set slightly forward, and most people would follow their momentum in an attempted dodge. Jumping backwards showed both speed... and knowledge.

The guards behind Jackson, who had stumbled backwards in surprise—or perhaps fear at their leader's flames—were staring at the spikes. A few of them looked warily down the tunnel, noting all the ground they would have to cross. Jackson's eyes lit in rage, and he stepped forward once more, flames gathering around him. They surged forward, the blazing light filling Garron's mind. In the real world, the orange-red of the flame lit the bend of the tunnel brightly for a moment, but no actual fire hit the opposite wall.

Andros had arrived.

When Garron returned to the projection, Andros was already in close quarters with Jackson. It was a difficult position, but staying down the tunnel would favor Jackson: the man's ranged techniques were far deadlier than anything Andros could manage.

The wind cultivator ducked under Jackson's punch, releasing a burst of air to push back the flames with one hand as another scraped against the floor below the spikes embedded in the wall. Dirt fanned out in the next moment, passing through Jackson's flames unaffected, and forcing the fire cultivator to close his eyes for an instant. "Sand? You *dishonorable*...!"

Andros used that moment to slip around the fire cultivator, so that he was between Jackson and the other guardsmen. Jackson whipped around, his flames already gathering around a leg, but Andros was tensing, head down to the side, shoulder pointed at Jackson. In a burst of wind, he shot forward a half-foot before slamming his elbow into Jackson's chest.

The fire cultivator went tumbling. Andros paused for a moment, rubbing his arm. His tunic had been blackened by Jackson's flames, but he seemed more bothered by the impact. He rolled his shoulder, then bent his knees and shot down the tunnel after his enemy.

"That would be my cue." Garron focused on the real world again, banishing Typo's projection. He took the remaining half of the tunnel at a run, dodging easily around traps. He was still worried about Jackson, but hopefully he would be able to slip past the man and deal with the guardsman behind first. He just wished he had some protection against the flames.

He slowed, and focused on a pair of images. <Typo, have we figured out shields? If so, I'd love one and a pile of rocks there.>

A round object slowly formed, resolving into a large wheel that rolled down the tunnel. Garron watched it go, trying to figure out why Typo was so happy about it. "Okay… I asked for a *shield*, and you made a… let me try and figure this one out."

<Mortification,> Typo sent helplessly as he tried again.

"You made something *wheeled*." Garron snapped his fingers as he pulled out the answer.

A fresh shield settled on his arm; a simple circle of water-saturated wood held by a strap. The rocks would be waiting at the end of the tunnel with the guards, ready for him to use. Garron took a deep breath, feeling as prepared as he could be.

He rounded the bend and was greeted by a wash of flame, and huddled behind his shield immediately, feeling the air become scorching around him. It took a moment to dissipate, and Garron dared to peek over the rim of the shield.

Jackson and Andros were clashing again, the sight reminding Garron of nothing so much as a pair of fish fighting in a still pond. The two moved in ways that shouldn't be possible, leaping over one another, twisting to avoid blows, each attack accompanied by a crescent of flame or a burst of wind to push the fire back.

As Andros jumped a flaming sweep, kicking against the wall twice before twisting and converting his momentum into an airborne kick at Jackson's head, Garron stepped forward cautiously. The fire cultivator raised a hand, the motion a blur, presumably intending to catch Andros foot, but in the last possible moment Andros loosed a burst of Essence, spinning midair and catching his opponent on the opposite side. For an instant, Jackson was stunned and Andros was on the offensive;

his feet already raining kicks as he reached for the blade at his side.

Garron ran forward. He wouldn't get a better opportunity, and celestials knew what would happen if he stood still and let the fight pass him. A blow like the one Andros had just delivered would have killed Garron outright, not just stunned him for a moment.

Andros shouted, even as he fought. "*Watch*—!"

Garron shrunk down in an instant, raising his shield. The air heated around him an instant later, and he held his breath tight lest he scorch his lungs. Andros grunted even as another word left his mouth, "Go!"

He ran halfway down the tunnel, stopping before the pile of rocks. Down at the other end, four guardsmen still stood, clearly unsure of what to do. Then they got their orders: "Kill the boy!"

Jackson's scream ended in a grunt, and the sound of rushing wind a second later told Garron that Andros was pressing the fire cultivator back again. He couldn't look, because the guardsmen had heard their leader's order. They stepped forward cautiously, fanning out in the tunnel, swords raised, testing each step. Garron scooped up a rock, but didn't throw it. Yet.

The lead guard was poking at the ground before him and to the side, stepping slowly and cautiously, eyes flicking around for any sign of a trap. His sword hit a solid plate, and a moment later a cage shot up, earth flying around it. The guards behind let out strangled yells, falling backwards, but none had been caught in the trap.

Garron grimaced theatrically. He took a step back, and looked around. Jackson and Andros had moved past the bend in the tunnel. That helped cool the itch in Garron's back, but he didn't let his relief show as he raised his rock at the guards.

"Take this!" He threw the rock. It landed short of the lead guard, landing with a dull thud.

"Just stand still, boy. If you come quietly… we'll just hold you." Garron noticed the note of discomfort in the guardsman's voice. He was actually sure they'd hold him. But that mercy would last only as long as it took Jackson to pass judgement. He threw another rock, managing to catch the guard on the arm with the stone. A grunt, and perhaps a small sigh, was all the response he got.

As the guardsmen moved slowly down the tunnel, Garron continued to lob his rocks continuously. Occasionally, he pelted the lead guard's shoulders, head, or legs, but many of his throws fell pathetically short. When one failed to get even halfway across the intervening distance, he let out a loud curse, dropping his shield and picking up a pair of stones.

He wound himself up dramatically, and threw with all his might straight for the guardsman's head. The man lifted his sword, wincing at the same time, but the throw went a little high. The guardsman let out a mutter too soft for Garron to hear, taking another step forward as he lowered his sword to the ground.

The second rock landed in that moment. He really was very glad Talia had convinced him to make some of the plates so sensitive.

A cage snapped the guardsman up like some great monster's claws closing around its prey, prompting yells and a few screams from his companions. The man cowered for an instant, then pushed at the enclosure in obvious panic. "What the abyss? Get me out! Get me *out!*"

Bird cages were all well and good, but hatching the iron so that the only openings were tiny squares too small for a finger to pass through meant that getting purchase on the cage from the outside was all but impossible. The guards spent an annoyingly long time trying to pry the cage open, one even trying to get his sword at the seam between the two half-domes. Garron responded by throwing rocks. Now that his ruse was up, every single one found a target, hitting home with all the strength he could muster, until finally the guardsman closest to Garron turned.

"That's *it*, boy!" He strode forward, jabbing his sword at the ground before him. Garron backed away slowly as he continued throwing rocks, grabbing his shield and strapping it on again at the same time. He let a trace of fear show on his face as the man triggered another spike trap, then moved until he was nearly at the bend in the tunnel.

The guard's sword jabbed into the ground. Immediately, cracks spread out from the holes in the ground, and a moment later the earth collapsed inwards, the guard sliding down as well. The man screamed as he fell, but it was soon muffled. He would land beneath a pile of earth thick enough to nearly bury him. Nearly, only because Garron was kind.

Typo pushed at his mind. <Warning!>

Roars and howls echoed down the hall. An image of Andros weaving around Jackson's attacks, his tunic burned and blackened in several places, filled Garron's vision. "No time."

Garron spared a moment of concentration for the dungeon. <Send Rai. Quickly.>

<Distracted confirmation.> Typo was focusing on Aiki, Garron could tell. Hopefully the huge lion boss would level the playing field between Jackson and Andros somewhat. The final two guards were reluctant to move forward, but they were edging slowly up at their caged companion's urging.

"Get the boy! Just *grab* him! He can get us out of this, and Jackson'll kill us if we don't—" Garron lobbed a rock gently, so that it landed at the guards' feet. He jumped back, screaming, but nothing happened. It was best to keep them on their toes.

It took precious seconds for Rai to come bounding up the tunnels, skirting traps with such grace that he wasn't so much as slowed. He stopped, rubbing his mane against Garron's leg, then snarled at the guardsmen down the tunnel. They had finished skirting the pit, where their fellow's angry shouts were echoing up, along with the sound of dirt being spit out of a grimacing mouth.

The guards looked at Garron, who was holding a rock, then at Rai.

"Roar," Garron whispered to his companion. Rai obliged.

The look of pure terror on the guardsmen's faces made Garron laugh. "Walk in a straight line down the tunnel and you'll hit two more cages. Up to you if you want to come over here and fight Rai. Jackson won't know that you got caught on purpose."

The guards looked at each other, then one broke into a run, flinching as a cage clanged around him a moment later. The final guard let out a defeated sigh and charged as well. Garron turned and ran down the tunnel, Rai by his side.

"Nice!" A salmon light appeared in front of him, matching his running speed through the air.

"Where the abyss have *you* been?" Garron didn't stop running. A week ago, talking to anyone while in a full sprint would have been impossible. Two weeks ago, speaking at all was a challenge. Not so much any longer.

"I... well, Andros was fighting four people. Then I wanted to make sure no one was waiting outside to ambush you two. It was very important," Talia insisted while blushing a light pink.

Garron snorted out a breath. "Sure. Well, now that you're done cowering in fear, let's go help Andros."

Talia in front and Rai looking for prey, Garron left the tunnel and entered the fray.

CHAPTER FORTY-TWO

Jackson vaulted over Aiki just as the great lioness charged toward him, her roar shaking the ground. Andros was there when the fire cultivator landed, striking upward with Essence-enhanced speed, but Jackson responded with a blast of flame that forced a swift retreat.

A Riverdancer laid whimpering by where Garron was standing, a great black mark burned into its flank. A Crystalfur was picking itself up across the room, moving slowly even for a stone wolf. None of the traps had been triggered yet. Not surprising, but it was something Garron could fix.

<Typo.> As he sent instructions to the dungeon, he lifted his rock. Andros jumped back as a blast of flame shot out from Jackson, barely missing his chest.

Garron realized that Jackson was using lethal force against Andros. He knew that the man didn't have the best control over his emotions, and perhaps he had a high estimation of Andros' sturdiness, but Garron would have thought he would have been more careful of damaging Andros than he was.

For a moment, Andros and Jackson stared at each other, feet apart, both heaving breaths. Then Aiki let loose a ground shaking roar. Jackson managed to keep his feet, but his balance was thrown off as Aiki turned, slamming a huge shoulder into the fire cultivator's side. His flames had vanished with his ranged attack at Andros, so he had no defense for the simple physical attack. The fire cultivator went down, grunting, and Rai shot forward from beside Garron with a snarl.

Jackson picked himself off the floor even as Aiki let out another roar that set the earth shaking again. His flames returned as he got to a knee. Just as Rai closed the space between them, the smaller lion let out his own roar and Jackson was immediately shrouded in steam. Rai entered the white cloud, unperturbed by the shaking ground. From the shout of pain, Garron knew the lion scored a hit.

"Don't die. Come on, Rai." Typo couldn't control Rai directly, like he could with Aiki. With his limited ability, that wasn't often an issue: Rai had the instincts of a predator and the intelligence of a growing monster. For something like this, Typo couldn't simply transfer Garron's intentions to the young lion's mind exactly. Rai had a task, and he would figure his own way to carry it out… or not.

The steam faded in a puff of flame, and Garron's heart froze as he saw Rai a breath away from taking a blazing kick to the side. His hand was up before he knew what he was doing, and he threw his rock even as Rai twisted away with his impossible grace. The rock bounced off of Jackson's shoulder, laughably weak, but it did have an effect. Where the fire cultivator's attention had been on Rai for a few moments, now he looked up across at Garron with blazing rage in his eyes.

He smiled, and flames gathered in his hand.

Garron had his shield up, but he jumped to the side anyway. He didn't know how many blasts of flame the simple wood could take before it dried and caught fire itself, and he didn't want to find out.

The column of flame screamed toward where he had just jumped, and Garron stopped himself a moment before the searing flame would have caught his side. He felt a scorching heat, and couldn't stop a sharp inhale. Immediately, he coughed, his lungs scorched by the hot air, and fear shot up his spine. Had he damaged himself permanently? Would he—

"Too slow, boy." Fire filled Garron's vision. His shield came up, too slow. He stumbled to the side, off-balance. His chest burned, and he couldn't get a breath. The flame reached him, but so did a beautiful sound.

When the lions roared together, it gave Garron the feeling of the forest. Of quiet, rolling fields and playful streams, of roaring waves crashing over rocks, and of rain hitting the leaves, each with its own unique note. Below that elemental music, he could hear a familiar shout.

"Garron!" Scalding steam washed over Garron first, and he almost screamed at the sharp pain that cooled an instant later. Air blasted toward him, and he opened his eyes and dropped his sluggish shield arm.

Andros was beside him, hand out, and chest heaving. Rai was on the ground between him and Jackson, a trail of muddied ground showing that he had just used his ability again. Jackson was screaming in rage as he wobbled on the ground, drawing back his arm for a punch at Aiki. The huge lioness was still roaring, pulling back her own claw for a slash. Garron knew which would land first.

"Hey! *Weakling*! Couldn't manage to kill me, could you?" Another spike of fear pierced him at the rasp in his voice, but he pushed it aside. That fear was old, selfish. He had friends now.

Jackson changed direction mid-punch, the flames surrounding his arm bunching up, preparing to be released. Garron was already running. "Brat!"

Andros ran beside him, and when the flames came shooting toward them, the Noble responded with wind, a gust almost strong enough to draw Garron in its wake. Andros sagged and stumbled. "Can't do that... so much, Gar. Let the mobs fight him."

Garron shook his head. "Stay there, Andy. Cover me."

"Wha...? Fine." Halfway through the word, Andros' tone switched from shock to tired resignation. He stumbled to a stop, and Garron kept running for all he was worth.

"Can't fight me close up, can you? Your *guards* were braver." They weren't, but Jackson didn't know that, and he was predictably incensed.

"You... fishy brat! If those idiots—" The enraged voice cut off suddenly, and Garron prepared himself.

<Typo. Rock?>

Jackson seemed to appear in front of Garron's path, a blazing trail at his feet. Garron came to a stop, a rock flying out of his hands. The guard captain lifted a hand, and his flaming sheath surrounded him again. Garron could feel the heat. "Jackson, you are such a—"

Jackson did a half spin and jumped back in a hard motion, too fast for Garron to follow. Three streaks of brown wood and flashing steel passed through the space where he'd been an instant before. Even with all his speed, a spurt of red followed two bolts as they shot past, the blood hitting the floor in the same moment the bolts slammed into the wall.

Jackson yelled, pain and rage mixing in his voice, but there was also a note of triumph. "Idiot boy. Didn't think I knew you'd try this? Didn't do... anything."

The fire blazed higher, and smoke appeared high on his arm and on his side where the bolts had ripped into flesh. The entire time, Jackson kept a wild, savage grin on his face, staring at Garron. The fire cultivator was frozen to the spot, healing his wound.

Garron screamed in his mind. <Now!>

It had taken a long time to absorb the cage, remove the spikes, and modify the ceiling so that the Elven mercenaries wouldn't realize where Andros would be dropping into the dungeon. But it hadn't taken the two minutes Garron bought for Typo. Most of that time had been spent modifying the rock-fall trap set to activate when someone fell through the pit, so that Typo could instead trigger it at will.

Garron jumped back an instant before the rocks fell. Jackson, held by his healing, didn't. It took a good few breaths for the rocks to fall, a sustained crash as stone and earth slammed into the ground, enough weight to bury even someone like Jackson.

As the rocks and earth continued to pour down, a tongue of fire shot out, and Garron started to run, calling out, "Okay, Andy, that's about it for me."

Instead of Andros, Jackson responded. "Good to *hear.*"

The voice was muffled, but it carried such anger that Garron turned instinctively. Jackson was blazing as he emerged from cracked and broken earth. Had he literally been smashing the rocks away as they came down? How much strength did the man possess?

The flames gathered at the man's feet, and Garron braced himself, holding the shield on his left arm aloft. As Jackson shot for him, he dove to the side and tossed the shield. He was out of rocks, unfortunately.

The stone cage fell with a resounding thud. He still felt the heat at his back when Jackson made his rage known, but for a moment hope surged. Had he been caught in the cage?

<Frustration.> As he ran, an image of Jackson rubbing a shoulder, his arm hanging limp, filled Garron's mind. "Well, that worked out better than the rockfall. And the crossbows. And the giant lioness. And Andros."

Jackson's chest was heaving, his face drawn in pain, but his flames were still gathering. The man was relentless, and even with their preparation, he was weathering every blow. The fire shot out in a column of roaring heat again, and something slammed into Garron hard enough to drive the breath from his lungs.

"You... okay, Gar?" Andros sounded... weak. Weaker than he ever had before. As Garron's vision focused again, he saw his friend's pallor had gotten even worse. They were across the room now, close to the exit leading to Typo's last room.

Garron's eyes widened. "Andy, are you—"

"I'll be… fine. Got enough left to beat this thief." Andros turned to face the man in question.

Jackson was screaming in incoherent rage, fire blazing around him, fallen stone cage behind. He was in the center of the room, and as Typo sensed Garron's intentions, both Rai and Aiki sprang into motion, bounding golden speed and slow unstoppable power. Both predators were silent, ready to kill. Jackson's scream cut off, his flames dropping away.

In a burst of wind, Andros shot forward with his knife leading the way. Jackson moved in a blur to meet the attack, and in the same instant Rai pounced on the guard captain from behind.

CHAPTER FORTY-THREE

Rai did his best to maul Jackson. Like Andros, the guard captain didn't wear the armor of his subordinates, relying both on his raw speed and the flames surrounding his body to protect him. This was a fatal mistake: Rai didn't care about a little *heat*.

His claws dug into flesh even as his own limbs began to smoke. The lion moved with such speed and grace that he avoided passing through the actual flames, finding gaps in the tongues of orange-red licking up to the ceiling. He didn't roar… Garron supposed that even monsters could get tired after using their abilities enough.

Aiki was able to show her worth as well. Garron could see that her ability would be particularly suited to dealing with groups of weaker enemies; her ability to destabilize attackers offsetting her slow movement, but she was a massive lion with claws and teeth of stone, strength to match her size, and a hide which didn't particularly care about getting scorched. All of that might not have mattered if Jackson could maneuver around her, but her raw power made every blow something to be avoided at all costs, and her durability made her nearly impossible to kill without absolute focus.

It was good, then, that Andros was pinning Jackson in place with sheer martial skill.

He ducked, wove, and attacked like the wind. He fought like a man possessed, and the few times in his spinning, mad dance with his enemy that Garron could clearly see his face... his eyes were wide, the whites showing all around the pupil.

Jackson's flames gathered, twisted, surged, focused... but nothing could touch Andros. He hardly had the Essence left for a true technique, but he attacked with precision that put Rai to shame, predicting each and every one of Jackson's moves perfectly, and finding openings in the man's defense to keep pressure on him while the lions focused solely on bringing the fire cultivator down.

The flame-wielder kept his left arm limp by his side, striking with all three of his other limbs, manipulating the fire around him like it was a living thing. He screamed in rage as he fought, but Andros wore him down, sliding past torrents of flame and punches blazing with heat. Garron wasn't clear on the exact technique Jackson was using, but he suspected that, for a D-ranker, it was far above the norm. The head guard had stolen a great deal from Lord Tet. The techniques the Tet family kept in the repository had made the man formidable. But Andros...

Jackson said that people called Andros a genius. Garron had suspected as much, but now he knew it was true. Andros stood toe-to-toe with a veteran of both cultivation and battle, and held his own.

Garron couldn't do all that much to help, but he ran around to get a good vantage, prepared to step in with a blast of Essence or a distraction to help Andros. Aiki was flanking Jackson, a wall he couldn't get past, and Rai pressured him from behind as he fought Andros. Garron covered the final avenue, but he was severely limited, his Center only full enough for a single blast. Garron had a thought and sent it along right away. <Typo, can you make more mobs?>

<Hesitant confirmation.> Garron got an impression of Typo's Center. Cayar's Essence had replenished him to an

extent, but not enough to make an endless army of monsters. But perhaps, it could be enough.

Garron nodded. <Wolves. Whatever you can make.>

<Agreement.>

Howls began to echo down from the exit tunnel. The first wolf to arrive was a Riverdancer that bounded along, flowing across the ground like a river. The monster was stronger than the original Riverdancers, in accordance with Typo's increased rank. With each movement, its form stretched visibly. When it opened its mouth to howl, fangs the size of knives suddenly flashed out, then retracted. Clearly this was the Malleable ability coming into its power at the wolf's higher rank. More howls echoed out, but as Jackson saw the first wolf, he let out an even louder scream of rage.

Andros ducked a wide, flaming swing, then slipped away from a focused jet of flame. Aiki brought a huge claw down the moment that Jackson's flaming shell vanished, and from behind, Rai leapt, claws raking down Jackson's back. Andros stepped away, chest heaving, for an instant's respite while Jackson dodged away from the attacks.

But Jackson didn't dodge.

Stone claws smashed down on Jackson's left side, and blood spurted out of his already wounded shoulder. Rai left huge furrows down the fire cultivator's back before leaping away as flames ignited once more. Jackson screamed and pivoted. His foot shot out with the speed and force of a lightning strike, blazing hot enough to shine white for a brief instant. Even so, Andros was fast enough to bring up an arm to block the strike. Across the room, Garron heard the crack when the arm snapped, saw the kick blast through and impact his head, and felt the air freeze in his lungs as his friend fell.

Essence blasted out of Garron an instant too late. Earth, water, and air shot toward Jackson's screaming form, and he stumbled at the wave of weakness as he sprinted forward, and refused to stop. The Riverdancer crossed before his path, running toward Jackson, but he didn't slow. He felt the blistering heat as he drew near. As he knelt down by Andros' side, the air was sucked from his lungs, and the roar of fire told him he hadn't been fast enough. He huddled over Andros, covering the other boy's body with his own. He took a final, deep breath...

"Go!" Talia's voice rang out over a grunt of surprise from Jackson. Garron didn't have to look to know that she was crowding the man's vision, distracting him; giving them a chance.

The roar of the flames ceased, and a moment later, Rai's roar replaced it. As Garron ran with Andros gathered in his arms, he passed a pair of Riverdancers. All had the same springy, malleable bodies and deadly cries. Even as the heat at his back faded and Aiki's roar joined Rai's, Garron kept running.

He was in the tunnel before his eyes had fully refocused. For a brief moment, he thought he could get Andros out of the dungeon, hide in the forest, perhaps escape while Jackson was bogged down by enemies. Then he refocused, and saw the cages holding two Elves, both unconscious, chests slowly rising and falling. "Abyss."

Garron wasn't as terrified as he should have been. It was a stupid plan, anyway: if Jackson could get away from the two birds, he could escape Typo and chase them down in the forest. He lowered a stirring Andros to the ground, and another wolf passed Garron, howling its cry anew. <Typo? How are you making more?>

<Confusion.> An image of Jackson kicking away and immolating a Riverdancer filled Garron's mind. Once again, hope dawned.

<Can you keep making them, keep replacing the ones that die?>

<Regret.> The image widened. The corpses of two other wolves lay at the fire cultivator's feet, his Aura preventing Typo from fully absorbing their energy. All that was left were Aiki and Rai. Typo's hunger was growing, and he had no more Essence left to use.

"You need more Essence." Garron looked around for a moment. His eyes skated over two bodies in cages, both incapacitated by Essence loss. Easy targets for the knife tucked back in Andros' belt.

Enough Essence, perhaps, to save them.

Garron shook his head, and started pulling Andros deeper into the tunnel, away from the fighting. He wasn't about to start murdering helpless people, not even to save his own life. Andros would be safe enough, even if Jackson was insane. Beyond Lord Tet's rage, killing a Noble would result in swift and certain punishment even if the kingdom had fallen apart. Nobles looked after their own.

As he dragged his friend down the tunnel, skirting the spike trap he'd laid, and pausing to pull him across the narrow stretch of safe ground at the pit trap, Andros spasmed in his arms, twisting hard enough to throw off his grip. A moment later, the young Noble was on three limbs, his broken arm clutched to his side, looking up at Garron with one eye closed, the other open but dazed. "What? Gar?"

"You got hit in the head." Garron grunted as Andros grabbed onto him, making it easier to hold him. "Let me get you past the pit trap. The mobs are fighting Jackson, we have some time."

<Warning.> Jackson kicked Aiki hard enough to break a leg, then another. He left the boss monster alive, her roars spent and coat glistening with sweat. He whirled, blazing like the inferno he'd set upon the forest, and brought his flames down on the last Riverdancer, the heat shriveling the creature even as it twisted away. All that was left was Rai.

Garron's heart fell. <Tell Rai to run away, Typo.>

Rai snarled, hackles raised, and opened his mouth. Nothing came out. Slowly, clearly fighting the compulsion, the lion backed away.

Jackson flashed forward and kicked him in the ribs.

Rai's bulk went flying at the strike, his coat smoking where it came into contact with the fire cultivator's foot. He landed heavily, without his normal feline grace.

<Tell him not to get up, Typo!> Garron knew he was screaming in his mind, but his fists were clenched, his palms sweaty. He felt the compulsion Typo sent to the young lion, and for a moment he almost fell himself. Rai stirred once, and fear filled Garron. Then he went still, and Typo sent Garron assurance. The lion was still alive. Jackson turned, and his flames calmed. He began walking to the room's exit. Toward Garron and Andros.

"He's coming, Andy." Garron knew his voice sounded defeated, broken. But Andros struggled to his feet, grunting.

"Stay behind me." Andros was swaying where he stood, though he pulled his knife out again. The blade shook slightly in his hand, and the other lay useless at his side, broken.

Garron snorted, stepping up beside Andros. <Typo?>

A pile of rocks appeared in front of them, just outside of Andros' Aura. He scooped them back toward him, picking one up. <Thanks.>

<Gratitude.>

Flames appeared down the tunnel. Jackson shot forward, past the cages in a blink. He passed another cage trap by sheer luck, missing the pressure plate. Garron threw his first rock, timing as best he could. Spikes shot out as Jackson passed the traps, but he knocked them aside with a burst of Essence. Garron picked up another rock and threw it as Jackson came to a stop before them, a trail of fire fading behind him. The fire cultivator tilted his head, and the stone sailed past him, clattering to the ground.

Useless.

Jackson raised his hand, and a blast of pure Essence slammed into Garron's remaining rocks, sending them flying outwards. Tongues of fire wrapped around the man's form once more, and in the confines of the tunnel, he looked like a spirit of death. He stood hunched, chest heaving, one arm limp and crusted with dried blood at his side. A line of blackened flesh was the only mark left of Aiki's attack, and Garron knew his back would bear the marks of Rai's assault as well. His eyes were half-slitted, his teeth bared in what seemed an involuntary snarl. When he breathed in, his flames grew until their heat nearly made Garron look away.

"Stop, Jackson. Please." Andros' voice was quiet. Pleading, even. Or perhaps just tired.

A mad grin split the fire cultivator's slender face. "Oh, now *that's* funny, brat. Begging, are you? See what happens to Noble pride when you face real power?"

Garron took a step back, then stopped. The ground beneath him shifted slightly. They were at a pit's weakened edge, meant to collapse when the victim stepped too far onto it. There was no retreat.

Andros was muttering something, but even Garron couldn't hear it. The blood was rushing in his ears. Jackson was raising a hand toward him. The flames were gathering. Surprise filled Garron from Typo's bond—the dungeon hadn't expected it to come to this, or just hadn't understood. Truth be told, Garron hadn't either.

A flash of light appeared by Jackson's face, and Garron tensed, grabbing Andros. Talia was giving them a chance to fight!

But... Andros wasn't surging forward. Jackson wasn't blinking and jerking away from the light, he was still gathering his flames. Nothing had changed.

Jackson let out a laugh. "Oh, just wait little *Wisp*. I'll come back for you in a few weeks. There are always buyers, looking to see if you little things are real. Worth the Mana net, if you ask me. But you aren't distracting me any more."

Andros sucked in a breath. "If you do this, my father will—"

"Your father's *dead*, boy!"

The words hung in the air. Jackson seemed to savor them, but Garron felt a piece of Andros break as his breath puffed out. A piece of himself broke away, too. Lord Tet was a good man, kind for all his power, and most importantly, the idea of his presence had always been a stabilizing one in Garron's mind. He was gone?

He had a hand out for Andros as his friend sagged. The young Noble couldn't have been paler or weaker, but tears fell to the ground below them, and when he spoke, his voice was choked. Ragged. "When?"

Jackson grinned at what he saw. "Two nights after you left. You know, I was angry that my idiot men couldn't manage to find you for so long, but after that… I was glad. I would have hated to miss the good news."

Still holding Andros, Garron spat at Jackson's feet. "Monster. I don't care if the kingdom's fallen, the other houses won't let you get away with robbing a Noble man and kidnapping his heir."

Jackson's grin grew wider. "Not the heir, fishie. The Lord. Such a *young* Lord, a child until he reaches the C-ranks. Everyone is so busy with the war, and that guardian of his, the one so *close* to the C-ranks, he is quite good. Better than them, even if they won't admit it. The perfect teacher. The perfect man to hold his estates, and enjoy the benefits of a Noble rank."

Andros let out a choked sound. A sob, Garron thought, until he let out another. A broken, terrible laugh. "A *Lord*? I thought we weren't fit to lick your boots. What do you want next, my cultivation technique? I'll give it to you, you know. If you let Garron go."

Garron stared at Andros' face. There was a grim smile on it, almost painful to look upon. Tears streamed down as he looked upon the flame-wreathed madman before him. "I will. I swear."

Silence. Was this it, then? After all this, Jackson just wanted the abyssal cultivation technique? A memory fell into place in Garron's mind—they had discussed that Jackson should have broken through before, but he hadn't. Now it made sense: he'd wanted something better to carry him past the C-ranks.

Jackson answered with a chuckle of his own. "Nice try, brat. You have as much chance of giving me that technique now as you do of killing me here. I'm not some peasant you can trick into letting your friend go. No, this fishie isn't the way to power. *You* are. Enough time, and they'll be calling me Lord Tet in your place. Then I'll get that technique myself, and show you what a real cultivator is."

The flames had calmed as Jackson spoke, but now they surged, gathered. Garron's eyes flicked around, but there was no escape. Talia still hovered, unable to do anything but crowd Jackson's vision. Typo's hunger and a powerful, nervous apprehension filled him. It almost mirrored his own. He closed his eyes. <Thanks again, Typo. Tell Talia. Grow.>

"Wait. I'll…" Andros' voice was quiet, but clear. It was choked off for a moment, and the heat grew. A shadow covered Garron's eyes, and he opened them.

Jackson screamed, "Get the abyss out of the—"

"I'll do it myself." Andros lifted the long, wavy knife, glinting in reflected firelight. The same blade, perhaps, that had touched Garron's throat before. His eyes were clear, but full of pain. "Sorry, Gar."

A clean, burning line of pain, a surge of hot liquid flowing out, and cold. Garron tried to take a breath.

He couldn't.

Where before it had taken minutes for darkness to close in, now shimmering black surged, covering the firelight. All he could do was put a hand to his own throat, and feel at the wound his best friend had left in it.

Something pushed hard at his chest, even as he fell. Andros' face was the last thing he saw, but he felt the earth give way beneath him, heard the ground collapsing, tumbling along with his body into the pit.

The last thing Garron felt was Typo. <Assurance.>

Everything stopped.

CHAPTER FORTY-FOUR

Ulysses felt as though he had aged a thousand years. He felt the weight of his armor on his shoulders. Or… was that the guilt?

His comrades, his fellow cowards, marched beside him. Their leader held an unconscious young man over his right shoulder, the head lolling slightly and the tongue out, but the chest still rising slowly. Andros, at least, was still alive. Quietly, so quietly he was almost mouthing the words, he whispered, "I'm so sorry, Garron."

Beside him, a short man with pointed ears limped along. He was quiet, perhaps from whatever wound he'd taken in the fighting, but he stared at Andros' sleeping face as it bounced against Jackson's back, the same as Ulysses. His partner stepped silent and cold on the mercenary's other side. Her gaze was stony.

They walked straight through the forest, toward the blackened and burned ground, and with a raised hand, the hungry flames guarding the way out parted to reveal a thin corridor of blackened ground, still hot but no longer scorching. The captain staggered, but he kept walking forward, and Ulysses kept following.

With every step and breath Ulysses took, words pounded in his mind. He'd heard them while he lay on the ground, barely conscious from the blow a boy braver than him had dealt. He'd remembered them when he woke to a kick from his leader, looking up at a ruin of black scars, a single young man slung over the monster's shoulder. "Remember your debt."

He entered the corridor behind the short mercenary, walls of flame dancing to either side. Ulysses nearly stumbled as the man before him paused for a breath, then kept walking. A moment later, he stopped himself.

"Remember."

The voice sounded in his ear from nowhere, the same voice that had whispered to him as he lay outside the dungeon entrance. The same one that had led him to the boys' hiding place. The voice he had already betrayed once.

"I will." He said the words, quietly, perhaps, but he said them. Not something he would have done even a day ago. But then, he would have to stop being so afraid, soon.

―――

Garron woke with tears in his eyes.

His head pounded, his throat burned with pain, and his mouth tasted like dirt. He shot awake, sitting up in a shower of earth, and touched his neck. There was a rough scar, not like he would expect from a cut so much as the mark of an imperfect artist. The skin felt as though it had been manually pulled together and pinched closed, rough and unwieldy. A mate to the scar on his side.

<Gratitude.> Garron was too tired for words, even in his mind.

<Joy, relief, welcome!> In spite of himself, Typo's simple happiness made him smile. It was watery, but there. Speaking of which…

<Water, please?>

Before he finished the projection, a simple stone bowl of

water appeared before him. He drank, and a moment later the bowl refilled, so he drank again. It took three more times before he finally set the bowl down, using the last of the water to splash at his face. The cool liquid felt good on his face. He needed it, to forget what happened.

"He swore an oath to Typo." Talia's voice was quiet, measured.

"I figured. Should have done it much sooner, honestly." Garron looked up. He was still in a deep pit, but Typo had cleared away all the loose earth that had covered him as he fell. He had a clear view up at Talia. "One clean cut, easy to close and replace the blood. Much easier for Typo to heal than burning to death, but still obviously fatal."

Talia let out a quiet snort. "Easy? You still almost died. Typo had to make sure you didn't come back too quickly, or Jackson would have noticed. Then the earth covering you… you almost choked."

Garron nodded and thought over what his friend had done for him. "But it hid my body. So he wouldn't wonder why I didn't disappear."

"It did." Talia flew a foot above him, voice still subdued. A golden-furred head poked over the side of the pit, purring. A bit of the knot in Garron's stomach loosened at the sight. Rai, at least, was alright.

Garron simply sat for a time, letting his mind wander. Andros was long gone, he was sure. Even if he wasn't, what could Garron do now? He'd played every trick he could, struggled hand and foot beside his friend, and in the end he hadn't been enough. Andros had saved him, and let Jackson take him prisoner once more.

Eventually, Talia floated down to him again. "So, what now?"

Garron let out a bitter laugh. Even asking the question, Talia had a hopeless note to her voice. "It's over. I lost. We lost. And it's my fault."

The Wisp bobbed. "It's not your fault."

"Whatever. Did you see those two fighting? How could I do anything even close to that? I'm out of Essence, Typo's out of Essence, and we can't do anything. We're not strong enough."

<Frustration.>

Garron caught the falling rock before it hit his head. In a burst of anger, he hurled it out of the pit. It landed with a dull thud. "That didn't work either, Typo. Nothing I did worked."

Everything fell quiet again. Even Garron's connection with Typo was dead silent.

Then, the dungeon spoke. <No.>

"Typo, I think—hold on, did you just *talk*?"

<Pride.>

Garron frowned. Had he just misinterpreted?

<No!> The dungeon shouted the words in Garron's head.

"He only knows how to say 'no.' Seems about right." The ground shook. Garron looked around, and found a rough slope carved into the pit's wall. A way out. But he didn't have the strength or the inclination to take it. "Typo, I—"

<No! Frustration, pleading.>

Rai let out a low growl; Talia bobbed slowly up and down. Dungeon, monster, and Wisp had all done more to keep him alive than he could himself. Far more.

<Demand.> The dungeon pressed him. Typo was right. He owed them a debt.

"Fine." Garron got slowly to his feet, then fell as blackness closed around him for a moment. But he rose again. The slope led further down the tunnel, toward Typo's Core room. With nothing better to do, Garron started walking, and soon both Rai and Talia were keeping pace on either side. They made it to the Core room, and for an instant Garron hesitated. Typo had made a pit spanning the first half of the room, at Garron's insistence.

<Assurance.>

He stepped onto ground he knew was false. It held him. He made it to the stone-covered well structure that housed Typo's

Core, looking around suspiciously for cracks in the floor. There were none. "What is it, Typo?"

Something smacked into his head, hard enough to make him wince in pain even as Talia laughed. "That's really getting old."

He looked down, and blinked. Not another rock, as he had expected, but a staff, short enough to be perfect for him. It was made of smooth wood streaked with gray stone.

He picked it up, swaying a little as another wave of dizziness overcame him, and leaned on it. Once the blackness faded, he looked at what Typo had made. The slender piece of wood was unremarkable except for its top. It flared out into a bowl shape, so that Garron almost expected a stone to be set in it. There wasn't one.

When he looked around, a glimmer caught his eye. Typo's Core, once hidden in its mud pit by a layer of rock, was now sitting unprotected. Inviting.

<Determination.>

Garron sighed. "Typo, I'm too weak to take him back."

After a pause, the dungeon responded. <Yes.>

Two words. They grew up so fast. "I'm glad you agree. It's a nice staff, but—"

A salmon light in his eyes stopped him. "Idiot. You're too weak *now*. You don't think Andros used to be like you? Jackson? Before you came here, Typo had zero mobs and I had the trap-design abilities of a clever rabbit."

Garron frowned and waved helplessly at the air above him. "So? Even if I get stronger, so will Jackson."

At his feet, Rai growled. Then the lion let out a quiet roar, and water splashed over Garron's face.

"What the…? Rai?" Garron wiped his face, trying not to think about the exact mechanics of the lion spraying him with water. Where did it come from? "Don't think about it."

<Mirth. Encouragement.>

Garron found himself smiling again. Despite its dubious

source, Rai's water was… refreshing. Cleansing, almost. He looked at the lion. "I am weak, you know."

Talia flew back, letting out a light laugh. "We can see those arms of yours. We know."

Garron took in a deep breath, and felt the power of his lungs.

"I'm stronger than I was, though. Thanks to Andy." He lifted the Core. "That's how it should be. Not the way Jackson treats his men. The strong help the weak."

Talia whispered something and he stopped, glaring at her. She bobbed innocently. "Nothing, nothing. Go on, King Garron."

"One day, I'm going to get you back for… everything." He picked up Typo's Core and pushed it into place with a light *snap*.

"We can't save Andros." He turned, dungeon Core in hand, and began walking back toward the entrance, Rai at his side. "Yet."

Talia let out a joyful chuckle. Garron whirled on her, pointing the Typo staff directly at her. "*What*? Also, how the abyss do you make sounds like that?"

She erupted into howling laughter. "Sorry. But you might want to wait a day or two, so Typo can slowly withdraw his influence from here and not, you know, cause an earthquake."

"Oh." Garron deflated slightly. "Didn't know that was a concern."

The Wisp flew to his shoulder. "But it was a pretty good speech! You just need to work on the delivery a bit."

"I don't hear you helping Typo absorb everything." Garron leaned the staff to the ground, feeling the surge of Typo's excitement at the novelty of being moved.

In a faux-deep voice, laughter still bubbling, the Wisp replied, "*Yet.*"

EPILOGUE

Garron had gone to a city far enough away from the Tet Estate—Andros' estate—then bought passage through a portal. Typo had supplied the necessary silver, thanks to some destroyed money pouches from the captured mercenaries. Apparently, they had been *very* vocal about the loss when Jackson had freed them...

For the young man, that meant a long trek across lawless land, stopping every few days and doing what he could to feed both Rai and Typo. He'd run into only one pair of bandits. With Rai at his side and his Center replenished by nightly cultivation, he'd left them unconscious on the ground without issue. That was how Typo had learned how to create copper coins.

"I think I found a spot!" Talia appeared before him, whizzing around excitedly. She'd been most of the reason he hadn't gotten in more trouble, truth be told. It had taken two weeks of travel to make it as far as they had, and it was thanks to her scouting that they avoided the worst fighting going on in the region.

"Go ahead." Garron followed the Wisp, a tired Rai padding along beside him. They walked through trees. In the distance was the foot of a great mountain, he knew, but so close all he could see were grassy slopes populated by trees and shrubbery, though everything had a windswept look to it. For fun, he scrambled up a rocky patch beside Rai, though the lion beat him handily. The ground sloped downwards soon later, until suddenly the rounded a copse of trees and the land unfolded.

For all that they were in the shadow of a great peak, they were standing before a green meadow dominated by a gentle hill, split by a rushing river. Garron stood at the top of a great slope, and to his left across a field of brown and green was a rocky face. The ground sloped down in the other direction, and far across the expanse Garron could see that there was another rising slope.

Garron whistled. "Celestial. That's a beauty."

Talia bobbed next to him. "No, my name is *Talia*. Easy to get it confused, I know. I think Andros will like this spot when we rescue him."

He rolled his eyes at Talia, but began negotiating the slope before him with vigor. An hour filled with taunts from the floating Wisp later, Garron was standing at the base of the hill, in an empty cave next to the river. He breathed in as the wind rushed across the meadow. Earth, water, and air, all strong, but in balance. Perfect.

He reached up to his staff, and pulled out the Core, setting it down before him. Typo greedily began to expand to his new surroundings, and soon his joy began to tickle Garron's mind.

Rai pushed against his leg, purring in a deep voice. His growth had slowed outside of Typo's influence, but with his mane grown back in, there was no denying that he was a true, adult lion.

As Talia excitedly made plans for building Typo's new body, Garron looked over the surroundings. A great place for the dungeon, yes, but he couldn't help noticing that it was fortified on three sides. The river was a steady source of water. Perhaps a mill near the meadow's edge could take advantage of it. The hill would offer a good view of the surroundings while also making its occupant visible to anyone else living in the meadow. Garron knew immediately where he would be sleeping.

In his deepest thoughts, the ones he kept hidden even from Typo, he thought back to what Talia had called him, weeks ago. He had really liked the sound of it, and had been playing around with the thought of it since then. In a whisper that even Talia wouldn't hear, he said the words swirling about in his mind.

"King Garron of the Lion Kingdom, first of his name, progenitor of the Lion's Lineage."

ABOUT ROHAN HUBLIKAR

Rohan Hublikar was born in Edison, New Jersey 20 years ago after the longest night of winter. The ice of that dark day has since flowed through his veins, making his teeth chatter constantly and the howl of a winter storm follow him through doors regardless of the season. This has made his studies at Rutgers University in the field of biomedical engineering difficult, but has given him plenty of inspiration to write, so he can't complain.

ABOUT DAKOTA KROUT

Dakota Krout, a heartwarmingly clever author known for weaving fun, punny, and clean humor into his LitRPG fantasy novels, brings joy and laughter to readers through his best-selling series: including Cooking With Disaster, Divine Dungeon, Completionist Chronicles, and Full Murderhobo! His work, celebrated for its wit and charm, earned him a spot as one of Audible's top 5 fantasy picks in 2017, alongside a top 5 bestseller rank that was featured on the New York Times.

Drawing upon his experiences in the Army, Dakota expertly crafts vast, imaginative worlds with intricate systems that captivate and delight. His background in programming and information technology not only infuses his writing with a distinct, logical flair; but also fuels his innovative spirit in managing his publishing company, Mountaindale Press. These unique perspectives shine through in his stories, making him beloved by fans of all ages who seek a wholesome and humorous escape.

Dakota's journey in publishing has been filled with gratefulness, and a deep desire to continue bringing smiles and laughter to his readers. "I hope you Read Every Book With A Smile!" - Dakota Krout

Connect with Dakota:
MountaindalePress.com

Patreon.com/DakotaKrout
Facebook.com/DakotaKrout
Twitter.com/DakotaKrout
Discord.gg/mdp

ABOUT MOUNTAINDALE PRESS

Dakota and Danielle Krout, a husband and wife team, strive to create as well as publish excellent fantasy and science fiction novels. Self-publishing *The Divine Dungeon: Dungeon Born* in 2016 transformed their careers from Dakota's military and programming background and Danielle's Ph.D. in pharmacology to President and CEO, respectively, of a small press. Their goal is to share their success with other authors and provide captivating fiction to readers with the purpose of solidifying Mountaindale Press as the place 'Where Fantasy Transforms Reality.'

Connect with Mountaindale Press:
MountaindalePress.com
Facebook.com/MountaindalePress
Twitter.com/_Mountaindale
Instagram.com/MountaindalePress

MOUNTAINDALE PRESS TITLES
GameLit and LitRPG

The Completionist Chronicles,
Cooking with Disaster,
The Divine Dungeon,
Full Murderhobo, and
Year of the Sword by Dakota Krout

A Touch of Power by Jay Boyce

Red Mage and
Farming Livia by Xander Boyce

Ether Collapse and
Ether Flows by Ryan DeBruyn

Unbound by Nicoli Gonnella

Threads of Fate by Michael Head

Lion's Lineage by Rohan Hublikar and Dakota Krout

Wolfman Warlock by James Hunter and Dakota Krout

Axe Druid,
Mephisto's Magic Online, and
High Table Hijinks by Christopher Johns

Dragon Core Chronicles by Lars Machmüller

Pixel Dust and
Necrotic Apocalypse by David Petrie

Viceroy's Pride and
Tower of Somnus by Cale Plamann

Henchman by Carl Stubblefield

Artorian's Archives by Dennis Vanderkerken and Dakota Krout

Made in United States
Troutdale, OR
07/24/2024

21513264R00215